The Zion Deception

Dr. Laurence B. Brown

ISBN: 1-4537-6211-6
ISBN-13: 9781453762110

Other Books

by

Dr. Laurence B. Brown

Fiction
- *The Eighth Scroll*
- *The Returned*
- *The Returned: Hard Boiled*
-

Nonfiction:
- *The First and Final Commandment*
- *MisGod'ed*
- *God'ed*
- *Bearing True Witness*

Author's Note, and Disclaimer

The Zion Deception is a work of fiction that expresses anti-Zionist views popular among Jewish revisionist historians (historians dedicated to correcting what they believe to be falsehoods of history that were designed to support the Zionist political agenda of a Jewish State). As for myself, I am neither a Jew nor a revisionist historian, neither a Semite nor anti-Semitic. I am a humanist and an author who recognizes a good premise for a story when I see it.

This novel touches upon controversial issues that challenge conventional wisdom regarding anti-Semitism, Zionism (the organized movement to establish a Jewish state) and the question of Israel's legitimacy. However, this is a work of fiction and, as such, I wrote it not to educate but to entertain. If you enjoy the action and adventure, then I have achieved my goal as an entertainer. If the premise of the story touches a tender nerve, I ask you to remember the spirit in which it was written. Lastly, if the content drives you to a closer examination of the issues, I have listed my sources at the end of the book. Read them and decide for yourself who and what to believe.

As the author, I neither affirm nor refute the claims advanced by revisionist historians–I simply make a story out of them. Hence, I declare the obvious: All incidents, situations and dialogue presented herein, and all charac-

Acknowledgements

I am very grateful to Rabbi Yirmiyahu Cohen, who assisted with some of the details on the Orthodox Jewish communities and their viewpoint on Zionism. Rabbi Cohen is a writer for the website: True Torah Jews Against Zionism (www.truetorahjews.org), which I have listed as a "must read" in my sources at the end of this book. I appreciate Rabbi Cohen not only for his valuable knowledge and self-less contribution to this work, but also for his sense of humor. He once joked that it was a good thing that The Zion Deception is a work of fiction, for if it wasn't, my communication with him and the TrueTorahJews website would put me on Mossad's watch-list. This is a joke readers will better appreciate when they get to the relevant passage of this book. Even then, they might sense that, like all good jokes, this one might contain a barb of reality.

I also would like to thank all those who, in their own ways, contributed to seeing this book to fruition. Due to the subject matter, most prefer to remain anonymous. I cannot blame them for taking this stance, because I have been warned to expect backlash from those who would prefer to see this subject suppressed. There is a point, however, when conscience overcomes fear for the sake of truth and humanity. For that higher goal, I pray that our Creator not let this work be in vain.

FOREWORD

When Dr. Laurence Brown approached me to ask if I had any suggestions on how to improve the factual content of his novel, *The Zion Deception*, I was humbled and awed. For several years, I have been involved in the writing and publishing of books on the subject of Judaism and Zionism (the political movement to establish a Jewish nation-state), but most of these books, as well as those of other authors on this subject, were intended for a relatively small audience of Jewish scholars. To my knowledge, *The Zion Deception* is the first work that packs the critical information into a fictional storyline intended for the general public.

The Zion Deception tells the story of a disaffected Jewish woman and her search for meaning to life and religion in modern society. But this is far from being a dry tale of self-discovery. On the contrary, the plot reads like a dynamic spy novel, leading the main characters through multiple armed conflicts and ultimately into a maze of intrigue involving a militant Zionist group, Nazi war criminals and Israel's Mossad. The plot is imaginative and highly entertaining, but the facts mentioned therein shed light on one of the most provocative controversies of the past century. The fact that this information is readily accessible in the real world–not zealously guarded by a paranoid

Mossad–only deepens the question of why most people continue to be misled by Zionist propaganda.

Those who choose to research the "secrets" revealed in this book will find that they have already become common knowledge among educated Jews (with the exception of the Khazar hypothesis, which is generally rejected by Jews). Among Orthodox Jews, numerous books have been published over the years; even among secular Jews, the Israeli newspaper Haaretz has published scathing accounts of Zionist conduct during the Holocaust, and revisionist Israeli historians have written extensively on this subject. In addition, numerous books and movies have been made about the Kastner trial. Nonetheless, much of this information is largely unknown outside of Orthodox Jewish and insular academic circles. For this reason, Dr. Brown's *The Zion Deception* may help to bridge the gap between facts and information. The facts are out there, and this book shows people where to find them.

The Zion Deception also opens a window to anti-Zionist, Orthodox Jewish communities. Readers are given a taste of the theology of Jews who believe in true Judaism, not Zionism, and who are committed to living peacefully among the non-Jewish nations where G-d has sent them until the coming of the messiah.

What strikes me most about this book is Dr. Brown's choice of subject. One would expect a Muslim author writing against Zionism to focus on the oppression of the Palestinians and other crimes against Muslims. But *The Zion Deception* contains very little on that subject. Its main characters are all Jews, and they reject Zionism because of how it has harmed Jews and distorted Judaism. He deserves credit for portraying a little known side of the story that desperately needs to be told.

If *The Zion Deception* spreads these facts to a broad audience, it will succeed not only as a highly enjoyable work of creative fiction, but as a tool to further religious tolerance and world peace.

Rabbi Yirmiyahu Cohen
True Torah Jews Against Zionism
(www.truetorahjews.org)

chapter I

"EVEN IN *our* business, head shots aren't common."

Private Sarah Weizmann stood at attention, flagpole stiff, her pale blue eyes focused in a million-mile stare over the post commander's desk, her mind even farther away. Colonel Farson's words brought her back. She chanced a downward glance at him where he sat, hunched over the papers on his spartan desk, his bald spot aimed at her like the mouth of a cannon.

"Sir?" she said. He raised his head, and she flicked her gaze back to the painting on the wall behind him, seeking refuge in the Renoir reproduction's smooth contours, but her mind popped and buzzed in the stress of confusion. Her peripheral vision registered Farson in a cocky pose: chin propped on the steeple of his fingers, lips pursed, eyes reading her with the intensity of a cobra preparing to strike. To each side of her stood a guard in desert camouflage, their sleeves rolled above their elbows and folded flat. These weren't military police, as her circumstance would normally warrant, but soldiers from her own unit.

She understood the significance of this from the moment they'd stripped her of her weapons and brought her here.

The drone of the wall-mounted air conditioner filled the room, and she felt the sweep of cold air from its oscillating vent chill the sheen of sweat at the back of her neck. Somewhere outside a bird chirped and whistled. Its incongruous song ended abruptly, as do most things of beauty in Iraq, lives included.

With a squeal of unoiled metal, the commander swiveled in his chair and rose. "I *said,* Private Weizmann, head shots aren't common. Even here. And *especially* not from behind." As he spoke, he strolled around his desk until he stood directly in front of her, his face in hers. Invisible vapors invaded her nostrils, and she remembered how she had once respected this man, if for nothing else, because of his taste for expensive and surprisingly understated colognes. But that was before she knew him for the dark horror he was.

Farson eased himself backward and sat on the edge of his desk, facing her. He floated a hand behind him, never taking his eyes off hers, and lifted the lid of a cherrywood humidor. From it he pulled an abnormally dark, bulbous stogie and swept it under his nostrils, inhaling. Then he wrinkled his nose and winked at her. "Mind if I smoke?"

"No, sir," she lied, "I don't mind at all, sir."

"Well, that just plumb takes all the fun out of it." He flicked the cigar behind him, where it rolled to rest between his inbox and a blue plastic stapler. "Now why should I risk gettin' cancer gassing a Jew if she don't pay no mind?"

"You're a true Southern gentleman, sir," Sarah said, struggling not to roll her eyes at his ridiculous faked Southern drawl.

"Well, shucks, little lady ... " He pushed himself off from his desk and stood, then jabbed a fist into her abdomen so fast she didn't have time to tighten it. With a savage twist of his wrist, he buried the knuckles even deeper.

Sarah crumpled to the floor as lightning streaks of pain drew her into a ball. She retched, but swallowed her scream. No way would she let him hear her wail.

"At ease, Private," Farson drawled, and through her gasps she heard the guards snickering as they stepped back. A camel-colored desert boot kick-rolled her onto her back, then laid its polyurethane sole on her throat. Instinct made her grab the rough leather with both hands, but she might as well have tried to push away an elephant's foot.

"Let me spell this out for you, Private." Farson had dropped the fake drawl. "I can understand *one* friendly fire incident. Chest wound, massive bleeding, death before your unit could access medical care—that sort of thing."

Sarah spat out, "He ran into my line of fire—"

A squeeze from his boot cut off her air. "But then there was the head shot incident. Heat of the battle, smoke grenade half-blinded you. Don't waste your breath, I read the report. You don't have anything to add about that one, do you?"

The boot lifted and Sarah sucked in a breath, but before she could speak he lowered his foot against the strength of both her arms pushing upward. She felt her face burning, panic tapping heartbeats on her eardrums.

"Didn't think so," he said. "Point is, I can understand guns going off by accident. What I can't understand is your *knife* going off by accident. Three times, into the same soldier."

Farson waited until she flailed her arms and a tinge of blue invaded her lips. He cocked his head with curiosity, as if conducting some sick medical experiment, and only then lifted his boot and sat back on the edge of his desk, his arms crossed over his chest. "Stand her up."

Each guard hooked an arm under one of her armpits and together they lifted her, bent at the waist and gasping for breath, to face him.

When she straightened enough to look him in the face, he said, "I don't suppose you have some entertaining story to cover your ... *assets* on that one, do you? Please, entertain me, I'm all ears."

Sarah waited until her breathing changed from shuddering to smooth, then swept a loose frond of auburn hair behind one ear with a tremulous hand. "Sir, it was self-defense. We were in a firefight, and I just happened to turn around as he was leveling his weapon on me. I swept it aside and he went for his sidearm. He was going to kill me first."

"Don't you mean, *before*?" Farson said, twisting a wry smile.

Sarah felt his jet-black eyes, as cold and vacuous as windows to Dante's frozen inner circle of Hell, shoot a chill through her. "Sir?"

"He wasn't going to kill you *first*, Private Weizmann. He was going to kill you *before*. Before, that is, *you* killed *him*."

She shrugged off the guards' arms as he circled his desk. He sat down with a shrill squeak from the chair, leaned forward, arms crossed on the papers in front of him, and leveled his gaze at her. "Private, you peed positive ten days ago. Maybe you thought you passed the random urine analysis, but you didn't. I scrubbed the result, because I need every swinging ... I needed all my troops in the field. But you peed positive. Imagine my surprise. Such a nice, clean Jewish bi—I mean, a nice Jewish *girl* like you. And there you go, popping your pee test. But then I saw what it was that you peed. Rohypnol. Had to call the doc to find out it was the date rape drug. So I'm thinking there was more rape than date in that drug. Why else would you be killing your fellow soldiers?"

Standing on her own, Sarah leaned forward and placed both fists on the commander's desk. "Sir, those—"

"Did I invite you to informality, *Private*?" His lips tightened, ice in his voice, malice in his eyes.

Sarah kept her hands on the desk, met his eyes and tried to match the steel of his gaze. "No sir, you didn't. I figured you just punched rank and decorum out of this room, sir. Those shootings *were* friendly fire, *sir*. As for Sergeant Kyle, I knifed him in self-defense."

Farson leaned back in his chair to the tune of a tortured metallic squeal, cradled the back of his head in the hammock of his interwoven fingers, elbows out, and nodded to one of the guards. "If she doesn't get off my desk by the count of three, break a fistful of her ribs."

Sarah jerked upright and stepped back. Farson nodded. "Let me explain something, you little Jew-trash. Number one, nobody, and I mean *nobody*, takes justice into their own hands in my command. 'Cepting me, of course. Number two, you samurai a fellow soldier to death, self-defense or not—and I'm saying it's 'not'—you're next on the friendly fire hit list. Number three, you never, ever, *ever* report your commanding officer to the JAG."

At the mention of the Judge Advocate General's office, Sarah felt all hope fly from her. For the past week, the unit had speculated over the identity of the whistleblower in their ranks. Somehow, Farson knew it was Weizmann.

"So this is how we're going to play this, Private Jew-trash." He leaned forward, picked up his previously discarded stogie and pointed it at her. "Where I come from, this here is what we call a Mexican standoff. As long as nobody does anything stupid, nobody gets hurt. So you're going to drop your case with the JAG, and I'm going to send you home a hero. But if you ever reopen your charges against me ... " He turned the stogie vertical and tapped the papers on his desk with it, leaving a dirty brown smudge. "You do that, I'll take you down with me. And then, while we're neighbors at Leavenworth, you doing life for three counts of premeditated murder, I'll bribe the dykes running your wing to make what those guys did to you feel like one of your Jew-trash Barbie love-dreams."

Chair squealing, he leaned back, flicked open a camouflage-pattern Zippo lighter and sucked his cheeks hollow. Then he puffed a toxic cloud from his stogie that obliterated all traces of his precious cologne.

chapter 2

EYES SQUEEZED SHUT, her lids furrowed into fans of fine lines, Sarah swore she could still smell the stink of Farson's cigar. *That was four years ago,* she reminded herself, and a different conflict, country and army. She knew she'd hardened in Iraq. It was such an obvious change, her friends now joked that despite her delicate fingers, her close-trimmed, unpolished nails could probably scratch glass. She cropped her auburn hair, denying the sensual, smooth waves it developed when shoulder-length or longer, and kept every muscle in her five-foot, eight-inch frame toned. Unable to rely upon others, especially men, she had crafted her supple, tanned body into a finely tuned weapon of war.

Weighing these considerations, she opened her eyes and wondered how, in just three short weeks, she had entered a hell nearly identical to the one she'd left in Iraq. She had expected to find fulfillment, perhaps even redemption, in her religion, and in military service to Israel. But her adopted country's recent actions had ended all that.

This time the military police were escorting her to the command post, where she would face her Israeli Army unit commander. The dim light of the armored personnel carrier's Spartan interior allowed her to sneak a glance at the senior MP across from her, and she felt he gazed at her with approval. Or was it admiration? One of her fellow soldiers had expressed open appreciation of her televised criticism of Israel's invasion of Gaza. Was it possible she had found another dissenter? She glanced furtively at the other MP, and felt she saw something completely different in his face. He looked embarrassed to escort her to what they all expected to be a slap-on-the-wrist reprimand. *The brotherhood of the objectors,* she reflected. Many soldiers opposed the wars they were forced to fight, but lacked resolve to do anything about it. To her, these MPs looked like they both were cut from that feeble, irksome cloth. *Or am I just imagining things,* she wondered.

The APC's stiff suspension jarred her spine. Nonetheless, she forced her eyes closed, as much to calm her nerves as to consider, in light of her bitter experience with Colonel Farson, how she should manage the upcoming confrontation with Major Simkin. Gritting her teeth, she muttered to herself, "I'm no victim. This time *I'll* take charge of the conversation." Steeling herself with this bold resolve, she started planning how to manipulate events to unfold in her favor.

***

Sarah stared at the concrete wall behind Major Simkin, bare save for mottled-gray blotches of mildew. Cracks of small-arms fire, staccato machine gun riffs and the muted booms of distant explosions played from one side of the room, the background soundtrack of modern warfare. She glanced through narrowed lids to both MPs and wondered whether she could count on them for moral support. *Probably not,* she concluded; they were committed soldiers. She shook her head and muttered, "Hypocrites."

"What?" Simkin glanced up from his desk.

She threw her shoulders back. "Nothing, sir."

He lowered his gaze again to his open laptop. "Don't you think we have a right to defend ourselves?"

A rhetorical question that didn't deserve the standard patriotic reply. Instead, she wondered how such a man rose to the rank of major. A head shorter than her and thinner at the waist, his shoulders only slightly broader than his hips, Simkin's dark beard seemed the only manly thing about him. Just a mousy man cowed by having to discipline a woman in uniform. Nonetheless, the fire of fanaticism burned in his heart, and she'd witnessed the ruthlessness with which he supported the Zionist ideal of a Jewish homeland.

"As I said in that interview," she pointed at his laptop, "this invasion isn't defense, it's terrorism. In fact, it's genocide."

Simkin swept a finger across the touchpad of his computer, tapped it once, then a second time, harder. As the screen cleared, he faced her, one hand resting on the top of the screen. "So you said. On CNN, no less. Higher command is furious. They want me to make an example of you. You know, I could have you—""Know and don't care."

He nodded and lowered his hand, snapping the laptop shut. "Weizmann, you're new here. This is our homeland. The Palestinians broke the truce. We had no choice—"

"*No choice?*" she said. "This is *their* homeland. *We're* the invaders. *We're* on occupied territory here. That's why it's called 'The Occupied Territories,' remember?"

He met her cold eyes for a moment, but then lowered his eyes to his desktop, chewing the corner of one lip. She inhaled deeply and blew it out like steam toward the ceiling, squeezed her eyes shut to focus.

"I've been studying, Major. If I'd done that before, I never would've joined. What I didn't find in the books, I've witnessed with my own eyes." Although what she'd found in the books was bad enough. Israel militarily occupied Gaza, the West Bank and East Jerusalem during the Six-Day War in 1967. The United Nations declared the occupation illegal, and ordered Israel out. One of *thirty-five* UN resolutions Israel failed to comply with in the forty years since then.

She dropped her eyes to his. Simkin raised a hand, but her glare made him drop it back to the desk. Just as she expected. During her six months in the Israeli army, she'd learned that rank had little practical significance in religious or political discussions. Not that they corrected their injustices, but they couldn't order a fellow Jew to silence. And she was ready to take full advantage of this chink in their emotional armor. She placed her fists on his desk. "Too much truth for you, *sir?* Here's some more. The Palestinians didn't break the truce. We did. And you know it."

She eased back to standing and glanced right and left to the MPs. Each in his turn avoided her gaze. Then she turned back to Simkin's bloodshot eyes and massive black beard, so long and scraggly it reminded her of tree moss.

"Hamas kept their side of the bargain, Major. In return, Israel was supposed to open the crossings in our apartheid wall, the same wall the International Court of Justice condemns. But we *didn't,* did we?"

Simkin stared at his desk and gave a weak shake of his head, his beard sweeping across his chest like a mop, and her ire turned to rage.

"For four months," she stabbed her finger in his direction, "for *four months,* the Palestinians couldn't get to their jobs, their schools, to outside hospitals, whatever. No work, no food, no medicine, no *nothing.* And then Israel killed six of them on November 4th—a targeted assassination—and another four two weeks later. All were killed *inside* Gaza. So Hamas went back to firing rockets. Who wouldn't? Now *who* broke the ceasefire, *sir?*"

Simkin slapped his desk with both palms and stood, still not meeting her eyes. "The Palestinians threaten our homela—"

She bent forward and pounded a fist onto his desk. "*We* threaten their *lives.* And it's their homeland, too. Their firecracker rockets are a joke, and you know it. Those ineffectual things kill two Israelis a year. *Two!* We kill ten times that many with every bomb we drop. We goad them into firing back, and invade them when they do—"

One of the guards grabbed her arm and tried to pull her back, but she pushed off from the desk, flung his hand aside and shoved him away with a slap to his chest. "Don't touch me, you hypocrite! You *know* I'm right. *We're* the criminals here, and God will see our deaths as justice for our crimes."

A cloud swept over the MP's face, and he stepped back and lowered his hands to his sides, his face to the floor. As much an admission of guilt as if he'd signed a confession. She whirled back to Simkin, who'd fallen back into his chair with a thump and a grunt, wide-eyed, his mouth an O.

"Oh? Oh, what?" she said. "We can commit genocide, but we can't say 'God'? *That's* our religion, is it? Well in that case, I guess I'm not a very good Jew, 'cause I *won't* kill innocent civilians but I *will* say 'God.'"

He raised both hands as if in surrender. "Private, calm down. Israel is about to declare a unilateral ceasefire—"

The mangled corpses of a slaughtered woman and her children filled her mind. "A unilateral ceasefire. After what? Israel *unilaterally* invaded and illegally occupied Gaza for the past forty years. Have you even *heard* of Amnesty International? They documented our illegal detentions. Tortures. Unlawful killings. Denied humanitarian aid. Blocked ambulances. Using civilians as human shields. All crimes against humanity. In the last three weeks we've *unilaterally* destroyed five thousand civilian homes and twenty mosques!"

"But—"

She unslung her assault rifle and flung it onto the major's desk, scattering papers with a clatter and a whoosh. She felt the guards move closer, but she didn't care. "So. We'll grant a unilateral ceasefire. What do you want, a medal? We *unilaterally* killed fourteen hundred Palestinians, most of them civilians, over four hundred of them *children!*"

She reached across her body with her left hand and stripped her sidearm from its holster. The guards pinned her arms to her sides. When they saw she only pinched the weapon between thumb and forefinger, they simply guided her hand to the desk. But she didn't release the gun. With a flick of her wrist, she threw it. It bounced off the assault rifle and started skidding. Simkin stabbed a hand at the weapon as it spun toward the edge of the desk, but he fumbled. The gun thudded on the floor at his feet. He looked at it, then at Sarah, eyes apprehensive, as though fearing she might throw something else at him if he bent over to pick it up. But her only volleys were her words.

"We've *unilaterally* murdered innocent civilians. Not to mention Red Cross and UN workers. We slaughtered over forty innocent refugees in that UN humanitarian aid center. Hey, we're great *unilaterally,* aren't we? Ask the media—they'll agree, because we've banned them from Gaza, *unilaterally.*"

His face reddening, Simkin pushed his chair back and bent down to pick up the gun ... and lingered there, as though preferring to hunker under the desk than meet Sarah's eyes. She directed her indictments at the top of his head. "What's the matter, Major? What is it we don't want the world to see? Genocide's unilateral too, you know, and that's exactly what Israel's doing."

Wincing, Simkin rose to sit upright, drew his chair forward to his desk, quietly laid the handgun in front of him and covered it with one open hand, then sank his drawn face into the other. He didn't see her fish her military knife from its scabbard, step forward and pound it into his desk with an overhand thrust. He jumped and scooted back in his chair while the guards grabbed her and hauled her back.

Pinned between them, she straightened and scanned the room with her eyes, then returned her gaze to Simkin, who stared at the swaying steel blade two feet in front of him. "Major, I quit."

When he raised his eyes to meet hers, she noticed his face held a mixture of ... she almost laughed, for the expression on his face truly was one of shock and awe. She turned her head a quarter-circle, first to one MP, then the other. "And all of you? All of you can go to hell, *unilaterally.*"

***

A nudge on her shoulder jolted Sarah out of her supremely optimistic day-dream, back to the musty grey interior of the armored vehicle. She shook off the apprehension that descended upon her and exited the APC's steel hatchway in a crouch. A strong hand clamped onto her bicep before she could even straighten, and tugged her toward a weathered concrete shoebox of a building she recognized to be the command center. She shrugged the senior MP's hand off and turned to push him away with a slap to his chest, a daring action that had established control in her day-dream. But before she could yell, "hypocrite!" he kicked her knee into a jackknife and swept her torso backwards as her lower half fell forward into the dust. Sarah tried to roll out of the painful position and away from her attacker, but he fell upon her and planted one of his knees into the small of her back, pinning her to the ground. In the same motion, he twisted her wrist into the excruciating stress position of a hyper-extended arm-bar. Leaning close from behind, his breath mingled the putrid odors of dyspepsia and fermenting plaque with that of a popular minty mouthwash. "Try that again," he growled into one ear, as he ground the other side of her face into the earth, "and I won't just break your arm. I'll break *all* of you!"

Through her pain and humiliation, all Sarah could think was how very much she had misjudged him. *So much for the brotherhood of the objectors,* she mused to herself, ruefully. *Not to mention, so much for me taking charge of the situation ...*

chapter 3

"SO WHAT'S THE punch line?" Katie asked, a forkful of Seafood Newburg poised at her lips. A waiter swept past behind her, starched white shirt flashing on black uniform as he twisted and swayed between tables, all the while balancing a loaded serving tray overhead on one hand.

Sarah snorted and felt her mouthful of Perrier pull an Old Faithful up her nostrils.

"Hey, don't stop there." Katie leaned into the tiny table for two, rumpling smooth ridges into the pink tablecloth. "I want to see you giggle Perrier out of your nose at the St. Moritz. That would be a first, for sure."

Sarah placed her glass in front of her and pretended to wipe her mouth on a napkin while surreptitiously rubbing the sting out of her nose. Her friend was the picture of femininity in her high-heeled, stressed-leather Italian boots and ecru linen bias-cut dress. Her *haute couture* wool coat and multicolor cashmere scarf hung on the back of her chair. In blue jeans and weathered leather jacket, Sarah felt better dressed for a hotdog stand than for one of Manhattan's best hotels.

Katie popped the creamed shrimp into her mouth and waved circles with the empty fork beside her head as she mumbled, "So, this Major Simkin, was he like, totally hot? I mean, did he ask you out after that?"

Sarah cracked a sober smile.

"Seriously," Katie said. "Some guys like hard women. Even pay for them to play dominatrix."

A pianist started playing, silencing the hubbub from the tables. Sarah pinched a millimeter of air between thumb and forefinger in front of a scrunched-up eye and said, "He wasn't exactly my type."

Katie speared a lump in the thick sauce of her dish, and found it to be a scallop. "Not your type? Oh, what ... you mean he didn't have a bullet in the back of his head?" Then she lowered her fork and looked up to search the instant silence from Sarah's side of the table. "Oh sweetie, I thought you were over that. I'm sorry, I didn't mean ... "

Sarah sucked a deep breath, forced a smile and waved her fingers as she looked down. "No problem. Water under the bridge. Or perhaps I should say, bad blood under the bridge. And yeah, I've dealt with it. Dead and gone. Ha, ha."

"Somehow ... I don't think so."

Sarah raised her eyes to Katie's lightly freckled face, and found powder-blue eyes studying her with concern.

"Somehow," Katie said, "I don't think you can ever joke away that kind of pain." She reached across the table and clasped Sarah's hand. "But tell you what, I'll always be here for you. You can cry on my shoulder and crash on my couch anytime."

"Yeah, but will you always feed me like this?" Sarah said, trying to force perkiness into her voice.

"Always. From now on, this will be our homecoming tradition. Nothing too good for my best friend. But next time, don't wait four years to look me up again."

With a deep sigh, she squeezed Katie's hand, then reached for her fork and knife. She ran her eyes over her perfectly seared sirloin steak and realized she hadn't even touched it. While she sliced into the meat, she said, "Oh, Kat, I thought when I—when they were dead, the nightmares would end. But they didn't. In fact, they got worse."

For a moment they sat in silence, pink juices oozing from the gash in Sarah's steak.

"You're ... " As Katie spoke, the piano music ended. The two women watched the pianist, decked out in black bowtie and concert tails, rise from his bench seat and strut toward the hotel lobby. Katie whispered, "What d'ya bet he picks his nose while listening to rap music in the break room?"

Sarah snorted, and felt the walls of stress that surrounded her crumble and fall away. A snicker followed, and then a laugh. For the rest of the meal they edged closer to the lighthearted, unrestrained friendship of their youth, but never completely recaptured it.

Over dessert, Sarah said, "You started to say something. Before Liberace left."

"Yeah. Hey, where'd he go, anyway? Man, if only *I* could get a job with half-hour breaks." Katie toyed with her strawberry sorbet. "I was going to say you're the strongest person I've ever known, man or woman. I don't know how you handle it."

"Anybody can pull a trigger, Kat."

"Not me. And one of the times, you pulled a *knife*. Stabbed the guy once in the gut and twice in the heart. You told me your commander made a sick joke of it. Said he could excuse the earlier shootings as friendly fire, but couldn't understand a knife accidentally going off three times."

"I told you that?"

"Yup. Guess you don't remember. You needed to unload, and weren't very cautious with details."

Sarah swept the room with her eyes, then leveled her index finger across the table. "If you ever say anything, I'll deny it. It'll be your word against mine, and my unit members and commander will testify on my behalf."

"Only to save their own skins. Your testimony against their war crimes could put them away for life. I remember that part of the story too." Katie bounced her eyebrows and shrugged her head in a tilt. "There's one thing I never understood. How'd you kill one of them without the other two figuring it out and crossing you off their list of worries?"

Sarah leaned back in her chair and braced herself against the table edge with a straight arm. Drumming the tabletop with her fingers, she studied Katie's face for a full minute. "Katie, you're my best friend."

"Goes both ways."

"You wearing a wire?"

Katie leaned forward with a sad smile and shook her head. "Honey, I'd never betray you, you know that. Don't go paranoid on me, okay?"

Sarah stared for a few seconds, then pushed her dessert away and tossed her napkin onto her place setting. "I think it's time for a bathroom break. Join me?"

"Nope, I'm good."

"You sure?"

"Yup. I'm fine."

"Just for old time's sake, I was hoping you'd let me see for myself ... that you're fine, that is."

Katie froze, bent over a spoonful of sorbet halfway to her mouth. Slowly, she lowered it to the dish, straightened, and stared. "You've *got* to be kidding. I'm *not* wearing a wire. I've never even *thought* about going to the police. I ... I ... Oh, for Pete's sake. Whoever *Pete* is." She threw her napkin onto the table and rose from her chair, snagged her purse from the floor and swung the strap over her shoulder. "It's okay. We're talking murder, after all, and you're the one who's on the line. Come on, let's get this over with."

They returned a few minutes later. "Sorry," Sarah said while she hitched her chair forward. "It plays with a person's mind. You begin to forget who your friends are. Trust no one. Doubt everybody."

Katie filled her mouth with a spoonful of sorbet and waved the apology away. "I've been wanting to show off my new lingerie anyway. So ... why didn't *they* kill *you?*"

Sarah took a deep breath and leveled her gaze. "Sergeant Kyle was away on two weeks' leave. He didn't know someone had spat in his eggs until he got back. By then the other two were dead." She swallowed hard, cleared her throat with more of a hum than a rasp. "Private Thomas came to me with tears in his eyes, begging forgiveness.

Said he couldn't live with the guilt, wished he was dead. But Private Carter was jubilant about it, reveling in rude innuendoes, and hinting he was going to do it again. He was the one who spiked my drink, and then took both first *and* last turns. What's worse, he was proud of it, and took every opportunity to offer me a 'real' date."

Sarah tossed her head violently, as if to shake off a shiver of fear. Then she steadied herself and stared at her hands in her lap, layered one upon the other like pale Autumn leaves, strangely calm at a time she thought her nails should be digging meat from her flesh. "It was Hell," she said. "I couldn't close my eyes to sleep, couldn't take a bite of food or a drink from my canteen without choking from fear. Carter was pure psycho. He saw me falling apart, and watched me like a predator waiting for its prey to weaken before taking it down. But at the same time, I could tell he was wary. He knew I still had some fight in me. If he had developed a suspicion I was out to kill him, he would've offed me in a second, even if he just read it in his tea leaves. So I killed him first. By that point, I knew it would be either him or me."

Katie waved an empty dessert spoon at her. "So why didn't Private Thomas turn and run, transfer into another ... what ... batallion? But in any case, get away from you. Surely he suspected he was next—"

"After that, Thomas might as well have been a zombie." Sarah paused, for she realized her own voice was that of a zombie—a robotic monotone that masked all emotion. She tried to dredge her soul for sympathy, but found none. "I'm sure he saw the hate in my eyes," she said. "I think he knew what was coming, but I think he wanted it that way.

He felt he deserved it and he wanted out—out of Iraq, out of his crime ... out of life. He was simply too guilt-ridden to care. Not just about me, but also about what the unit had done in—Well, anyway ... "

"I'm not wearing a wire. You checked, remember?"

Sarah shook her head. "Believe it or not, Thomas told me he used to be an altar boy. He saw President Bush speaking from on top of the Twin Towers rubble, bought his lies, waited a couple years until he came of military age, and then signed up. Stupid kid."

Katie's dessert had melted into a sorbet island surrounded by a moat of juice. Sarah stretched an arm over, dipped into it, and fed a spoonful of the stuff into her friend's mouth. She smiled bittersweetly while Katie swallowed with a nod. Then she leaned back in her seat and crossed her arms over her chest. "A lot of grunts couldn't handle Iraq. Many took their own lives. But Thomas was a strict Catholic. He believed suicide is the one sin God won't forgive. He got peer-pressured into what he did to me, a repressed altar-boy, drunk for the first time in his life, trying to fit in with the guys. But he couldn't end his own life, even though he wanted to. You know what he said to me the day he died? We were paired up and had to advance. He grabbed my arm, looked me in the eye and said, 'Into your hands I commend my spirit.' Then he stepped in front of me and just sort of *sauntered* into the smoke. Like he didn't have a care in the world. Stupid ... "

"Kid."

Sarah cocked her head at Katie. "Yeah. Exactly."

"Sergeant Kyle?" Katie leaned forward.

Sarah sighed, reached across the table and lifted Katie's dessert schooner, stirred the sorbet into the juice and drank the mix in two gulps. "Kyle figured it out when he got back. A no-brainer, really. Tried to kill me first, but, well ... "

"Stupid kid."

Sarah wagged a finger at her. "No. Smart. Scary smart. And nothing *kid* about him. But slow. And now very, very dead."

"Could've been you," Katie murmured. "Like I said, you're the strongest person I've ever known. But now ... well, I just don't seem to know you anymore."

"How do you mean?"

Katie gave her a sideways glance from beneath blonde eyebrows. "It's like you've been transformed into something ... different. I wish you could hear how coldly you speak of this, almost as if you were stomping cockroaches."

"I was."

"See, that's what I mean. Whatever else they were, they were human beings. Especially this Thomas guy. Why didn't you just go to the authorities and let *them* take care of it?"

Sarah clasped her hands together on the table and lowered her head over them, as if in prayer. "Look, nobody I know left Iraq the same person as when they entered. An unprecedented number of Iraq veterans returned home and ended up killing themselves and/or their families. PTSD, drug addiction, suicide, violent crime—it's off the charts. Iraq didn't just change people, it *warped* them."

"And it made you ... "

"Scary." She raised mournful eyes, sat back and crossed her arms on her chest. "Actually, I don't know what it made me. A vigilante? A monster? I'm trying to figure that out. Before Iraq, I wouldn't have thought myself capable of killing a mouse, much less another human being. I joined the Army for the discipline—"

"You joined to escape Nowheres-ville, USA."

She shrugged both shoulders and one eyebrow. "Yeah, well, that too. But the recruiter lied, and instead of being posted to California, I got Iraq. Ever since ... "

"I thought that only happened in the movies."

"The recruiter lying? Me too. That's how he suckered me into enlisting. Since then, I've learned to trust no one. That's why I had to, well, you know ... " Sarah waved a hand in her direction.

"Check out my lingerie?"

Sarah's face relaxed into a dopey expression. "For a wire, bleach-brain. What I was saying was that ... ever since Iraq, I've been struggling to rebuild myself."

Katie perked up and smiled wide, eyes twinkling, "And Israel didn't work out, so ... what army are you joining next? Give it up. Huh, huh, which one?"

Sarah glanced down at her plate. "Well, actually ... "

Katie's smile dissolved. "Oh, no. No. I was just kidding. You can't be serious."

"Not an army, no. I was thinking the JSA."

"The Jewish Soldiers Alliance? Are you bonkers? They're a bunch of right-wing Jewish terrorists! That group's been accused of everything from hate crimes to bombings and murder! The JSA's sister organization, *Kahin ... Kacha ...* "

"Kahane Chai."

Katie snapped her fingers. "What you said. There was a big article about them in the newspaper just the other day. They've been designated as a terrorist organization by both the U.S. State Department *and* the Israeli government! Heck, the JSA's so radical, many of their fellow Jews disown them *and* their ideology. You *are* kidding about joining them, right?"

Sarah shook her head. Katie threw her hands into the air and sat back so forcefully she bounced against the seatback. On the rebound, she leaned forward and braced both hands on the table edge. "Sarah. You know nearly nothing about New York City. And I don't care if you're Jewish, you know nothing about Judaism."

"I know history." She glanced away. "Anyway, people learn best when they get involved. I didn't last long in Israel, so I think I'll try the JSA."

"Oh, Christ."

"Isn't that blasphemy for a Christian?"

"Some say it's sacrilege. Do you know the difference?"

Sarah shrugged.

"Didn't think so. Hon, why do you keep bouncing between extremes? Remember how I used to call you 'pilgrim'? You used to be the most innocent, naive person I knew."

"Sheltered upbringing."

The waiter approached, and both women went silent while he arranged a tea service between them with the tinkle of fine china. As soon as he left, Katie said, "Sheltered upbringing? I'll say. I was there, remember? You and your pleasantly weird kid sister. Your divorced, struggling mother. Your disappeared and oh-so-deadbeat dad. It doesn't get much more sheltered than the outskirts of Leola, Pennsylvania, in the heart of Amish country. Not bad for a Christian." She tapped her own chest with her fingertips. Then she pointed across the table at Sarah. "But absolute isolation for a Jew."

"Believe it or not," Sarah said, "Israel wasn't much better. The Jews were so divided, I left more confused than when I arrived. Now it's time I learned my religion."

"Not this way." Katie pushed her cup of tea away. "It's like you're trying to kill yourself, but I'm afraid you'll kill someone else first. What's happened to you? It's like something twisted you, and now you can't get your noggin screwed on straight again."

Sarah dropped her head. "I ... I don't know what's happened to me." She raised her eyes and stared across the table, but not at Katie. "Remember that swim in the lake when we were kids? When you got the cramp?"

"And you saved me from drowning? Sure. Who can forget? I owe you my life."

Sarah floated her eyes toward the ceiling, her head tilted to one side. "After that, I thought I'd spend the rest of my life helping people. But after Iraq, I don't feel whole unless I'm putting my life on the line for something. I can't relax, or even enjoy myself for more than a few minutes. I want a relationship, but can't hold on to one for more than a couple weeks. I want fulfillment, love, atonement. But I can't find those either."

"Well, you certainly won't find them in the JSA."

She lowered her eyes to Katie again. "I'm desperate. Drastic situations call for drastic measures."

"Honey, don't do anything now. What's the rush? You've got a decent place to live, a good job. Why not just let things skate for a while? Or hey, maybe even just join a synagogue, stick your toe in the water first. You're confused, and—"

"I'm going to do it. I'm going to join the Jewish Soldiers Alliance. I can't explain why, because I don't understand it myself. It's simply something I have to do."

Katie shook her head as she reached for the delicate china cup in front of her. "You're going to join the most hardcore Jewish group in this city? Just because you 'have to'? In that case, you're not confused. You're crazy."

chapter 4

*STOP BEING SUCH **a man** ... .*

One leg tucked under her, Sarah sat on a cheap brown sofa in the Brooklyn apartment some members of the Jewish Soldiers Alliance jokingly referred to as their temporary field office. The rest of the group were in deep conversations that didn't include her, but she didn't feel slighted. She was the newbie, and it would take time for her to earn their confidence. Besides, she didn't understand Yiddish, so the background conversation in the small apartment meant as little to her as the piano music had at the St. Moritz.

Silently, she ruminated over Katie's parting words three weeks ago. *Is that what I'm trying to be—just like a man?*

Voices rose and she cast her eyes to the two men in the corner. Three JSA youths sat to one side of her, silently observing the pair, hands stalled in midair from picking at the plate of tortilla chips and salsa that lay between them. Sarah didn't need to understand Yiddish to realize the two men were in disagreement. The tall, dark and muscular Benyamin, the resident of the apartment, towered over Hymie, who at five foot two was so slight of build, he was doomed to wearing "tweens" clothing for the rest of his life. Woody Allen looked like Mr. Universe in comparison. Benyamin, the leader and unabashed bully of the group, barked his words and stabbed a finger into Hymie's chest, driving him backward even with that insignificant gesture. Hymie backpedaled, arms spread wide, palms open and up, his face drawn into lines of innocence and perplexity. When he recovered, he spoke softly in return, shoulders slumped, a quaver to his voice. Benyamin turned and waved him away without even looking in his direction.

Voices now lowered, the three youths returned to their chips and dip, and Sarah allowed her mind to drift back to her conversation with Katie: "So you grew up self-sufficient," Katie had said, "always needing to dominate any relationship, never able to trust a man in your life. But hon, you'll never find happiness until you become the woman you were born to be."

"Maybe I *am* the woman I was born to be," Sarah had countered.

They'd stood on the sidewalk outside the famous hotel on Central Park South, Katie's eyes filled with love and concern. Her words came out in puffs of vapor in the chilly winter air, whisked away by a cool breeze from the park that stirred the scent of horses and greenery into the city streets. "A woman needs a man for her life to be complete," Katie said. "And if you reign over your man like a tyrant, he won't be a man anymore. He won't respect himself and, in time, neither will you. You don't need to learn how to love, Sarah, you need to learn how to trust—how to trust a man enough to let him lead the relationship, be the man he needs to be. Did you ever ballroom dance?"

Sarah shook her head, an amused smile twitching her lips. "Amish country, remember?"

"Yeah, well, when you ballroom dance, only one person can lead." Katie wove the fingers of her hands together and allowed one hand to lead the other in a wave-dance. "If you both try to lead, you don't end up dancing, you end up fighting." She pulled from both ends and her hands separated. She held up the newly divorced hands and said, "Is that how you want to spend your life? Think about it...."

Benyamin's voice exploded in anger, yanking Sarah from the sofa and to her feet. The bully whirled on Hymie with a backslap that spun the small man's head in a flail of wavy red hair and flung his yarmulke across the room like a Frisbee. Benyamin reversed his arm, but the JSA youths were upon him before he could land a second slap. The overturned plate threw up a confetti-cloud of tortilla chips and dashed a red gash of salsa on the carpet before landing with a clatter.

Sarah rushed forward to where Hymie cowered, both arms protectively wrapped over his head like a human pretzel. While the youths wrestled Benyamin into a corner, Sarah pulled Hymie away, chased by the bully's thundering shouts. Hymie's slight form stayed bent over while she led him into the short hallway and snatched up his crocheted yarmulke from the cheap shag rug. She left him propped against the wall, replacing his yarmulke with trembling hands, and stepped back into the room. No way would she stay here, and it was clear that Hymie needed to leave too.

As she whisked her leather jacket from where it lay draped over the sofa back, she glanced into the corner, where the wary youths held restraining hands on their leader. Benyamin shook them off and thrust out a muscular arm, sighting along its length, his finger pointing past her and straight between Hymie's eyes. Benyamin's face, flushed red with anger, reminded her of a cartoon character whose next breath inevitably comes out as steam. Instead, he shouted a single line in Yiddish she couldn't make out, and then turned his back on them.

She had committed herself to the JSA, but she never, ever tolerated a bully. She shouted at Benyamin, "Coward! Try that on someone your own size ... . Try that on *me*, for that matter, and see what happens!"

When he didn't turn to face her, she plucked a paperback novel from the coffee table and flung it at him, yelling, "Yeah, I thought so!"

The book tumbled in the air and opened with a flutter of pages. It struck him in the lower back, but he stood immobile. Huffing in indignation, she threw on her jacket while she strode the few steps to Hymie and pulled him from where he leaned against the wall, blood trickling from one corner of his mouth. Then she draped one arm around his shoulders, marched him out the door, and slammed it behind them.

***

She threw open the aluminum-and-glass doors of the apartment building and pulled Hymie out onto the sidewalk. The cement underfoot was colored gray by the gloom of the winter day, the macadam street next to it boot-polish black. She cast a look back and, as they had in the weeks she'd been coming to the JSA meetings, her eyes settled on two bullet holes in the aluminum door trim, scars the building wore of some long-forgotten shooting.

She inhaled deeply, and the crisp winter air freeze-dried her nostrils and sharpened her senses. She glanced at Hymie while she led him by the elbow to a nearby coffee shop, and saw it was the same for him. His gait seemed steadier, and the tremble she'd felt in his arms had disappeared.

When they entered the Chez What? café, he headed directly to the bathroom while Sarah waited at the counter. He emerged minutes later with a harlequin face, one cheek pale and freckled, the other crimson and puffy. When he slipped onto the stool beside her, she drawled, "Stranger, you look like you could use two fingers of espresso."

He shook his head, red hair swaying, and affected a smile that didn't quite hide his misery, even when he said, "Anything stronger than tea, ma'am, I get mean and start looking for trouble." He snatched a paper napkin from the counter, dabbed at the corner of his mouth and found it clean of blood. With a sigh, he dropped the ball of his hand to the counter, blooming with petals of the white tissue.

"Trouble?" Sarah said. "I'd say you already found it. What happened back there?"

He dropped his attempt at humor; hunching farther, his narrow shoulders hovered above the level of the counter, his eyes down. Speaking to the countertop, he said, "Do you believe in what the JSA is doing?"

"I've decided to quit."

His eyes lifted and at last his shoulders relaxed a bit. "Me, too. You look at our extremist approach, it doesn't take an Einstein to understand why we're not liked, even by our fellow Jews." He snorted in disgust and turned to her, squaring his slender shoulders. "Einstein. Know what *he* said? In 1948, one year after the creation of Israel. Or maybe I should say, 'the Zionist state of Israel,' because that's really all it is, isn't it? Israel's nothing more than the Zionists' choice of a Jewish homeland—"

"You were saying?"

He gave an embarrassed shrug. "Anyway, one year later, Einstein denounced Menachem Begin's Zionist Freedom party as, and I quote, 'closely akin in its organization, methods, political philosophy and social appeal to the Nazi and Fascist parties.'" He snapped his head in her direction and raised one eyebrow. "Hey, did you ever read *51 Documents: Zionist Collaboration with the Nazis*? I have. Can you imagine? Einstein basically equated Begin's party with the Nazis and Fascists!"

Sarah hadn't known, but she got it. "Wow," was all she could come up with.

"Wow, indeed. And he was speaking about Menachem Begin, who later became prime minister of Israel."

He motioned to the counter attendant, who stepped over, order pad in hand. "What can I getcha?"

"I'll order," Hymie said, which was fine with her. They'd killed time there before, waiting for Benyamin to return home and open the JSA's temporary field office. By now both of them could fill in the order blanks for the other. "Tea for me and assorted cookies," Hymie told the man. "House blend for the lady with an extra shot, and a raspberry scone."

"Gotcha." The waiter turned and yelled over his shoulder, "Hot earwax and a plate of UFOs, cup of midnight with a sledgehammer, one cinderblock with smallpox."

His counter-mate sauntered over, a frothing pot of hot milk in one hand. "Watcha yammering this time, Loco?" Not waiting for an answer, he took the order slip in his free hand and walked away, shaking his head as he digested its contents.

Neither spoke until the counter attendants split in opposite directions. Then Sarah said, "Is the world crazy, or is it just me?"

"Nah, it's just him." Hymie nodded toward the attendant nick-named Loco. "Heck, it's a boring job. Got to spice it up somehow. Maybe he's saner than the rest of us."

"Back to the subject," she said, rapping a clenched fist against the counter. "So that's why Benny belted you? Because you decided to quit?"

"You're the only one who gets away with calling him Benny, you know that?" Hymie smiled for the first time since leaving the apartment. "But I kind of like it. And yeah, that's why. I just don't believe in what we're doing anymore. We started out trying to protect our people, but became terrorists ourselves. Benny ... " Hymie smiled again. "Benny ... If he heard me call him that, he'd hit me again. Anyway, Benny called me a traitor. Said I should be killed."

She raised her eyebrows in alarm. "Would he? Kill you, that is."

"Nah. Just talk. Know what he shouted at me as we left?"

She shook her head while taking a bite of her scone.

Hymie pulled in a ragged breath. "He said, if I make trouble, he'll break Roni's legs."

She froze her scone in midair, then lowered it to the crumb-dusted plate while she struggled to chew and swallow. In her mind's eye she saw Hymie's youngest brother. Nine years old, half-blind from birth and both mentally and physically retarded, he was one of the sweetest kids she'd ever known. The two of them bonded the day they met. "What's Roni got to do with this?" she asked.

"Nothing. Nothing at all. Just bully stuff, I guess." Hymie sipped his tea, then dunked a cookie and bit a half moon in it. "Wanted to hit me where it hurts."

"What're you going to do?" She leaned back in the stool and rolled her coffee mug between her palms.

"Don't worry, Benny's harmless. Mostly." Hymie finished the cookie and sipped his tea. "Hey, here's an idea. There's a protest at the Israeli Consulate this weekend. Want to go with me?"

"A protest against ... ?"

"The recent war crimes in Gaza, against the Palestinians. Look, we'll go dressed as Muslims. I passed for a fair-skinned Syrian a bunch of times, when we'd infiltrate and disrupt Palestinian demonstrations."

Sarah showed him a blank face. "Explain."

"What, you don't know about this? We dress as Arabs and work our way into the crowd. Then we agitate. Sometimes we get the demonstrators to pick a fight with the other side. When we got lucky, we start full-blown riots. The Palestinians' peaceful demonstrations made us look bad. This turns the tables, and makes *them* look like the aggressors. But the point is, I can pass for a fair-skinned Syrian, or even for a Palestinian."

He peered at her face. "As for you, there are plenty of Caucasian Muslims. Think Russia, Albania, Bosnia, Kosovo ... even Western converts. You'll be covered head-to-toe in black, but even if they notice your eyes, they'll think nothing of it. And maybe ... maybe if you and I protest for the *Palestinians* this time, that will atone for some of the mistakes we made while working with the JSA. What d'ya think?"

She sipped her coffee. "Won't Benny and his gang be there? On the Israeli side?"

He shrugged. "Sure. But, well, you know ... nothing ventured, nothing gained. Anyway, I know their tactics. We should be able to steer clear of them."

She gazed at him and felt a warm glow invade the core of her being. Atonement. Wasn't that what she'd been looking for? And what better way than to protest Israel's war crimes against the Palestinians? The spirit of mischief twitched the corners of her mouth, then spread a full smile across her face.

chapter 5

"HOW DO I look?" Sarah spun around in the tiny rectangle where her Murphy bed would normally lie when it wasn't folded against the wall. The third-floor studio apartment was small, but it was two blocks from Central Park and gave her everything she needed, including a quick commute to her new job. Besides, the job Katie had landed for her meant she could afford it. She never imagined herself selling fur coats, but the commissions were generous and the hours flexible. She still wore her venerable tan leather jacket to work, but that didn't stop her from accepting the mink earmuffs Stwarroff's gifted her in appreciation of her first sale. Both items were far different from what she wore now.

"How do you look?" Katie said from where she sat cross-legged on the floor, "Take that tent off and I'll tell you."

"No, this is great." Sarah spun another turn in her Islamic dress. The black, full-length *abaya* covered her from neck and wrists to ankles, and with her face and head hidden beneath a black *hijab* and veil, only her eyes showed through slits. "I can see you, but you can't see me," she mused. "I wonder if that's the point. And where's your *abaya?*"

Katie rolled her eyes, stood, and spun a circle in her full-length block-print dress. "Talk to me when Armani goes Muslim." She pointed down. "Hey, at least I'm not showing any leg. So, we're going to meet this, what's his name? Heinie?"

"Hymie. And don't make fun of him. He's very nice."

At this, Katie cocked her head, and Sarah could almost imagine her social antennae going up, her radar sweeping the horizon for blips. "Is he, like ... ?"

"Totally hot?" The two locked eyes, and laughed. "He's very nice," Sarah said, "but a complete nebbish."

"Hey, that's Yiddish, isn't it?" As she spoke, Katie settled herself back down to sitting on the floor, her dress swept into folds in her lap. "Where'd you pick that up?"

Sarah snaked her arms into black elbow-length gloves. "JSA talk: Be a man, not a nebbish. But Hymie's a living example of nebbish-dom. Nerdy, inept, almost effeminate. Really not JSA material."

"Sounds like your kind of a guy. Easy to boss around, and there whenever you need him for diaper changes and takeout pizza. Your very own Mr. Mom."

Sarah wove her hands together to hitch the gloves into the webs of her fingers. Then she turned them inside out with a stretch of her arms and a rapid fire of multiple knuckle cracks. "I'm only going along to keep him out of trouble."

"Uh-huh." Katie uncrossed her legs, rocked forward onto her feet and stood. "You stick with any man long enough, it's *you* who'll be in trouble." As she spoke, she swept her hands over an imaginary balloon-sized tummy and then, bracing it from beneath, waddled across the room to the mini-fridge under the counter.

"Marriage or nothing, babe," Sarah said, and then lowered her voice to a murmur. "And the way my life is going, I'm betting on nothing." Then she raised her head and watched Katie scout through her refrigerator's meager offerings. "Do me a favor and finish that cheesecake."

"Specific crave," Katie replied, emerging with an apple in one hand and a wedge of cheese in the other. While she nibbled the cheese, she rubbed her imaginary balloon-tummy appreciatively, if clumsily, with the hand holding the apple.

Sarah stepped to the door and unlatched the deadbolt with a metallic click. "So ... are you coming?"

"Let me think about it," Katie mumbled around her cheese, pausing only a split second before adding, "Okay."

"You're weird."

"Love you, too."

Sarah grabbed a posterboard sign from where it lay propped against the wall, and held it up by its wooden handle. She pointed to the sign, which simply read Again? above a drawing of piled corpses beside an open mass grave. She said, "The Jewish Soldiers Alliance borrowed their motto from the Jewish Defense League: 'Never Again,' referring to the Holocaust. But they're only thinking of Jewish lives. In 1996, the Israelis killed a hundred refugees in a UN compound in Qana, Lebanon. *Refugees*, Kat. Innocent civilians. Last month, they did it again, in Gaza. The UN told the Israelis about the refugees, even gave their GPS coordinates, to avoid them being shelled. But the Israelis shelled them anyway. And some say they used white phosphorus, a violation of international law. They killed forty refugees, mostly women and children."

"You were there, weren't you?"

She nodded soberly. "Not *right* there, but near enough to hear about it afterwards. Seems like a lifetime ago, but it was only last month. What seems unreal is how quickly I was allowed to leave Israel. Almost as if they *wanted* me gone after I did that interview. But that was then, this is now."

She swung the door open and Katie tossed the apple core into the trash, stepped past her and turned in the doorway. "Just so you know, I haven't been to a demonstration since college. If my wimp-o-meter swings into the red, I'm gone."

"Wimp-o-meter?" Sarah grinned.

Katie's face turned grave as she laid two fingers on Sarah's chest, indenting the thin fabric of the black *abaya*. "Look," she said, peering into Sarah's eyes through the slits in her veil, "I'm serious. I don't quite know you anymore. Unlike you, *I'm* not bent on self-destruction. If I sense danger, I'm leaving, with or without you. Don't hold it against me. My help is limited to telling you we shouldn't be doing this. It's risky."

"You don't have to come."

Katie dropped her fingers from the *abaya* and huffed "Huh" with a jerk of her head. "No, I do. I *do* have to come. It's my turn to save *you* from drowning."

She stepped from the doorway and turned down the hallway in the direction of the elevators. Sarah studied her purposeful stride, and considered how hard it must be for Katie to do this. Then she pulled the door closed behind her and followed.

***

"Oh, *boy*, this could turn ugly," Katie said as they neared the edge of the crowd of protesters. They'd caught the subway to Grand Central Station and exited on 42nd Street. Sarah led the way, resting her protest sign on her shoulder. The moment they turned the corner onto Second Avenue, they saw two crowds facing off on opposite sides of the street in front of the Israeli Consulate. The protesters were predominantly Arabs, with a smattering of other nationalities.

Most demonstrators carried signs and shouted slogans. The crowd of Jewish men, some in frock coats and hats, others wearing yarmulkes, milled angrily in front of the consulate. Both sides were restrained by their own leaders, complemented by a moderate police presence.

Katie stopped beside a lamppost and hooked one arm around it like a newfound aluminum friend, and her face told Sarah she was struggling to hide her anxiety. Even so, she wondered if Katie planned to use the lamppost for cover or support, in case a wave of protesters threatened to sweep her away. "Turn ugly?" she said. "I've seen ugly, and this ain't it."

"Maybe not, but ... "

Now, her friend's face held the fear she'd been suppressing since they turned the corner. "Listen, Kat, you don't have to be here." She glanced at her watch, then at the building address behind them. "This is where we agreed to meet. Hymie should arrive any minute now, and I can catch up with you later."

Katie swallowed hard, and her head bobbed with the effort. "I'll stay."

Sarah saw her force a brave face, but figured a little hardship would do her good. She reached out and squeezed her shoulder with one hand and said, "Atta girl. Now look, you stay here. I'm going to check out the Palestinian side of the crowd, see if I spot any JSA faces."

Katie's eyes unglued themselves from the crowd and bored into Sarah's. "You told me Hymie said the JSA wasn't going to do fake protestors this time."

"Benny might've changed his mind. But don't worry. Anytime you want to know where I am, just look for my sign above the crowd."

Katie reached out and grasped the sign's handle. "Let me hold it. You'll move more freely without it."

Sarah relaxed her grip, but then realized the sign might draw unwanted attention to her best friend. "That's okay." She patted Katie's hand, then teased her manicured fingers from the handle. "I'll fit in better if I carry it. If I'm not back in ten minutes, it either means I've found Hymie, or there's trouble."

"What—?"

"Kidding! Either way, don't come looking for me. If I'm not back in ten, go home and wait for me there."

"How about I just call you on your cell?"

Sarah glanced at the milling crowd as they waved their signs and chanted their slogans, so loudly they threatened to drown out even her thoughts. "I doubt I'll hear the ring," she said, and turned to leave.

"Wait." Katie waved a hand toward the other side of the street. "Just remind me what we're up against here."

"Okay." Sarah rested the sign on her shoulder and locked eyes with her. "The other side are all Zionists, meaning those who support the political idea of a Jewish homeland—in other words, Israel. Most are Jews, but some are fundamentalist Christians, maybe a few ill-informed sympathizers. The JSA is one small, radical faction of Zionist Jews. What works in our favor is that the Zionists are divided into many groups, and they don't always work together. What's working against us is that the JSA, and groups like them, are very good at tricking the others into following their lead."

She turned her gaze toward the crowd. "Hopefully, this will remain peaceful. Hymie thinks it will, and he's been to plenty of these. We'll protest Israel's war crimes, and the other side will pretend Israel's innocent. Speeches, a little yelling, maybe a little pushing. Or ... things could turn violent. Let me go check the crowd. Back in a few."

She turned and stepped into the mass of milling protesters. She passed people of all ethnicities, a multicultural cross-section of the cosmopolitan city. The din of their chants and the clutter of their protest signs engulfed her, and she soon realized Katie probably wouldn't be able to see either her or her sign in the crush. She wove herself through the crowd until she was satisfied none of the anti-Zionist protestors presented a familiar face. Then she returned to the lamppost, where she found another woman, dressed modestly and wearing a headscarf, speaking politely with Katie. "*Assalam alaikum,*" Sarah said, playing out her Muslim cover, "Peace be upon you."

The woman turned, swept Sarah's black *abaya* with her eyes, smiled and said, "Shalom."

"What?" Sarah felt her head swim at the Jewish welcome, and involuntarily took a half step back. "How did you know I'm—?"

Shouts from the crowd washed her words away, and the stranger extended a bare hand. "I'm sorry," she said, "I'm not Muslim, like you. I'm Jewish. But like Muslims, Orthodox Jews cover." She gestured to her headscarf and drew a circle around her face with two fingers. "So do many Palestinian Christians. Sometimes it's hard to tell all of us apart, but in any case, I'm on your side. By the way," she said, pointing above their heads, "great sign."

Sarah took the woman's hand in hers and shook it, her mind numb. She struggled to think of something to say, but just then a frail form, his head and face wrapped in the Palestinian checked scarf known as a *guttra*, ran to her side, shouldered her lightly and rebounded. She regained her balance with a quick sidestep and turned as the man gasped, "The ... the ... the son of a ... "

Sarah realized with surprise that the man was Hymie. She grabbed both of his arms and pressed them to his sides, steadying him. Stooping slightly, she drew his eyes into hers. "What happened?"

He flicked his gaze across the street, back again, then pointed with a finger that trembled all the way to his shoulder. Sarah followed it to where Benyamin stood in the opposite crowd. "See ... " he panted. "See him?"

She involuntarily sucked in a breath, then jerked a nod. Hymie pressed a block of something cool and rough into her hand, saying, "Here, hold this."

She glanced down. "A brick?" She turned her worried gaze to where he stood beside her, bent at the waist, hands on knees, sucking air. When he straightened, Sarah saw wet blotches on the *guttra* below his tear-reddened eyes. "He found out," he panted, voice quavering. "I don't know how, but he found out we switched sides."

She recalled flashes of horrors she'd witnessed, wrought by the brutal hands of vengeful men, and cringed. Deep inside, she felt her inner being curl up in a corner, hands over ears, but she willed herself to say, "What? What did he do?"

"Roni." His little brother's name came out in a shudder. "Roni. Benyamin ... he shot him in both legs."

"He shot him in ... " Her mind flooded with questions. The first thing she wanted to know was Roni's condition. Instead, she asked, "What's Benny doing here, then? Didn't you call the police?"

"Of course. But they can't arrest him. Nobody saw him do it. The doorbell rang, Roni answered, bang-bang-bang and the shooter was gone. We found Roni collapsed, screaming, in the doorway. The police are searching for witnesses, but so far nobody saw anything. Roni almost died from blood loss and shock. He's in the hospital. Both legs shattered." Hymie began to cry. "Remember how Benny said he'd break both his legs? I just *know* it was him!"

"Christ," Katie muttered, but Sarah only faintly heard. The walls of her world closed in upon her. First the shouts from the crowd, and then the crowd itself fell from consciousness as her mind focused on one point, everything else obscured in a gray blur. She peered into the crowd. Centered in the tunnel of her vision, Benyamin turned from where he chatted with one of the JSA youths on the other side of the street. Decked out in faded dungarees and a denim jacket over a loose rugby shirt, he struck a cocky pose as he scanned the field of protesters. He took a hard drag from his cigarette, and the JSA youth by his side laughed as Benyamin said something to him, smoke trickling out with his words. And then his eyes settled upon Sarah. Straightening, he cracked a wide smile, winked, and blew her an exaggerated kiss.

Sarah bellowed something between a scream and a war cry, and flung the brick in her hand with all of her strength. As it arched across the street, she launched herself forward, gripping her sign like a spear.

The crack of an explosion shocked her to a stop as a cloud of smoke and dust partially engulfed the consulate side of the street.

"Bomb!" somebody yelled from the other side. "They're trying to kill us!"

"Defend yourselves!" another voice bellowed. "Attack!"

As a group, the JSA members threw themselves forward. The police closed ranks, and their line buckled outward as they absorbed the charging demonstrators. For a moment Sarah thought the line would hold, but then the rest of the Zionists followed the JSA lead and surged forward as well. The dam of policemen broke in one weak spot that turned from a crack to a chasm in a split-second. The Zionists exploded through the opening, knocking some police off their feet and pushing others aside. They swept across the street in a flood of humanity that engulfed Sarah in its mass. She felt strong hands grab and carry her;

other hands tore at her clothing. Something hard struck the side of her head and threw a dozen suns into her vision. Then she felt herself thrown to the ground. She struck her head again as she belly-flopped and rolled into the gutter, the asphalt clawing at her flesh, her rag-doll arms and legs flailing in different directions.

She tried to shake the fog from her mind and eyes, but found her entire body turned to rubber. Every movement swayed farther than she intended, then rebounded involuntarily. After a moment, she succeeded in lifting her wobbling head to witness a scene of chaos and insanity. Protesters from both sides battled with their fists and signboards, milling around in pockets as if on a Middle Ages battlefield. She didn't see any police until her gaze reached the edge of the battlefield. Her mind struggled to connect her thoughts. Then she realized that by working the edge of the crowd, the police not only protected their backs, but held their position between the crowd and the consulate.

Searching for Katie and Hymie, she swung her head around as she tried to raise herself up on rubber arms that rebelled against her attempt to control them. On the third try, she succeeded at propping herself up on her elbows. She struggled to keep from falling, but couldn't get rid of the sway in her arms that threatened to capsize her. Looking around, she found a single lamppost that suddenly split into two, and then slowly merged back into one. *Double vision*, she thought. *A concussion for sure. Maybe even brain damage. This isn't good.*

Then, remembering where she last saw Katie, she followed the lamppost to the ground with her eyes. Katie wasn't there, but the Jewish woman they had met lay on her back on the ground at its base. A youth stood over her in stonewashed jeans and tails-out shirt, his head bundled anonymously in a black-and-white Palestinian *guttra*. The woman stretched both arms upward, palms open and waving, pleading as the man leveled a pistol at her face. Sarah felt a heave in her chest as a wave of blood slammed into her brain.

The hammer of the gun rose, so slowly she could see the shake in the assailant's hand. She screamed, "NOOO!" but her scream seemed swallowed by the din of the battle around her.

The hammer fell. As if a series of freeze frames, a jet of flame blew a funnel of smoke from the barrel and the gun rose in recoil. Sarah blinked, and once again saw life in real time. On the ground, the woman's headscarf billowed outward, then contracted as her head bounced on the pavement once, then lay still. Her limp arms stretched skyward and gently swayed in the current of her departing soul. Then, with a spasm that shook her entire body, her arms fell to the pavement with a double-slap.

The youth stepped from where he straddled her body and sprinted away, dodging protesters like a running back headed for the goal line. Three bobs and weaves, and he disappeared into the crowd. Sarah watched him go, sometimes as one man and sometimes splitting into two, and then sank her face into the crook of one tremulous arm, heaved a sob and longed for unconsciousness to return.

chapter 6

"EAT SOMETHING."

Sarah wanted to shake her head or turn away. Instead, she lay on one side in the Murphy bed, staring as Katie held the soup spoon to her mouth.

"Something. Please. *Anything*. It's been three days." After a moment with no response, Katie dropped the spoon into the bowl with a slosh and a clatter. Sarah's head jerked, but she didn't respond.

"The doctor in the emergency room warned me you might still be suffering from combat fatigue. So you might be a little, ah, difficult." Katie tried to smile at Sarah, failed, and added, "Know what else she said? 'Either way, Sarah needs peace, quiet, and understanding.'"

Sarah didn't need reminding. She'd also overheard Katie's side of the call to the triage nurse two days ago, when Sarah refused to leave her bed for her follow-up appointment at the hospital. Katie had called the Emergency Room. "Yes, she's walking," Katie replied to the nurse's question. "Not talking much ... well, almost no talking. But no, no dizziness, no more double vision ... .

Yes, I know the first brain scan was normal, but how will we know what's going on if she refuses to come back for the second one?"

Now, smoothing her trumpet skirt with both hands, Katie stood and paced the small floor. "The doctor was probably right about the combat fatigue," she said. "Poor thing. You've been through enough to break Rambo." She pulled one of Sarah's arms from beneath the blue fleece blanket and peeled back the sleeve. Then she leaned close and inspected the scrape on Sarah's cheek. "You're healing. No signs of infection."

"Tell me again," Sarah rasped out, cleared her throat and repeated, "tell me what happened."

Katie sighed. "You tell me something first. When you were in Iraq, why didn't your commander have you killed? Why'd he cut that deal with you, and send you home a hero?"

Sarah closed her eyes, as if in sleep. She didn't feel any shift in weight on the bed, and opened her eyes to find Katie still waiting, watching her intently. "You're a good friend, Kat."

"The best. Don't forget me in your will. Now, about your commander?"

"I have a headache."

Katie took in a quick breath. "That's new. Maybe you're dehydrated. Drink something. If that doesn't work, I'll drag you back to the hospital for another MRI."

"I'm tired."

"You haven't eaten. Keep this up and I'll put you in a hospital with a tube up your nose. A *biiig* tube. I'll ask them to make it ribbed, for added discomfort."

Sarah rolled her eyes, then grimaced from the vicious ache in her orbits. When she glanced at Katie again, she saw the resolve written in every line of her friend's face. She sighed deeply, pushed herself to a sitting position and propped herself against the wall with a pillow. With one hand she straightened the lapels of her oversized flannel pajamas. "Okay. Give me that soup."

Katie bent over and retrieved the bowl from where she'd placed it on the floor, along with a plate of finger sandwiches, the crusts tastefully trimmed off. Sarah took the bowl in her hands, and Katie propped the plate on the bed beside her.

"Okay. Why didn't my commander have me killed? First of all, killing an American was murder, but the army taught us the Iraqis weren't human. In the American soldier's eyes, they were animals. It's the same old story. In World War Two the Germans were Krauts, the Japanese were Nips, the Chinese, Chinks. In Vietnam, the Viet Cong were gooks. In every conflict, the military think-tanks dehumanize the enemy, to make it psychologically easier for the soldiers in the field to kill them. After the war, we meet them, maybe managing the corner convenience store, and realize they're just as human as we are. That's when the war-crimes trials start. Well, sometimes … ."

"Okay, I get that part of it." Katie leaned her chin onto her open palm. "Now, back to my question?"

With a sigh, Sara continued. "A lot of guys offed Iraqi civilians just for kicks, or to vent their frustration. But killing me? That would've been tough. They saw me as one of their own. And a girl at that. Anyway, it would've been too suspicious. I'd already reported Colonel Farson to the JAG—the Judge Advocate General. I told them about his war crimes, as well as those of his unit."

She slurped a spoonful of soup and felt the broth warm her all the way down. Realizing how hungry she was, she took another spoonful, mumbled, "Mmm, that's good," then took a third. Finally she handed the spoon to Katie, cradled the bowl in both hands and guzzled the contents in one swig. Katie stood and took the empty bowl across the room to the countertop stove.

"So what would've happened if I was killed by the same unit I reported?" she called to Katie's back. "Sure, Farson might've gotten away with it. But I told him I'd mailed a more detailed report home, with names, dates, places, and my mother had delivered it to a lawyer for safe-keeping."

"A bluff." Katie spoke over her shoulder as she poured soup from the pan.

"Of course. But Farson couldn't risk it." She waved a hand dismissively. "For that matter, none of my unit members could risk it. So he overlooked my 'friendly fire' killings, including the stabbing, and in return I dropped my case against him with the JAG. I was the only soldier who stepped forward as a witness to his war crimes. When I with-held my testimony, the case went away. If the truth be told, there was so much negative publicity coming out of Iraq at that time, the JAG was *happy* to let it go. The last thing the army needed was another scandal. Farson shipped me home; end of story."

Katie returned with the soup and reclaimed her seat on the bed, her back bowed to keep the bowl balanced. "How do you feel about it now?"

"What, having left that monster in Iraq to continue his atrocities, just to save my own skin?" Sarah's face collapsed in grief as tears welled in her eyes. "How do you *think* I feel? It tears at my guts. But back then, all I could think about was lethal injections and electric chairs."

She buckled forward at the waist and hugged her knees. "I told you, Iraq *warped* people. God forgive me, I just wanted to get out of there in one piece, and to hell with the cost. Now I wonder how many Iraqis suffered and died from my selfishness. I left those monsters free to commit their horrors."

"What did your unit do that was so terrible?"

A moment passed. "You don't want to go there, Kat."

Katie nodded but held up a hand, palm out. "Maybe not now. But someday I want to know what he did that was so terrible."

"Oh, Kat, it's not what *he* did. It's what *we* did."

They locked eyes for a moment, and then Sarah dropped her gaze to her lap. A single tear slalomed down her cheek, chased by two more. Her shoulders heaved and her whole body shook, and suddenly she was consumed with sobs. Arms wrapped around legs, she buried her face between her knees. Katie placed the bowl of soup on the floor, shifted closer and wrapped her arms around her as though comforting a child. Sarah rocked in her arms for a moment, and then let go of her legs and threw her arms around Katie instead.

Katie continued to rock her until Sarah's great, shuddering sobs turned to plaintive mewls between small hitches of breath. Sarah heard Katie say, "Whatever's happening, it's for the best. You've been holding something inside you for too long. Someday, kiddo, you'll have to talk about it."

"Not now," Sarah said. "Maybe not ever." The tears broke free again, but this time, after a few minutes, she felt her breathing return to normal. They slowly broke away from one another, a palpable embarrassment in the air. Sarah dropped her hands, and one knuckle rapped the plate of sandwiches beside her with a clunk.

"Now *that's* the Sarah I remember," Katie said. "The one who cried not over *her* puppy, but over *my* puppy when it was hit by a car and had to be put to sleep. You've been playing the cold, hard killer for so long, you've lost your sweet, caring side. Now that you have it back—and I'm hopeful you do—don't lose it again."

Sarah wiped her face and eyes with a handful of tissues, and then blew her nose wetly. Then she held up a sandwich in one hand. "No crust?" she said with a weak smile. "What is this, a tea party?"

"Shut up and eat, soldier."

She saluted, stuffed the wedge of bread and cheese into her mouth and chewed. "Hmm," she hummed, and motioned for the soup. She took a spoonful, and swallowed with a jerk of her head. Then she took another sandwich and dunked it into the broth before biting off a piece. "My throat's dry," she said, then caught Katie's look.

"Told you, you're dehydrated."

"Okay," Sarah said, and took another bite. "Your turn. Tell me again what happened at the protest."

Katie's eyes narrowed. "Are you checking my story?"

"I need to mentally put myself back in the mix. We're missing something—something that doesn't fit, but I can't figure out what."

chapter 7

"FROM THE BEGINNING?"

Sarah sat back in the bed and closed her eyes. "Like we're doing this for the first time."

"Really, we should have Hymie here for this."

Sarah's eyes fluttered open. "I wish. When he called to check on me, he told me he's busy with Roni and the investigation into his shooting. Anyway, he thinks it's best for us not to be seen together for a while. Obviously, we couldn't discuss more than that over the phone." She shut her eyes again and leaned her head back against the wall. "Now, start."

Katie plucked a sandwich from the plate in Sarah's lap. "Okay. What do you remember before going all Braveheart on Benny?"

"Hymie told me to hold that brick-thing while he caught his breath. But it wasn't a brick. It looked like one, but it was too light. When I heard what Benny did to Roni, I completely lost it. I just threw that thing and charged."

"Intending to spear Benny with your poster stick?"

"I ... don't know what I intended."

"Well, whatever it was, it wasn't ... polite."

Sarah glanced at Katie through the corners of her eyes, a smile drawn tight on her lips. "Now I understand the temporary insanity plea. And I think I'd qualify."

"What next?"

Seeing that Katie wasn't feeling like joking, she lowered the shutters on her eyes. "An explosion. Dust and smoke. Everything stopped. Then the crowd on the other side ran forward, broke through the police barricade and hit me like a wave. Someone bashed me over the head with something hard. Everything went limp, even my neck muscles. They stripped off my Muslim gear and dropped me in the gutter. I hit my head on the ground a second time when I landed. They left me wearing just the street clothes I'd worn underneath. No headscarf, no veil, even the *abaya* was gone. Oh, and the gloves. All stripped off me."

"Wait. Gloves are pretty hard to remove."

"Both. Clean off. I never saw them again."

"Why did they undress you?"

Sarah shrugged. "To humiliate me?"

"Did they molest you?"

"Ix-nay to the copped feel-ay."

"So much for the humiliation hypothesis. So what was their point?" Katie stood and paced the floor, cradling her chin between thumb and crooked forefinger of one hand. When she reached the far side of the tiny room, she turned and pointed a finger. "Were *any* of your street clothes pulled away?"

"Nope."

"No torn fabric?"

"Not even a popped button. What're you thinking?"

Katie arched one eyebrow. "Not sure. But it doesn't make sense. It's like they didn't want you looking like a Muslim. But if that's all they were after, why'd they conk you over the head? Unless they knew you were a former soldier and didn't want you fighting back. But how would they know *that*?"

Sarah remained silent. Katie stepped back to the bed and sat on the edge. "In any case, they did you a favor. If they hadn't stripped you down, the police would've identified you as the bomber, and I'd be sending you soup in jail instead of sharing sandwiches in bed. All the same, it's weird. And I don't like weird. So ... you're down to your street clothes. Then what?"

Sarah flinched.

Katie leaned forward, sandwich in hand. "And after? You buried your head and cried."

"No. Babies cry. I wailed. Like the lost soul I am. I've joined three conflicts in five years, and in each case innocent people were murdered in front of my eyes." Sarah knew Katie was reading her face, but kept her eyes shut, her face immobile. *Just the facts, ma'am,* she told herself, *just the facts.* "Okay. I did what you asked. Now tell me what you saw."

Katie snapped her fingers. "Right. My turn. *Ahh* ... when you threw the brick, I was behind you. Hymie yanked something like a small TV remote control from his pocket. He pushed a button and it detonated. I—"

Sarah held up a hand. "It detonated *in* the crowd, or over their heads?"

"Over their heads, but close."

Sarah nodded. "Continue."

"The Jews ... "

"Zionists. Israel's supporters."

"Have it your way. The Zionists surged forward, so I kicked off my shoes and ran."

Sarah had to smile at the memory. "High heels at a demonstration. Katie, you're one of a kind."

"Slave of fashion, hon. Somebody's got to do demonstrations right."

"Then?"

"I only went thirty yards or so. We were on the edge of the crowd, remember?" When Sarah nodded, Katie continued, "I stopped and turned around, and Hymie was directly behind me. I grabbed him and told him we had to go back and get you."

"So you came back."

"Sarah, I swear, from the look of him, I wouldn't have thought Hymie could carry a bag of groceries. But he threw you over his shoulder and *ran* with you. I wouldn't have believed it if I hadn't seen it."

Sarah opened her eyes as Katie bit into her sandwich. "Adrenalin rush, maybe. But I agree. Something's not right."

Katie snorted. "Yeah, well, Hymie Milquetoast Nebbish having the strength to carry you is what springs to *my* mind."

"No, something else." They sat in silence for a moment, the only movement Katie's chewing.

"So we agree," Sarah said. "Hymie intended to kill Benny with that bomb, but when I threw it instead of him, he panicked and detonated it too early."

"Maybe he meant to kill a bunch of people."

She shook her head emphatically. "No way. If that's what he wanted, he would've packed that sucker with nails and ball bearings. Come to think of it, was *anyone* hurt?"

"Not by the bomb. There was nothing in the papers about your Benny, so he must've gotten clean away. A few demonstrators were hospitalized from the fight, but the only one killed was ... " Katie bowed her head.

Sarah pushed the plate of sandwiches from her lap and swung her legs to the floor. "The only one killed? Wait a minute. Was *anyone* else shot? Anyone besides that woman?"

Katie grabbed another sandwich and watched while Sarah padded barefoot across the room to her closet. "Nobody mentioned in the papers."

Sarah turned, a flannel shirt in hand. "Why would the assailant only shoot one protester? That doesn't make sense."

"Unless ... " Katie swallowed her bite of sandwich. "Unless he thought she was you? I mean ... like, maybe your commander didn't get over having to let you off so easy? Maybe he's been biding his time—?"

"Very funny, Sister Sunshine." Sarah color-matched a pair of her old tactical pants with the shirt. "No. Her death's got to have something to do with the demonstration. I can't imagine the newspaper headlines reading, 'Protester Killed in Random Act of Senseless Violence.'"

"Oh, no," Katie said, and stood from the edge of the Murphy bed. "The papers ran it as a Muslim woman—that would be you, by the way—bombing the Israeli Consulate, and in the ensuing riot, a Palestinian terrorist murdered an innocent Jewish woman. The way they spun the story, they made it sound like she was on the side of Israel."

Sarah sighed. "More sympathetic press for Israel."

"Who says Zionists don't have friends in the media?"

"Just friends?" Sarah said with a snort, "I thought they practically controlled it." She strode toward the bathroom, but then turned. "Hymie was dressed like a Palestinian."

"Yeah, but it wasn't him. He was with me, remember?"

"*Yesss*," Sarah said, thoughtful, "I'm just thinking it doesn't matter that he's red-haired and white as rice. Bundled up, anybody can look like a Palestinian ... ." She hefted the clothes draped over her arms. "You know, maybe we should drop in on the JSA and see what they're up to."

chapter 8

As they entered Chez What?, Sarah swiped the sunglasses from her face, folded them with a snap, slipped one temple-piece inside the neck of her flannel shirt and let them hang.

"You know," Katie said as she drew alongside, "if I could accessorize just half as well as you do your Secret Service act, I'd be a supermodel."

"Tea?" Sarah said.

"With two biscotti."

They sat at the counter and Tony, code name Loco, sidled over. "What can I getcha?"

Sarah gave Kat's order, followed by her usual house blend with a shot of espresso.

"And a raspberry scone?" Tony asked. She nodded in a head-tilt, one eyebrow arched, and he said, "Gotcha covered." Then he shouted down the counter, "Toasted tap juice with two rockers, hot lava with a lurch and a pink keystone."

His friend cruised the counter in their direction and gazed over Tony's shoulder at the order pad in his hands.

Tony rolled his face and eyes skyward, and shared his head-shaking frustration with the heavens. His countermate walked away muttering "Loco. Pure loco." Tony thumbed over his shoulder at his friend's retreating back and said, "No imagination," then slid down the counter with an artificially huge side-step to serve some neighboring customers.

"How long are we going to be here?" Katie said.

"Hour, hour and a half. Benny's apartment building's just down the street. This is where we used to gather. I want to see who comes and goes."

"The shooter. You said he wore stonewashed jeans with shirttails out. Shoes?"

"He had 'em."

"Yeah, but what kind?"

"I don't know," Sarah said, thinking. "Sneakers, maybe."

"Like that guy?"

Sarah spun on her stool and looked out the broad front window, reached up and slowly lowered Katie's pointing finger. "Never point."

"Is it him?"

Sarah shrugged. "Who knows? It's not like that clothing combination is exactly unique."

"Right height and build?"

"Maybe. Yeah, I guess. Just like a million other guys in the outer boroughs."

They watched him step from the sidewalk and enter Benyamin's apartment building, and turned to one another. "Or," Katie said, "just like a few dozen guys in that building. At least we're narrowing it down. What about his gait, his walk?"

"The guy I saw, he didn't walk, he ran." Behind them, Tony placed their order on the counter. Sarah spun on her stool, grabbed her order and led the way to a window table.

For the next forty minutes, they sat and watched. Sarah pointed out the JSA members she knew, and listed all the arrivals on a notepad. The sky was unusually clear for a winter day in New York City, but had just begun to darken with sunset when two of the JSA youths stepped from the building entrance and headed straight for the café.

"Here's the coffee run," Sarah said. "See what you can overhear, and come get me when they're gone." She took a quick double-sized bite from her third scone, this one walnut-raisin, and a swig from her coffee. Then she turned to the one place she figured she'd be hidden from their eyes.

After ten minutes of curious glances from women who found Sarah loitering in the ladies room, Katie opened the door and stepped inside. Sarah snapped her cell phone closed and arched one eyebrow in silent inquiry. "Still no answer?" Katie asked, and motioned her out with a sideways jerk of her head.

"Maybe Hymie sees who's calling, and doesn't want to talk." Sarah pushed her way through the door while speaking over her shoulder. "It really hurts. I'd like to see Roni, but I don't even know what hospital he's in. And now Hymie's not answering. That worries me."

"You're right to be worried. Those guys? They were talking about, quote, paying Hymie a visit a little later tonight, end-quote. What does that mean to you?"

Without replying, Sarah threw some bills on the table, grabbed Katie's winter coat from where she'd draped it over a chair and handed it to her friend. Then she spun and pulled Katie out of the café. As she punched through the door, she asked, "What'd they order?"

"Coffees and a half-dozen bagels. Sides of hummus and cream cheese. Then they headed back to Benny's building."

"That should slow them down a bit. We've got to get to Hymie first."

"I thought he said it wasn't safe to meet so soon after the ... event."

"Based on what you just told me, if we don't find him now, we might never meet again." She stepped one foot off the curb and raised an arm. A yellow cab swerved two lanes and screeched to a halt at the curb, and they piled in.

***

The lights were timed for traffic to run them on the green, seemingly for every car but this one. Sarah glanced at her watch, and wondered how it was possible that the driver caught every third traffic light on the red. Twice she asked him to speed up, normally an unnecessary request, and both times the next light saw them coming and switched red. Eventually she gave up, sat back and watched the concrete forest of apartment buildings sweep past, while her cell phone cycled through an unanswered series of auto-redials.

They arrived at a squat gray apartment building, anonymous in the cluster of residential buildings. Sarah read the meter, tossed some bills and bolted from the taxi. Katie trotted from her side of the car, but only caught up to her at the lobby elevators.

They stepped in and Sarah punched 4. From one side, an elderly lady shuffled in their direction, back bowed, her blue-tinted white hair certain evidence of cataracts. Katie caught Sarah's eye, but Sarah gave her a tiny headshake and tapped the door-close button. As the steel walls glided together, a scarred metal cane swung into the narrowing slit. The jaws of the doors closed upon it, bit with a clang and reopened. Sarah rolled her eyes as she stepped back, and the woman shuffled inside. "Don't feel bad," the woman said, swinging a sweet smile from Sarah to Katie. "It happens all the time. I saw you trying to hold the elevator for me, but that door-open button hasn't worked for years."

While the doors slid closed again, she laid an arthritis-gnarled finger on the 2 button, and gently rubbed until it lit up. Sarah shifted weight on her feet and exchanged sideways glances with Katie.

A minute later they exploded from the elevator and sprinted the length of the hallway to Hymie's apartment. "I hope we beat them here," Katie panted.

"They said later tonight, right? I guess it depends on how fast they can wolf down those bagels." She held up a finger for silence and laid her ear against the door. After a few seconds she said, "No sounds of trouble," and tapped a quick triple-knock on the door while pushing the doorbell. Then she sidestepped to the window at the end of the hallway. Pressing one cheek against the glass as she looked out, she tried to calculate whether the fire escape platform reached the windows of Hymie's apartment. If the others arrived while they were still here, they might need a back way out.

Katie asked, "How many subway stops is it?"

"From there to here? Five."

"That's not many."

"And we caught a lot of red lights." Sarah stepped back to the door and gave it a harder triple-tap.

"Sarah?" Katie stood to one side, nervously working a fingernail against her teeth. "How long does it take to make a bomb?"

"Footsteps," Sarah said, her ear to the door again. "A bomb? What, like the one I threw?"

"Hymie said Benny had just shot his brother. But then he already had ... could he have made a bomb that fast?"

Sarah felt a chill climb her spine as the short hairs on the back of her neck stood up and screamed an alarm. She pulled her face from the door and realized Katie's powder-blue eyes had paled to gray. "It was something like a brick, but lighter. Plaster, maybe. He might have baked it dry."

The metallic chunk of someone fumbling to unlock the deadbolt reached them through the door. Katie's voice trembled as she said, "Can you bake a bomb? I mean, wouldn't it explode in the oven?"

Sarah felt her temples squeeze. She knew very well that dynamite could be "baked," but it was extremely risky. In the old days, many miners' careers ended when their ramshackle huts exploded in a fireball of splinters and minced meat. The doorknob turned with a click just as she realized something was terribly wrong. She blurted, "Oh, barnacles!"

The door jerked open and she found herself looking down, directly into little Roni's half-blind, searching eyes. His chalk-white eyes swept her face three times before he stuttered, "S-s-sarah? Sarah-so?" His face lit up. "Sarah-so!" He lurched forward and wrapped his arms around her thighs. Then he took one of her hands, held it against his cheek and crooned, "Sarah-so."

Katie took a step back. "Sarah. His legs. There's nothing wrong with them. Hymie said they were shattered."

Sarah felt her heart melt with relief; but at the same time her mind filled with confusion. She crouched down and ran her hands over Roni's legs through his blue sweatpants. "No bandages or swelling," she said over her shoulder. "Maybe the bullets just grazed him ... but I can't imagine a kid getting shot while answering the door, and then fearlessly answering the door again three days later, can you? He should run and cower under his bed every time the doorbell rings."

A woman's voice called out from somewhere inside the apartment, "Who is it, Roni?"

Katie crouched down beside her. "Hymie set you up," she whispered. "He must've *planned* to murder Benny, far enough ahead of time to make that bomb."

"Tartar sauce," Sarah said. She read the quizzical look on Katie's face. "'Tartar Sauce' and 'Barnacles.' SpongeBob's swear words. To sea creatures, the only thing more offensive than barnacles is tartar sauce." She head-nodded toward Roni. "I picked it up from his favorite cartoon."

"You've been here before?"

"A couple of times." She caught Katie's speculative gaze. "Well, maybe a little more than that."

"What do we do now?" Katie said as she got up.

The voice called out again, this time closer, "Roni? Who is it?"

Sarah stood also and drew Roni to her, his head nestled against her hip. In return, he hugged her legs. "Look, Hymie must have planned to kill Benny as payback for his bullying. He couldn't throw the bomb himself, because the other JSA guys might've recognized him, despite his disguise. They'd played Palestinian dress-up before. So he tricked *me* into throwing the bomb instead. Maybe he figured I'd get away with it, since I was just one of many women in that crowd dressed anonymously in black. But he detonated it too early. Benny got away, and the riot followed instead."

Katie nodded uncertainly, her brow deeply furrowed and her lips pursed in thought.

From the back of the apartment came footsteps. Sarah said, "With his mother home, the apartment's probably safe to enter. All the same, wait outside at that corner convenience store. If you don't see me in half an hour, call the police."

"Why not call them now?"

"You'll get me in trouble, too—No. Call me first. If I say I'm fine, that means I'm not. If I say I'm upset, that means I'm okay. Got it?"

Katie nodded, checked her watch, then turned and headed back down the hallway toward the elevators. The apartment door swung open to reveal a matronly middle-aged woman, pushing the wheeled walker that supported her prematurely rheumatic knees. Sarah sucked in a deep breath, smiled, took one of Roni's hands and allowed him to draw her into the apartment, past his bewildered mother.

chapter 9

"HE'S IN THE shower," Hymie's mother said, wincing as she shifted weight from one stiff leg to the other. The hint of a welcoming smile played between the lines of pain permanently etched in her face. "I'll let him know you're here. Please, have a seat."

"It's urgent, Mrs. Levine," Sarah said. "Can you tell him it's an emergency?"

Her eyes registered alarm, and she reflexively drew Roni to her side, the bars of her walker wedged between them. "Is everything okay?"

"Everything will be fine," Sarah said, realizing the best way to avoid discussion was to downplay her fears. "It's just ... something personal." She wanted to run down the apartment hallway and beat on Hymie's door, but Mrs. Levine motioned her to the sofa. Then she tottered off, leaning heavily on her walker, with Roni close behind.

A few minutes later, Sarah felt ready to claw the sofa to shreds. Roni entered the room and handed her a plate of cookies and a mug of hot tea, beaming. "I fixed you a snack by myself, Sarah-so."

Kids. Sarah felt the tension ease, and released her death-grip on the sofa seat cushion. *Now I know how a race horse feels when his trainer puts a goat in his stall to calm him down.* She exhaled the deep breath she'd been holding, thanked him, and watched the back of his head after he sat inches in front of the television and swept the screen with his eyes. She didn't understand what their bond was. They didn't read books or play games together. Roni just liked having her around. He always welcomed her dearly, and cried when she left. For as long as she was in the apartment, however, he just sat and watched television, his back to her.

She glanced nervously at the window that opened to the fire escape, then at her watch. *Four minutes. Is he ever going to finish in the shower?* She set the plate of cookies and mug of tea on the end table by her elbow and stood, resolved to drag him from his room if he wasn't yet ready. The pad of footsteps stopped her. Hymie appeared in the doorway wearing lounge pants, a towel draped over one shoulder. Even with his hair wet and tousled, he wore his crocheted yarmulke, spiked red hair shooting from beneath in all directions. This was the first time she'd seen him without a shirt, and for a moment she felt disoriented. Belying his slight frame, his pale skin was drawn tight over bunched muscles, his abdomen a full six-pack.

"Mom said you have some kind of emergency?" He leaned into the doorframe, hands stuffed into his pants pockets. She couldn't help thinking that if he were taller and darker, he could be a model. But the coldness of his greeting surprised her. The last time they met, they exploded a bomb, touched off a brawl in which an innocent woman was murdered, and narrowly escaped arrests and beatings. Nonetheless, she realized she had discovered his lies, and could no longer know what to expect from him. She took a half-step in his direction. "Hymie, we've got to get out of here. Benny's coming over with the JSA guys, and I don't think they're coming for tea."

For a moment, his poker face registered nothing. Then he blinked and cracked a smile. "I'm glad you're all right. Wait a minute while I throw something on."

He disappeared down the hallway and she reclaimed her place on the sofa. Roni glanced over his shoulder from where he sat on the carpet, seemed satisfied she was still there, and returned to eye-sweeping the television.

She cast her eyes around the apartment and reminded herself that someone in Hymie's family had done well for themselves. The spacious apartment was well furnished, and stocked with higher-end electronics.

Hymie reappeared in tan chinos and a polo shirt. "Let's go."

"What a relief," she said, rising from the sofa. "For a minute, I was afraid you thought I was joking about Benny beating a warpath here."

Nodding, he slapped the flip-phone in his hand shut, slipped it into a hip pocket, and grabbed a jacket from the foyer coat rack. Then they paused at the door as he stood on tip-toe and glanced through the peephole. "Perfect," he said. One hand on Sarah's back, he swung the door open and gave her an insistent push forward. Behind them, she heard Roni's plaintive cries, "No, Sarah-so, no. Don't go."

She stumbled a half step forward, caught herself inches from the man who stood blocking the doorway, and stared straight into Benyamin's meaty face and amused brown eyes. Three JSA youths stood behind him, arms crossed. Benyamin said, "Hi, Sarah," in a voice that reminded her of the psychiatrist in *The Terminator*. Then he placed a hand in the center of her chest and pushed her back into the room, across the floor and to the sofa. She landed in a controlled fall and pressed herself back into the sofa cushions, instinctively increasing the distance between them. She glanced toward Hymie, not understanding anything but hoping he would know what to do.

Benyamin turned from her as Hymie closed the door behind the JSA youths, who took up positions by the door and apartment window. Then Benyamin held out a paper sack toward Hymie and said, "Your mom's favorite bagels and spread."

Hymie bolted the door, tossed his jacket onto a chair and took the bag with a nod. "As long as you keep Ma in bagels, she'll remember you in her prayers. Hey, Roni? Take these to Ma."

Roni stood and lurched over to his oldest brother, studied the bag with tilted head, sniffed and said, "*Baygals?*" Then he took the sack and disappeared in the direction of the kitchen.

chapter 10

Hymie leaned back against a wall as Benyamin lowered himself into an overstuffed chair opposite Sarah. "Thought you were pretty smart, didn't you?" he said. When she didn't reply—she couldn't; shock wouldn't let her—he continued.

"We had you pegged from day two. Not day one, mind you. Day one, we checked you out. We traced your military service in Israel to Major Simkin, and he told us all we needed to know. We couldn't figure out why you wanted to join the JSA when you couldn't stomach the war in Israel, but that didn't matter. What mattered is that we realized we couldn't count on you, and you wouldn't last with us anyway."

Sarah hitched forward in her seat, understanding at last. "So you set me up."

"Careful, now," Benyamin said, and held out an open hand in her direction. "Be a good girl, and nobody'll get hurt."

She sat back again, and he nodded. "That's better."

She glanced at Hymie, then back at Benyamin. "You needed someone to start the riot. Someone expendable. You used me."

"And I'm guessing that's never happened before, huh?" He leaned back against the overstuffed cushions and craned his neck behind him toward Hymie. "Boss, you want to take over?"

Sarah jumped to her feet. "Boss?"

"Uh, yeah." Hymie sauntered forward to stand in the center of the room, between her and Benyamin. "Every group has an elected leader, and I'm it." Benyamin nodded, and one of the youths by the door snorted a chuckle, his head bobbing. She glanced between the two of them, then back at Hymie.

He stepped within arm's reach of her. "Look, Sarah, I like you. You might be mixed up in your religious convictions, but at the end of the day you're one of us. Or at least, you used to be. But the fact is, we needed you to throw that bomb, and you wouldn't have done it if you'd known the reason. We had no choice. We *had* to set you up. Of *course* we used you."

She felt her arms tremble, her hands ball into fists by her sides, her legs quiver with the familiar weakness that accompanies both fear and extreme anger. "You needed a fake Palestinian to bomb the Israeli Consulate. That's it, isn't it?"

"Thanks to you," Hymie said, nodding to her, "we're one step closer to convincing the world that all Palestinians are terrorists. Even the women."

"And it was you," she said, turning to Benyamin, both her temper and voice rising, "*you* bashed me over the head in the riot?"

"Sorry about that." He rubbed his chin and grimaced. "I didn't mean to hit you that hard. We knew you'd fight, but we needed to strip off your Muslim attire. Otherwise the police would've identified you as the bomber and arrested you. But *we* needed you to get away. If they arrested you, the police would have learned you're a Jew, not a Palestinian, and that would've blown the entire deception."

"So you suckered me into turning a peaceful demonstration into a lie. *You're* the terrorists, but now the world sees it the other way around."

Hymie shrugged. "As they say, the first casualty of war is truth. Believe me, you made great footage. Every news channel in America carried it. Not only did we have cameras on you, but we sold the footage to CNN. We got our media plug, and got paid for it. So be happy—you served our cause in two ways."

Her response was to spin toward the window and wave the JSA youth away from it with a, "Move, you stupid lump." She gave him an unnecessary shove as he sidestepped out of the way, then she leaned both hands on the windowsill. Outside, the street had grown hazy with a winter mist that snuck in on the tail of twilight. The streetlights cut the mist, but she didn't see Katie anywhere. She spun from the window. "Why me? Any of you guys could've done it, without all this ... this ... " She waved her hands, and Hymie said, "All this elaborate planning?"

"Yeah."

He shrugged. "We've been faking Palestinian *men* for *decades*. Both here and abroad. Now we're upping the ante. We're working to make the media demonize not just Palestinian men, but women as well. We're working for the day America will see all Palestinians, even their *children*, as devils. Then they won't object to our wiping them off the face of the earth. Hey, it's the American way. It worked with the native Indians, it'll work with the Palestinians."

"Massacre mentality," she whispered hoarsely. "Create so much hatred and fear, people will kill anybody they believe to be the enemy, women and children included. Like in Vietnam."

"And now, in Israel. We need to get people to believing we're not killing babies, just Palestinians."

She felt the strength drain from her limbs, chased out by a cold hatred. "You're … you guys are simply … "

"Fanatics?" Benyamin said. "Oh, now *there's* an original thought."

She sat back against the windowsill and felt the chill of the glass seep through her leather jacket. "Actually, I was going to say 'evil.'"

"No, Sarah," Hymie said. "We're not evil. We're chosen."

She glanced into his eyes and read the same crazed fanaticism she'd seen in the eyes of too many megalomaniac soldiers—those suffering the psychosis of an ideology warped into something demonic. "Chosen?" she said. "Oh, yeah, excuse me. We're the chosen people, right? Sorry, I must've forgotten." She pushed off from the windowsill and strode back into the center of the room. "Remind me, will you? What, *exactly*, are we chosen for? To kill the prophets, commit genocide and spread countless evils through the land? Your stupid stunt got an innocent woman killed. A Jewish woman, no less."

Benyamin coughed into his fist, in what could only be an artificial tone. Hymie shot him a glance, but then returned his gaze to Sarah while squaring his narrow shoulders and planting his feet. "She was on the wrong side."

For a moment nobody moved. Sarah felt electricity play in her arms, a sensation she'd felt before, and knew she was on the verge of striking. At the same time, a dull realization invaded her thoughts. *I'm on your side*, the Jewish woman had said to her, just before she was killed. When she spoke those words, she had thought Sarah was Palestinian. *A Jewish woman, protesting on the side of the Palestinians?* Sarah didn't understand back then any better than she did now. It didn't make sense, it simply was.

Hymie's mother called out from the kitchen, "Dinner's ready, boys."

"Later, Ma."

"It'll get cold."

Hymie glued his eyes to Sarah but called over his shoulder, "Ten minutes, Ma."

"Never mind me. I'll just put it in the oven to keep warm."

"Love ya, Ma." Hymie nodded to Sarah with a condescending smile. "Join us?"

She shook her head. "You knew someone might get killed in the riot. That's what you mean, isn't it?"

Benyamin looked down at his feet. Hymie shifted his weight from one foot to the other. She scanned the faces of the youths, but none of them met her eyes. The electricity that played in her arms jumped to her spine and shot straight down to her toes. "Oh ... my ... God. You meant to kill her. That's it, isn't it? One of you dressed up as a Palestinian and killed her. You knew the media wouldn't know, wouldn't even care which side she was really on. They'd just naturally assume it was a Palestinian murdering a Jew. And you didn't give a damn, because even though she was a Jew," she wagged her head and shifted to an imitation of Hymie's voice, *"she was on the wrong side."* She spun on the three youths and shouted, "Which one of you did it? Huh? Which one of you's going to burn in hell for this—?"

"Sarah."

Benyamin's calm voice spun her around again.

"Listen. We could never admit such a thing, but we applaud the one who did it." He turned from her and winked at the three youths, now bunched together at the front door.

Sarah followed his gaze, not to the youths, but to the door they blocked.

"You're different, don't worry." Benyamin said, as if reading her thoughts.

She turned to where he sat and locked eyes with his as he continued. "You're wondering if we're going to let you leave this apartment alive. Number one," he began ticking off his fingers, "we never kill our own—meaning, a JSA member—even if they switch sides, as you have. Number two, if you go to the police, it'll be your word against ours. Three, if you're dumb enough to go anyway, the police will put two and two together and come up with fifteen—fifteen years to life, that is, for you and your act of *terrorism.*" He spread both hands wide. "After all, you threw that bomb, and an innocent woman was killed ... by a *Palestinian,* of course."

One of the JSA youths coughed loudly and another snickered. Benyamin flicked a glance in their direction. Sarah didn't bother. He shrugged his eyebrows and threw her a snide smile. "Specifically, if you try to turn us in, we'll arrange for your Muslim clothes to be found. Dust on your glove will match residue from the bomb you threw. Fingerprint technology's so sensitive nowadays, your fingerprints might even be lifted from the inside of the gloves. No fingerprints? No problem. No doubt there are hairs, maybe even blood on the headscarf where I hit you. That will DNA-match you all the way to jail. We've got, well, let's see ... "

He bounced his finger around the three youths at the door, counting, "One, two, three," finishing with Hymie and himself, "four, five. Five witnesses who'll place you at the scene, all of whom will vehemently deny your wild, *completely* unsubstantiated conspiracy theory. And when the pressure's on, I bet even your *shiksa* friend, what's her name?"

"Katie," Hymie said, standing to one side.

"Katie. I bet the police won't sweat her for ten minutes before she admits that you threw that bomb."

"She'll also tell them that Hymie gave it to me," Sarah said, jerking a thumb in his direction.

"What, the little guy with his head wrapped in a *guttra?* Think the police will honor her identification?" He dropped his voice an octave, imitating a hard-nosed NYPD interrogator: "Let's go over this one more time,

Miss *Shiksa*. You said the man who handed the bomb to Miss Weizmann had his head and face wrapped in a *guttra*, and you could only see his eyes? How, then, can you positively identify him as Mr. Hymie Levine?"

Sarah dropped her eyes to the floor. "You ... you sons of ... "

"Oh, hey, look, it's not all bad," he said as he stood. "Look at it this way: If you go to the police, we'll get another round of fantastic media. No doubt the press will talk about how far Israel's enemies—and that would be you, the consulate bomber—will go in their vain attempts to discredit the defenders of the Jewish homeland. Defenders like, oh, say, *us*—the Jewish Soldiers Alliance, for example. So please, by all means, go to the police."

Hymie picked up the plate of cookies from beside Sarah's cup of cold tea and sidestepped between them. "Don't think too deeply about all this," he said. "You were just a pawn in this play." He held out the plate to her. "Cookie?"

Anger exploded inside her and she threw a fist at his face, her full strength behind the punch. She expected a bone-jarring jolt, but the strength of her blow yanked her forward when she connected with nothing but vapor trail. Hymie had swayed to one side, then dropped into a perfect back-stance. She spun and kicked at him, but he whirled to the other side of her and stabbed three fingers into the back of her knee. One leg kicked into the air, her other leg folded and she fell, swinging at where she knew him to be. She landed on nothing but carpet, sprung up again and found him standing in front of her, the plate of cookies still in his hand.

Her cell phone rang, but she barely heard as she feinted with her right, jabbed with her left, spun to the side he slipped off to, threw a roundhouse punch and then kicked, elbowed and pummeled her way to ... nothing. Her cell phone now silent, she spent the next twenty seconds flailing, her full strength behind each attack. Eventually she bent over, braced both hands on her knees, and sucked air.

"Hitting Hymie's like trying to catch a puff of dust in a high wind," Benyamin said. Hymie smiled from where he stood in front of Sarah, breathing shallowly and through his nose, and stretched his arm behind him to his lieutenant, proffering the cookie plate. Benyamin picked through the cookies with exaggerated calm until he found the one he wanted, then sat back holding it. Sarah scanned the floor and realized not a single cookie had fallen from the plate.

"A puff of dust?" she panted. "I think ... it's harder than that."

Benyamin nodded. "Nobody hits Hymie unless he lets them. When we spar, he beats the Bill Clintons off me."

Her cell phone rang again and she slumped back onto the sofa, dug the phone out of her pocket on the third ring. "Yeah. Hey, thanks for calling back."

"Longest three minutes of my life," Katie said from the other end. "How are you doing?"

Sarah rolled her eyes behind closed lids. "I'm ... upset, but I'm okay."

"Wait a minute. We were talking in opposites. 'Fine' meant you're not. 'Upset' meant you're okay. What does 'okay' mean?"

"It means I'm okay."

"You don't sound okay. I'm calling the cops."

Sarah gripped the phone tighter. "No, no. Listen, I'm upset, okay? I mean, I'm just upset. Really, really upset. A little winded, but just *upset*. Got it? Don't call the cops. I'll see you in ten."

She clicked off. Hymie waved her to stand up, saying, "Yeah, I think we're done here," and head-nodded her to the door. Instead, she stepped up to stand facing him. Keeping her eyes on his, she took a cookie from the plate he held between them and popped it into her mouth. Then she jerked both shoulders at him. He didn't flinch, but his eyes turned cold. "Next time, Sarah, I'll hit back. Don't push your luck."

"Say goodbye to Roni for me."

"I will."

"I care for him."

"I know."

"And ... I think I used to ... love you."

Hymie jerked his head in surprise and blinked hard. In the next instant, the plate flew from his hand and her concealed uppercut caught him square on his chin and lifted his feet from the carpet. He fell to the floor in a heap and she dropped with him, her knee landing full in his crotch. She saw blood spurt from a split lip, again from a battered eyelid while she pummeled every tender spot the US and Israeli armies had taught her. But then strong hands pinned her arms and lifted her. She landed another two kicks before the youths dragged her to the door and hurled her out. They slammed the door behind her, but she rebounded off the opposite apartment door and threw all her weight behind a stomp-kick that landed directly beneath the doorknob.

The door burst inward with the splintering of wood and a squeal of bent metal, and she halted in the doorway. Benyamin and one of the youths held Hymie, who was moaning, in a semi-sitting position in the middle of the floor. The two youths who'd thrown her out stood immediately inside. Roni swayed in the kitchen doorway, his chin raised as if scenting the air for clues.

She thrust a finger at Hymie's dazed face. "I'm *not* one of you, and never will be. *I* am an enemy of your cause, you got that?" Then she whirled around and strode down the hallway. As she pushed through the door to the stairs, she glanced back and found Roni standing in the hallway, one hand braced on the splintered doorframe. He called out, "Sarah-so. Don't go, Sarah-so." She stepped into the stairwell, tears filling her eyes, a painful sting in her nose. With a sob, she started down the stairs. The door swung closed behind her, cutting off Roni's cries.

chapter II

THE JAMAICAN TAXICAB driver maneuvered through the dense evening traffic with the comfort of a soldier running a familiar obstacle course. Sarah sat beside Katie in the backseat, dabbing tears, not sure if she was crying more from humiliation or from helplessness.

"Barnacles," she said, drawing in a deep, liquid sniff.

"I told you, at the demonstration Hymie threw you over his shoulder and *ran*. Deep down, we knew things didn't add up. Now we know why."

Sarah sniffed again. "He must be some kind of martial arts master. He moved like the Tasmanian Devil."

"And yet, you nailed him in the end."

Sarah raised her fist, saw the first two knuckles reddened and swelling. "Yeah, but I had to trick him."

The driver, his dreadlocks partially bundled inside a multicolored Rasta beret, glanced into the rearview mirror, intense curiosity in his eyes.

"*Sooo*, why'd you keep pounding him after he was out cold?"

"I wasn't playing for what he could feel *then,* which was nothing, but for what he would feel when he came to."

"*Oof,*" Katie said as she shook one hand from the wrist. "Vicious."

"Don't get on my bad side."

"Deep down, you're an old softie."

Sarah snorted and dug a fresh tissue from her jacket pocket.

"*Sooo,* what're you going to do now, become a white supremacist? There's got to be some wacko militant group out there you haven't joined yet. Just don't go the tattooed-skinhead route, 'kay? They might not let us into the St. Moritz anymore."

Sarah sniffled. "I don't know what I'm going to do. All I know is, I've got to hang up my guns. They bring me nothing but trouble."

Katie dug through her purse and pulled out a container of breath mints. "I don't mean anything by it, but take two." Katie glanced at the rainbow-colored Rastafarian 'Lion of Judah' flag hanging from the car's rearview mirror, then leaned forward and offered mints to the driver through the pay slot. When she sat back, she took Sarah's hand and said, "Remember how we used to daydream together when we were kids? I wanted to be a princess, you wanted to be Jane Bond 008. Save the world, all that stuff?"

Sarah nodded, and Katie said, "Hon, if by hanging up your guns you mean avoiding militant groups and living a normal life, you should've done that years ago. Every group or army you joined, you just became a pawn in their agenda. You need to stop trying to save the world and just save yourself."

"If I knew how to do that, I wouldn't be in this mess, would I?"

"Are you open to suggestions?" Katie noted her sullen nod and said, "Get back in touch with your warm, fuzzy side. I'm talking teddy bears, perfumed soap, bubble baths and long walks in the park. Stop to smell the flowers and watch the children play. Instead of trying to stamp the evil out of this world, find the peace and beauty, and build on it. Whatever you do, don't go the Hollywood stereotypical loser route of burying yourself in the deep end of a bottle."

"Don't worry," Sarah said. "I swore off the stuff after I was drugged."

Traffic at a standstill on the Manhattan Bridge, she gazed down into the East River's murky waters, and remembered the last drink she inflicted upon herself. She'd been new both to the military and to Iraq. She hadn't been inside the Emerald City—America's walled-off enclave in Baghdad—long enough to know the dangers. When one of the guys in her unit invited her to an impromptu "hail and farewell" party, she attended without suspicion or caution. Innocent to a fault, she reflected; "Pilgrim," to quote Katie.

When she arrived at Sergeant Kyle's room, there were only two other privates there, both men. They gave her a drink and assured her the others would arrive shortly. The room seemed barely large enough for a gathering, but she sipped her drink and laughed at their jokes until her world went black. She awoke alone, in pain, and found blood where there shouldn't be for the next two weeks.

Still groggy, she realized the treasure she'd saved for her future husband had been torn from her.

From the moment she swung her legs over the edge of the bed and sat entangled in the bloodied bedsheet, a primal bloodlust for revenge welled up inside her. She contemplated calling the MPs, but decided against it. The soft justice of jail with early probation simply wouldn't suffice; one of the few Old Testament teachings she remembered rose up inside her and demanded their deaths. She knew if she reported the rape, she couldn't kill them if the military's justice system failed; her motive would incriminate her. Her only chance of getting away with murder lay in keeping quiet.

Over the next week she congratulated herself on her decision; she learned that rape inside the Emerald City was as common as murder outside, and both were routinely hushed up. The only hope for justice, she became convinced, lay in her own hands.

Ten days later, her unit shipped out to one of the many local hot zones. The first few days passed in a blur of fear, fatigue, and the shock of witnessing the horrors of combat for the first time. During one skirmish they advanced on foot through a rural village, rooting out insurgents while they wove through dirt roads, shadowed alleys, and ramshackle mud-brick homes, trying to avoid a sniper's bullet. Hunkered down behind a wrecked car left to rust at the side of the road, she watched Private Carter advance in front of her. She checked over her shoulder and found they were alone—the situation she'd been waiting for.

She leveled her weapon across the vehicle's mangled hood and lined up the sights on the center of his back, as she'd done a half-dozen times that day. And she choked. Her finger trembled as she tightened her pull on the trigger. *No,* she thought. *There must be a better way.*

As she raised her eye from the gun's sight, a jet trail shot a steel football past her head in a streak of smoke and blew out the brick wall behind her. The RPG's blast made her flinch and her M-16 erupted in her clenched hands. The weapon's muzzle climbed skyward while it unleashed its deadly fusillade on full auto. Private Carter flew forward, chest out, arms thrown open and legs pedaling against empty air, as if rushing to embrace the angel of death. Then he collapsed in a cloud of blood-mist and dust, and all hell broke loose as the enemy laid fire down on her position.

Four years later, and her hands still trembled thinking about it. Willing them to be still, she lowered her gaze to the taxi's floorboard and shook away the memory of gun blasts, the sparks and dull bangs of jacketed rounds punching holes in the car that had served as her cover. "I'm not as coldblooded as you might think, Kat," she said, eyes down. "It's not like I would've gone through with the killings. I just ... I just got caught up in them."

She looked up to find a question etched on Katie's face, saw the taxi driver's eyes dancing between the road and her reflection in the rearview mirror. Ignoring both, she remembered how Private Thomas' murder seemed to simply flow from Carter's death. Considering the load of guilt Thomas heaped upon himself, she almost believed his murder a mercy killing. One thing was certain, though:

each killing made the next easier, as though the ball of vengeance, once set in motion, wouldn't stop until it ran full course.

When Sergeant Kyle returned from leave, he realized the danger immediately. She could still see his eyes change from predatory conceit to confusion the day she spun around, swept aside the rifle he'd aimed at her and buried her knife in his chest. She stabbed him two more times before he dropped his weapon and fell to his knees. And she could still recall her exact thought, watching him clutch at his wounds as the life drained from him in bloody pulses. *I'm not your victim any more, you sick troll. You don't own me.* In her mind, her action was as much self-defense as self-defense ever got, regardless of the events that led up to it. So why was that crushing hand of guilt working its way from her heart to her throat, even thinking about what happened?

"Oh, barnacles," she said with a deep breath. "Kat, if I don't pull myself out of this tailspin, it'll suck me down until I auger in."

"Language *you* no doubt understand." Katie gave a wave of her delicate fingers. "But I get the gist of it."

"Help me, will you? Help me to be a woman. A *womanly* woman."

Katie flashed a brilliant smile. "Now *that's* my kind of challenge! And, well, fur coats and designer accessories will help a lot with that. You might say you're already positioned for a successful transformation."

chapter 12

THE NEXT TEN days brought fair weather and a deluge of dinner and theater invitations from Katie. Mink and sable coats seemed to fly from the racks during Sarah's shifts, and Stwarroff's store manager took heightened interest in the employee who formerly broke sales commission records, but now doubled them. He observed her blowing a funnel in the fur of a mink coat, to demonstrate to a customer that the roots of the fur didn't show the telltale color change seen in dyed furs. Another time he found her peeling back the lining to show the leather side of the hides, explaining that narrow hides were female skins, thinner, lighter and justifiably more expensive. "Furthermore," she said while she shrugged the coat on, closed her eyes blissfully and luxuriated in the caress of the high collar, "female skins are more sensitive and *caring*."

The customer laughed—and bought the coat. The next day Sarah convinced an environmentalist socialite that the minks weren't slaughtered, but recycled. They were farmed mink, not wild, so harvesting them to make room for the new brood was no different from a logging company that planted a tree for each one it cut down. Another sale. She convinced a rabid feminist to buy a male-skin mink coat ("Because those cheating little weasels deserved to die, didn't they?"), and a movie star to purchase a silver fox coat because it matched the interior of her Rolls Royce. Two more sales.

A Muslim sheikh the manager later learned was a prince of Brunei produced the most lucrative sale. While his petite wife modeled a fur in front of the five-paneled mirror, Sarah stepped to the prince's side and murmured that she understood Muslim men could have up to four wives. When he demurely acknowledged this fact, she asked if he had room for one more. She laughed, he smiled and lowered his gaze. "No, I regret to inform you the positions are all full."

"Of course," she said, "after all, a man of your stature ... but Your Highness, doesn't your religion teach that a man has to treat all of his wives equally? Equal time, houses, cars? Equal money, jewelry? Equal ... fur coats?"

For the first time the modest man raised his gaze and stared straight into her eyes. "Yes," he said, and lowered his gaze once again. "That is precisely correct."

When his wife made her selection, he nodded to Sarah and said, "In that case, Ms. Weizmann, I'll be needing four of these."

"Will that be three for your wives, and one for your revered mother?" she asked, her face bowed over the counter while she scribbled the order on a pad.

The prince leaned forward and said, "Ms. Weizmann, I believe you have a career in politics ahead of you. No, what I meant to say is that I'll need four of these, one for each of my four wives. But of course, I will also need the finest, most expensive fur in your store for my *highly* revered mother."

The next day, a courier dressed in the distinctive livery of the Sultanate of Brunei brought Sarah a gift box laminated in gold leaf, tied with a green silk ribbon and sealed with a solid platinum medallion. To everyone's great disappointment, she took it home unopened.

The ultimate challenge, however, came in the form of a famous death metal vocalist, the last person her manager ever imagined purchasing an upscale fur. Hair in ratty tendrils, more tattoos than skin tone, facial piercing so dense it qualified more as body armor than decoration, she bought a sable coat most people couldn't afford without taking out a second mortgage on their house, and many couldn't afford even then. Again, it was Sarah's joke that did it. She assured her the coat was the finest rat fur that money could buy, much better than a nutria swamp-rat coat. She even offered to infest the fur with fleas for an extra thousand dollars, an exclusive service Stwarroff's provided only to the most discriminating of their counter-culture customers. The clincher was her suggestion.

"Picture this," she said. "Your band strikes up something classical ... let's say, Mozart. Or Tchaikovsky. No, definitely Tchaikovsky. *Marche Slave*. You step on stage in your new sable coat. Strut a circuit from one side to the other, then turn a spin at center stage. Suddenly, the lights go epileptic, the music morphs to acid, the front man smashes his guitar against the stage, the percussionist kicks a boot through a drum, throws a cymbal down and jumps on it. At the same time, you strip the fur off and a couple rockers run in from the side and help you tear it into strips, and you toss the pieces to the crowd. Your audience will go home with souvenirs of the best Russian rat ever sewn."

The manager, infuriated at the prospect of a prize fur being publicly desecrated solely because of what he imagined to be Sarah's greed for a generous commission, called her to his office when he heard what had happened.

"Look," Sarah explained, "last year Gory Harm and her band, The Bloody Muses, trashed a Lamborghini on stage, and the crowd went wild. So did the press. The story ran in every major news outlet in the world, along with an official statement from Lamborghini. Imagine the free press you'll get." She held up both hands and stroked air quotes with her fingers. "We are not surprised that when Ms. Gory Harm sought out a prize fur coat to trash on stage, she chose a Stwarroff. While we are saddened to see a coat of such noble and unique craftsmanship destroyed, we recognize her as our customer, alongside other top celebrities and world leaders who rely upon Stwarroff's for unique products of style and distinction."

As he listened, the manager's face cooled from crimson to calm. His eyes drifted up from Sarah's face to a focal spot on the ceiling. When she finished speaking, he thoughtfully drummed his desktop with a Montblanc pen, and the hint of a smile played on his lips.

The next day, he promoted her to department manager.

Despite everything else going right, she left her smile in the coatroom when she departed work each day, and spent her off-hours in a deep, inconsolable funk.

What she'd learned from Kate was helping her make huge amounts of money. But despite Katie's chirpy and ongoing reassurances, neither of them could figure out how to pull Sarah out of the emotional tailspin she was in. But that didn't stop her best friend from trying.

"How do you *do* that?" Katie asked, leaning forward on the park bench and peering at the side of Sarah's face.

Sarah looked up from twiddling her spoon in the whipped cream that topped her scoop of ice cream. "Hmm. What ... how do I do *what*?"

"How do you eat Häagen-Dazs with a frown? That violates Einstein's theory of real-ativity. Meaning, it doesn't seem real."

Sarah balanced her dessert beside her on one of the wood bench slats. Then she hitched herself up, turned toward Katie and sat back down, one leg folded beneath her. "It's the movie we just saw. I can't get it out of my mind."

"I can't get the prices out of *my* mind. Remember when you didn't need financing to go to the movies?"

"Your dad died and left you rich."

"Yeah, but while he was alive, he taught me to think poor." Katie loaded her plastic spoon with Cherry Vanilla and took it in one bite.

"Thinking poor. Maybe that's why we get along."

"Anyway ... "

"Yeah, anyway. You remember the theme of that movie?"

"Basically, get a life." Katie stirred the remainder of her ice cream into the consistency of soft-serve. "Honest, I didn't know it was a message movie. It just looked fun." She hunched over her cup and scraped up the last of the melted mass with her spoon. "You done with that?" she said, and motioned behind Sarah's back.

Sarah reached behind her, retrieved her cup, handed it over, and watched Katie holster the full cup into her empty one, scoop out the whipped cream and flick it into the trashcan at her end of the park bench.

"Hey, that's the best part," Sarah said.

"Sorry. That's a judgment call. You've got to know which calories are worth dieting for." She raised the ice cream in her direction. "Here's to getting a life."

"A *new* life. Katie, I meant what I said before. Maybe not that womanly change-thing. But I've got to make a change. Something big, bold, dramatic. Do a spiritual makeover, maybe."

"Become a Rastafarian?" Katie said, and dug her spoon into the cup. "Maybe I can hook you up with that taxi driver. Or, no, wait. A voodoo priestess. I can just see you dancing in loose rags, a python draped over your shoulders, flailing a freshly killed chicken in one hand and the bloody knife in the other. So there's an idea. Become a voodoo high priestess."

Sarah narrowed her eyes into slits and sighed. "I was thinking about becoming a better person. Remember that woman? The one who was murdered? Maybe I'll go visit her grave."

"Huh? *That's* 'big, bold, dramatic'?"

Sarah shook her head. "No, it just … it seems like the right thing to do. Something I maybe should've already done. To close the book on my past."

"Maybe," Katie said, but they both knew it was a half-hearted response. It was a "maybe" that held loyalty to a friend, but little enthusiasm.

chapter 13

SARAH SAT CROSS-legged in the center of her bed in over-sized flannel pajamas, hunched over her laptop computer. The consulate bombing article from the online *New York Times* gave the murdered woman's name as Leah Cohen. The following day at work, she called the funeral home named in the obituary and learned the cemetery and gravesite address. *"If only there was something I could've done,"* she said to herself as she lowered the phone into its cradle on the glass-top counter. But then a woman entered her department and started running her hands through the rows of fur coats, and she ambled over to help.

On Sunday, shortly after sunrise, she strolled into an independent Jewish cemetery in Queens, found Leah Cohen's gravesite with the aid of a plot-map, and stood at the foot of the freshly mounded earth, head bowed to the ground. "I'm sorry," she whispered. "I'm just *so* sorry." She wished a voice would reply, tell her it wasn't her fault, but all she heard were the chirps and warbles of songbirds celebrating a new day.

"Well, what did you expect," she muttered, "a spiritual lift? Instant atonement?" A sting in her eyes brought tears, but she blinked them back and shuffled her feet in the dew-laden grass, glanced skyward, and then bowed her head again, this time in prayer for the deceased. Then she turned to leave.

A quick movement at the edge of her vision seemed utterly out of place in a graveyard. The action reminded her of a child peeking from its hiding place behind a tree while playing hide-and-seek, and then ducking back out of sight when spotted. *Which one of them is it?* she wondered, though she was already certain of the answer.

She sauntered over to the majestic oak tree, where the last of the morning mist soaked into the warming air. "Hi, Hymie," she said as she rounded the thick trunk.

He stood, hands in pockets, his back against the tree. One knee was cocked, his foot braced behind him against the sturdy trunk. "No 'Shalom' for an old friend?"

"*Shalom* means 'peace.' That's not what you've brought me."

He nodded soberly.

"How long have you been following me?"

He raised open hands in her direction. "Did you get your licks in last time? Or do you still need to pummel me?"

"Are you here for revenge?"

He dropped his hands to his sides and lowered his face to the ground. "You were always safe with me, Sarah."

She nodded in the direction of Leah's grave. "She wasn't."

"As I said before, she was on the wrong side."

"Now *I'm* on the wrong side. So why am *I* safe?"

He pushed himself off from the tree with his foot and raised his eyes to meet hers. "You said ... you thought you might have loved me."

She jerked her head as the flash of understanding slapped her consciousness. "It was a ruse," she said, and planted her feet squarely in front of him, her thumbs hooked into the waistband of her gray wool slacks. "I needed to throw you off your guard."

His head bobbed up and down three beats. "Thought it sounded too good to be true. But I had to check. You see ... ." He shuffled his feet in the grass and kicked one of the few fallen acorns the squirrels had missed. "Well ... I *did* love you. Crazy, huh, considering what I did to you. But there it is."

The gauntlet thrown, he stared into her eyes, but she put daggers into her gaze and shook her head. "I hate you," she said, "and everything you stand for. And I'll oppose you to the day I die, with everything I have at my disposal. Now, am I still safe from you?"

He shrugged and turned away. "From me? Probably. From the others ... ?" A sigh, then, "Look, we might never see one another again. But if you ever need me, you know where I live." He took two steps, stopped, and looked back over his shoulder at her, sadness writ large on his face and in his eyes. "Shalom, Sarah." Then he turned toward the cemetery exit and ambled off.

She watched his lean figure weave through the grave plots, struggling for something to yell at his retreating back. Nothing came. She took a deep breath and let it float back out. *Put away your guns,* she reminded herself, and unclenched the fists she now found balled up at her sides. With a mind of its own, her right index finger twitched, as if searching for a trigger to pull. A smile snuck onto her lips and she bounced one eyebrow in wonder. "I guess you never put away your guns for good," she muttered.

She sat on the modest border wall that surrounded a weathered ledger stone at her feet. The morning had brightened to the bronze glow of a sun that promised an unseasonably warm day. She popped open the magnetic snaps on her oversized purse, pushed aside a sandwich and a bottle of tea and extracted a prayer she'd written to place on Leah's grave. Grinning, she thought, *The groundskeeper will probably have me fined for littering.*

Sarah raised her head and swept the grounds with her eyes. Rather than spotting a groundskeeper through the forest of headstones and monuments, she saw a man at the foot of Leah's grave. He stood in a black suit, bent at the waist and consoling two young children, their backs to her. The little boy was dressed in a jet-black suit, the mirror of his father's. The girl wore a gray dress with black accents at the collar and cuffs. "Daniel?" Sarah muttered to herself, but it didn't sound right. She dug through her purse and extracted her printout of the *New York Times* obit. Not Daniel. David. She lowered the page to her lap. "A good man, this David Cohen," she muttered in his direction. "Rested the Sabbath on Saturday, visits his wife's grave on Sunday."

She watched him crouch between the children and enfold them in his arms. The children's sobs wafted in her direction, but then waned. The heaves of their little chests shallowed, and the man gave them a bouquet of flowers to arrange in the graveside urn. After they placed the flowers, they turned, and Sarah saw their faces. Both dark-haired, the boy's lips were drawn so tight they were invisible at a distance. A storm of anger and grief filled facial features that seemed remarkably mature for a boy she judged five, maybe six years old. The girl's black hair hung to her shoulders, and although her oval face also showed grief, it was more on the level of sadness. Sarah couldn't pinpoint exactly how she could tell, but the little girl seemed more reconciled with the loss of their mother, or perhaps just didn't fully understand it. Blinking at unexpected tears, Sarah glanced down at the paper in her hands and whispered, "Yosef and Miriam. Five and four years old, respectively. Huh. Why'd they put the boy's name first? Chauvinists."

She looked up in time to see the man straighten, take the kids' hands in his and turn to lead them back down the path. As he turned, Sarah saw his face. She felt the blood drain from her own face, her vision dimmed, and for a moment her world buckled, slanted and spun. She closed her eyes until the nausea of a near-faint passed. When she opened them, the sad trio was approaching a curve in the path, the man moving slowly to accommodate the children's short strides, in the direction of the exit. The little boy's free arm was rigid by his side, his hand balled into a tiny fist. With every other swing of her free arm, the little girl rubbed a handful of tissues across her face.

And she doubted her own eyes. Sergeant Kyle was dead. She knew this because she had killed him. But the face she'd just seen was his. The thick, dark hair, the slight curve to an otherwise square jaw, the thin lips that could twist in a way both sensual and cruel, even the swarthy Mediterranean tint to his skin.

As they disappeared around the curve, she jumped up and ran to the grave, looked around frantically for a rock to weigh down the page of prayer. "You have *got* to be kidding," she muttered. "All this dirt, and no stones? What do they do, sift them out?"

She swung her purse off her shoulder, popped the snaps and dug inside. All she could come up with was the perfume atomizer Katie had insisted she start carrying as part of her feminizing regimen. Hastily, she placed the prayer on the middle of the mound, the atomizer on top. She turned and jogged a couple steps down the path, but just as quickly spun around and ran back. She grabbed the atomizer and sprayed shots of mist over the head of the grave. "Hope it's your scent," she said, and replaced the perfume on the paper. Then she sprinted across the grass to a different path. She knew this path was longer, but was certain she could beat them to the exit. After all, she wasn't hampered by children—especially those slowed even further by grief over losing their mother.

chapter 14

DAVID COHEN STOPPED outside the cemetery and motioned his children to stand back from the curb. Sarah turned left and quickstepped twenty yards before hailing a taxi. As she got into the backseat, she glanced through the windshield and confirmed her guess was correct; he'd also hailed a cab. She watched while he ushered the children inside, then climbed in after them. This time, she spotted differences. The more aquiline nose, the angle and spacing of the full, dark eyebrows, and most of all, the eyes. Sergeant Kyle's eyes had been close-set and narrow, a feral animal's. David Cohen's eyes looked the same when he squinted into the sun, as he had when she first saw him. Now they were relaxed, and appeared more widely spaced and soft. When their cab started to edge away from the curb she said, "Follow that car."

"I've waited all my life t'hear that," the driver said and sat up straight, as if electrified. He pulled out into the near lane, first with a glance over his left shoulder at traffic, then with a glance over his right shoulder, at his passenger. "Hey," he said, and then 'do, do-do-do'ed' the James Bond theme song, "Are you KGB, or Specter?"

"I sell fur coats," she said with a sigh.

"Oh. Well, dat's even worse—"

"They're getting away."

"Relax, I got'em in my sights. Hey," he said, with another glance over his shoulder, "isn't dis da part where you promise me a twenty not t'lose'em?"

"I'll give you fifty."

"Yo, fifty! Well, in dat case … " He flipped open his cell phone and punched a number as he caught a light on the yellow. "Hey, Tommy. How ya doin'? Got your cell on speakerphone? No? Good, keep it dat way." He turned and bounced his eyebrows at Sarah, then returned his attention to the traffic. "Listen up, I'm getting fifty not t'lose ya. Can you slow down? Tanks, buddy, you're in f'ten … . What? Highway robbery, dude. Okay, fifteen and my wife's lasagna. Later."

Sarah sat back and shook her head with a smile. "You hustled me."

"First time in da Big Apple, lady? Yo, you gotta have da streets wired to survive in dis town. Look at it dis way: now you can relax and enjoy da ride. Gotta be worth something."

When David's cab drew up to a subway station ten minutes later, Sarah paid and stepped from the taxi. The cabbie waved the fifty at her and called out, "Go get'im, sister."

She followed the family through the subway circuit, keeping one train car behind but watching them through the window in the connecting doors. They exited at

Delancey Street, and she noticed how the boy came alive in what she presumed was his own neighborhood. His father and sister looked crumpled by the weight of their grief, but the boy lost both the droop in his shoulders and the fist by his side. He swung his arm more than his pace required and bounced in his step. Sarah only realized her distraction by his boyish energy when his father abruptly stopped to guide the two children into a Jewish deli. She'd drawn within a couple of paces and almost bumped into him, but turned sideways at the last moment and slipped past unnoticed.

She backtracked while she waited outside, and window-shopped a Jewish grocery two doors down. Her attention was drawn to the row of window posters at the bottom: A few were advertisements, but most of them were political statements. Half of the political statements were in English and the other half in Hebrew, but she could tell by the images that all of them were against Israel. Some called for protest or boycott of Israel, others appealed for Jews to denounce Israel's claim to represent all Jews, and still others condemned particular Zionist policies or pro-Israel politicians. She recalled her own indignation of the crimes she had witnessed in Gaza, but wondered why the Orthodox Jews of this area seemed to be united against Zionism. *What do they know that I don't,* she mused to herself. As if to interrupt her thoughts, she abruptly recognized the two eyes that stared straight back at her from one of the posters. It was Leah's face on the page-sized flyer inside the display window. The cheerful eyes stared out at Sarah, and a caption beneath the picture asked anybody who'd been at the demonstration for information regarding her murder.

She glanced to the side. The store window next door held similar posters, including the one of Leah. When she turned a half-circle, she spotted them on lampposts and in storefront windows across the street as well. "Must be a tight-knit neighborhood," she muttered. Scanning the area to case out her surroundings more carefully, she saw the street was lined with Jewish businesses and synagogues. Hebrew signs dominated the storefronts, and Orthodox Jews were everywhere—the men in their long black coats and hats, the women in kerchiefs, full-length skirts and brown stockings. "A tight-knit neighborhood, indeed," she said.

As she turned back to the grocery, she withdrew a pen and notepad from the inside pocket of her tan leather jacket, jotted down the email address and phone number at the bottom of the poster, and then glanced to her left. A potbellied middle-aged man with shoulder-length gray hair, Borsalino black hat and long side curls stepped out onto the sidewalk, rubbing his hands on the lap of his greengrocer apron. "Know anything about that?" he asked with a nod at the flyer.

"I just want to help," Sarah said as she pocketed the pen and notepad. "I have a friend who might've been there. I'll ask."

He dropped his apron and braced his hands on his hips, swept his eyes from her short-cropped hair to the razor creases of her straight-legged slacks. She felt his appraisal was more curious than intrusive, and noticed that his eyes dwelled upon her unadorned ring finger. "Jewish?" he asked, with a slightly bowed head-thrust and cocker-spaniel eyes pregnant with hope. She nodded, and he straightened with a smile. Then he said, "Well, if you really want to help ... " He jiggled a finger at her as he disappeared back into the grocery, and reappeared moments later with a rectangle of paper, tack marks in the corners where it had been pinned to some communal corkboard, fingers of tear-off tabs at the bottom with two missing. He presented it to her in both hands, slightly bowed forward, as if bestowing an honor upon her.

She took the paper and skimmed the advertisement for a part-time caretaker for two children, one boy and one girl, aged five and four respectively. Then she read it again, more slowly. She glanced between the phone number on the advertisement and that on the poster and realized they matched. "I'm ... afraid I can't help," she said, and handed it back.

"Shame," he said with a solicitous nod. "But maybe you have a friend who can. The children's father is recently widowed. And he doesn't have much family to share his burden."

Behind the greengrocer, David Cohen emerged from the deli with the children and headed down the street, a small paper bag in each child's hands, a larger one in his.

"I'll ask my friends," Sarah said hastily as she maneuvered around the grocer. He glanced over his shoulder, spotted the object of her attention, and hooked one of her arms as she came abreast of him. "Oh, sorry," he said, and lifted his hand from her arm. "It's just that ... well, it's more than his children that's needing care."

She felt her forehead tighten. Sergeant Kyle's face jumped out at her, and the memory brought another wave of nausea. She swallowed and shook it away. "If I know of anybody who can help, I've got the number. Thanks."

He shrugged with a friendly smile and then nodded down the sidewalk, to where the boy had stalled the family in front of a kosher sweets shop. "They're good kids. The best, in fact. Shalom."

The family continued their trek down the block and Sarah rushed to catch up, not completely understanding why.

***

"Stupid woman." The Mossad occurrence analyst, one of many in a field of cubicles housed in a warehouse-sized office in Tel Aviv, reread Benyamin's emailed account of Sarah's altered loyalties, and her subsequent betrayal of the Jewish Soldiers Alliance. She tapped the keys to her computer and pulled up the reports of Sarah's treasonous wartime testimonies to various war correspondents and CNN, and then sat back chewing her lip, staring at the monitor.

"Stupid, stupid woman," she repeated. "But not dangerous." She adjusted her trapezoid eyeglasses with both hands, and then hitched forward in her seat. Sweeping her Star of David cursor across the screen with her mouse, she bundled the reports into one file, and clicked and dragged it to a basket titled, "No immediate threat—register report only."

"Careful now, baby," she said as the file disappeared from the screen. "Another hit or two, and you'll make the official threat list. Then your troubles will start, big time."

chapter 15

"When you saw Hymie, weren't you afraid?" Katie said through a mouthful of corned beef.

"Face your fears, Kat, face your fears." Sarah saluted her friend with the pickle wedge from her plate, then bit into it with a crunch. She waved her hand as the tart juices took over her senses. "The JSA, they're not a bunch of unthinking hoodlums. No, they're very *intelligent* hoodlums. They know I can't go to the police. What happened, it's over ... I think. On the other hand, if we ever cross swords again, things could go nuclear. In any case, this is the deli I followed David to. It turns out, he does most of his shopping here, and at the grocery down the street. That's where I met Mr. Klein, by the way."

"The teddy bear of a grocer? That is, teddy bear with a black hat and curly ... " Katie twirled a finger beside the edge of her jaw, "things."

"Um, Yeah." She put down her sandwich and took a long sniff, her nose practically dancing from the mingled scents of kosher meats, pungent spices and fresh-baked breads. "You know, I bet I could gain weight just breathing in here."

"Okay, reality check. What're you doing doubling as babysitter?"

"Trust me, it was the last thing on my mind. It just kind of happened. I think what it is ... " She put down her fork and leaned into the table, hands on the edge. "It's just that all my adult life has been about death. Even at work, I sell dead animal skins. This ... this is about life. Two fresh, beautiful little lives. If you just saw these kids ... "

"Oh, so it's about the kids, is it? Nothing to do with David?"

Sarah waved her hand and shook her head at the same time, mouth full. She swallowed and said, "Sometimes I see him from a certain angle, with a particular expression on his face, and he looks so much like Sergeant Kyle I want to scream. Other times I only see a faint resemblance. But Kyle looked edgy whereas David looks ... well, softer." She shrugged. "Either way, I can barely stand to be in the same room with him. I can't forget what Kyle did to me."

"Not to mention what you did to him," Katie said, and shot a finger-gun at her across the deli table. Sarah saw no reason to remind her that Kyle died by a knife.

Katie's eyes crawled over Sarah's off-white blouse, from the high neckline to the billowy sleeves and frilly cuffs. "So if it's not David, then what did it take to get you out of tactical pants and into ... well, what is that, anyway?"

"DKDC."

"Don't you mean DKNY—Donna Karan, New York?"

"No, I mean DKDC—Don't Know, Don't Care. Got it on sale at a modest-clothing boutique around the corner. Want a laugh? It's called 'Girls Gone Mild.' I'm just trying to make a good impression on his kids."

Katie returned her overstuffed sandwich to her plate, wiped her fingers daintily on a napkin, and attacked the corned beef with a fork. "So how're you holding down both jobs?"

"By the skin of my teeth." She fanned herself with one hand and spoke around nibbles on her sandwich. "In the interview, I learned David's some kind of computer programmer. Self-employed. He works at home, so he needs someone to keep the kids out of his hair in the mornings. His sister takes over around noon. The kids and I play games, do a little home pre-school, that sort of thing. Then I've got ninety minutes to catch lunch and run uptown to Stwarroff's and start my shift."

"And his father?"

"The kids call him Grandpa J. He's nice to have around, but you can't rely on him to watch the kids, on account of his age. He's a Holocaust survivor, believe it or not. And even if his memory didn't fuddle up every once in a while, I don't think he'd want to commit to watching them every day. He spends most of his time visiting old friends."

Katie gave her a sideways glance. "So you don't see David much?"

Sarah sat back and held up both palms in surrender. "Enough, already. No, I don't, and thank God for that. Maybe he's a workaholic, maybe it's how he deals with losing his wife—he's polite and all that, but not friendly at all. He just hides out in his office, and that's fine with me."

***

Two more weeks passed before Sarah said anything more than "Hi" or "Goodbye" to David. She found his father gregarious by comparison. Though Grandpa J clearly had his own interests, he usually returned from his morning forays with bagels or sweet rolls for her and the children. Twice, when he returned close to the end of her shift, he brought a deli lunch, which they shared before she departed. The first time was her third Thursday on the job, when he came home with a grocery bag that trailed tantalizing aromas. She could hear the clatter of plates and silverware in the kitchen, but he declined her offer of help. When he called her and the kids to eat she found him bent over the kitchen table, spooning salads from deli containers onto plates heaped with pastrami. His pale hands shook, but he again refused her offer of help. "Drag our little Einstein out of his cave, will you?" he said with a glance in her direction.

She grimaced. "He doesn't like me to disturb him when he's work—"

"No guts, no glory." He scratched where a few strands of gray sprouted from beneath his black yarmulke, and then returned to spooning salads.

The office door was half-open. David sat with his back to her, chin cradled between thumb and forefinger, elbow propped on the desk. His other hand held a pen to one side, motionless as he stared at one of the scores of pages that papered every wall—gibberish to her, but at least she recognized the scribbles as some kind of computer language.

She knocked gently, but he neither spoke nor moved. When she knocked again he flicked his head and eyes in her direction. She forced herself to meet his gaze. "In Japan," he said, "you only disturb people when they are working. You never, ever disturb someone deep in thought."

"It's time for lunch."

"I'll eat later."

"Your father wants you to join us."

"Honor thy father," he said, and pushed away from the desk. With a last look at the wall, he stood and turned in her direction.

She realized she blocked the doorway, but the elaborate flowcharts demanded a question, if not an answer. "What are you working on?"

He reached behind and dropped his pen on the desk. "It's pretty complicated."

"Try me."

"Know anything about programming?"

"Not a thing."

His wide smile made her forget any similarity she previously saw between him and Sergeant Kyle. "You know nothing about it, and you think you can help me with this?"

She shifted her weight to one leg and leaned against the doorframe, arms crossed over her smocked-sleeve blouse. "If you air out your thoughts, the answer might jump into your head."

"Hm. Well, in a nutshell, all computer language is in binary code. Everything is coded with a sequence of zeros and ones. No matter what you see on the screen, it's ultimately coded in a chain of zeros and ones. With me so far?"

Seeing her nod, he turned to one of the wall charts. "The problem is, these code numbers become very long, and applications use so many sequences that the numbers of digits involved become astronomically large. If we had a better code, computers would work faster and require far less memory. But devising a better code isn't simple. Not only does the new code have to be superior in all respects, it has to integrate with preexisting computers and applications."

"*Sooo*," Sarah said, "you need to make long numbers shorter."

"In a nutshell, yeah."

"Sounds like you need a computer equivalent of casting out nines."

David stared at her, his face blank. "What's that?"

"An ancient Arabic invention. A way of crossing a mathematical chasm in a single step. Imagine you have a lengthy addition problem, and you want to verify that the answer you computed is correct. You can either add up all the numbers again, which takes forever, or you can cast out nines."

She pushed off from the doorframe and stepped into the room. "You take all of the digits of all the addends, throw out anything that equals nine, such as a nine, an eight and a one, a two and a seven, or any equivalent combination, and keep doing that until the sum of the digits is reduced to a single digit. Then you do the same for the equation's total. If you get the same answer for the addends as you do for the total, then the total's correct."

"Wow. And that works?" Eager for the answer, he stepped toward her. His face lost its smile, and Sergeant Kyle invaded his features. She stepped back, out of the room and into the hallway. "Works like a charm," she said, pivoted on one foot and retreated down the hallway.

chapter 16

DAVID WAS AS distant as ever during the lunch, and she didn't see him again for a full five days.

"Don't mind my son," Grandpa J said, as he rocked his maroon recliner in the family living room. "He's just ... distracted."

Sarah sat cross-legged on the floor at his feet, one hand resting on Miriam's back as it rose and fell in sleep. The children had played past midnight at a friend's house the previous evening, and only lasted an hour into their home preschool before crashing on the living room carpet, still in their pajamas. She nodded and said, "He's been through a lot."

"Maybe so," Grandpa J said, "but that doesn't bother him as much as you might expect."

She cocked a quizzical eye at him.

"My son ... he's a genius—an overachiever who has already been more places and done more things than most people achieve in their entire lives. The problem is that he's successful in everything but life. Sometimes I think he doesn't know how to be happy. Oh, he misses her, but more out of practicality."

Not understanding, Sarah said, "He didn't love her?"

He drummed the armrest with one pale, withered hand and then said, "David ... he's never loved anybody. I don't think he knows how."

She'd been looking at Miriam's sleeping face, but turned her eyes to him. "Then why did he marry her?"

Grandpa J scrunched his face as a mixture of grief and regret played upon his features. For a moment, she thought he was going to cry. But then he relaxed again and said, "Leah was a beautiful girl. I thought she would make him happy."

"He married her for you?"

He nodded slowly. "It's our tradition. He trusted my choice but, well ... " He flapped a hand on the armrest and turned his head away, his lower lip quivering.

"I bet he was a lot happier with her than he would've been without her," Sarah said. "And now the world has two little treasures it might never have had otherwise." She gazed at the sleep-mottled rose in Miriam's cheek as the child's lips wriggled dream-talk, then looked back up at Grandpa J.

He stared back at her with his brows drawn closer together, the stunned expression of a man whose heavy burden had just been lifted by a complete stranger. Then he dropped his gaze into his lap and murmured, "Sarah, you bring light into this house. Thank you."

She felt a lump rise in her throat. *If he only knew. But I can never tell him. It would break his heart.* "She must've been a brave woman," she said. "Few people are blessed to die fighting for their convictions."

He rose from his chair and lifted a throw-blanket from where it lay draped over an arm of the sofa, shook it open and covered Yosef with it. Then he returned to his lounger.

"It was a tragedy," he said with a shake of his head. "All her adult life, she opposed Israel and fought for Palestinian rights. David worked a stint in Israel, and returned sharing her opposition views. But when ... "

"He spent time in Israel?"

"A couple of years. He doesn't like to talk about it, and I don't push. What I do know is he returned with reformed smoker's syndrome." He glanced at her and shrugged. "The strongest ideological opponents are frequently those who start out loving something, but then they see its ugly side, and come to hate it. I don't know the details, but that's what happened to him. As for Leah, like me, she always opposed Israel purely on religious grounds."

In the back of her mind, Hymie's words jumped out at her: *She was on the wrong side.* "On *religious* grounds?"

He nodded. "Most people think all Jews are Zionists, and all Zionists are Jews. Not true. Some of the strongest critics of Israel and Zionism are Jews. There are over ten thousand Orthodox Jews in this neighborhood, another hundred and fifty thousand scattered around communities in Brooklyn, like Williamsburg and Borough Park. All of them oppose Zionism. There are even Orthodox Jews in Israel, many of them descended from Jewish communities that pre-dated Israel, back when the Turks ruled Palestine. They had nothing to do with the founding of the State of Israel, and they wish Israel were dissolved. The state only makes their lives difficult, and its wars drag them into harm's way."

He paused, as if to let his words sink in. "In any case, a *Muslimah*—a Muslim woman—threw a bomb, and the protest turned into a riot. In the melee, one of the Palestinians must have assumed Leah was one of the enemy, and killed her ... ."

He pursed his lips in thought, then said, "Strange, though. She had attended many protests before, even had friends among the Palestinians. But maybe it was someone new, ignorant. A fanatic."

Sarah had to say something. If she didn't, she would blurt out her association with Leah's death. "I saw her picture on the posters. She was completely covered and wore a headscarf. Her clothing was more colorful, but all the same, she looked like a Mus—"

He cut her off with a single stroke of his hand. "Maybe to you. A hundred years ago, all women in the Holy Land covered. Jews, Christians, Muslims? They all considered it part of their religion. Now it's rare to find them dressed that way, but the few Jews who *do* cover tend to wear something identifiably Jewish, like a snood, *tichel* or bandana. Leah wore a headscarf but, like other Jewish women, tied it differently from Muslims. Anyone familiar with the dress code could tell a Jewess from a *Muslimah* at a glance. For sure, the killer knew Leah was a Jew."

For sure, Sarah thought, heart lurching. *For sure he did.*

She felt the warmth from Miriam's back seep into her hand, and the heady scent of baby shampoo and clean-child wafted from her soft body as pure as innocence. "I don't want to intrude, but ... why was Leah protesting against Israel in the first place?"

Grandpa J leaned forward in his recliner, collapsing the footrest with a clunk. "Did you read that booklet I gave you, Sarah?" When she nodded, he said, "Well, what did you learn?"

She thought for a moment. "Judaism is a religion, Zionism is a political movement." *But, of course, I already knew that. Well, most of it, anyway.*

"Zionists follow an *agenda,*" he said, "not scripture. They want a homeland and to hell with the cost. Which is precisely the price they're going to pay for it. Torah-True Jews—those faithful to the Jewish scripture—recognize Zionism as contrary to the Jewish religion. Rabbi S. R. Hirsch said the Torah 'forbids us to strive for the reunion or possession of the land by any but spiritual means.'"

He stopped speaking and closed his eyes, and she thought he was finished. He wasn't. He opened his eyes, met hers and said, "The Romans destroyed our Holy Temple at Jerusalem two thousand years ago. Since then the Jewish people, as a body, have lived in exile from the Holy Land by Divine decree. The Talmud orders us not to return to the Holy Land as a nation until the Messiah appears, and not to take the Holy Land by force. Those who do will be doomed."

Sarah nodded. "I found 'True Torah' and 'Torah-True' Jews on the Internet, along with a bunch of other anti-Zionist Jewish groups: Jews Against the Occupation, Jews Against Zionism, Jewish Friends of Palestine, Orthodox Jews United Against Zionism, International Jewish Anti-Zionist Network, Naturei Karta Jews—"

She stopped when Grandpa J leaned back again and lifted a glass cup of sweet green tea from his chair-side table. "You're a quick study. So, you likely also know that Zionism is only a hundred years old. Before World War Two, chief rabbis of several European countries condemned Zionism. After the war, most of them weren't around to voice their objections anymore."

"The Nazis killed them?"

"Nazis, Zionists, what's the difference? They both wanted us dead. The Nazis killed us because we were Jews. The Zionists wanted us dead because we opposed them."

Something cold and ugly ran an ice-cold hand down her spine, and held it to her lower back. "You can't possibly mean ... "

"Oh, the Zionists didn't kill us *directly*. But they have our blood on their hands."

She closed her eyes and saw the gun explode, saw Leah's head bounce on the sidewalk. She didn't remember having seen a pink mist surround her head, but she saw it now. "I ... I have to ... " She stood and stooped to pick Miriam from the floor. "It's almost time for me to leave. I'll just put the kids in their room."

***

After making the children snug in their beds, she passed David's office on her way to the kitchen. The door had been closed for the past five days, but today it stood ajar. She glanced in as she passed, but took another two steps down the hallway before the vision in her mind threw her gears into reverse. Quietly, she retraced her steps and peered in. Sure enough, David sat at his desk, rolling his bowed head on the pillow of his crossed arms resting on the desktop.

She knew her steps had been silent on the thick shag carpet, and in any case they would have been muffled by the talk show playing on the radio beside him. Despite her certainty that he couldn't feel her presence, she didn't know whether to retreat or to advance. He appeared in the throes of some private agony, and she hadn't been invited.

He's not Sergeant Kyle, she told herself. She remembered Kyle's face, so handsome in her eyes before the ... crime, so abhorrent after. *But he's not Sergeant Kyle, he's not!* She tapped on the doorframe with a fingernail.

At first, he didn't move. Then he straightened and turned, his eyes red and puffy but without tears, his unshaven face bearing the haggard look of someone who hadn't slept or even changed clothes in days.

"I—I'm sorry," she said, "I was passing and I couldn't help noticing. I just wanted to say ... well ... something."

The more he stared at her, his face an unreadable blank, the more any explanation seemed futile. But she had to try. "I ... I mean, your father, he just told me I bring light into this house. I guess I was hoping to say something you wanted to hear. But now I'm at a loss. I'm sorry." She turned to leave.

"It wasn't my fault."

She glanced back over her shoulder and he added, "That's what you wanted to say, isn't it? That it wasn't my fault that Leah was killed." As he spoke, he reached out and clicked the radio off.

She turned back to him and squared her shoulders, crossed her arms and leaned into the doorframe. "Yes. That's exactly what I wanted to say."

"But I already know that. I had to be at a meeting that day. So I wasn't at the demonstration, and I doubt I could've done anything if I had been there. Anyway, that's not what I'm wound up about. This ... " He picked up and hefted a scientific notebook in his hand. "*This* is what I'm upset about."

Oh, right, she thought sadly, as she recalled Grandpa J's assessment of his son. *He's a globe-trotting, overachieving genius who cares more about his work than he does about people.*

He got up from his desk chair in a way that made him look both old and tired. Then he crossed the room to her in four quick strides, eased beside her and opened the notebook between them. She felt overcome by the mingled odors of fatigue, stale sweat and unchanged clothes, but tried to keep her attention on the maze of flowcharts as he flipped the pages.

"Casting out nines," he said. "I've been working on it day and night, ever since you told me about it. It's brilliant. I've never seen anything like it. I'm a programmer, not a mathematician. The moment I grasped the concept, I felt like I had the key. Like playing Scrabble, where you just *know* there's a killer word sitting on your tile rack, but you just can't put it together. And that's the problem!"

His hands stilled upon a notebook page, where the flowchart ended. "That's the problem," he said, seemingly to himself. "The problem is ... " He snapped the book shut and turned to face her. "The problem is that it just ... doesn't ... work."

His face contorted, and he whirled away from her and flung the notebook across the room. It glanced off a wall, caught one edge of his computer monitor and toppled it with a crash, upsetting a mug full of pens as it tumbled to the desk. He stomped back across the room and leaned over the desk, hands braced on the edge.

Sarah felt the muscles in her legs paralyzed with indecision over whether to stay or run away. "I'm sorry," she said. "I didn't mean to waste your time ... ."

He waved over his shoulder without turning around. "No, no. Like I said, it's brilliant. The problem's not with you, or with the idea. The problem is me. I just can't make it work. And now ... " He righted the plasma screen, tapped his keyboard and received a blank, black stare from the screen, then turned back to her. "And now, it looks like my monitor's busted. Know what we call that in my business?"

His movements were of someone frustrated, but in full control. Authoritative. Self-certain. *Manly.* Sarah fought to keep an expressionless face, though her heart was trying to climb through her throat. She shrugged.

"In my business, we call that break time." He sat, leaned back in the swivel chair and rested the back of his head in the basket of his fingers, elbows out. "So. What's on your mind?"

For the first time, she stared into his eyes and saw nothing but David. Something warm and soft spread out from the core of her being, and warmed her all over. She felt her head swim, and lowered herself to sit cross-legged beside the door. "On my mind? Your father said something about the Holocaust."

The words came out so shaky, she hoped he would believe she just needed time to gather her thoughts. In fact, she took a moment to flush the confusion of a major brain-rush from her mind. *He's stinky, disheveled and, and ... and what the heck am I thinking?* The thudding in her chest shrank to a flutter, but she had to force her eyes to meet his. *Stupid puppy-love heart*, she thought. *Every time I've had this feeling before, it was nothing but trouble.* She swallowed hard and said, "Grandpa J. He said the Zionists have Jewish blood on their hands."

David blinked hard, then nodded. "You've seen his death camp tattoo?"

"Once, when he wore short sleeves."

"Well, about Zionists having Jewish blood on their hands? He should know. He was the only one of his family who survived the Nazi internment."

"Is that why your family opposes Israel?"

He stood from the chair and stretched, one shirttail out. Then he paced the floor, head down, hands behind his back. "Look, I'm not the best one to talk about this: I was more secular and less religious until a few years ago. My religious convictions are still maturing. But the point is that the Holocaust happened once, and it can happen again. Torah-true Jews believe it was our Creator's punishment upon all Jews for the crime of Zionism. That our Creator punished the Zionists for trying to return to the Holy Land by force, before the Messianic redemption. Furthermore, He punished the rest of Judaism for not working harder to stop them."

He halted in the middle of the room and ran one hand through his unruly hair as he turned to face her. "In addition, Zionists rekindle hatred for the Jews through Israel's crimes against humanity. Currently, against the Palestinians—Muslims, Christians, Atheists ... all of them. Crimes they justify with their claims of racial superiority as God's 'chosen people.' Just as the Nazis forever tainted the world's view of Germany and Germans, the Zionists are doing the same to Judaism and Jews. But not all Germans were Nazis. And not all Jews are Zionists ... ."

He shrugged and sat on the floor facing her, legs crossed. "That answer your question?"

For an Orthodox Jewish man, touching or being touched by a woman was forbidden. That much she knew about being Jewish. He was less than an arm's length away. If she didn't leave right now, she realized, she might give in to her urge, maybe tap him on his oh-so-close knee while making a point. Or more than that. "Ah, yes. Yes it does," she managed to say. "Talking to your father ... what you said ... definitely answered my question." Moving carefully, she pushed herself to her feet. "I better get going, check on the kids."

She got one step down the hallway before she heard him call, "Oh, and Sarah?"

She back-stepped and peered around the doorframe to where he sat, now with one leg stretched out in her direction. He leaned back with one arm braced on the bare wood floor behind him and balanced an elbow on the bent knee of his other leg. "You *do* bring light into this house."

She stared at him, and for the briefest of moments wondered why he didn't dress like the other Orthodox Jews she had seen. No side-curls, no hat, and she'd seen a yarmulke on his head only once or twice. *Huh. I guess his religious convictions really haven't completely matured yet. He's only Orthodox on the inside.*

As she returned to the children's bedroom, she realized she had a bounce in her step that wasn't there before. She found Yosef curled up in bed, his blanket on the floor beside him, and remembered wistfully the pleasure of sleeping until noon as a child.

On Miriam's bed there was nothing but a jumble of covers. She stooped to check the little girl's favorite hiding place, under her bed, when she heard the muffled click of a light switch behind her. She turned as the bathroom door opened. Miriam swayed, framed in the doorway. She shuffled forward, flip-flopping pajama sleeves longer than her child-chubby arms, the oversized pant legs bunched at her ankles. She hugged Sarah's thighs, yawned while she rubbed one eye with a fist, and then belly-flopped onto her bed, one arm draped over the side.

Sarah stood for a moment, drinking in the sight of children sharing the sleep of the innocent. Yosef suddenly giggled, and Miriam started to laugh along with him. She'd heard the children laugh in their sleep before, when she babysat on occasion at night, and had always thought it the happiest sound in the world. This, however, was the first time she heard it in chorus. "I think," she whispered through a smile, "I've finally found something worth fighting for."

An indeterminate time later, she glanced at her wristwatch, which informed her she was a half-hour late for work at Stwarroff's. In the next instant, she realized she no longer cared.

chapter 17

FIVE DAYS LATER, a dowdy-looking functionary of one of the world's most efficient secret services sat at his desk in Tel Aviv, nursing his fourth cup of morning coffee, reflecting over the fact that nothing exciting ever happened in his office. He never had to make a critical decision, write a new policy, or stick his neck out in any way. He just spent most of his days slurping coffee, warming a chair at meaningless meetings in which he was never called upon for an opinion, and shuttling computer files from one department to another. It was a job so boring, he barely considered it work. "And that suits me just fine," he muttered to himself, when he realized an exciting job means stress and headaches—two things he definitely didn't want.

He smoothed the rumpled lapels of his outmoded suit with both hands, glanced at the wall clock and calculated the number of hours left in the day. As he did, his computer beeped and one of a double-row of LED lights mounted above his desk switched from red to green. With a sigh, he turned to the screen and jiggled his mouse. The screensaver blipped off and a spreadsheet of incoming files presented itself.

In a mundane job, this was his most boring task. The files that downloaded onto his computer reported the daily roster of Internet hits on sensitive websites—sites in which Israel had critical interest. Some were related to tourism, others to publicity or public opinion, still others to the activities of Israel's neighbors and enemies. This particular batch of files cataloged Internet hits on anti-Israel websites. Each hit was assigned a weighted interest value. Longer webpage views indicated greater interest on the part of the viewer, and were assigned higher interest values. Repeat visits to the website, extensive browsing of content, downloading material and email to the host all racked up higher interest values, with monetary donations carrying the highest score on the scale.

At least Meyer didn't have to worry about assigning these scores, and for that, he was grateful. Website hits and interest values were automatically fed into a diagnostic matrix that cross-compared with data from different websites in same or similar categories. The deeper the matrix analyzed, the more it narrowed down the list of interested parties. The result, the master merger file, listed the individuals with the greatest cumulative interest values over the past week, and it was this file Meyer was tasked to flesh out for his superiors.

Humming a nameless tune, he opened the master merger file and scanned the Media Access Control, or MAC, addresses, and other indicators that identified the electronic fingerprint of the computers on Israel's watch list for this week. Then he dumped the data into a tracking tool that traced the computers to their owners. A technician once explained that this utility traced computer owners through multiphasic collaborative analysis.

Meyer had nodded knowingly, but the tech guy must have misread his vacant stare for interest. Meyer didn't ask—he knew he didn't need to know, and he *definitely* didn't care—but the tech apparently felt honor bound to bombard him with every bit of knowledge he possessed. So Meyer learned how every computer has multiple pathways by which a hacker—in this case, Mossad—can identify the owner/operator. He also learned that the Internet server alone identifies the owner, as do software registration records and identity-specific documents like tax and financial records, and business and personal correspondence. Most users access their email accounts when online, allowing hackers to determine whether the owner and the operator are one and the same. Chat rooms, social networking and Internet telephony added to the many pathways by which Israel's automated hacking utility tracked and identified computer owner/operators. Images gained from tapping into Internet cameras and fingerprint readers rendered the operator's identification conclusive.

Meyer had listened politely, but didn't really care how the system worked, as long as it did. Without the automated IDs, his job would have been more boring than it already was.

As he did almost every day, he questioned the competency of his employer. *How can Mossad be so perfect,* he wondered, *when they can't even figure out that a computer could do my job?* Once upon a time he'd been on the verge of asking his superior why Mossad needed him to process these files. All he did was dump files into utilities and then forward results to the appropriate office. In short, he was an unnecessary link in the chain. Thankfully, he realized in time that he'd be out of a job the moment his boss recognized his redundancy. So he kept quiet.

A rapid double-beep brought him out of his reverie, and he looked up as entries on the list of gibberish on his screen morphed into names and addresses. He leaned back in his chair and closed his eyes, waiting for the second double-beep that would signal completion. Once again, he reflected that whoever thought he actually read the list was paying him a salary he greatly appreciated, but little deserved.

The computer double-beeped once again. With the fingers of one hand he typed in his selection, then the command to dump the names into the next utility, a detailed profiling tool. This was the final step. As he fingered the Send key, he wondered if this week's search would unveil any investigative journalists, talk-show hosts, politicians or public personalities—those who, armed with the wrong information, could pose a threat to Israel's media image.

As he felt the key sink and reach its detent beneath his finger, he glanced at the screen. One name jumped out at him and he felt a heave in his chest. But then it was gone, along with the entire list. Eyes wide and fixed upon the screen, hands frozen on the keys, he wondered if he'd read the name correctly. For a moment, he considered canceling the utility so he could recheck the list. But as soon as he conceived the thought, he dismissed it. He had learned never to cancel a process, unless he was prepared to explain his action. In the same way that Mossad trusted nobody outside the organization, it trusted nobody *within* the organization. Reversing a process without justification was certain invitation to scrutiny.

Seven minutes of fidgeting and frustration later, the computer returned the list. Each name was followed by paragraphs to pages of biographical information, so he had to scroll down to search the list. He found the name at the bottom, nestled between two other last names beginning with *W.* He glanced at the photo, pirated from her laptop webcam, leaned back and shook his head in disgust.

"Traitor," he muttered, and slapped his desk so hard one end of his keyboard jumped and landed with a clatter of keys.

chapter 18

SARAH STARED THROUGH the rental car's bug-spattered windshield, her eyes fixed on the seemingly endless belt of highway slipping beneath her. The concrete jumble of New York City was imprinted on her memory, the same way staring at a lightbulb temporarily bleaches an impression into the vision. But now, she reminded herself, the car's nose was pointed toward the heart of Pennsylvania Amish country.

"Wow," Katie said from the passenger seat. She placed the last page on top of a misaligned stack of loose papers, stood them on her knee and tamped the edges flush. "So now you're on the run?"

"It's not that bad," Sarah said. "I just have to take this show on the road if I'm going to dig any deeper." She thought back over the last few days, and winced. David had done something he'd never done before, according to Grandpa J, not even with Leah. He tore himself from his work and joined her with the children on occasion, even bought lunch for her and his family every day since their talk in his office. She didn't think the change had anything to do with the electricity she'd felt that day; each day that passed convinced her that he had failed to read her feelings, which relieved her. Since then David never said much, and she could tell that although he struggled to make time for them, his mind never completely left his office. Twice she'd caught him gazing through her, as though she blocked his view of some great celestial mystery. Both times he snapped out of it the moment she waved a hand through the path of his stare. She bought his explanation, but his mind having wandered was as evident as the fact that his eyes hadn't. And she questioned the significance of this.

She shared her Internet findings with him yesterday. Less than four hours later, he called her back to his apartment and sat her down for a talk.

Today she was on her way to bid goodbye to her mother.

"So he told you to leave town?" asked Katie. "Exciting."

"No, I told you, it's not like that." *Or is it?*, she wondered. David had read the stack of printouts now cradled in Katie's lap, visited the anti-Zionist websites from which she downloaded the information, pulled some Internet-guru moves, and decided what he had to tell her couldn't wait until the morning.

He'd paced the floor while she sat in the only chair in his office, his desk chair, until he waved the stack of papers in his hand, and then handed it to her. "Sarah, this is dynamite. But like dynamite, it can blow up in your face."

She cocked an eyebrow at him, and he continued. "I investigated the websites. Most are legit. But two aren't.

Two are hosted through a government server in Israel, but not openly. I ferreted it out."

"In Israel? But why would ... ?" Mentally, she answered her own question. His next words only confirmed it.

He stopped beside a three-drawer file cabinet and draped his arm along the edge of the open top drawer. "Those two websites are redundant. Meaning, they contain nothing original. In fact, their content only echoes the most insignificant information. But you registered with them to access their content, so they know who you are."

"Mossad?"

"No doubt." David coughed into his fist. "I ... I know something about how they operate, and this has Mossad written all over it."

Yosef and Miriam's faces flashed through her mind, chased by the memory of their mother's fight for peace in the face of Zionism, and how that fight ended. "I'm not quitting," she said.

"I'm not asking you to," David replied. "But if you insist on continuing your research, you're going to have to do it offline."

"Jane Bond, 008," Katie said, jerking her back to the present. "Don't ask *me* for help. The sidekick always gets killed."

Sarah swiped a hand across her eyes. "How many times do I have to tell you it's not like that?"

"Keep saying that, and you might begin to believe it. When you told me what you're into, I did a little research of my own. Do you know just how bold the Zionists have been with some of their assassinations?"

She cocked a jaw and shot her friend a sideways glance through narrowed lids. "Hunh-uh."

"Wait, hold that look." Katie held out her hands and sighted Sarah through a rectangle of thumbs and forefingers. "Honey, you ever want to jumpstart some guy's engine, remember this look of yours. It's got serious woof-factor."

"Woof-factor?"

"Yeah. You know. *Woof-woof?* I'm telling you, hon, you've got untapped wells of femininity inside you. That look can be your secret weapon. Save it for when you need it."

Sarah punched her lightly on the shoulder. "Girl, you're weirder than I knew."

"Me? You're the one who just made Marilyn Monroe turn over in her grave and check her woof-look in a mirror."

"I don't think she'll like what she sees at this point."

Katie tilted her chin with a stretch of her slender neck. "In any case ... the assassinations. It's scary stuff. Lord Moyne, Count Bernadotte, the former Dutch diplomat Dr. Jacob Israel de Haan, and the list goes on. We're talking high-profile people who were friends of the Jews and/or revered rabbis. But the moment they opposed the Zionist state of Israel, even though they did so on the grounds of basic humanitarian values or the Jewish religion, Zionists killed them. Take Count Bernadotte, for example. He was a Swedish diplomat. Have you ever heard of him before this?"

Sarah cocked her jaw again, a smirk twitching the corners of her lips, and shot her another sideways glance. "Hunh-uh."

Katie shook her head, wonderingly. "I'm telling ya, major woof-factor. In any case, me neither. And I don't know how my college history courses skipped over this guy." She glanced down at the top page of the stack in her lap. "Vice president of the Swedish Red Cross during World War Two. Rescued over thirty thousand prisoners from German concentration camps ... ."

She looked up again. "It's hard to be a bigger friend of the Jews than that. Bernadotte was such a prominent diplomat, Heinrich Himmler conveyed Germany's early offers of surrender through *him*. After the war, the United Nations appointed Bernadotte their mediator in Palestine, because of his war record of good relations with the Jews."

Her eyes went back to the page. "In 1948, he brokered a truce in the Arab-Israeli War. And yet, the moment he proposed fixed borders for the state of Israel, and the Palestinians' right to either compensation or return to their homes, a militant Zionist group, headed by Israel's future prime minister, Yitzhak Shamir, assassinated him. This is the same so-called Stern Gang that had already murdered Lord Moyne, the British secretary of state to Cairo, seven years before. Moyne's crime? Implementing anti-Zionist policies. Shamir was even reported to have killed an unreliable member of *his own group*—"

Katie stopped reading and threw both hands in the air with a snort of disgust. "Heck, did you read that part about Menachem Begin—another future prime minister of Israel? He had a Zionist terror group too—called Irgun. When negotiations didn't give them what they wanted, they bombed the King David Hotel in Jerusalem. They killed around ninety people, roughly half of them British delegates or personnel."

Katie thumped the sheaf of papers with her finger, and then reached behind her and slapped them onto the backseat. Then she thumbed over her shoulder in their direction. "Honey, they're not shy to assassinate *diplomats* when it suits their purpose. Whoever transports that information from the Internet to the mainstream media will become Public Enemy Number One in Israel. Like I said, I'm not volunteering for sidekick duty on something like *that*."

"Not that I asked you to," Sarah muttered, but she kept staring through the windshield, her mind more on the information she'd read than on Katie's bantering: She had learned that the term Zionism was invented only a little over a hundred years ago. Also that Orthodox Jews worldwide condemned Theodor Herzl, the so-called "father of Zionism," on the grounds that Zionism replaced Jewish religiosity with nationalism, a "false concept" of the goal of Judaism. The chief rabbis of Vienna, Belgium and England joined in; they openly opposed the Zionist concept of Jewish nationalization. Decades later Rabbi Hirsh, of Jerusalem, published an objection in the *Washington Post*. His statement was so succinct, so chilling, she had memorized it.

Zionism is diametrically opposed to Judaism. Zionism wants to define the Jewish people as a national entity ... This is a heresy. The Jews have been entrusted by God with a mission, not to return by force to the Holy Land against the will of those who live there. If they do so, they will suffer the consequences. The Talmud says that this violation will turn your flesh into the prey of deer in the forest ...

She allowed her hands to slide down the slope of the steering wheel to her lap. But all this wasn't what Katie seemed so worried about. None of this would get Sarah killed. No, what might get her killed were far darker secrets: secrets already responsible for the deaths of hundreds of thousands, if not millions. Secrets that were out there on the Internet, if only people knew where to look.

Or if they just stumble across them, like I did. Her finding them, without knowing she needed to shield her identity in case the wrong people were monitoring the website traffic, was why David demanded she get away from New York City as quickly as possible.

Which, surprising to him, didn't terrify her as much as he had expected.

Mossad's Public Enemy Number One, she thought, peering through the windshield. *Huh. Well, I've always wanted to rank first at something.*

chapter 19

THE STEEL-GRAY CHEVY Lumina slid to a halt, its front tires teasing the limit line at a four-way intersection on the outskirts of Leola, Pennsylvania. The crossroad ran in both directions between shoulders of untended grass, bordered by scanty woods. Through the trees on both sides, they could see fields stretching to the hills beyond. Behind them lay the highway. Ahead of them, lush greenery gradually gave way to scattered warehouses and industrial parks.

"Waiting for it to turn green?" Katie asked.

Sarah glanced at the stop sign to her right. "Something like that."

"If you're looking for an excuse not to go, you can blame something on me if you like."

Sarah shook her head, her eyes on her hands at the bottom of the steering wheel. "No. I asked you along to help me through this."

A horn toot-tooted behind them. She glanced in the rearview mirror, eased her foot from the brake, pulled to the right and crossed the intersection at a crawl. The other car swerved around and passed, and then flashed a left blinker followed by a right.

"I think that means 'thank you,'" Katie said.

Sarah grinned at her. "Guess we're not in New York anymore. In the Big Apple, it might mean something considerably different."

Katie turned in her seat and pulled her shoulder harness loose from where it bit into her neck. For a moment, Sarah felt her friend's eyes probe her. Then she said, "Look, we can go get you one of those tight military haircuts. Your mother might not recognize the new, Davidized you."

Sarah swept her new bangs behind one ear. "I'm not growing my hair for David. I told you, there's nothing between us, and never can be. I just ... decided to let it grow a bit, see what it's like."

Katie squealed. "For the first time in your adult life? Like I said, hon, untapped wells of femininity. I can't wait to see you in a floral-print sundress." She sighed and her eyes went distant. "Yes. Yellow sundress, sandals in one hand, palm of your other hand pressing a wide-brimmed sunhat to your head as you skip along the water's edge at the beach with childlike abandon ... ."

"Just don't squeeze me into a bust-out blouse and Daisy Dukes and have me wash David's car. Okay, we're here." Sarah swung the Lumina into the driveway of a two-story concrete building that ranked, on an architectural scale, midway between a county hospital and a rundown retirement home.

Ten minutes later, they sat together in the waiting room of the State of Pennsylvania-sponsored Barnett-

Kidley Mental Health Facility. The television in the corner cycled nature videos. At the moment, a pod of humpback whales cruised shimmering blue surface waters to the tune of their eerie songs.

Katie bit her lip and glanced at Sarah. "Has your sister visited your mom recently?"

"Carla?" Sarah shook her head. "After she weirded out and joined that throwback- to-the-seventies flower-children cult, she kind of dropped off my radar. She emails every year or so, but I don't even know where she lives anymore."

"Another casualty of Nowheres-ville, USA." Katie poked Sarah's arm. "Stwarroff's is going to miss you."

"They said I'm welcome back anytime, but I don't think I can stomach it anymore. The money was great. And don't think I'm not grateful you helped me get the job. It's just that every time I saw a fur coat sashay out the door, the commission side of my brain heard '*ka-ching,*' but the tree-hugger in me heard the screams of the animals that died for fashion. I guess when you start asking yourself what's wrong with synthetic fleece, it's time to get out of the fur business."

"Gotcha," Katie said. A long pause later, "So. Your mom?"

Sarah ran her gaze around the waiting room. The furniture and carpet were varying shades of blue, the walls the subtlest shade of pink. All the wall decorations depicted forests, meadows or waterfalls, and were bolted to the underlying concrete. *Soothing,* she thought, *very soothing.* She lowered her eyes to her lap and shook her head.

"Mom's prognosis? Very little hope at this point. Doc says she needs sedation before she can see us."

"What happened?"

She shrugged both shoulders and eyebrows. "You know the stress she was under while we were growing up. No help from anybody, barely making the bills from one month to the next. When Sis and I got out of the house and on our own, she ... collapsed. The doc thinks stress carried her through, but once it was lifted, something inside snapped. Unfortunately, the doc tells me schizophrenia rarely rebounds, especially when it's this bad."

A heavy silence crept between them, but then Katie said, "I forgot how old you were when your dad died."

Sarah shrugged again. "Fifteen or sixteen. I can't remember exactly. But I was old enough to want to go looking for him. You know, find out who he was, why he deserted us, get his side of the story. That's when Mom told me he had died ... in one of the skirmishes."

"And that's why you eventually joined the Israeli Army? To follow in his footsteps?"

"More to justify what he did, I think. I wanted to show he didn't die in vain. But ... "

"But he did?"

A shake of the head and a deep sigh. "I just wanted to find something good to say about the guy, you know? In the end ... " She shook her head again and said, "He must have been an incredible jerk."

"It's a terrible thing to condemn your father."

"It's worse to defend a country of criminals."

Behind them, something feeding into the television rebooted, filling the screen first with static bars and then, after a blink of snow, with a flock of butterflies beside a tropical pond. Katie said quietly, "You never found him?"

Sarah turned to her, feeling the heaviness drip from her voice, face and eyes. "Not a trace. Mom told me he started a new life when he moved to Israel. Complete zealot. He changed his first name, joined a kibbutz, then the army. Somehow she kept track of him, but she didn't share. I couldn't even find his army records when I went to Israel, much less his grave. Do you know how many Weizmanns there are over there?"

"One less now, I guess."

Sarah snorted a laugh, caught the twinkle in Katie's eyes, and laughed again. "And that, Kat," she reached over and stroked circles on her friend's back, "that's why I brought you along. You make me laugh at the strangest moments. If anyone else said that, well, it just wouldn't work."

Out of the corner of her eye, Sarah saw a lab-coated woman approaching. Dr. Fouler greeted them, then said to Sarah, "She didn't require much sedation. She's more catatonic than combative at the moment, but seeing you might raise her anxiety level." With one hand, she bade them to follow her down the hallway.

"Is she talking?" Sarah asked.

"Rarely, and never on-topic. Just a heads-up: she probably won't understand a thing you say. She might not even recognize you. She's disoriented times three, meaning to person, place and time. That's not a problem *per se*, but if she becomes agitated, the next step might be a full-blown panic attack. So follow my cue, okay? If I say it's time to leave, believe me, you won't accomplish anything good by staying."

Dr. Fouler stopped beside a metal door inset with a thick Plexiglas window. At her nod, Sarah peered through at the gray-haired woman she barely recognized anymore. Her mother was seated in a heavy wheelchair in the middle of the room, between a hospital bed and a ceiling-mounted television. She swayed rhythmically and jagged her head from one side to the other, and appeared to be held erect by a yellow chest-restraint tied to the chair's seatback.

Sarah turned to Dr. Fouler. "The restraint. That's new. Is she—?"

"Oh, don't worry about that," Dr. Fouler said. "That's only to keep her from slipping out of the chair if she falls asleep." She locked eyes with Sarah. "Are you up for this?"

"She's aged ... tremendously."

Dr. Fouler nodded. "The stress of mental illness can do that. Come on, let's go say hi." She pushed through the door and led them inside.

***

An hour later, Sarah and Katie sat opposite one another in the booth of a local diner, barely touched dinners spread before them. Katie reached across the table and covered Sarah's hand with her own, and squeezed. Then she retracted her arm and toyed with her chicken fried steak. "Remember the good times," she said. "Hold onto how she used to be."

"Tortured?" Sarah said cynically. "Suffering? At least now her worries are over. The state takes care of her, even though she doesn't know it. Did you notice how she was disoriented and confused, but not in a bad way?"

"Yeah." Katie thought for a moment. "Dr. Fouler called it 'pleasantly demented.' If you're going to be demented, that sounds like the way to go. I'm sorry she didn't know you. But at least you got to say goodbye to her."

Sarah nodded. Neither said anything for a long while, only watched their plates growing colder. Then Katie reached across the table and tapped Sarah's hand with her finger. "So, where are you going next?"

Sarah picked up her utensils, sliced a chunk of turkey breast from the slabs piled on her plate, then held it aloft at eye-level, impaled on her fork and dripping gravy.

"Where next? Into the Devil's lair. And deep."

chapter 20

By late March, Sarah completed her tour of the concentration camps in Germany, and moved on to Poland. Many of the camps were in ruins; many more were overgrown, reclaimed by the forests in which they'd been built. From Dachau to Mauthausen, Flossenburg, Buchenwald, Sachsenhausen and Ravensbruck, she covered all the major German sites, taking detours to the lesser-known camp sites whenever convenient. In Poland, she ran a circuit from Chelmno to Treblinka, Sobibor, Majdanek and Belzec, leaving Auschwitz for last.

Her goal was simple: to investigate Grandpa J's accusation that Zionist Jews contributed to the Holocaust. She had already witnessed Israel's crimes against innocent Palestinians. Now she wondered if Zionists contributed to an even greater genocide ... against fellow Jews in World War Two. Was Israel fighting on the side of the angels, as its leadership professed, or was it a partner to Satan? And was her father's death in the Israeli Army in vain, like her own time there?

Her bus departed Krakow for Auschwitz in the gray fog of mid-morning, and she reflected that the only thing she'd gained so far was an education. She'd learned that the German concentration camps were of different categories. Some had been labor camps, others hostage or POW camps, still others re-education facilities for political dissidents. Contrary to popular belief, the extermination camps weren't in Germany, but in Poland. Spread throughout all of these camps had been a diversity of "undesirables": Catholic clergy, Jehovah's Witnesses and Jews, Communists, Socialists, Democrats and other political dissidents, Gypsies, incorrigible criminals, outspoken journalists, homosexuals, handicapped and the mentally ill.

And then, of course, there were the captured enemy soldiers, predominantly Poles and Soviets. She put her guidebook down as the tour guide's voice took over.

"Prisoners at forced labor died from starvation, exhaustion, freezing and disease, most commonly typhus," he said, speaking into a handheld microphone at the front of the bus. "Executions were conducted at all camps, by shooting, hanging and lethal beating. It was in the camps in Poland, however, that the gas chambers and furnaces ran day and night. In all, between five and six million Jews are reported to have died or been killed, a quarter of them at Auschwitz, under the command of Rudolf Hoess, one of the most notorious mass murderers of all time. The camp routinely gassed and cremated 10,000 prisoners in a twenty-four hour period, on occasion rising to its peak efficiency of twice that number."

A heavily tattooed teenager in punk dress, decked out in blue-and-pink spiked hair and steel facial piercings, whispered a snide remark to his equally attired seatmate, who sat slouched against the window. The pair snickered rudely, then laughed even harder when heads turned to stare at them in consternation. Sarah glared at them, but the tour guide just shook his head from where he stood in the entry well of the bus and continued.

"Auschwitz was notorious not only for genocide, but for Josef Mengele, the 'Angel of Death.' Mengele conducted unspeakable horrors under the guise of medical experimentation. His favorite subjects were twins, whom he would frequently dissect side-by-side, alive, without the benefit of anesthesia. He would remove their sexual organs, inject dye into their eyes to change their color, and harvest their organs. As you can see from your fellow travelers," he said, pausing to point the cordless microphone in his fist at the two punk rockers, "there were a few unfortunate survivors."

The busload of tourists burst into laughter, Sarah included, while the two punks squirmed in their seats. The guide raised his muscular bulk from the entry well and sauntered down the aisle. "Mengele even went so far as to remove limbs and stitch siblings together."

He scanned both sides of the bus, locking eyes with the tourists as he spoke, the microphone virtually lost in his great ham of a fist. Sarah felt the bus become deathly silent, the only sounds his cold voice and the wind-rush outside as all eyes followed him.

"What perversity drove him to commit such unspeakable acts? Believe it or not, he was trying to create conjoined twins. And he didn't work alone." He squeezed his bulk sideways between the seats as he worked his way down the aisle, slowly approaching the punks, who sat up straight and darted nervous glances at one another. "No, Mengele commanded an entire team of doctors. They simulated battlefield injuries by inflicting horrific wounds and performing amputations without anesthesia. Then they rubbed sawdust, dirt and ground glass into the wounds to study the healing process."

"Please feel free to repeat that experiment," he said as he drew alongside the rude youths and nodded down at them, "on yourselves, that is. And if you lack the stones for it, I'm sure some of us will be happy to perform the honors for you, right here on this bus."

He cracked a smile that showed two chipped front teeth, then turned his back on them. As he retraced his steps down the aisle toward the front of the bus, the punks slouched deeper into their seats. Watching their expressions, Sarah was certain that this time they weren't hunkering down out of rudeness, but simply trying to disappear. Meanwhile, the guide had raised his voice to a more convivial tone, and she felt the entire tour group relax.

The bus eased to a halt outside Auschwitz. A few minutes later Sarah approached the main camp entrance on foot, and a crowd of visitors in clothing as varied as the flags of their countries surged past. Suspended above the metal gate were the words, *"Arbeit Macht Frei,"* spelled out in wrought iron against an overcast sky. "Work will make you free," the guide translated for them. He told them this was the gate through which the prison laborers entered and exited on their way to their daily assignments. For a moment she wondered what this false promise must have meant to them. Twice a day, starving, diseased inmates trudged beneath these words, knowing their only foreseeable escape wouldn't be freedom, but death. She fingered the folded envelope in the slash pocket of her tan leather jacket and reflected that soon, she might know better how they felt.

For the next few hours she toured the camp's grounds. The SS had collapsed two of the crematories with dynamite, a last-ditch attempt to conceal their war crimes. Crematory number one, however, remained intact, complete with gas chamber and furnace, as well as the iron carts used to shuttle corpses from one to the other. Outside, beside a small grouping of trees, stood the gallows where Commandant Hoess was hanged for his crimes. In addition, the execution plaza had witnessed the deaths of roughly twenty thousand, and bullet scars pockmarked the stone wall backdrop. The saddest spot, to Sarah, was the unloading ramp, where arriving prisoners were herded from the railroad cars and divided into two lines. To the right meant slave labor and slow death. To the left, the path trailed off toward the walled entrances to the crematories.

The tour group left through the same gate they'd entered, beneath the same disingenuous words. Sarah felt a mental numbness and shook her head to clear it, but all it did was stir the mud between her ears. For a moment, she questioned why she'd come. She did not feel she had accomplished anything, or learned anything she didn't already know. Was there any point in visiting the locales she still had on her itinerary? Then her fingers touched the envelope in her pocket, a reminder of the promise she'd made to Grandpa J.

While the tour bus eased back onto the road and aligned its spine with Krakow, she gazed past her reflection in the side window and watched the electric double fence of Auschwitz slide past. Like a stream of music that ends in a sudden crescendo, the camp's fence ended in the somber bulk of a long-deserted guard tower, then was gone. Rather than encouragement, she now expected the letter she had carried with her to read like a condemnation—that she'd failed in her goal. But she had promised to read it, and she owed Grandpa J that much.

She shook off a chill, turned from the window, and fished the letter from her jacket pocket. Slowly, as if contemplating the correctness of her action, she unfolded the envelope and read the shaky handwriting: *Open only after seeing Auschwitz.*

Holding the envelope to the light of the afternoon sky, she tore an empty strip off one end, extracted the letter between two fingers and unfolded it in her lap with a rustle of dry paper. She was surprised to find an ATM card nestled in its deepest fold.

David's father had started the letter with, "Dear Sarah," and for reasons she couldn't quite grasp, tears came to her eyes at those words. She blinked them back and started reading, noting that despite the occasional wavering line, his bold, fluid script reflected an age when people took pride in their penmanship.

Dear Sarah,

When we first met, I liked what I saw. I remember telling my son that despite your outward rigidity, the softness of your features betrayed sensitivity and kindness that you preferred to keep hidden. At the same time, the line of your jaw and the glacier-blue tint to your eyes spoke of steely resolve when you have committed yourself to a course of action. I was mindful of this when I tried to talk you out of your present undertaking, because I soon realized nothing my son or I could ever say would stop you. So I have decided to support you instead. The PIN for the enclosed ATM card is 8243. Take whatever you need, and don't think twice about it. What you are doing is worth more than money, but I worry it also might be worth your life. So take care.

One additional word of caution. By now you have toured the death camps, and such visits make the horrors of the Holocaust more vivid. But I remind you of your purpose. Don't waste your time recycling the Nazi atrocities. That is a story well known, and the few Nazi war criminals still at large are no doubt suffering the ravages of old age. It will serve little or no purpose to bring them to justice now, because they will face G_d's wrath soon enough. More importantly, their evil ended long ago, whereas the evil you wish to expose is very much alive.

It is the Zionist collaboration with the Nazis, both before and during World War II, which exposes Israel for what it is—a threat to the Jewish people, to the Jewish religion, and to world peace. That is a story people need to know. Unfortunately, it is also a story the Zionists will kill to suppress.

From an aged Holocaust survivor to a determined young lady whom I would grieve to lose, I ask you to do what I did— survive, and return to expose the truth.

Shalom,
Grandpa J

She refolded the letter, hitched to one side in her seat and slipped it into the rear pocket of her jeans. Then she realized the ATM card was still in her hand.

Plenty of fur money left, but just in case ... . She slid the card into a side pocket of her patent leather clutch purse. "Never keep the PIN with the card," she muttered while she mentally ran through formulas by which she could remember the PIN. *8243, 8243 ... hm.* She consulted her cell phone and tried to spell a word from the keypad, gave up quickly on any word beginning with a *U* or a *V,* and gave up a moment later on the *T.* Then she tried mathematical formulas, beginning with eight divided by two equals four, but was stumped on how to work a three into the equation. Eventually she leaned back in her seat and watched the foliage fly by. A moment after she released the burden of the task, a fitting formula crept into her mind and curled her lips into a sly smile.

"Ah," she whispered, "Grandpa J, your secret's out." *8243. The date of the inmate rebellion at Treblinka death camp: 8/2/43—August 2, 1943.* Few of the escapees survived, but if her guess was right, Grandpa J was one of them. His letter was laced with an old man's regret—the grief of someone who had survived the camps, but the weight of responsibility and later, age and infirmity, had prevented him from completing his lifelong mission. His goal had now become hers.

chapter 21

MEYER NEVER ATTENDED a meeting without a mug of coffee. Being an eight-to-ten cups a day addict, it wasn't just the caffeine that kept him awake, but also the habitual sipping. As usual, he sat at the far end of the table, virtually ignored. The section chief, known only as "Chief," had his secretary review the minutes of the previous meeting, and then launched into the new business. The drone of the chief's voice as he worked down the list of names on Mossad's watch list washed over Meyer like a lullaby, and he felt the familiar fatigue settle upon him. He sipped his coffee reflexively, but then lowered his mug to the sudden realization that the room had gone silent. And that everyone in the room had fixed their gaze upon him.

"Meyer. I asked you," the chief said, as he laid a file flat on the table and then vaulted one hand over it in an umbrella of fingers, "what you think we should do in her case?"

Chief is asking for my *opinion?* Meyer thought. *That's unprecedented.* Unfortunately, he didn't have any idea who "her" was, or that she had a case, or even what the case was about. "I'm sorry, I didn't ... "

The chief sighed and lifted the top sheet from the folder in front of him. "Sarah Weizmann. Near the bottom of your watch list. I asked what you think we should do with her."

Weizmann! The traitor's name jumped out at Meyer, freshening his senses. Then the question came: *What are you asking* me *for?* Then he realized what was happening. Every once in a while, the masters at the agency tested their employees. Those who demonstrated loyalty and insight moved up one more rung on the institutional ladder.

His mind replayed the first time he'd seen Sarah on television. He sat slouched on his rust-colored overstuffed living-room sofa, channel surfing. With a click of the remote CNN filled the screen with Sarah in a drab-olive Army uniform, rifle slung diagonally across her chest with the gun-butt below her right shoulder, her back to Gaza in the near distance. Fireballs burst in the dark night, flames and smoke billowed up from behind her. And yet she'd stood strong, self-confident and determined against the backdrop of Israel's siege, feminine in face but hard in jaw and ice-cold in her eyes.

The perfect Israeli woman-soldier, he'd thought. *One more brick in the foundation of the Zionist state of Israel.* Just as he was thinking she was the most beautiful thing he'd ever seen, CNN announced in the crawl at the bottom of the screen that she was Private Sarah Weizmann, soldier-witness from the front line.

Meyer's two daughters were wrestling on the carpet in front of him. He shouted to hush their squeals and thumbed up the volume. A moment later, he wished he hadn't. Words like "atrocities," "genocide" and "crimes against humanity" rolled from her lips, condemning him and his employer and the entire country of Israel. Instantly, his heart shriveled up and spat at her. *Traitor.* He'd wanted to smash the television screen. Instead, he threw himself back into the sofa cushions and cursed her.

"What if I asked you to make this decision?"

"Er ... what, Chief?" he said.

The chief raised an eyebrow at him. "Our road workers tell us she went from touring the Internet in America to touring the concentration camps in Germany and Poland. She's up to something. So, what if I asked you to make this decision?"

Meyer reflected how he'd waited years for an opportunity to prove his commitment to Israel, to the Zionist ideal. He knew the chief was probing him, to see how strong he was. In particularly, the chief needed to know how far he would go to support his political convictions. *This is my chance. I have to appear decisive, dedicated and strong, no matter the cost.*

"Take her out," he said. "Kill her."

Silence descended upon the room like a vacuum. On both sides of the long table, the attendees stared at him, as frozen in their facial expressions as they were in their seats.

The chief ruffled the stack of files in front of him. "That seems harsh and more than a little premature, don't you think? After all, she hasn't really done anything yet, has she?"

In all his years with Mossad, Meyer had never heard a death sentence pronounced in the meetings to which he was privy, and he felt proud to be the one to speak the words. Of course, death sentences were passed down all the time, but always from higher, more secretive levels. Having demonstrated the strength of character to make such a pronouncement, he felt his chest swell with a feeling of importance. "She's a traitor," he said. He gestured to the stack of files beneath his superior's crossed hands and added, "You saw the report on her wartime interviews with CNN. The woman is a menace. Kill her for the honor and protection of our homeland."

He watched as the chief nodded soberly, then scribbled a note inside Sarah Weizmann's file. *Finally*, he thought. *Finally somebody listens to me!*

As he wrote, the chief flicked his eyes in Meyer's direction, over the rims of his reading glasses. "Thank you for your opinion." Then he glanced down and read his note: *Hands off, continue surveillance. Note to self—Meyer's an idiot.* Then he slapped the file closed, shuffled it to the bottom of the pile and flipped open the top folder. "Next case."

***

Meyer returned to his office humming a tune that put spring into his step. He settled into his chair and then began swiveling it, half-empty coffee mug cradled in both hands, imagining a future in one of the posh executive offices upstairs. *You're on the way up, now. Someday soon—*

He froze. His mind had stopped on the unfortunate cost of his career advancement, what he imagined would be the sad fate of Sarah Weizmann. But then his computer double-beeped and he found the red LED lights above the monitor blinking green. He grabbed the mouse and jiggled it, and eagerly scanned the list of names that appeared on the screen, hoping to identify another traitor to cement a promotion.

chapter 22

THE ONLY FURNITURE in the hostel room in Krakow was a miniscule composite wood desk with mis-matched chair, and a low bed shoved against the wall in what can only be described as faux-prison cell design. Sarah had spread stacks of papers along the bed's free edge, overlapping like roofing tiles to create a dateline. Other pages lay scattered on the desk, the chair's seat and the floor. Before she could fulfill Grandpa J's request, there was homework to do, and lots of it.

She stood in the middle of the mess, ran her finger along the papers, determined to commit each word to memory. Before she left America, David had placed a bewildering array of security features on her notebook computer, but somehow the printouts, arranged by date, helped organize her thoughts better than any computer spreadsheet could.

She leafed through the first stack, scanning the highlights and memorizing the data that told the story of Germany in the post-World War I period. Seeing the number of highlights, the depth of Germany's plight washed over her. Combined with the war reparations stipulated by the Treaty of Versailles, the First World War cost Germany more than any other country–thirty-nine billion dollars, over a trillion dollars in year 2000 money. The country's loss of men, money and industry practically destroyed it. The international community shunned trade with Germany, making raw materials difficult or impossible to obtain. Machinery was obsolete, if it worked at all, and factories were poorly staffed due to the war's attrition of manpower.

Rebuilding the economy after the First World War required Herculean effort, so it only made sense that the global depression over the next two decades affected Germany more than any other country in the world. The Weimar Republic tried to buy itself out of the Great Depression by printing money. The result was hyperinflation and mass starvation. Inflation was so extreme that the exchange rate approached one trillion German marks to the American dollar. Germans fueled their wood-burning stoves with stacks of bills because, pound for pound, money became cheaper than wood. Two things this twice-shattered nation really could have lived without were an economic boycott and a malignant totalitarian leader. Unfortunately, it got both.

Sarah put down one stack of papers, picked up a microfiche printout of London's *Daily Express,* dated March 24, 1933, and read the front page article titled "Judea Declares War on Germany."

"Jesus ... H ... Christ," she muttered, and then laughed at the realization of what she, as a Jew, had just uttered. "Jesus H. Christ. *Hok-kay*, moving right along ... "

She turned a quarter-circle and paced the narrow floor while she read how Jewish leaders had declared an economic boycott on Germany. The boycott's intent was to cripple the Nazi government and force regime change. Only two months before, on January 30, the president of Germany, Paul von Hindenburg, had appointed Hitler as Chancellor of Germany. On March 23, the new Nazi leader gained totalitarian powers.

But to her surprise, Hitler didn't launch a campaign of Jewish persecution right away. At first, he didn't even restrict Jewish rights. Oh, sure, there were random acts of anti-Semitism in Germany, just as there were all over Europe. That was simply par for the two-millennium course of anti-Semitism in Europe. But none of the scattered hate crimes were officially sanctioned by the new coalition government. That wouldn't come until later.

I wonder, Sarah mused, *how much the Jewish boycott fueled Nazi anti-Semitism. Was Hitler going to have his Holocaust anyway, no matter* what *the Jews did? Was the Jewish economic boycott a justifiable effort to unseat the Nazi dictator before he could commit a foreseeable genocide? Or did the so-called Jewish economic war provoke Hitler to atrocities he would not otherwise have committed?*

She halted at one end of the room, laid the papers on the tiny desk and highlighted where the article described the boycott as an "economic crusade." Then she replaced the stack in the dateline sequence on her bed, extracted the inflammatory statements by Samuel Untermyer, a New York lawyer and a prominent Jewish leader, and stroked her fluorescent-pink highlighter over the passage where he called Jews of the world to unite in a "holy war" against Hitler's regime.

"Crusade," she whispered, then "holy war."

She leafed through the next stack of pages, found one announcing the Jewish declaration of economic war against Hitler's government and the German nation.

The next day, Hitler accused Jewish instigators of vilifying the German people for what he claimed were fabricated atrocities. *And fabricated they must have been,* Sarah mused: according to her timeline, Germany hadn't yet committed any of the crimes for which the Nazi regime would later become notorious.

Hitler responded to the Jewish declaration of economic "holy war" with a one-day German boycott of Jewish businesses on April 1. The international Jewish leadership declared Germany's boycott a naked act of aggression and spun history to reflect that lie, overlooking the boycott they had themselves launched just one week prior.

Wait a minute, she thought. *Did the Jews play into Hitler's hands, giving him the provocation he felt he needed to launch his genocide? Or did they bring his wrath upon themselves, not only through their economic revolt, but also through their misrepresentation of events?*

She teased a page from the end of the timelined papers, plunked a stocking-covered foot on an empty space on the wooden chair seat, and leaned into the Thinker posture, elbow on bent knee and chin on fist. One of the many quotes she'd downloaded from the Internet was spoken by the future first president of Israel, Chaim Weizmann.

"Chaim Weizmann," she muttered. "Same last name as mine. No relation, I hope. Especially since he'd been quoted as promising British Prime Minister Neville Chamberlain that the Jews would 'stand by Great Britain and will fight on the side of the democracies.'"

She looked again at the article's date: September 6, 1939, only five days after Germany invaded Poland, which kicked off World War Two. And Weizmann, president of the International Jewish Agency and the World Zionist Organization, had pledged Jewish support to Great Britain, in their war against Germany.

Her eyes closed of their own accord. *Hardly the best of timing, if you're hoping to shelter Jewish lives in Poland and Germany.*

The Thinker position was suddenly too passive. She snatched a sheaf of papers from the seat and straddled the chair. Blowing out a breath, she glanced at the papers on the bed. "I'm beginning to understand why Hitler started his persecution. The Zionists declared war on him, then promised to fight on the side of his enemies. Hm." *But, barnacles and tartar sauce, that's not even the worst of it ... .*

From her perch on the chair, she swept a bunch of unordered papers from the floor and sorted through them. The first advised her that the Jewish boycott practically crippled Germany, the second reminded her of the infamous "starvation riots." The next page referenced a quote allegedly from the Jewish newspaper *Natscha Retsch*:

The war against Germany will be waged by all Jewish communities, conferences, congresses ... by every individual Jew. Thereby the war against Germany will ideologically enliven and promote our interests, which require that Germany be wholly destroyed.

Wholly destroyed. Not "stopped." No attempt at developing a mutually beneficial political or economic alliance. No, the writer of that article wanted Germany obliterated.

She looked for the date of the quotation, couldn't find one, balled the page up and tossed it into the corner with a high hook. It did a perfect two-wall carom and dropped into the woven plastic trash basket with a rustle.

The next few pages contained more quotes, and in almost every one, the word "war" was prominent.

German biographer, Emil Ludwig Cohn, stated: "Hitler will have no war, but we will force it on him, not this year, but soon."

A citation from the National Chairman of the United Jewish Campaign read: "We Jews are going to bring a war on Germany."

And on June 3, 1938, New York City's *The American Hebrew* described how the "sons of Israel will be sending the Nazi dictator to hell."

"Well *that* certainly set the tone," Sarah whispered while she shuffled these pages to the bottom of the pile. Then she read the next sheet, dated March 29, 1939. Less than six months before Germany's invasion of Poland, the *New York Tribune* quoted Brigadier General George Van Horn Mosely as having said, "The war now proposed is for the purpose of establishing Jewish hegemony throughout the world."

For a moment, her brain flooded with supremacist ideology: the Nazi concept of Aryan superiority versus the sanctimonious Jewish concept of being God's elect. The Nazi "master race" versus the Jewish "chosen people." One source even equated Zionism to "the concept of a racial state—the Hitlerian concept."

From some deep and dusty file cabinet in her mind, she dredged up UN Resolution 3379, which in 1975 declared Zionism to be racist. In 1991, the UN revoked the Resolution, which made her wonder if people were actually fickle enough to believe that when a concept became politically incorrect, it also became untrue.

She blinked long and hard, trying to abort her memory, but the vision of Gaza filled her mind. She'd been standing guard on one of the many anonymous street corners, known to her unit only by its GPS coordinates. Half a block from where she stood, their unit tank sat in the middle of a residential strip of brick houses, gouged and perforated with the craters of gun and tank fire. The black pistol grip of her M-16 assault rifle felt cool in her hand, the butt of the weapon braced firmly against her shoulder, the textured stock solid in her left hand. She rested her right index finger outside the trigger guard and angled the barrel down, so as not to obstruct her view while she scanned the empty streets for movement.

Willing her eyes to penetrate the windows and shadows, she commanded her ears to sift the sounds of danger from the surrounding silence. She expected to hear explosions and small-arms fire in the distance, but the day was strangely still and quiet, devoid of any apparent threat. At other sites, she'd suffered the suffocating dust of pulverized concrete, polluted with the bite of cordite and the stink of burning rubber. That day, an incongruous sweetness of blooming flowers drifted in from somewhere and floated a ribbon of sensuous scent beneath her nostrils. *Someone must've broken a bottle of perfume,* she thought, with a glance at the cold blue winter sky. Then she turned her gaze back in the direction of their tank.

A door opened to the house facing the tank from across the street, and a Palestinian woman stepped onto the tiled landing, waving a white flag. *Muslim? Christian?* Sarah wondered, but couldn't tell from the distance. Four girls followed her, fanning out to each side of the woman, all waving white flags. The two youngest were dressed head-to-toe in white prayer clothes, looking like the closest thing to angels Sarah could imagine. The smallest folded herself into her mother's ankle-length skirt; the other girls glanced between the street and the doorway they'd just exited. Like their mother, the two older girls wore colorful headscarves and full-length winter coats, modest in cut but stylish in design.

Sarah glanced at her partner on the opposite street corner and saw that from where he covered her position, he couldn't see the family of girls. She glanced back and saw the Palestinian mother mouth something and gesture questioningly to one of the soldiers who stood guard beside the tank. He shrugged, nodded to the empty doorway behind them and then looked away. Almost as an afterthought, he turned to the tank and yelled something up to the unmanned turret.

A head popped up from the turret manhole, then disappeared. Sarah glanced again at her partner across the street, scanned her field of view and found it quiet, and looked back to see the tank commander's head and chest rise clear from the turret. He lifted an assault rifle from below, swung it to eye-level, and set his sights straight at the group of women.

The mother raised her white flag in one hand, her other hand open in surrender, and yelled something. The three oldest daughters, who'd been running their gazes up and down the street, turned to her as one and raised their hands, instinctively following their mother's lead. With four white flags in the air and an equal number of empty, open hands, and the youngest girl cowering in the folds of her mother's skirt, the commander unloaded the full clip from his American-made M-16 in an eruption of flame and bullets.

The automatic fire was so fast, the explosions of the individual shots ran together. The bullets didn't. The youngest girls collapsed in heaps of white prayer clothes, splashed with patches of blood and gore. The older girls twisted, tumbled and fell, the bullets blowing puffs of blood and brains on the concrete wall behind them.

In the center of it all the mother fell to her knees, and her body bucked and twitched as the bullets tore through her. Echoes of the slaughter screamed down the empty streets, then silence once again threw its cloak over the scene as the mother convulsed once, then collapsed upon the bodies of her dead children.

When the carnage began, Sarah ran a few futile steps forward but stopped, one arm flailing helplessly, the other dangling her M-16 by its pistol grip, when she saw the children fall. She took another running step forward, but stopped again when the mother collapsed. While the sergeant lowered his rifle and casually exchanged the spent clip for a full one, she stood and stared, her arms limp at her sides, her mouth open with a formed but unspoken word.

"No," she said, and then realized she was still in her hostel room in Krakow. The room was cold, but her forehead felt damp, and she reached her free hand to wipe at it. She glanced at the paper in her other hand, found herself staring at a quote from Theodor Herzl, the so-called father of Zionism: "The loftiest moral aim does not reside in the progress of all humanity, but in the realization of a more perfect human species among the elect."

For a moment her mind returned to her Jewish parents, and she wondered how they would have fared in Nazi Germany. Especially her mother. Her mental illness would have branded her an undesirable. *Immediately expendable.* Her mind conjured up a sweeping image of the gas chambers and ovens at Auschwitz, and she shivered.

"A 'more perfect human species among the elect'?" she said, recalling the quote. "Aw, get off it, Herzl."

Something just like Katie would have said, but Katie wasn't here. Her belly and chest wouldn't stop quivering. She lunged from her chair, covered the distance to the bed in two strides and inserted the various pages into their appropriate places in her dateline. As she stooped to pick another pile from the floor for sorting, the shrill wail of a police siren filled the room.

chapter 23

SARAH SNATCHED HER cell phone from the bed and thumbed the connect button, cursing the smart aleck phone salesman who'd programmed the police siren as a ringtone. She punched the speakerphone button and said, "Did I do something wrong, Officer?"

David's voice floated out of the device. "Most likely. So, you still haven't changed the ringtone?"

"Haven't bothered. That practical joker deleted all the other tones, and it's too much trouble to download a new one. The phone's prepaid anyway. I'll ditch it as soon as the minutes run out. For now, every time you call I think I'm going to get a speeding ticket."

"Maybe you should slow down."

"Tomorrow I'm off to—"

"Can we talk?" he interrupted.

"Can we ... I mean ... isn't that what we're doing now?"

"No. I mean, face-to-face. I'm here in Krakow. Tell me what hotel you're in, and I'll take you out to the best dinner in town. Have you eaten?"

"You're here ... ." She pinched the bridge of her nose with a tight eye-clench. "Um, what are you doing here in ... " She waggled a finger in the air. "No, forget that."

"Have you eaten?"

"A granola bar. I was going to grab a Big Mac later."

"A Big Mac. You're joking. Why didn't you just pack a suitcase full of Army MREs?"

She turned a circle while scanning the room. Her eyes settled on the half-empty box of granola bars beside her suitcase. "Very funny. But no, I'm not joking. There's an intriguing McDonald's just a couple blocks away. It's constructed on multiple levels in an ancient underground cellar. You'll love it."

"Not. Look, Dad told me where to take you for the best *naleceniki* in Poland. That's fruit-and-jam-filled omelets, something like crêpes. For dessert, of course, but I'll throw dinner into the bargain. What d'ya say? In an hour?"

Sarah read him the hostel address from a brochure.

"Just one thing," he said. "I've got some important papers with me. I need to deliver them to a lawyer for safekeeping tomorrow. Can I leave them in your room while we're out?"

She shrugged. "No problem." As she thumbed the end button, she was surprised at the warmth that washed over her. She was no longer alone in a strange city.

An hour later, she was doing a last-minute hair-check in the room's mirror. The bare edges were scalloped with the creeping corrosion of cheap manufacture, and an S-shaped crack cut across the bottom right-hand corner.

Huh. He called from his computer, using the Internet. How was I to know he's here in Poland?

She swept her hair behind an ear on one side and teased a bang free above one eye, shooting for the casual-disarray look. "Nah," she muttered, and brushed it back with two fingers. But it seemed to like its new friend of an eyebrow; the strand fell back down to join it. She flicked it up again, it fell back down, and she turned away with a huff of disgust and smoothed her buff-colored watered-silk blouse with her hands. She twisted in front of the mirror, scanning her straight-legged wool trousers for lint. Satisfied, she surveyed the room and debated picking up the papers from the bed and stacking them neatly on the desk. Decision made, she bent to the one closest just as a triple-knock jerked her upright and swung her face to the door. She gave herself one last look over, flattened a high-riding collar-tab and reached for the knob.

An hour later, neither her hair nor her annoyance over David's surprise arrival mattered. The hotel restaurant's steaming hot *krupnik*, a barley soup seasoned with vegetables and smoked meat, reminded her how poorly she'd eaten during her travels. Nonetheless, the soup didn't fully prepare her for the best stuffed cabbage she'd ever tasted. Known as *golabki* ("It means 'little pigeons,'" David told her), the tart juices perfectly offset the sweetness of the *kaczka z jabłkami,* baked duck with apples. Side dishes of potato pancakes and buckwheat groats rounded out the flavors in their own spectacular way. Each dish teased different taste buds, in the end thrilling the full extent of her palate.

"So this is the best restaurant in Krakow?" she asked while she mopped the aromatic juices from her plate with a sponge of fresh-baked bread. "I believe it."

"Nice to see you come up for air," David said, smiling. "Best restaurant? It's got to be. It's kosher."

She cocked her head at him. "This isn't the only kosher restaurant in town, you know."

"I needed this hotel's Wi-Fi."

"Oh. Well, now that you mention it, I don't mean to complain, but you've spent more time looking at that thing than you did at me." She gestured to the open laptop beside him. "I've put up with some strange dinner guests in my time, but that one's a little off-putting. Are your stocks doing badly, or what?"

He shook his head as he glanced at the screen for the umpteenth time that night.

"So what are you watching?" She reached across the table to turn the laptop in her direction, but he deftly picked it up and held it to the side, beyond her arm's reach.

"All in good time," he said, "all in good time."

She sat back and threw an arm over the seatback. "So, what brings you to Krakow?"

"A few things. For one, I simply had to get away." He resettled the laptop to his right, flicked his eyes at the screen and then back at her.

"How're the kids?"

"Doing fine with Katie. She's a live wire, as you know. Beautiful, energetic, full of laughs. They adore her."

"You're messing with me, aren't you?"

"Deal with it." He stared, and she felt him reading her. When she held her poker face, he nodded and said, "They miss you."

"And you?" She cocked her jaw and slipped him a sideways glance through narrowed lids.

"*Ye-ouch*, that's your woof-look, isn't it?"

"Now I *know* you're messing with me."

"Katie told me about it. She told me to 'woof' if I ever saw it. It sounded childish to me, but now that I see it, I understand."

He flicked his eyes again to the computer screen, then back to her poker face. "The kids wake at night sometimes, crying for their mother. But during the day it's you they miss. I think they understand Leah isn't coming back, but they can't understand why you don't. Katie's trying hard to fill in, but she doesn't click with the kids the way you did."

"And you?" She shot him her woof-look. When she could hold it no longer, she leaned forward and laughed. He relaxed, and she propped both elbows on the table and rested her chin on her fists. "Is that why you've come? To try to take me back? For the sake of the kids, of course."

"Uh, no." He leaned back and, mirroring her previous pose, hooked an elbow over the corner of his seatback. "No, I needed to talk to you in person. Apparently, you buying a new laptop wasn't good enough. I hacked it a couple days ago through the Internet and found out you're being monitored. Also, someone's pinging your cell phone."

She felt her eyes and voice turn to ice. "Explain."

"Right." He leaned forward and lowered his voice. "Somebody got your new computer's MAC address, and they've been following your Internet traffic ever since. Also, they're pinging your cell phone to track you. It tells them where you are, using GPS."

She forced a breath in, then slowly out. "Who?"

His eyes flicked to his laptop screen. "As I told you before, I have some ... familiarity with how Mossad works. So my guess," he spun the computer to face her, "is this guy. And his friends, of course."

It took her a split-second to realize that his laptop screen showed her room at the hostel. A dark-haired man faced directly toward her while his gloved hands systematically flipped pages on the tiny desk, photographing each page with a digital camera. David's briefcase lay on the floor behind the intruder, fully open, amid the assorted piles of her papers.

David waved her back down into her seat. "Careful, Sarah. Someone might be watching us right now. That's why I took this corner table in the back."

She hadn't realized she'd risen from the chair in response to seeing the man in her room, but now she eased back down, saying, "So, this is why you told me to leave my laptop open on the desk. And connected to the Internet."

He shrugged and gave a tense nod. "I hacked your laptop camera and microphone. Better still," he pointed toward his screen, "I'm recording this."

She lifted a steak knife from her place setting and tested the tip with her finger. "Um, David? Did you record anything else off my laptop camera that I should know about?"

"Complete gentleman," he said, and held his hands up in surrender, unable to stifle a chuckle. "Tempted, but I resisted."

She sighed out her breath of air and felt herself relax, but then he said, "I resisted recording, that is. But as for just watching ... "

Her eyes went wide and she slapped the knife flat onto the table. "Did you—"

He winked. "I'll explain the sacrifices I've had to make to insure your safety later. Just remember I did it all for you. Not for me—for you. Of course, I did find your private birthmark somewhat charming ... "

"How did you know about ... . Did you see—"

The mirth left his face and this time it was his eyes that went wide. "Whoa," he said, raising both hands again. "Kidding. Really, I was just kidding. Geez, Sarah, your reactions give away your secrets more than a computer camera does."

She looked at him skeptically, but he rolled his eyes and said, "A little trust, okay? Now, back on point." He motioned to the screen. "Remember when we talked on the phone? When I said I had important papers I'd leave with you, but only for this evening? Well, it's nothing of great value. I just said that to bait them. And it worked. Now this guy's photographing the cutting-edge facilitation software I was carrying. He's using the desk to lay out the papers, so the laptop position is perfect."

"And he doesn't realize it's watching him?"

"Hiding in plain sight. Computers are so ubiquitous, people don't give them a second glance any—" He tensed, eyes still on the display. "Okay, he looks like he's wrapping it up."

On screen, the man slipped his digital camera into a zippered pocket of his denim jacket, assembled David's sheets of computer language and replaced them in the briefcase. Then he stood the briefcase by the door, where David had left it. He peeked through the peephole, and then opened the door and slipped out. As the door swung closed behind him, Sarah said, "Wait. Why isn't he photographing *my* papers?"

As soon as she asked the question, she realized the answer.

David saw her sudden understanding and nodded as he began typing. "He's been in your room before, no doubt. That's probably how he got your computer's MAC address."

"What're you doing now?"

She waited, trying not to fidget, while he typed furiously for two minutes, then shut the screen with a slap and a click. "Covering my tracks. If they know I'm onto them, it could be trouble for both of us." He pushed the laptop to the side and crossed his arms on the table in front of him. "They probably tracked you through your passport activity, picked up your trail at one of your transit points."

She blew out a worried breath. "I've been watching, but I haven't seen anyone following me."

"I'm guessing you won't, unless they want you to. I hacked back the Internet trail, and it's definitely Mossad we're up against. Remember, you're trouble in their eyes, especially after those CNN interviews you did. And they now know you're researching the most damning Zionist cover-up of all time. Can you say 'Increased threat level'? Speaking of which, what have you learned so far?"

"I ... was working through the dateline when you called. I'd just passed the point where quote, Judea, unquote, declared war on Germany." She leaned back as the waiter settled a plate of poppy-seed bread pudding before her.

As soon as the waiter left, David said, "That was in March, 1933. Did you get to Herschel Grynszpan's assassination of the German diplomat, Ernst vom Rath?"

She nodded. "November 7, 1938. Five and a half years into their economic 'Holy War,' a Jewish youth assassinated a German diplomat inside the German embassy in Paris. Stormtroopers responded by laying waste to Jewish homes, businesses and synagogues in Germany. Scores were killed, and the streets were covered with so much broken glass it became known as *Kristallnacht*—the 'Night of Broken Glass.'"

"Not exactly a proportionate response," he said.

"Well ... " When she looked up and caught the surprise on David's face, Sarah quickly added, "You have to remember, the assassination of one man, Austria's Archduke Franz Ferdinand, touched off World War I. Given the temper of the period, what would you expect after five years of economic boycott, which in the eyes of *any* government would be little less than treason, followed by the Jewish assassination of a German diplomat?" She shrugged. "There was a lot of distasteful rhetoric bandied about back then, by both sides. From what I've read, each wanted the other gone. That's hardly a recipe for proportionate responses."

"More like a recipe for war."

"Precisely."

"You know ... " He raised his hand to her, his eyes focused past her shoulder. She turned to find the waiter approaching with a small tray, upon which sat two sherry glasses filled with a plum-colored liquid.

"*Śliwowica,*" the waiter said as he placed the drinks before them. "Compliments of the hotel."

After the waiter departed, David raised his glass and said, "To the truth."

Sarah sat, hands in her lap and eyes glued to the table, and repeated his words in a monotone.

He cocked an eyebrow. "I didn't picture you as a recovering alcoholic."

"Recovering, yes. Alcoholic, no. But I can't stand to even see the stuff."

He lowered his glass unsipped, waved the waiter over and returned the drinks, and ordered coffee.

She raised her head and smiled, and then poked her bread pudding with a fork. "What happened to the *naleceniki?*"

"Crepes are made with eggs."

"So?"

"We ate duck, remember?"

She mentally flipped through the neglected Kosher Rules folder in her mind, couldn't find a connection, but decided to nod knowingly and not pursue it. "In any case, that brings us to—"

"The Transfer Agreement," he said, sipping his coffee, "wherein the Zionists collaborated with the National

Socialist government to allow Jews to emigrate from Germany to Palestine."

"But only to Palestine, and for a price."

"Which they paid, gladly. Think about the shape of things at that time. Zionism was forty years old, and it was failing. Orthodox and Reform Jews alike condemned it on the basis of religious teachings. The Zionist leaders were all marginal Jews, at best. In fact, many of our sages and saints classify them as disbelievers or atheists. The Holy Land was still known as Palestine: the British didn't give it to the Zionists until after World War Two. That's when it was renamed 'Israel.' So Zionism lacked religious support, a Jewish majority, and a country. Among the Jews, Zionism was nothing. Until the Holocaust, that is, after which it became everything."

"Only with blood shall we get the land," she whispered.

"Exactly." Rare emotion crossed his face, and he bowed his head and nodded deeply, as if on the verge of crying into his coffee. "My mother's family was safe in America, but the Holocaust wiped out Dad's family. It was their blood, at least in part, that paid for Israel." He looked up mournfully. "And we didn't even want it."

chapter 24

THE NEXT MORNING, Sarah waited in the Renaissance-period courtyard of the Royal Castle on Wawel Hill, thinking about what she'd learned about the landmark. The coronation and burial site for Polish kings for centuries, it exemplified the country's pride in architecture and the arts. She reflected on what a thriving city Krakow must have been when it was Poland's capital, from the eleventh to the seventeenth centuries. Back then, Krakow's market square was the second largest in Europe, exceeded only by St. Mark's Square in Venice. Sarah didn't wonder why UNESCO's World Heritage list included Krakow among its twelve sites. The city was a central hub of culture, art and science.

She took a deep breath of crisp air and gazed down the Planty, the oval city park that surrounded the Old City, where the fortified wall and defense towers had once stood. Somewhere in the crosshatch of streets outside the morning mist-filled Planty, she knew David was making his way from the historic Jewish Kazimierz district, where he was staying, to meet her.

An elderly British couple shared her bench as they huddled over a tourist map, commiserating over which of the city's thirty museums to visit next. Sarah mostly kept her gaze on the footpaths and taxi stand, but wondered if her fate included ever being part of a couple. Would it be lonely, at the end of her life, if she had no one to share memories with? What if she never learned to follow a man, as Katie had chided her on that day a lifetime ago? What if she was hard-wired to only lead? At journey's end, would she regret being strong and independent, insistent on following her own path and no one else's?

The answers were too elusive. She forced her mind to the previous evening's discussion. The thought of how an ostensibly religious group could ever become so cold and calculating in the face of abject human misery made her shudder. Under the terms of the Transfer Agreement, the Zionists paid a thousand dollars for each Jew permitted to emigrate from Germany to Palestine. Yet once the war started, it seemed as though they wouldn't save a life that didn't serve their cause. Their focus became establishing a Jewish homeland.

She watched the British couple rise from the bench and stroll toward the line of waiting taxis. Then she fished a small stack of index cards from her jacket's inside pocket. As she flipped through the stack, she stopped at one and read how, in 1940, with World War Two well under way, the executive vice-president of the Zionist United Jewish Appeal, Henry Montor, declined aid to a shipload of older Jewish refugees. In words more fit for a eugenicist than a vice-president of a humanitarian aid organization, he said,

"Palestine cannot be flooded with ... old people or with undesirables."

"How Hitlerish of you, Herr Montor," she said aloud, disgusted.

The next card reminded her that twice, once in 1941 and again in 1942, the Gestapo sought to partly resolve the "Jewish Problem" by deportation. They offered to allow European Jews to emigrate to Spain, and from there to America and the British colonies. The cost: the Jews had to surrender their property, pay $1,000 per family, and agree not to settle in Palestine. Knowing that refusal equated to death, the Zionists denied ransom unless Palestine was made the destination, and stated the need for European Jews to suffer and die in order for the Zionists to trade world sympathy for the Holy Land after the war.

With the gas chambers working day and night in 1944, the Gestapo repeated their deportation offer regarding the Hungarian Jews. Separate offers were made to sell the lives of the Romanian, Slovakian, and Balkan Jews. In virtually every case, the Western Zionists refused, and the gas chambers continued to run at full capacity. The prevailing sentiment seemed to be best expressed in a letter attributed to Nathan Schwalb, representative of the Zionist Hehalutz organization in Geneva, in which he allegedly stated, "If we do not sacrifice any blood, by what right shall we merit coming before the bargaining table when [the Allies] divide nations and lands at the war's end? ... only with blood shall we get the land."

The bench shifted and Sarah turned to find a stocky European man, in his mid-thirties in years but well past his belt line in belly, seated at the other end. He nodded his flabby double-chin in her direction and winked. With a sigh and a shake of her head, Sarah stood and strode in the direction of the gardens. Once there, she couldn't take in the wintry view in front of her. Her gaze kept going back to the cards in her hand.

"Cramming for final exams?"

She whirled around, stumbled over her own feet and stepped back with a jerk. David stood, hands in jacket pockets, blue scarf looped once at his neck, studying her.

"Don't *do* that," she said while she shifted the cards to her other hand.

"Edgy?"

"Didn't sleep last night." She motioned to one side, and they strolled off into the grounds. "I kept worrying that creep might come back."

"Nah. As I told you, if that had been his intention, he wouldn't have risked a break-in beforehand. Anyway, after what we said in your room last night, I assume he believes you're going to drop it."

"Assuming he was listening."

"He'd be a pretty poor spy if he wasn't. Here, add this to your collection." He held out an index card, and she took it. After reading for a moment she said, "Wow! He actually said that?"

David reached toward her hand and bent the card in his direction. "Ben Gurion, Israel's first prime minister. He actually said, 'If I knew it was possible to save all the children in Germany by taking them to England, and only half of the children by taking them to Eretz Israel, I would choose the second solution. For we must take into account not only the lives of these children but also the history of the people of Israel.'"

She peered at the card that bridged their hands. "1938. Before the war. Oh ... my ... God."

"Yeah, well, leave Him out of it," David said with a shrug. "The Zionists sure did. They were willing to deal with anybody just to get their precious Israel, even if it meant linking forces with the devil of Nazi Germany. We Jews say in our prayers that 'Because of our sins we were expelled from our land,' but the Zionists want to take the land back against the will of our Creator, and without messianic redemption. That's not just a sin, it's heresy. Did you know that our saints and sages tell us that Hitler was sent as a scourge upon us because of the apostasy of Zionism?"

She narrowed her eyes at him. "You're getting heavy on me."

He dropped his hand from the card. "As Herzl said in his diaries, 'Anti-Semites will become our surest friends, anti-Semitic countries our allies.' That's what Zionism became: a manipulation of history, an amplification of anti-Semitism to justify a Jewish state."

They were approaching the early eleventh-century Romanesque building known as the Palladium. Sarah stopped walking. "Why were you late this morning?"

He faced her with reddened eyes and blinked forcefully. "I nodded off this morning. I didn't sleep last night, either."

"Same reason?"

"Sort of."

"Is that like 'maybe pregnant'? It's a yes or no question."

He scuffed the pavement with one shoe. "Actually, I was watching your door."

"You were ... "

He leveled his gaze on her. "Watching your door. I took the room across the hall from you. Sorry, but I couldn't take the chance."

She saw something in his eyes she'd never seen before, a warmth and openness that reminded her of a window to a garden. She realized this was her chance to tell him everything: about her rape and vengeance in Iraq, the war crimes she'd witnessed in Gaza, even Leah's death and her role in the riot. If she missed this opportunity, it might never come again. "David," she said, "I ... I have to tell you something."

He blinked, and she could swear it was as if a shutter fell across the windows of his eyes. Reflexively, she took a half step back.

"I just spent eight hours glued to the peephole in my door," he said. "The next few days, we'll find out if Mossad considers you a serious enough threat to try to disrupt your work or, worse yet, to silence you. Right now, I'm wondering if we will live to tell the truth of one of the greatest conspiracies in history, or if we'll die trying. So. Do you really think this is the right time?"

Sarah had never seen such steel in a man before, and like steel, such coldness. As she digested his words, she realized he must have expected her to say that she loved him. Although that was not her intention, the conviction fell upon her like a brick that, indeed, it might have come around to that.

He seemed to read her thoughts through the transformation in her face, for he nodded and said, "The time might come." Then he turned and scanned the castle grounds. "Now," he said, as if there were nothing more important to discuss, "the myth is that Krakus killed a dragon somewhere around here. Think there are any more dragons?"

"Why?" she asked. "You tracing your ancestry?"

He smirked. "Are we talking dragons, or knights in shining armor?"

chapter 25

THE CHIEF DID have a name, but few at Mossad headquarters used it. To his subordinates, he was "Chief." To other department heads he was "Professor," not because of his educational level, but because of his owl-shaped glasses and ever-present Dunhill pipe. To the director of Mossad, he was Landau, and to the Israeli prime minister, and *only* to the prime minister, he was Simon.

Dinner with Prime Minister Rosenfeld had wound down to that pleasurable hour old friends enjoy after the meal and business are concluded, but before other obligations call. The chief had his family to return to; the prime minister was scheduled for a necessary appearance at a state social event.

Landau would never have bothered the previous prime minister with the details of his more mundane cases, but PM Rosenfeld was different. He was not only a lifelong friend, but he held a sincere fascination with investigations. Between them, they traded moves in the various scenarios of Landau's cases in the way other friends might spar over a game of chess.

On this occasion, they sat commiserating over Sarah Weizmann's case, including their G4's rash suggestion of assassination. "Exactly *why* did our army allow her to resign?" the PM asked.

"Damage control," Landau said. "Her superiors knew they couldn't silence her. They just didn't want to see her on TV again wearing an Israeli uniform, with Gaza burning in the background. It was a good move on their part. The moment she was demoted to civilian status, she became just one more war protester and the media lost interest in her."

PM Rosenfeld nodded soberly. "And this G4 clerk? What's his name ... Meyer? A bit of a *nebbish*, is he?"

"No," Landau said. "He's not *nebbish*. Just a weasel."

"Granted," Rosenfeld said, "but going purely on instinct, I have to say he might be right in this case. What's his angle?"

Landau reached to the hand-painted enamel ashtray beside the fireside wingback chair in which he sat. He pulled the ashtray onto his lap and knocked ashes from the bowl of his pipe with a dull clunk. "Meyer? He's bucking for advancement. My read is that he's watched too many gangster films, and imagines Mossad to be some kind of mafia where he has to make his 'bones.' The man has no concept of reasonable assessment and threat-based directives."

PM Rosenfeld nodded thoughtfully, plucked nuts from an elaborate Murano glass bowl on a chair-side candlestick table, and rolled them in his fist. "Still ... "

Landau leaned forward. "The most recent emails suggest that her significant other is trying to talk her out of this. Her own missives are mellowing, even showing hints of sympathy with the Zionist point of view."

"Do you believe it?" the PM said between crunches of nuts.

"It's the usual." Landau looked up from scraping out the remnants of his burnt tobacco plug. "They either suspect or know they're being monitored, and are trying to divert suspicion. I'm thinking of taking a 'broken-heart' approach with them."

PM Rosenfeld stood and turned his back to the fire, hands behind him. "Take care, Simon. You've always been a little too soft-hearted for your job. Remember, we can't afford to have another Lenni Brenner out there."

Lenni Brenner. The chief's hands stilled over his pipe at the reminder. Brenner, a dissident Jewish author, had been one of his early cases—a case that nearly ruined his career. When Mossad's information radar picked up Brenner as a blip on its potential threat screen, Landau launched a "broken heart" demoralization campaign. Such campaigns typically recruited Zionist sympathizers from among the activists' friends and family, and directed them to discourage the activists from continuing their anti-Zionist activities. Hate mail and threats might enter the fray, but the most important step was for the Zionist web of media control to blacklist the person from radio and television. Then, the Zionist-controlled publishing industry ensured that book proposals and manuscript submissions were returned with the harshest criticism and the most unflattering reviews. Should the opportunity present itself or the need arise, a good house or office fire could destroy all of an author's research. Forty years ago, when Brenner was just starting, this could even have taken out an author's only working manuscript. Few persevered in the face of such adversity, but Brenner turned out to be one of those persistent few.

Landau shook his head. By the time he realized he had grossly underestimated the man, it was too late. Brenner poured four books and numerous articles into the underground press, and co-founded that damnable 'Committee Against Zionism and Racism.' His work eventually gained recognition, and his books became mainstream. By then he'd become outspoken and authoritative, impossible to silence. If Mossad had eliminated him early, he would have died in obscurity. Once his works were known, assassinating him would have turned the man into a martyr.

Landau angrily tucked fresh tobacco into the bowl of his pipe with one finger, then compressed it with a tamper.

"I told you to eliminate him," the prime minister said while he rocked on his feet in front of the fire. "But you delayed until it was too late. Be careful not to repeat your mistake, Simon."

"I just wonder if she isn't more of a talker than a doer," Landau replied.

"Tell you what … ." The prime minister pulled himself as tall as his five feet, six inches allowed, then pointed a finger at Landau. "Watch her information trail. If she learns anything new or uniquely threatening, you know what you'll have to do."

The chief nodded slowly, and then did what he always did when faced with a tough decision: He slipped his pipe into one corner of his mouth and, one hand cupping the bowl, sucked the tapered flame from his Dupont lighter into the tobacco. Then he puffed out an aromatic cloud of smoke, and allowed his thoughts to drift in the swirl of vapors.

chapter 26

THREE SLEEPLESS HOURS were enough. Sarah swung her legs onto the cheap hostel carpet and stood, flicked on her desktop lamp and paced the small floor. She wondered if David was having better luck with sleep across the hall. Deciding she'd find out soon enough, she grabbed up papers and clothes and stuffed them into her suitcase and shoulder bag.

Then she triggered the mousetrap.

It had been David's idea. He'd wound a string around the door handle and tied it to a mousetrap trigger. Then he stretched another piece of string between the mousetrap jaw and the room's light switch. When she was alone, all Sarah had to do was weigh down the mousetrap with a book, set it, and make sure the lines were drawn taut. Anyone who so much as jiggled the doorknob would trip the trigger, and the room's light-switch as well.

Despite this security measure, she couldn't sleep. She visually swept the room to be sure she hadn't left anything behind, and spied a half-eaten granola bar. It was still in its wrapper, and she kicked it beneath the bed. Then she thought better of it and got down on hands and knees to retrieve it. She'd just stretched her arm to its limit in the tight space beneath the low bed, her hand doing a spider's dance searching for the bar, when there was a light rapping at the door. She instinctively jumped, wrenching her arm and banging her elbow on the underside of the bed. The bed's legs resettled to the floor with a thump and a scrape at the same moment that David's voice drifted through, saying, "Sarah, it's me, David. Don't worry."

"Barnacles." She sat back on her haunches and cradled her wrenched elbow in her other hand. Then she rose with a swing and a stumble, and yanked the door open. David stood, hair mussed but otherwise his normal self, in the hallway.

"Why's the light on?" he asked.

"Don't worry, I did it." She rubbed her elbow with her hand and searched his face with her eyes.

"Couldn't sleep," he said. "Came across to check on you and saw the light on under the door. Did you sleep badly?" He pointed at her arm.

She dropped her hand from her elbow, leaned into the doorjamb and crossed her arms on her chest. "Granola bar."

For a moment, his eyes registered a blank. Then they twinkled. "Sarah, you're a woman of unexplored mysteries. Tell me about it in the car, okay? Let's get out of here before another granola bar attacks."

***

She woke once at the Czech Republic border, again at the Austrian border. Both times because they had to step inside the roadside customs house to arrange visas.

All she recalled from the Czech border was entering to find the supervisor berating his subordinate. When he finished throwing his rank around, he turned to face them across the work-worn counter. Sarah had the impression that beneath his beady eyes and cruel, thin lips, he was an even more malicious person. The unsmiling man placed a meaty palm over the gray metal stapler on the counter between them, nodded over his shoulder to his subordinate, and said to Sarah and David, "He like stapler. Only work when I press on him."

The Austrian border brought smoother roads and breathtaking early morning scenery, but Sarah didn't awaken again until they entered Vienna. She stretched as well as she could inside the box-like Lada, elbowing the door on one side and punching the roof-liner on the other. She chuckled at what Lada considered to be an SUV, then turned to David. "I hope the rental company isn't charging you for distance. How're you doing?"

He ran his forearm across his eyes. "Nothing a liter of espresso won't fix. So here we are. Vienna. Home to Sigmund Freud, Gustav Mahler, Franz Kafka and Theodor Herzl. Also renowned for its waltzes, sweets, espionage and anti-Semitism."

Sarah yawned. "What're we doing here?"

"This is where Simon Wiesenthal founded his Jewish Documentation Center."

The Lada's heater did little to blunt the chill of the air that seeped through the floorboards. She yawned and stretched again, then gathered her leather jacket about her in a self-hug. "Simon Wiesenthal. Famous Nazi-hunter. But he died in 2005. His center was shut down and moved to Los Angeles. Hm. Los Angeles. Where's it's always warm."

David shrugged. "They moved the Center, not the people. I want to see what his former employees can tell us."

It took the better part of the day and visits to the Jewish Welcome Center, the Jewish Museum and the two main synagogues, the Stadttempel and the Leopoldster, to find the men they sought. Retired to his violin and study of the Jewish scriptures, Zelig Novak had served as Wiesenthal's assistant and secretary for over forty years. A Holocaust survivor himself, Novak's work had been less a job than a devotion.

David introduced himself by phone, and they agreed to meet the next day for lunch at one of Vienna's preeminent kosher restaurants, the Alef-Alef. Late that afternoon, David stood in the doorway of Sarah's room, the door to his room across the hallway wide open behind him, and wiped his fingers on a thin hand towel. "I offer you the best hotel in Vienna, but you chose *this?*"

She turned from rearranging items between her suitcase and shoulder bag. "How do you afford five-star hotels on a computer programmer's pay?"

"I consult in a highly specialized area of mobile telecommunications. Low overhead, serious money. I make my own hours, and as long as I have a laptop and Internet connection, I can work from anywhere in the world. My income can cover three-star hotels all month long, a five-star as an occasional treat."

She pulled a handful of clothes from her suitcase, tossed them onto her bed and spoke over her shoulder.

"Hostels are simple and uncomplicated, and so are the people in them." She turned, hand braced on hip, and felt the full focus of her being drawn into his eyes—eyes she wasn't expecting to be suddenly liquid with longing. In that moment, everything outside of his covetous stare blurred. With a mentally crushing rush, she felt as though her mind had downloaded his thoughts, down to the intimacy of his soul.

David dropped his hands to his sides and leaned into the doorjamb. She stumbled a half step backwards and plunked down on the edge of her bed. Her mind now overloaded and fuzzy, she glanced up to find him still staring at her. The longing remained, but now, it was overridden by befuddlement.

"Wow," he said with a shake of his head. He playfully blotted his bone-dry forehead with the hand towel. Then he fanned himself with it while rolling his eyes. "Is it hot in here, or am I just—?"

"Tired. You're tired."

He looked down at where she sat, smiled again. "I might be tired, but I'm not dead. I think, maybe ... "

"Did you turn in the Lada?"

He nodded. "Big bucks for mileage and crossing borders. Taxis make more sense now that we're in an unfamiliar city."

"You drove hundreds of miles and half the night. Get some rest." She lifted her head halfway, stared at him with upturned eyes, and willed him to do the last thing she wanted him to do: leave. She tried to stiffen her voice as she said, "I'll go out for some chow. Give me a knock on my door when you wake up and I'll share. But right now, you're sleepwalking. Go to bed."

He nodded, pushed off and spun from the doorjamb. Striding the few steps across the hallway, he mumbled, "Go to bed. Go to bed." Then he half-turned and spread his arms wide. "If only those words worked on my kids when *I* say them ... ."

She watched his door close, then rose from her bed and swung her door shut with a metallic click. She stood for a moment, contemplating the fact that what brought her and David together would just as quickly divide them, if he ever learned of her role in Leah's death. The thought of losing him and his children drove her to the floor, where she propped herself up, her back to the door. Then she bowed her face between her knees and cried.

Thirty minutes later, she threw her leather jacket over a flannel blouse and left her room, forcing her eyes away from his door as she strode past. At the elevator she tapped one foot impatiently and debated the utility of stairs. With a *ding* the doors slid open, and she stared straight into the face of a twin she knew she didn't have. Sarah instantly tensed, but the other woman only stared back, her hand frozen halfway inside her purse. The doors started to close again, and the stranger withdrew her hand from her purse, holding a room key by its number tag. She punched a button inside the elevator as she stuck her foot into the narrowing space.

The doors opened again and she stepped out, staring wonderingly into Sarah's equally amazed face.

chapter 27

OVER DINNER, SARAH learned that Hava Östberg was in her final year of medical school at the University of Bratislava, in neighboring Slovakia. She visited Vienna for the occasional weekend vacation, which stretched her student finances, but also her mind. The two marveled at the similarity of their appearance, down to their height and weight. Aside from that, their lives were remarkably disparate. When they parted after an evening of laughter and discovery, they exchanged contact information and the promise to keep in touch.

The next morning Sarah found a note under her door from Hava, which Sarah exchanged at the front desk for a "remembrance gift" consisting of a miniature bouquet of multicolored crystal flowers encased in a solid glass egg. She returned to her room to find another note, this time from David, saying he would be out for a couple of hours. He ended it with, "I worry when you're out of my eyesight."

She pursed her lips and savored the line, though she knew it had a wholly different meaning than he'd intended. *Or does it?* Regardless of which meaning, she relished that, for once, she wasn't fighting a battle on her own.

With a glance at her watch, she tucked Hava's gift into her suitcase and once again headed out the door.

***

It took a half-hour search to find a suitable boutique. One thing she knew about Europeans was that they prized leather goods inordinately. Thinking that Hava probably had never received such an expensive gift in her life, she purchased a hand-stitched leather purse with matching wallet. As she turned to leave, her eyes fell on a black cavalry coat with mandarin collar, embroidered with an exquisite floral pattern.

"Ah," the saleswoman said as Sarah stared longingly at the mannequin. "People think the French are the only Europeans with style. Here in Vienna, we have over two hundred balls every year. Our fashion sense makes the French look like peasants or, worse yet, like Americans." She flashed a 'just kidding' smile.

"Do you have one in my size?" Sarah asked, breathless.

"And only in your size," she said, and reached to strip the coat from the mannequin.

"I'm afraid to ask the price." Sarah slipped the coat on. The material surrounded her like a warm caress.

"Price?" The saleswoman tossed her head and laughed, in what seemed to Sarah to be an exaggerated gesture. "What will price matter, when the man you love sees you in this? But you're in luck. It's the last one, and on sale. Anyway, with what a Russian would pay for your leather jacket, you could buy two of these, if we had them."

Sarah arched an eyebrow in her direction. "But that would be secondhand—"

"Oh, yes, but don't you know? Russians would practically kill for a stylish American leather jacket like yours."

A dim lightbulb in the back of her mind suddenly glowed brighter, with Hava's smiling face in the center. "What about a Slovak?"

The saleswoman tilted her head questioningly.

"I mean, which would a Slovak prefer?" Sarah waved a finger between the cavalry coat and her own jacket.

"Ah, I see." The woman cracked a sly smile. "Well, in your country you'll never find a masterpiece like this." She ran a crooked finger down one of the cavalry coat's sleeves. "But in her country ... " she nodded toward Sarah's tan leather jacket. "Even secondhand, she'll think it a treasure."

***

Did you know Hitler was Austrian?" David said after they stepped from the taxi outside the Alef-Alef restaurant, in the center of Vienna.

She nodded. "Of course. That's the first thing I learned about him."

David admired the nearby synagogue in the midday light and added, "Odd that this country should be home to both Theodore Herzl, the father of political Zionism, and Adolf Hitler, the leader of the Nazi movement. Herzl's family moved here from Pest when he was eighteen, roughly ten years before Hitler was born."

"It takes two flints to make a fire," she said.

As prearranged, they found Wiesenthal's assistant, Zelig Novak, at the window table nearest the door.

White-haired and stooped from a lifetime of deskwork, he shared one side of the table with a man Sarah judged to be twenty years his junior in age, thirty to forty years younger in health and vigor. Novak introduced the man as Ari Pinsk, formerly one of the assistants at the center.

"It was just a three-room office," Novak explained, "with a staff of four. I assume you don't mind, but I invited Ari along to help with my memory." He tapped his forehead. "It just isn't what it used to be."

Sarah chose the seat next to the window and draped her tan leather jacket over the back of the chair. Glancing around the restaurant, she regretted having left her new coat in her room. But she'd decided to save her surprises until that evening, and she supposed wearing her old jacket one more time was a good enough way of bidding it farewell.

When she glanced back across the table, she found Pinsk watching her through narrowed lids. With a blink his chiseled features changed from analytical to amicable. *Somewhere behind his fifty-something years*, she thought, *beneath that slender, athletic frame, he's hiding something.*

Over the meal, she learned it was only Novak's short-term memory that suffered from his age. In particular, he seemed to have difficulty with her name and David's. Otherwise, he didn't seem to have forgotten a thing. He described how Wiesenthal's Center had brought a thousand Nazi war criminals to justice. The most notorious, Adolf Eichmann, had been head of the Gestapo's Jewish Department and chief implementer of the "Jewish Solution." On a tipoff from the Wiesenthal Center, Eichmann was captured in Buenos Aires and transported to Israel, where he was tried and executed in 1961.

"Nonetheless," Novak said, "the vast majority of the 90,000 documented Nazi war criminals were never brought to justice. Some escaped with ironclad aliases. Many more found refuge in indifferent or sympathetic countries. And the world in general lost interest around the time of the Cold War, when there were simply bigger, more threatening issues to worry about."

Toward the end of Wiesenthal's life his greatest enemy became not apathy, but time. Novak explained as they walked out of the restaurant: "He suffered ill health, as did many of the war criminals he hunted. So one might think there are few left worth the effort of indicting, but that's not true."

Leaning heavily on his cane, he led them with stiff, shuffling steps to his modest second-floor apartment two blocks away. David and Pinsk walked ahead of them, but Sarah slowed her pace to accommodate Novak's, and was struck by his unusual gait of two cane-taps for each step.

Inside the sparsely furnished apartment, he ushered them into the spare bedroom that served as his study. The room was filled with file cabinets, a folding card table for a desk and three gray epoxy deck chairs. The fourth chair of the set sat askew in one corner, crippled by a broken leg.

"Please, sit," he said, and waved the three to the table. Sarah and Pinsk eased into the deck chairs, but David stood in the doorway, his jacket open, blue wool scarf looped once around his neck, the loose end tossed over his left shoulder. He leaned into the doorframe, one leg bent at the knee and crossed, foot balanced on toe. Sarah ran her eyes from his head to his feet. By the time her gaze returned to the level of his eyes, he'd turned his own gaze upon her, a sly smile on his lips. He winked, and she turned away as nonchalantly as she could, fully aware that the sudden burn in her cheeks betrayed her.

Novak opened the top drawer of a fire-engine-red file cabinet, fished out a plastic bowl of pastilles, and absentmindedly popped one in his mouth as he set the bowl down beside him. He hummed as he slid the top drawer shut and opened the middle drawer, and tucked another pastille between his lips. Suddenly he raised his head. "Oh, sorry." He grabbed the bowl and offered it around, saying, "If I were married, my wife would probably nag me about my poor manners. Of course," he added as he turned back to the open file drawer, "that's probably a good part of why I never married."

All the hanging files inside the middle drawer were yellow, except one thin green folder, which Novak removed. "Here we go," he said, cheerfully, as if the sweets had instantly raised his spirits. "A standout color for a most unusual document." He extracted a single sheet from the folder, then shuffled over to his fax machine. He fed the page into the machine with tremulous hands and pushed the copy button. When the two sheets slid out, he returned the original to the file cabinet. Hunched over even more than usual, he extended the copy to David.

Pinsk opened his mouth to speak, but Novak raised a hand in his direction to silence him. Then he handed the page to David, lowered his shaky frame into the remaining chair and draped his hand into the bowl of pastilles.

"That," he said, pointing a crooked finger at the paper in David's hand, "is a list of eleven Nazi war criminals, their aliases, and their last known locations. Three have been crossed out, because they have died. The remaining eight, so far as we know, are alive and still living at those locations."

"Why is this one circled?" David turned the page in their direction and stepped into the room. The name he pointed to was both circled and crossed out.

"Ah. One of Eichmann's direct subordinates. A technocrat who implemented his orders. Eichmann's defense at his war crimes trial was that he was just following orders. Well, Felix Schroeder just followed *Eichmann's* orders. All the same, they're both mass murders."

"How do you know Felix Schroeder is dead?"

"We have ... unofficial helpers within Mossad."

"Ah. So why haven't you been able to bring the others to justice?"

"That," Novak said as he popped a pink pastille into his mouth, "is what makes this list so interesting."

Novak explained that the Jewish Documentation Center had always faced obstacles. "Too many," he said. "Indifference from authorities, pro-Nazi sentiment in some countries, anti-Semitic sentiment in others, various political considerations. All of these have obstructed justice in the past." To circumvent these obstacles, he explained, the Center learned how to manipulate the media. They had frequently played the publicity card in the past, to force authorities to take action.

"But the individuals on that list?" he said, pointing. "Nothing has worked. The shock wasn't that local authorities wanted nothing to do with these war criminals. The Center had faced apathetic governments before. No, the shock was that *Israel* didn't want to bring them to trial."

"So what do you do when local officials or their governments refuse to take action?" Sarah asked.

"Again, the publicity card," Novak replied. "The Center takes their evidence to the press. But in these cases, the press refused to run the stories." As a matter of fact, he added, the names on Novak's list seemed to be on another list as well: a media blacklist.

Sarah stood, stepped to David's side and read over his shoulder. She was shocked to see that two of the names were listed as residing in America, one in Chicago, the other in Miami.

"There's a perfectly natural explanation," Pinsk said as he leaned onto his elbows on the card table. "Those names are small potatoes. They're not worth the trouble of indicting and extraditing."

Novak shot him an annoyed look. "Eichmann's number-two man, a small potato? He might be dead now, but he was very much alive when we were trying to nail him."

Pinsk shook his head. "They're old men. They'll most likely die waiting for trial."

Novak turned to David. "At least they'll die in prison. But the point is, Israel pursues Nazi war criminals, even when they're *dead*. When Israel learned that Dr. Aribert Ferdinand Heim, a.k.a. Dr. Death, had died and was buried in Egypt, they petitioned for his *bones*."

Pinsk stood, his face a mask of harsh resolve. "I'm sorry, Zelig, I didn't know what you had on this paper. Now that I *do* know, I don't feel you have the right to give out such sensitive information from the Center." He stepped forward and swiped at the paper in David's hand, but David swung it to one side and placed an open palm on the man's chest. From beside him, Sarah slipped the paper from his hand, folded it, and slid it into the inside pocket of her leather jacket. Then she took a half step back, her thumbs hooked into the belt loops of her straight-legged jeans.

Novak braced himself with the card table and rose, shaking both his own frail frame and that of the table. "This isn't a *center* anymore, Pinsk, and I'll give my life's work to whomever I choose. Whose side are you on anyway?"

Pinsk whirled and thrust his arm at Novak, pointing with the full blade of his hand. "I'm on the side of ethics and decency, and don't forget it. Me? I stand for truth, justice—"

"And the Israeli way?" Novak tottered forward, tap-tapping with his cane. "Israel is defending the men on this list, and you're defending Israel. What does that say about the 'decency' of your intentions?"

"Defending? *Defending?*" Pinsk's face turned purple with rage. For a minute he spluttered incoherently, an engine that turned over but couldn't quite start. He swiveled from Novak to David and back again, his body language shouting, "Can you believe this?" When he finally spoke, what came out was an insensible string of obscenities. Then he threw himself back down into his chair and glared into empty space.

chapter 28

DAVID THUMBED HIS cell phone off and slipped it into the breast pocket of his shirt. Thin and light, it barely made a bulge. "Novak says he'll see us again tomorrow, same place."

"It was the right time to leave." Sarah glanced around the café from the corner table they occupied. "That Ari guy, what's his last name?"

"I guess Novak isn't the only one with memory problems. Pinsk. Ari Pinsk."

"Pinsk's a problem, but I can't figure out exactly why. I thought he was about to explode."

"I thought he did."

"Yeah, well ... " She glanced around again at the spaced tables and patrons. "What are we doing back in a café? We just ate."

"Dessert. A Viennese tradition. Take a look." He gestured toward the refrigerated display case, and although it wasn't particularly large, she realized it contained the most mouth-watering assortment of desserts she'd ever seen. She half-stood from her seat for a better look, then lowered herself back into her chair.

"You're paying?" she said. He nodded, and she shook her head wistfully. "You might regret that. You've never seen me turn my stomach loose on a dessert cart."

***

At roughly the same time that the waiter took David and Sarah's order, Chief Landau closed his briefcase on a long day at work in Tel Aviv and headed for the door. He got halfway down the hallway before his assistant called him back with an urgent communiqué. Head down and briefcase knocking at his knee, he shuffled back to the office. He tossed his case onto an empty leather sofa and sat on its twin with the communiqué in hand, and read Ari Pinsk's report about the content of Novak's letter. He also read that David Cohen and Sarah Weizmann now possessed the damning information.

Landau stripped his glasses from his face and rubbed both eyes with the backs of his hands. Then he glowered up at his hovering assistant, who stood with pen and paper in hand. "Call my wife, tell her I'll be late. Then order up a thermos of black coffee and dinners from the canteen."

"Yes, Chief."

His assistant clipped his pen to his notepad with his thumb as he turned to the adjoining office. Landau stopped him with his words, almost as an afterthought, "Oh, and send a coded message."

The assistant about-faced in the doorway, pen and paper instantly at the ready.

"Tell our road workers in Vienna I need a pair of toothpicks on this." Landau stared up at the ceiling. "Absolute containment, extreme prejudice. Zelig Novak, Sarah Weizmann, David Cohen, in that order. Recover the list and code C Novak's apartment."

His assistant turned to his office, still writing, and returned with a typed page three minutes later. The chief read, signed, and handed it back. The man disappeared back into the adjoining office and Landau slumped in his seat, plucked a pipe from its stand on the end table and started to work his way through his tobacco ritual.

***

Talk eventually turned to the kids. David mentioned his deceased wife midway through dessert. Instantly, Sarah felt the good mood crumble, and a flood of history overwhelm her. A familiar sting in her eyes and a choke in her throat forced her to lay her crème-smeared fork beside the object of its assault. She took a deep, shuddering breath and tried to blink the sting away. When she realized it wasn't leaving, she bunched the napkin from her lap on the table in front of her and pushed away. "Please excuse me," she said, her gaze to one side, and strode from the restaurant. She stopped at the counter to grab a handful of paper napkins from a stack beside the antique brass register, then pushed through the door.

Hair and scarf tossing in the wind, David caught up with her partway down the block. He drew alongside and stuffed his hands in his pockets, but said nothing.

She dabbed at her eyes and then blew her nose wetly into a paper napkin. "I'm sorry. You didn't do anything wrong."

He shrugged as he strode beside her. "I know." Then he stopped and turned to her, arms wide. "I *know* I didn't do anything wrong. So I'm wondering what, exactly, *is* wrong." Head askew, he locked eyes with her through narrowed lids.

Now or never, she told herself, and nodded down the street. "Walk with me, will you?"

He fell in beside her again. She crossed her arms on her chest to ward off the chill that descended upon her, and started talking.

She started with the My Lai-like massacre her unit had committed in Iraq, one of many Colonel Farson had hushed up but openly condoned. She described how her unit members clubbed another soldier and her to the ground and then PlastiCuff-ed them, hand and foot, when they tried to intervene. How they'd sucked and swallowed dust as they rolled around on the ground, screaming for the others to stop the senseless murders. When the last man, woman, child and babe-in-arms was grenaded, shot or knifed to death, the soldiers planted captured Kalashnikovs to make the battle look legit, then called in a phosphorus "shake and bake" airstrike to destroy the evidence.

She described the atrocities of Gaza, some of which made the horrors of Iraq pale in comparison, and her escape from both the American and Israeli Armies. She concluded with Leah's murder, and her own inadvertent role. Finally, she explained how she found her way to the cemetery that day, and later, into his household.

By the time she finished, darkness had drawn its shade over the city. They found themselves walking in a park along a narrow path straddled by willows, a trickle of a brook bubbling beside them. Neither spoke for a full five minutes, until David said, "I'm glad you didn't tell me this before. In any case, what's done is done. Anything else you need to tell me?"

When she didn't reply, he glanced at her from the side and added, "I find it hard to believe there might be more, but if there is, you might as well get it off your—"

"No!" She wrapped her arms across her chest, hoping to recapture the feeling of how her mother had hugged her nightmares away when she was a child. The little girl inside her would've given anything to feel that warmth again, but life had taught her to toughen up.

"No," she repeated, and wrapped her arms tighter around herself. What Sergeant Kyle and the others had done to her, and she in turn to them, flicker-framed through her mind, and became unbearable. "No—I mean, yes. There's something else ... worse."

When she finished telling about her rape and subsequent vengeance, David broke the silence that followed. "Let me see if I've got this straight." He halted beside a lamppost and leaned against it. Behind him the wind whispered through an umbrella of willow fronds, carrying the clean scent of running water. As he spoke, he ticked the items on his fingers. "You've served in two armies and witnessed multiple atrocities, all of which you tried to avert and/or expose, but none of which were your fault. Three of your fellow soldiers drugged and violated you. In return, you executed them, which you justified by Old Testament law. Next, you joined the Jewish Soldiers Alliance, despite your best friend's admonishment that it's a terrorist organization. They suckered you into throwing a bomb that triggered the riot in which my wife was killed. Lastly, you found your way into my home, and sought atonement by raising my children in place of Leah, for whose death you feel partly responsible. Did I miss anything? Perhaps your contribution to global warming or to the worldwide economic crisis?"

She stood and faced him, hands in jacket pockets, shoulders slumped and head bowed. "That's all of it."

He snorted to one side and turned back to face her. "Well ... exactly what do you expect from me after hearing this?"

To forgive me. To keep me in your life, your kids' lives, so I'll never have to go another day without seeing their sweet faces, and yours ... . For you to love me, anyway.

Words she could think, but never speak. How could she expect anything but utter contempt from him after this?

He pushed off from the lamppost, forced her chin up with one hand and held it between thumb and forefinger. Staring into her eyes, he shouted, "I *SAID*, WHAT DO YOU EXPECT FROM ME AFTER THIS?"

She dragged her hands from her jacket pockets and let her arms dangle by her sides. Then she hooked a thumb into a belt loop and shifted her weight to one foot. "Hit me," she whispered.

He dropped his hand from her chin and leaned closer, hands on hips. "What?"

Her head bowed to the ground, she mumbled, "Hit me. Please. Or ... or ... "

"Hit you?" He spun a full circle, fanning his arms out from his sides. "*Hit* you? How is that going to ... ?"

She raised her head and shifted her weight to her other leg, tears streaming down her cheeks. From some hidden recess, the little girl deep inside her found voice. "Or hug me. Please. But do something! Don't just stand there looking at me like that."

He jerked his head to one side and snorted mist into the chill evening air. When he turned back to her, he raised his face to the heavens, cocked his head as if listening. Then he lowered his gaze to meet hers once again. Cautiously, as if unsure of himself, he closed the gap between them with a half-step. Gingerly, he folded his arms around her.

She stood frozen for a moment, then lowered her face to his shoulder and buried it in his neck. She knew they were breaking the rules, but some brittle weakness shoved that realization into a mental closet, closed and locked the door.

Her arms floated up and slender fingers hooked his shoulders and pulled him close. Behind them, the willow fronds waltzed in the breeze, and the little brook carried the whisper of its secrets downstream.

***

David glanced at her, from where he stood by the road that ran past the park. "You know that was forbidden, don't you?" He stepped from the curb and raised an arm, but the approaching taxi flashed its lights and continued past.

He was distant again. *Better play this cool. And ignorant.* "What, a hug? A hug's forbidden?"

"Orthodox Jews don't even shake hands between the sexes. You have to be family to touch."

She grimaced. "I'm not there yet. Give me time, okay?"

He sighed. "Yeah, I know what you mean. I've been trying harder since Leah ... well ... you know. In any case, it takes commitment and serious effort. But our sages tell us anything less is selling our religion for our desires." He raised his arm again. This time the oncoming taxi pulled to the curb and stopped.

When he opened the rear door for her, she stepped into the opening and held the door between them. "Can you accept me," she said, "considering all that I've done?"

He searched her face and said, "You realize, of course, a time will come when we'll all be asking our Creator that question."

"Can *you?* Accept me?"

He lowered his gaze to where his hand rested on the door. "That's going to take time, Sarah. I can ... think about it. I *will* think about it."

She reached for his hand but stopped short. She noticed he flinched, but didn't pull away, and she realized that if they were going to touch, she would be taking the action upon herself. As a compromise, she laid her hand a hair's breath from his on the edge of the door, close enough to feel his warmth. "Whatever happens, David, I want you to know that I ... I—"

"I know." He blinked his eyes closed for a long moment, as if to sort out his emotions. "You don't need to say it. And I feel the same. It just doesn't mean that we're meant for one another."

"Time," she said.

A sigh, then, "Yes. Time." He raised his hand and withdrew. "See you back at the ranch, Sarah."

Of course he doesn't want to return to the hostel. Not with me. Not now. She clenched her teeth behind tight lips, nodded, and lowered herself into the taxi. He pushed the door shut and stepped back as the car eased away from the curb. The vehicle rumbled into the black of a moonless night, scalloped at the edges with yellow half-domes cast by evenly spaced streetlights.

chapter 29

A FEW MILES distant, tucked away in an unmarked office at the far end of the Israeli Embassy's Immigration wing, two men stood huddled over a table covered with sheets of paper and empty Styrofoam cups. "You twit," the older one said. "That 'Mr. Smith'-bull-your-way-through-with-luck-and-muscle routine only works in movies. In real life, you've got to have finesse."

"Oh, so you're *Mrs.* Smith?"

Hawk, nicknamed for his hooked beak of a nose and sharp facial features, shouldered his companion a half-step out of balance. "Come Friday, I'll show you who's the missus."

Quasar nodded good-naturedly. Although ten years younger, he rarely squeezed a draw out of their weekly boxing match. Hyperactive even in adulthood, his legs tended to quiver during a fight, and always left him the slightest edge off-balance. For Hawk, this provided the opening he needed for his jackhammer jabs and kiss-the-mat roundhouse.

"Look here," Hawk said. As he spoke, he ran a finger over highlighted sections of a city map blowup. "Building and lamppost surveillance cameras cover the sidewalk from here to ... would you hold still for one blasted minute?"

Quasar, nicknamed for that poorly understood but incredibly energetic matter found at the edge of the universe, stuffed his hands in his pockets and shifted his weight from one foot to the other.

"Okay," Hawk said. "The hostel has cameras in the lobby and hallways, so forget about trying anything indoors. Outside, building and lamppost surveillance cameras cover the door. But these stretches of sidewalk are clear, from here to here, and here, and on the other side. Got it?"

Quasar bit a fingernail. "How are we going to get the list—?"

A decoder the size and shape of a desktop calculator beeped, and the laser printer beside it fed out a page. Hawk ripped the page from the printer with a zing of rollers. "The chief's latest clarifications. He says we should get the list if possible, but not worry if we can't. He says the big concern isn't the list, but what our marks might do with it. Once they're out of the picture, it becomes a non-issue. If the Vienna police contact our guys, Mossad'll say the list is old news, that they already followed up on these leads and hit dead-ends, blah, blah, blah. Nobody hunts Nazi war criminals except Israel, so when our guys say those leads didn't pan out, nobody else will pursue it."

"Okay, so we do Novak first—"

"He's the authority who can validate the list, so he's number one. Then Sarah Weizmann and David ... " Hawk brushed papers aside, scanned one page. "David Cohen. They're six feet under but just don't know it yet."

Quasar stepped back from the table and walked a circle on the carpet, his hands dancing wild gesticulations in front of him. "I've ... never killed a fellow Jew before."

"Heck, kid," Hawk said from where he stood, hunched over the table and leaning on one arm. He half-turned from scanning the papers in front of him and scratched a day's worth of stubble on his narrow jaw. "You get used to it."

chapter 30

SARAH WOKE THE next day to find no note, and no answer to her hesitant knock on David's door across the hall. As she turned back to her room, Hava stepped into the hallway two doors down. Sarah called out a morning greeting, asked her to wait and ducked back into her room. She returned a moment later with her leather jacket and the new purse.

"I know you're leaving today," she said, "and I wanted you to have something to remember me by. As we say in America, something old, something new."

Hava's eyes went wide, and she immediately stripped off her own jacket and flung it through the open doorway onto the floor of her room. Then she slipped on Sarah's jacket with an ecstatic, shoulder-raising self-hug. She twisted first one way, then the other. Then, squealing her thanks, she threw her arms around Sarah's neck and kissed her on both cheeks. She paused on the second cheek, and then laid another two kisses on for good measure. As an afterthought, she picked up the purse and admired it.

"Come have breakfast with me," she said. "I was just going for a bite across the street."

"I'd love to, but I'm waiting for my travel mate to show up," Sarah replied. "We ... lost connection last night, and I want to make sure I'm here when he gets back." *If he ever comes back.*

"Tell you what," Hava said, nodding eagerly, "I'm just going to the place across the street. I'll bring breakfast back for both of us. How does that sound?"

"Sounds great," Sarah replied, and with a "Be right back," Hava practically skipped down the hallway, stroking the arm of her new leather jacket with delight.

***

Quasar watched their number-two target line up to cross the street at the crosswalk. When the light turned green he followed two paces behind her and to the left, within easy striking distance. The street was crowded with early risers. For all appearances, he was just another tourist taking in the sights of this disappointingly dreary city. When the target entered the café opposite the hostel, he peeled off to one side and stood, window-shopping. She returned the way she'd come a few minutes later, carrying a brown paper takeout bag. He stepped in close behind her and felt the tingle of excitement in his legs and arms that always preceded a kill. Once again, however, she sloughed him off at the door, this time when a couple with huge backpacks walked out of the hostel. Together with their pack-bearers, they forced him to veer off to one side again.

He pulled a cell phone from his jacket pocket but paused as a niggling doubt surfaced. *Something different about the angle of her jaw? The set of her eyes?* He slipped a photograph from his pocket and studied it, then shook his doubts away, reminding himself that in his business, indecision was deadly—to the assassin, that is. He speed-dialed a number on his phone and cradled it to his ear.

"Dry run," he said into the phone. "She didn't step outside camera coverage." He listened for a moment, then said, "No, he hasn't come out yet. I figure if I do her in one of the blackout zones down the block, that'll flush him out of the hostel. I can wait for him in the crowd that gathers."

Another pause, this one longer, and he said, "No problem. You do your end, I'm here for the day, if need be. Oh, and I've been within striking distance twice. That's twenty points, and *that* puts me in the lead for the month."

He smiled as he thumbed the disconnect button, imagining that familiar pained expression on Hawk's face whenever he had to pay for the steak dinner they played for each month.

***

After a breakfast she barely tasted, Sarah left Hava's room for her own. Head down and heart lower, she entered to find the message light on her phone unlit, dark and depressing. She nibbled a corner of one lip and debated calling David on his cell, but decided not to. Twirling around in her room, arms spread wide, she said, "If you love somebody, set them free. Right?" As she lay down on her bed in her clothes, she sank her head into the pillow and muttered, "And if he doesn't come back, hunt him down and ... *beg.*"

She didn't intend to fall asleep, but the sleepless night before conspired against her. Three hours later, she awoke to the hornet's buzz of her cell phone vibrating on the hardwood floor beside her. She swung her legs over the bed's edge and snatched it up.

"What do you think of promises?" David said.

She scratched behind one ear. "Not much."

"Me, too. So I'm not going to make any, okay?"

"Okay."

"Meet me in thirty minutes, we'll see how it goes. In the meantime, we've got to finish what we started."

She jotted down the address he gave her, primped in front of the mirror, and then threw on her new coat. She paused to run a finger along the embroidered black collar. "No promises, huh?" she muttered. "Well, if he's giving me even the smallest of chances, it's still more than I deserve."

Then she shrugged, pushed her insecurities from her mind and reached for the door.

While waiting for the elevator, she remembered Novak's list. She started back down the hallway just as Hava came out of her room.

"Lunch?" Hava asked as she pulled the door shut behind her. "Last chance. I'm heading for the train station in an hour."

"I'd love to," Sarah said as she whizzed past, "but I've got a date." She spun, a runway model in the hostel corridor. Her coat flared outward, and she glanced over her shoulder saucily. "How do I look?"

Hava shook her head with a smile. "To die for."

Sarah gave her a farewell hug, then returned to her room. She grabbed Novak's list from her bedside table, stuffed it into her shoulder pack and waltzed back out the door. Outside the hostel, she hailed a taxi. As it coasted to the curb, she saw Hava disappear into the crush of the lunchtime crowd at the café across the street. Silently wishing her well, she lowered herself into the waiting cab.

chapter 31

"Two more in-the-zones, for twenty more points," Quasar reported into his cell phone.

"She's still keeping to the safe zones?" Hawk asked.

"She'll get tired of that café sooner or later," Quasar said, casting a look first at the hostel's door, then around the street at the pole-mounted security cameras. "Funny thing, though. I still haven't seen the guy."

"He'll surface. In the meantime, I'm on Novak. His apartment's about to do a code C, and that's good for fifty points. Novak will be a hundred."

"Seventy-five. He's feeble."

"Okay, seventy-five. In any case, you've got some catching up to do."

***

Sarah found David seated on a sidewalk bench two blocks from the Alef-Alef restaurant. He stared across the street and didn't rise when she exited the taxi, so she walked up and stood over him. His face drawn with fatigue, he scanned up her new full-length coat to her face, then his eyes grew wide with recognition. He pulled himself out of his slouch and patted the empty wooden slats beside him, so she gathered her coat around herself and sat down, leaving a discreet few inches distance between them.

"I needed time to think," he said. "I walked for hours. It got pretty late and I couldn't find a taxi back, so I crashed at a bed and breakfast. But I didn't forget this appointment with Novak."

"You look like you slept in your clothes."

He waved her observation away. "Sarah, they played you. The JSA. And if you hadn't played along, they would've pulled off that consulate bombing some other way. Leah was targeted. She would've been killed no matter what. What I'm saying is ... it wasn't your fault."

She felt a rush of hope, and her voice came out in a hoarse whisper. "Do you truly believe that?"

He looked straight into her eyes. "Yes, I do."

With a hard swallow, she felt her normal voice return. "Because if you're ever going to blame me for what happened, it would be better to call it quits now."

He nodded and then stood, stuffed his hands into his jacket pockets, glanced down the block in the direction of the restaurant. "No calling it quits, Hon. We've got work to do."

She jumped up, grabbed his jacket lapels and pulled him to face her. "You called me 'Hon.'"

"I ... " He searched her face. "No relation to Attila, I take it?"

"Too late—you called me 'Hon.' That's a Freudian slip if I ever heard one."

He reached up, gently shook her hands from his lapels, turned and guided her down the street. "Freud's dead, and he was a twit when he was alive. Look, it's short for *Honskukle*, an obscure Austrian colloquialism for over-bearing women who eat granola bars and look stunning in long black coats."

"Is not. Look, if you're going to—"

"There he is," he said, and nodded across the street and a half-block down. Sarah turned to look, and immediately recognized Novak's tap-tap step, tap-tap step just as he shuffled into a crowd, his wooden cane pacing his gait like a metronome. As she watched, something changed. The mass of people puffed out, and then instantly contracted in upon itself. In the same moment, the crowd congealed into an unmoving clot on the pavement.

David ran across the street, dodging honking cars. Sarah followed, slowed by the traffic and greater caution. As she pushed through the crowd, her quickening pulse told her what she'd find, but that didn't lessen the shock. Novak lay on his back in a spreading pool of blood, his face as gray as the pavement, his glassy, unseeing eyes staring into the sky. His arms and legs twitched as his soul shook itself loose from his body, and after one huge convulsion he lay still.

Two men from the crowd were on their hands and knees over the body, and a sharp-faced man stood shouting for the police, an ambulance, anything, over and again, in between bewailing the horror of the murder. David stood to one side of the sharp-faced man, watching him cautiously. As Sarah scanned the crowd, she caught the same man watching her from the corner of his eyes while he continued his histrionics. He averted his gaze, but in the same instant David stepped forward and swung the open blade of his hand in a wide arc that ended in a crushing chop to the base of the man's spine. His head whiplashed from the force of the blow, and he pitched forward to land on top of Novak's legs.

The crowd puffed outward again, and David stepped into the empty space. "It's him," he shouted. "He did it, I saw him!"

Not comprehending, Sarah could only watch while David fell to his knees, patted down the man's pockets and then flipped his jacket open. There, on the left side, lay a body-hugging sheet of hardened leather. When he peeled it away from the man's chest, another sheet of leather lay underneath, with a bloody dagger sandwiched between the two, trailing a wide elastic ribbon in the direction of the man's armpit.

David leaned back so all could see the knife and shouted, "Nobody touch this." When he saw only blank stares, he waved his hand in the air, fingers splayed, and said, "Fingerprints. Don't touch the knife."

The crowd had already stepped back upon seeing the knife, but now half the faces lit up with understanding. From the back, someone in the crowd yelled words of translation into German.

Returning his attention to the body, he yanked the man's jacket halfway down to pin his arms behind him, in case he regained his senses before the police arrived. A stocky woman stepped forward from the crowd, stripped shoelaces from their eyelets, and started to tie the assassin's ankles together. David smiled at the communal effort, and quickly tapped a number into the cell phone he'd lifted from the man's pockets. The moment his own cell phone buzzed, he disconnected. Then he leaned over the assassin, hands on his chest, as if to check his breathing. When he straightened, Sarah noticed his hands were empty.

In the distance a siren wailed, then a second from another direction. "I'm going for an ambulance!" David shouted as he stood. Then he grabbed Sarah's elbow and together they pushed through the crowd.

They crossed the street at a run, then slowed to a quick walk. He pulled her around a corner and slipped his arm around her waist. She reflexively reciprocated, and was surprised when he recoiled. He fell back beside her and said, "Sorry, it's just for the cover. They won't be looking for a couple."

"When they bag that guy with the knife, they won't be looking for *anybody*. Where are we going?"

"Novak's apartment. We've got to take a look at his files—No. No!"

He dropped his arm from her waist and sprinted toward the end of the block. She glanced ahead of him, saw a broad column of smoke swirling over the rampart of rooftops, and ran to catch up. She caught him at the corner and they stood side-by-side for a moment, watching fire and smoke billow out of the windows of Novak's second-floor apartment. She grabbed his elbow, spun his back to the scene and nudged him in the opposite direction.

"They'll be after us next," David said with a glance behind them. "We can't go back to the hostel."

She tapped the strap of her shoulder bag. "I've got everything I need right here. Your passport?"

He nodded as he stepped from the curb and hailed a cab. "Novak's list?"

"With me. Where're we going?"

"Egypt," he said as he ripped the passenger door open.

"In a taxi? What's up with—?" Sarah felt a rush up her spine. "Hava," she sputtered.

David stared at her, his face a blank.

"I gave her my jacket. Just this morning. A goodbye gift. They'll think she's me."

The taxi driver shouted something in German, and David leaned down and motioned him to wait. He straightened with a pained look on his face. "If we go back, they might kill us."

"If we *don't* go back, they *will* kill her."

He blinked once, then said, "Jump in."

chapter 32

QUASAR WAS TEMPTED to call Hawk, but in the slang of their profession, his partner was in a bombing run, on final approach. Any last-minute distraction could throw Hawk off, so Quasar nervously jingled the keys in his pocket instead, and kept watch on the hostel door from across the street. He wasn't surprised when his mark exited the building, crossed to his side and entered the café. The only break to her pattern was that this time she carried a small suitcase.

***

"So, Hava is leaving this afternoon?"

"Any minute now, unless ... " Sarah was already cupping her cell phone to one ear.

David turned to the driver. "Can you go faster?"

"No," the driver barked. David pleaded, but the man just shook his head. When David extended a handful of Euros over the seatback, the Austrian straightened his right arm against the wheel, hunched his shoulder and turned his face away, as if insulted by the offer.

David sat back grumbling as she thumbed her phone off. "She's not answering her cell. The front desk says she just checked out."

He motioned to the driver. "He's driving safe. Nothing'll move him."

Sarah leaned forward, tapped the driver on his shoulder and said sweetly, "If you get us there in time, I'll give you a kiss." Then her voice ground its blade on a whetstone: "But if you're late, I'll kill you."

He shot her a startled look, eyes wide in the rearview mirror, flashing his gaze between the traffic and her steely gaze. Then he faced the road, leaned into the steering wheel and the car lurched forward.

"Your version of carrot-and-stick?" David asked as she settled back in the seat beside him.

She teased the wad of bills from his hand. "How do you think I get your kids to take their naps when I tell them to?"

***

The target left the café with her suitcase in one hand and a large carry-out cup of coffee in the other. As she turned down the street in the direction of a bus stop, heading into a long stretch of dark zone, Quasar pushed off from where he leaned against a parked car and followed, his legs tingling with excitement, his hands twitching in his pockets.

She halted, lowered her suitcase to the pavement and fiddled with the plastic cover to her cup. He nonchalantly turned to the storefront beside him. In the reflection of the glass, he saw her pass the cup to her other hand, wincing in pain, and then shake spilled coffee from the first hand. She licked a couple of drops from two fingers and then adjusted the plastic cover. He could see that each time she pushed down the edge on one side, the other side popped up. Eventually she checked her watch and, switching the cup between hands again, she bent and hoisted her suitcase from the pavement. More slowly now, with the stilted gait of someone who can't walk without sloshing her beverage, she resumed her path toward the growing crowd at the bus stop down the block.

***

"How the heck did you know that was the guy who killed Novak?" Sarah asked.

David watched the traffic streak by. "I told you before, I know something about how Mossad operates. All the same, I've only ever read about the Sicarii—a secret society of Jewish assassins who eliminated their enemies with short, easily concealed daggers called *sicae*. They were the ninjas of the Jewish underground. The books tell us the Sicarii died out in the first century CE, during the Jewish revolution against Roman rule, roughly two thousand years ago. But now we know they've been resurrected, don't we?"

"Uh, no. No, we don't know anything of the kind. Why couldn't that guy be any other kind of assassin? What makes him a ... Sickery, or whatever?"

He hunched his shoulders. "Si-ca-ree. Sicarii. What gave him away was the same tactic they used to evade detection two thousand years ago. After making a kill, rather than run away—which would declare their guilt—they were the first to shout "Murder." Then they'd stand over the victim, lamenting the crime, directing rescue efforts and pointing to the direction they claimed the assailant escaped. The Jewish community quickly learned that the standout "good Samaritan" in the crowd was usually the Sicarii assassin. But it wasn't until I saw that guy scoping you out, as if he was surprised to see you there, that I was certain."

"Wow." Their taxi jagged between lanes, tossing her against the door first, then toward David as they swept past the other traffic. "Pretty sharp," she said, straightening herself. "Even if I'd known their history, I'm not sure I would've made the connection. So ... if we run into another of these Sicarii, how will I spot him?"

"Or her. They usually work in crowds, so their assault is as concealed as their weapons are. They only strike once, but that's all they need."

"And if I get close to him? Or her?"

"Don't. Remember, he wants you more than you want him. Okay, we're here. Get ready to jump."

Sarah leaned forward in her seat and checked the meter. It showed less than a third of the money she held in her hand. She reached over the seatback and dropped the wad of bills beside the driver as he pulled to the side, jumping the curb with one wheel. "Sorry," she said with a wink in David's direction, "I'm trying to be Orthodox, so that's the only kiss you'll ever get from me." Even before the car came to a full stop, she lunged out the door.

chapter 33

QUASAR CLOSED THE distance from his mark as she angled toward the crowd at the curb. Moving in her blind zone behind her and to the left, he approached to within a half step as he calculated his attack, knowing that as soon as she broke the circle of the crowd he could slip even closer, unnoticed by her and by others. The first bump she felt from him would be the last thing she would ever feel.

He snuck his right hand inside his coat, between the hardened leather plates shaped to his chest, and his fingers found the stickiness of the thin, tape-covered handle. As she passed the first pedestrian on the edge of the crowd, Quasar pulled against the resistance of the mobiband, a highly elastic ribbon used by physical therapists in strength and mobilization exercises. He eased the short dagger to the center of his chest, calculating the thrust that would take the blade through her back and into her heart. At the instant of release, the blade would snap back into the leather sandwich on his chest and he would grab her as she fell, shouting "Murder!" Though well-practiced, he reminded himself of the importance of grabbing her,

because it would explain any accidental blood on his clothing or hands.

***

Sarah spun one direction, then another as she
scanned the sidewalk outside the hostel. David ran inside
and returned to her side a minute later, shaking his head.
Craning her neck and standing on her toes, she spotted a
flash of tan down the block, on the other side of the street.
Then, through the shifting figures, she glimpsed her tan
leather jacket for sure. As she watched, it disappeared into
the crowd, with a man close behind. Doing the only thing
she could at that distance, she took a deep breath and
screamed loud enough to break glass.

***

Quasar felt himself slip into The Zone, an expression only those in the killing business truly understood.
Everything around him faded in a blur of light and sound,
the only thing in his mental crosshairs the target in front
of him. He closed the final half step, brought his chest to
her back, and pushed forward for the thrust.

The dagger flew forward, slicing leather and   …
the only thing his mind registered was that it felt wrong.
Something had spun him to the right, and his adrenalin-
pumped brain was unable to compute the change.

His training taught him to store the knife after the
first thrust. His instructor's face flashed in his mind's
eye, screaming spittle into his face with the words, "You
never, *ever* take a second thrust!" He released the blade
and felt the dagger snap back into its hiding place on his
chest. Reflexively, he reached forward to grab his target as
she fell, but she twisted and thrust her Styrofoam cup at

him instead. The plastic lid flew off and a stinging bath of scalding-hot coffee drenched his face. His ears filled with a rush of screams and shouts and he spun frantically, his brain screaming *Run!*

In the next second he felt nothing but air and a whooshing rush as the ground dropped out from under him and gravity sucked him down. He hit the pavement with his hands and face, instantly pushed himself up to a sprinter's crouch, but felt his legs kicked out from under him once again. Panicked into disregarding his training, he rolled onto his back and reached for his knife, only to see a crazed lady swinging a suitcase at his head with all her strength.

He blocked with his left arm, but his forearm shattered under the blow. The suitcase flew open and dumped its contents on his face, and he raised his good arm to sweep the clothes away. His entire body exploded in pain, radiating from his abdomen and out. He rolled in one direction, but whoever had jumped on his stomach then landed on his side, and he both felt and heard his ribs crack. He rolled again and stuck an arm up, screaming for the first time in his adult life.

Somebody grabbed his wrist, twisted violently, and rolled him into a half nelson. But whoever it was didn't stop forcing his arm up until his elbow popped from its socket. The weight lifted from him again, but this time it jumped onto his back. Everything from his waist down screamed, but on the second jump there was the crack of an elephant's knuckle popping, and his legs went still and numb. He tried to lift an arm to his face, but the pain shut his joints down. Suddenly recognizing the futility of his condition, he closed his eyes and wished for death.

Sarah pushed her way through the crowd to find Hava struggling against a lumberjack of a man who had her arms pinned in a bear hug-from-behind. At her feet lay a sobbing heap of scattered clothing, bruised flesh and mangled limbs. David stood to one side, bent double at the waist and bracing his weight on his knees with bent arms. Most incongruous, he was laughing, sucking air between each guffaw.

When she saw Sarah, Hava's face lit up. She stopped struggling, spoke over her shoulder to the lumberjack-type, then wriggled free and rushed into her arms.

chapter 34

THE POLICE TREATED Hava to a detour via the hospital, where she had a quick swab-and-stitch job on the shallow four-inch cut on her back. "Just enough of a scratch to put your DNA on the knife and the jury on your side," the escorting police sergeant said. An American born of Austrian parents, Sgt. Gretel Koubek emigrated back to her parents' homeland seven years ago. Due to her bilingual fluency, she was assigned to their case by default. "I did more paperwork than police work when I lived in Chicago," she explained. "One day I broke my fist on an AIDS-infected crackhead's jaw after he kept spitting at me. I called it self-defense, but he won an excessive-use-of-force case against me. That's when I decided it was time to get out of Dodge."

Sarah, who'd never left Hava's side, nodded sympathetically, even as she marveled at how their Austrian-American policewoman built their case. Koubek sat Hava up for the photographs of her wound. When Sarah asked why, she said lightly, "Because blood streaking down her back looks more dramatic than drops pooled on the surface when she lies flat. You've got to think of what will make the biggest impression on the jury." Not satisfied with the cut's innocent appearance, Koubek squeezed it bloody for the photo. When red rivulets ran down Hava's pale skin, she said, "That's better."

Hava glanced over her shoulder first at the wound, then at the sergeant, and they both laughed. Sarah and the nurse caught the infection, and the room took on more the mood of a party than of a crime investigation.

A few minutes later, after the wound was cleaned and swabbed with disinfectant, the emergency room physician examined her and stated the cut was so shallow it didn't even deserve sutures. Sterile skin tape would suffice. Koubek took him aside and spoke with him in serious tones, with a great deal of head nodding on the doctor's part. After a moment he returned to her bedside, and Koubek flashed a wink and a thumbs-up sign to Hava from over the doctor's shoulder.

"Multiple, interrupted sutures. The nurse will numb you up."

He stepped out of the room and Sarah asked, "How is that better?"

"When the jury reads that the wound was taped closed with Steri-Strips, they'll know it wasn't serious," Koubek said. "I told the doctor to suture, and really pack them in close. He said he could do it in six stitches, I told him to make it twelve." She glanced at Hava. "Hey, don't think you're going to have all the fun. You beat the creep up on the street, but we're gonna kill him in court."

The doctor returned and closed the wound with twenty passes, after which it looked like a quilt stitch.

They repeated the documentary photographs, complete with wound squeezing to freshen the blood. "To make it look," Koubek said to Hava, "as though, without these sutures, the wound will split open and your life will gush out."

The doctor wrote the number of stitches in the file, complete with an order for their removal within ten days.

"Here comes the good part," Koubek said with a wink. The doctor turned his back on Hava and reached for the suture tray. He turned back with scissors and forceps in hand, and removed every stitch.

"Within ten days," Koubek said, with a smirk and a shrug of her eyebrows.

"Now," the doctor said to the nurse as he stripped off his gloves and headed for the door, "put some tape on that."

Sarah slapped one hand to her face and held it, smiling broadly and gazing incredulously at the policewoman. "Sisters," she said.

"Just doing my job," the sergeant replied, with another of her face-scrunching winks.

***

While Hava gave her statement inside one of the police station's offices, David caught up with Sarah in the waiting area.

"Our essentials are in this bag," he said, setting a carry-on bag at his feet. Then he sat on the wooden bench beside her. "The hostel staff will pack up the rest and bring it later."

"She heard my scream," Sarah said with a smile.

"Who didn't?"

"She was nearly a block away, in a busy city." She dropped her face and wove her fingers together in her lap. "She said it was as clear as an air-raid siren, one of those rare miracles that remind people of God and Providence. Her words."

"So she turned, he missed, and your shaped-charge of a friend detonated on him."

"That's about it."

"Remind me never to date a Slovakian."

Sarah shot him a smile from her eyes. "I've killed before."

"In a police station?"

Hava stepped from a nearby office and sauntered over to where they sat. They stood as she approached and she hugged Sarah, nodded to David, and then sat beside them. They waited in silence while another police officer entered the office she'd just left, a couple sheets of paper flapping in his hand. A moment later Sergeant Koubek appeared, followed by her colleague. She motioned for the threesome to stay seated and walked over to where they sat together in a line on the bench.

"I thought you might want to hear how your assailant is doing," she said.

"Skin tape?" Sarah asked, innocently.

Koubek smiled. Her colleague beside her squeezed his lips together in a tight line, and looked like he was about to burst with laughter. "Not exactly," she said. "First and second-degree facial burns. Concussion. Compound fracture of the right radius and ulna. That's the arm bones ... ."

She looked up from the page, and then down at Hava. "I wouldn't have thought anybody could swing a suitcase hard enough to do that kind of damage. A baton, maybe. But a suitcase?" She scowled and shrugged her shoulders. "Women must be built different on your side of the border. Anyway, to continue, dislocated left elbow with spiral fracture of the radius. Fracture of lumbar vertebrae two and three with avulsion of spinal cord—"

"That's not good," Hava said, leaning forward, her medical training surfacing.

"Depends on how you look at it," Sarah said.

Hava turned to her, a shade of regret in her eyes. "He'll be spending the rest of his life in a wheelchair and diapers."

"See what I mean?"

Sergeant Koubek cleared her throat, and together they looked up at her. "Sorry, Hava. I forgot you're a med student. In any case, he'll only be in a wheelchair and diapers if he lives."

"If he *lives?*" Sarah asked.

She dropped her eyes back to the page in her hand. "Fractured ribs. Tension pneumothorax, right side. Collapsed lung, in other words. Ruptured spleen. Sternum fracture with laceration of the liver by the xiphoid process ... that's a new one on me, but lacerated liver seems to be the key there." She shrugged. "I suppose we can skip all the bruises and multiple-organ contusions. He's in surgery right now, but his condition is ... " She flipped to the second page. "Let's see, spinal and hemorrhagic shock, unresponsive to painful stimuli, blah, blah, blah ... oh, here it is: clinically unstable, with extremely guarded prognosis."

Hava grunted. "Huh. I didn't mean to … ."

Sergeant Koubek swiped her reading glasses from her face with one hand and pointed them at David. "You know, if you hadn't nailed that other assassin in Old Town, the one wearing the same knife getup, we wouldn't know who to arrest here. You want this?" She held the papers out to Hava.

"What for?" she asked, even as she took them.

"Frame it," she said, and slapped her colleague on his broad back. "I would." They turned back to her office and she shouted over her shoulder, "And Hava? Let me know if you ever need a letter of recommendation."

The three of them stood to leave, and they all noticed the waiting area had gone quiet. Officers at the nearest desks watched Hava with open interest, the nearest gave her a nod of respect. Two officers in Kevlar vests escorted them to the elevator, and from there to the sub-basement parking lot, where an armored GMC Suburban awaited them.

"Armored?" Sarah asked, without breaking stride.

David stepped through the open rear door and slipped back into the third seat. "They're not taking any chances, now they know we're targets."

chapter 35

"DOES HE ALWAYS laugh like that in the face of disaster?" Hava asked while the Suburban swept through the streets of Vienna, en route to a police safe house. As she spoke, she rolled her eyes toward David, seated directly behind them.

"Only when he sees a member of the frailer sex torquing a trained assassin," Sarah said.

"It was a nervous reaction." David leaned forward and rested his arms on their seatback, his head between them. "Stress letdown. There we were, flying from Novak's murder, Sarah saying, 'She needs us,' and 'They're going to kill her,' and stuff like that. I sprinted over thinking I was going to save your life, only to find you playing break-the-Barbie with the guy. I swear, when you finished with his arms, I expected you to twist his head off next. Then you started jumping trampoline on the guy's kidneys, and I don't know what came over me, I simply cracked up."

"I wish *I'd* seen it," Sarah said. "Whatever you did, Hava, it wasn't enough." She turned to David. "They're going to ship us out of Austria. Are we done here?"

He nodded. "We have Novak's list. Next stop, Egypt. Actually, they're doing us a favor by giving us safe passage." He bowed his head and spoke with a slight quaver to his voice. "It's sad about Novak. He seemed like a nice guy."

Sarah shook her head. "He spent his life tracking down Nazis, only to be killed by a Zionist Jew. If that's not irony, I don't know what is." As she spoke, she watched Hava sweep a finger along the surprisingly small tear in the leather jacket bunched in her lap. She tapped her on the arm and said, "I'll send you a new one, soon as I get back to the States."

Hava looked up, eyes wide, and held the jacket protectively. "You can *never* replace this. Other jackets may be newer, or have a different style, but this one has history!"

***

Chief Simon Landau sat with his elbows propped on his paper-strewn desk in Tel Aviv, cradling his head in his hands. A spectacular blue-and-gold mid-April sky edged toward a cheerful sunset in the window facing him from across the room, mocking his foul mood. He realized this was worse than his failure to stop Lenni Brenner's books. Not since Mossad's 1997 failed assassination of Khalid Mishal in Amman, Jordan had his department so thoroughly botched a job. He didn't want to think about it, but his mind roiled, imagining how events would unfold from here. Austria's Chancellor, Bruno Zuckerkandl, was a principled Socialist, devoted to human rights. There would be no polite negotiations. He would contact Israel's Prime Minister Rosenfeld, and would back the Zionist country up against a wall and hold it there with a knife at its throat. Israel would offer reconciliation, but Bruno would refuse until he squeezed the last possible political and economic consideration from this windfall of an opportunity.

Three Austrians had died, including a young mother and child who perished in the fire at Novak's apartment building. The Israeli agents would stand trial as common murderers and quietly disappear into Austrian jails. Assuming, that is, that Israel satisfied Chancellor Zuckerkandl's demands. If not, Austria would parade them through the world's media as spies and international terrorists, trained and employed by the Zionist state of Israel. Either way, once the dust settled, PM Rosenfeld would split somebody's cabbage with a cleaver, right here on Landau's desk. And, he feared that *he* would be that somebody.

With this morose thought in mind, the red phone beside him rang. Instead of answering, he stared at the direct line to the PM's office as if it were Dante's gates of Hell opening just for him.

***

The next day, the Austrian police escorted David and Sarah to the airport and placed them on a Lufthansa flight to Cairo, via Frankfurt. Leaving nothing to chance, they escorted them to their seats on the plane.

"Nice of them to give us our choice of destination," Sarah said once they were settled.

David checked his watch. "Hava should be home by now, and safe. Mossad won't make that mistake twice."

"Do you think *we're* safe?"

"Nope." He boosted himself up in his seat and checked out their immediate neighbors. When he resettled himself he said, "They're shipping us out to get us off their turf. If Mossad makes another attempt on our lives, they don't want it to happen in their country. If we're as safe as they said, why are they arranging a police escort in Frankfurt, just for the plane change?"

"On the other hand ... "

"Yeah, I know. Mossad's probably in damage control mode right now."

She rested her head back against the contoured headrest and stared at the ceiling. "So they might suspend their order for our assassination."

"Or make it an even higher priority." He sat with eyes closed, hands clenched on his knees. "Look, why did they try to kill us in such an open, public way?" He turned his face to hers. "It was a message killing, meant to warn anybody working with us not to pursue this project. Their message is out now, so I'm betting they're going to switch to trying to fake an accident."

"But nobody *is* working with us," Sarah said.

"They don't know that. And others *do* know what we're doing. My dad. Katie."

She nodded, suddenly worried. "Katie and I joked about her being my sidekick, but—"

"The point is, if Mossad doesn't remind them of the dangers involved, they both might be tempted to try to complete our work after we're gone."

She pulled her shoulder-pack from where it rested at her feet, slipped Novak's list from a side pocket and unfolded it on the armrest between them. "Okay, you chose Egypt." She scanned the list and noted that of the eight names still listed as living, only one was in Egypt. She placed her finger beside the name. "Okay, so you want to find Leon—"

"No." He pointed to one of the crossed-off entries. "This one."

She pulled his finger from where it partially covered the name. "Felix ... Schroeder. But he's dead."

"Look how much we learned from Novak, even though Wiesenthal's center in Vienna is officially closed. Furthermore, Felix Schroeder used to be Eichmann's right-hand man. That makes him the biggest name on the list. So why was *Israel* blocking his arrest?"

***

Two days later, Sarah sat in the living room of their rent-by-the-week apartment and watched David groom the keys of his laptop computer. She cast her eyes out the open French windows over the rooftops of the small Egyptian neighborhood of Beni Suef, and sighed. "Felix Schroeder was last seen here. We've asked every shop owner and visited every street café and sidewalk restaurant. We've spoken with apartment supervisors, laundry and grocery clerks. We even scouted the open-air market. Everywhere we've gotten the same benevolent, unknowing smiles. This guy wasn't a man. He was a ghost. So what're we missing?"

"Maybe we need a photo." David spoke above the click of keys, not looking up from his laptop.

"We *have* a photo—the one you downloaded from the Internet. What're you doing now, looking for something more current?"

"There *is* nothing more current. We've got to make it."

She stood and walked a question mark to the back of his chair, bent to look over his shoulder. "Explain."

"Facial aging software. I don't know why I didn't think of this before. This is what the police use as a profiling tool. I pulled it from the Internet just now. Let's see if it works."

She watched as he digitally sliced the 1944 head-shot of Felix Schroeder off at the neck, freeing him from his Gestapo uniform. Then he dragged and dropped the man's face into the software, where it faded into a maze of broad pixels that gradually shrank and coalesced into a fuzzy portrait. The image cleared to show a gaunt white-haired man with the severe, unsmiling face and intense blue eyes typical of German war photos. Except this particular German was eighty-eight years old, and his photo now looked it.

***

The next day, the first market clerk who saw the photo stared with wide eyes, but then dropped his chin to his chest and shook his head. When David tried to press the clerk, he simply turned his back and walked away.

Clerks and shop owners acted the same way all down the block. More than one slammed the door when Sarah and David stepped from their place of business back to the sidewalk. They never made it inside one store; as they drew near, a nervous-looking man hastily flipped the "Closed" sign with one hand and turned the door locks with the other. David waved to grab his attention, but the man was gone before he and Sarah reached the door.

"Can you believe this?" David said when the next door closed on their approach. "Who was this guy—the local Count Dracula? He's dead now, so what's the problem?"

"Unless he's not really dead," Sarah said, her voice low.

"Interesting thought. Interesting, and incredibly scary. Misplaced loyalty, more likely. Maybe he bought these peoples' affection. Maybe he left a family behind when he died, and the locals want to protect them."

"Or, he left a family behind that are more horrible than he ever was. And now here we are, wanting to interview them."

As they strolled back up the block, they heard a hissing and turned to see a shadowed figure in the doorway of a café. The man surreptitiously motioned them closer, but stood inside and spoke around the edge of the doorframe, nervously wringing his fingers. His voice a hoarse whisper, he said, "If you want to know about the man in the photograph, I can introduce you to ... someone who might help you. Come for coffee this afternoon. Two o'clock. But now you have to go. Please!"

He glanced nervously behind him, then peeked over their shoulders and down the street. He waved them away, then ducked back into his café.

"I don't know about you," David said while they walked back to their apartment, "but I think he was overacting."

"Maybe he's seen too many spy movies."

"Or our Nazi ghost."

chapter 36

THEY ENTERED THE café at two o'clock, after window-shopping the block. The owner, a middle-aged Egyptian, walked with a stoop that suggested a lifelong burden of troubles. He bustled up and directed them to a table in the center of the small room. Sarah and David scanned the nearly empty café and exchanged cautious glances. A matronly woman who appeared to be the owner's wife sat on a stool behind the counter, fidgeting with her hands but doing nothing productive so far as they could see. Only one of the other tables was occupied, by a pair of Egyptian youths dressed hip-hop.

The owner returned with glasses of mint lemonade and a plate of assorted nuts. "My compliments," he said while he arranged the refreshments on the table. "My friend should be here shortly."

"How shortly?" David asked.

The man's head snapped up as if he'd been slapped, and fear flicked across his face. "A few m-minutes," he said, and then retreated to stand beside his wife, behind the service counter.

Sarah reached for her lemonade, but David raised his hand from where it lay on the table and patted the air in her direction.

"I'm not stupid," she whispered. "I was only going to fake a sip, for appearances." She nudged the drink to one side.

"Do me a favor," he whispered back. "I'm going to call him back over here. You go talk with his wife. Keep looking back to check on me, but keep your back to us at all times, and keep your hands inside your jacket, where we can't see them. Got that?"

"Let's see … ." Sarah said, "What you're saying is, you want me to act threatening and pretend I've got a gun. Is that it?"

"Was it that obvious?"

"Pretty much." She stood and sauntered over to the counter, and David motioned to the man. Looking befuddled, he shuffled over to the table, and Sarah heard him ask if anything was wrong.

"I'm just wondering what this is," David replied, and motioned to the drink.

The man's face relaxed, the worry lines smoothing out. "A local specialty. A sweetened blend of fresh mint leaves and lemon, over crushed ice."

David nodded. "Is it good?"

"Please, have a taste. Your wife, too. Here, allow me to take it to her." He reached for Sarah's glass, but David thrust his arm forward and clamped the man's hand to the glass, pinning both to the table. He locked eyes with him, and Sarah saw the man's chubby face become a mass of twitches.

"Do you see my partner over there?" David asked.

The man glanced over his shoulder to where Sarah stood, leaning sideways into the service bar in front of his seated wife, half-turned in their direction. She held her right hand tucked inside the open flap of her black cavalry coat, at waist-level. Her face cold, she glanced in turn at the wife, whose smile was pleasant but befuddled, and at them.

David said, "Now, look back at me."

The man refocused on his face, but only after a reflexive second flick-glance over his shoulder. David said, "If I say the word, the next sound you'll hear is my partner pumping a bullet into your wife's head. Do you understand?"

The man started to shake, but nodded.

"Good." David uncurled his fingers from the man's hand on the glass and nodded toward it. "Now ... drink."

The man's eyes bounded between the glass and David's face. "What? No, I—"

"Drink."

"Sir, please, I can't. Please, if ... "

David glanced at Sarah and raised his eyebrows slightly.

"No!" the man shouted. "No, please." He swung his head around, and his wife jumped from her barstool. Sarah stuck out an arm to bar her way, locked eyes with her, and gave a slow shake of her head. The woman, now terrified, backed up against a small prep counter, her hands shaking as if with palsy.

"No, sir, please," the man blurted, his whole body quaking. "Please, I ... *we* have children."

David pushed his chair back and stood, head-nodding Sarah to the door. "Let's get out of here."

She backed out, her hand still tucked inside her coat, keeping both the man and his wife in her field of view. When she came alongside David, she spun and they both stepped toward the door.

"Playing it for all it's worth, aren't you?" David said as he reached for the doorknob.

"Nothing by halves," she said, and then her eyes went wide, staring past him.

Two monstrous-sized men pushed the door open, forcing them back into the room. She flicked a glance over her shoulder to find two more goons entering through the kitchen and sweeping around the counter. As she turned back to the two at the door, a quick whistle ended in a flash of thunder and light, and then blackness.

chapter 37

SARAH OPENED HER eyes again, and this time her mind was clear enough to process her new surroundings. She found herself sitting, slumped sideways but held upright by bands of duct tape that criss-crossed her chest. She felt coolness at her back, and glanced over her shoulder to find a vertical steel I-beam serving as both her backrest and anchor. She also saw David taped to the opposite side. The loops of duct tape encircled both of their chests, with the I-beam sandwiched between their backs. She could glimpse David by craning her neck, and although she could not see his face, she could tell by his lolling head that he was still unconscious. Furthermore, her wrist was handcuffed to his on each side, behind their backs, so together they formed a human ring around the metal support. The only light sifted in from two mud-splattered slit windows set high in the walls, barely enough to tell her they were underground, in some kind of basement.

She raised her head wearily and pulled her legs up from where they lay splayed out in front of her. Her jeans rasped on the rough concrete floor, but it felt good to brace herself with bended knees. Gently, she tugged at the handcuff on one hand, then the other. Feeling the dead weight on the other end of each, she sighed. But then she got a tug in return, and she felt her heart jump in her chest.

"Are you okay?" she asked.

"*Mmph.*"

She felt tugs on the duct tape around her chest, and realized he was shaking himself awake. "Don't pull on the ... Ouch! Don't do that!"

"What is ... Where are we?"

"A basement ... somewhere. They must have drugged us after they knocked us out."

"How are we tied?"

"We're duct taped back-to-back, on opposite sides of a structural steel beam. And don't bother looking. It runs uninterrupted from concrete floor to concrete ceiling. And they handcuffed my hands to yours on each side of the beam. So don't yank your end of the chain like that again, unless you want to hurt me."

David was silent for a moment, then said, "Your nose itches."

"*What?*"

"Your nose itches," he repeated, and this time chuckled.

"Don't *do* that. Are you crazy?"

He laughed out loud, and she felt his idiocy tease a laugh out of her as well. "Your nose itches," he said again, through gales of laughter.

"Oh, for ... " But she had to laugh; yes, her nose *was* beginning to itch. She yanked her end of the handcuffs and got a satisfying "ouch" from his side, followed by more laughter. Then she leaned forward as far as the duct tape around her chest allowed, and brought up one knee and rubbed her nose on it. "Have you gone *nuts?*" she said. "Or did that blow to your head scramble your brains?"

His laughter subsided into silence, and then he said, "Sorry. It looks like we're not going anywhere soon, so we might as well make the best of a bad situa—"

The door at the top of the stairs opened with a ghastly groan, as if the room itself was in pain, and a shaft of light cut through the dim interior. Silhouetted in the lit doorway at the head of the stairs, a broad-chested, thick-limbed man stood stock-still. Then he stomped down the bare wooden stairs, each footfall reverberating through the clammy, shadowed basement like a drumbeat of doom.

A second monster of a man descended into the basement, and after him, a slighter figure appeared at the head of the stairs. He stepped lightly down the staircase, without use of the railing, and strode purposefully to the center of the room. He stood over and between Sarah and David, where both could see him with a turn of their heads. With a nod to one side, the nearest thug flicked a switch and flooded the basement with light.

For a moment, Sarah thought her eyes deceived her. She blinked to adjust, but with each blink she was able to hold her stare longer, until she was convinced.

"Felix Schroeder," she said, aghast.

"At your service, *Fraulein.*" He clicked his heels together with a nod of his gaunt, white-haired head.

"Wiesenthal's list records you as dead," David said, staring up from where he sat on the cold floor.

"Wiesenthal only knew what Mossad told him," Schroeder said. "And *they* don't want me on anybody's list but theirs. But you know that already, don't you?"

"Why should we know that?" Sarah asked.

"He thinks we're Mossad," David said over his shoulder.

"Ah," Schroeder said through bloodless lips, drawn tight in a thin, cruel smile, "and now the game begins. I accuse, you deny, the stakes of the game being our lives. Such an amusing contest, and up to this point I have always won. But I do so enjoy the Mossad cover stories. They are always so exhaustively researched, so extraordinarily creative. So please, by all means, tell me yours, so I can educate myself before I kill you."

Sarah sighed and leaned her head back against the post. "Should we tell him?"

A short pause, and David replied, "No reason not to."

At the end of their explanation, Schroeder nodded and said, "Imaginative. Very imaginative." Then he turned and started to climb the stairs.

Sarah yelled at his back, "What can we say to convince you that we've told you the truth?"

Schroeder turned on the stairs, laid his hand on the railing for the first time, and smiled sadly. "Nothing, my dear *Fraulein*. Absolutely nothing."

The two goons followed, one of them turning out the light and leaving them in semidarkness.

Sarah looked up, wishing she could see though the ceiling. "What do you think they're doing right now?"

"Loading their guns? Sharpening their knives? How should I know? Dang, I've got a monster of a headache."

"From what he said, you might not have to put up with it for much longer."

"Yeesh, talk about gallows humor."

She hitched herself higher, into a full sitting position, and then felt behind her for his hand. He squeezed her fingers and she felt they both understood: They knew the rules, but they trusted the Creator to understand moments such as these.

"Hopefully they're checking out what we've told them," he said. "If they confirm your expulsion from the Israeli Army and our adventure in Vienna, they'll realize Mossad is hunting *us* more than they're hunting *him*." After a pause, he added, "What happened to the two witnesses at the restaurant? You know, those two young guys?"

She shrugged. "They probably bolted like frightened rabbits. Schroeder's got his little fiefdom sewn up tight. I'm betting he murdered anybody who ever came looking for him. Some of the townsfolk, like that café owner, wimped out and turned informant."

As close as Sarah could guess, two hours passed before Schroeder returned, dressed in faded khaki pants and shirt. She couldn't tell whether the stains on the sleeves were old blood or new dirt. Then she realized it didn't matter. *Gardening or killing clothes, neither one sounds good.*

He glanced first at Sarah, then at David, and she was shocked to see admiration in his eyes. "I must say," he said, "Mossad gets better each year at trying to eliminate me."

As he spoke, one of his goons appeared at the top of the staircase, holding a prisoner by the arm in each of his thick hands. The young man and woman had their hands cuffed behind their backs. The huge thug manhandled the pair down the stairs as easily as if he were helping an old lady cross a street.

The young man missed the next-to-last step, stumbled and dove to the concrete floor at Sarah's feet. He then rolled over, one cheek deeply abraded and bleeding. The goon thrust the second hostage forward; she tripped over her companion and fell to her knees beside him with a cry of rage.

"Your stories are much more imaginative than what these two dreamed up," Schroeder said. He lightly kicked the man with a worn canvas boot. "Like the two of you, their cover is that they're on holiday together."

"We're not on holiday," Sarah said. "We have a mission."

"And so do they," Schroeder said. "So do they."

The nearest goon pulled the two hostages to their feet and backed them up against the far wall. The woman stepped forward, said something in protest, and he buried his fist in her gut. As she buckled forward, he raised his knee to meet her face with a meaty slap. She fell in a miserable bundle, crumpled and crying at the feet of her companion. Her attacker stepped back to admire his work, a bored expression on his broad, apathetic face.

Schroeder pointed to the man who stood with his back against the wall, his cheek dripping blood to one shoulder. "Do you notice how there's no sympathy, no chivalry, no 'Honey, are you okay?' What kind of a man doesn't even offer a word of comfort as his wife rolls at his feet, crying?"

"A Mossad man," the goon said, his voice thick and blubbery.

"Exactly."

"How can you be certain?" Sarah asked as she strained against the chest-tape.

"*Certain?*" Schroeder turned to her, one brow cocked in a question mark. "Why, they confessed. Not in the beginning, of course. But with a little encouragement, and after they learned what we found in their hotel room."

He snapped his fingers imperiously. One goon stepped to his side, holding a serving tray. Schroeder plucked a pen from the tray and said, "A work of art. The classics only get better with time." He stroked the pen in his fingers, then said, "The ink cartridge contains pressurized poison. Twist the barrel of the pen to extend the tip, and it writes. But push the clip, and it shoots a jet of nerve poison. Most imaginative."

"But this is art," he said while he replaced the pen and lifted a cigarette from the tray. He snapped the cigarette in two to reveal a hardened fiber core. "You can get three puffs out of it safely. After that, the fire ignites a charge that shoots a shower of microscopic crystals. When they penetrate skin, they dissolve into a deadly cocktail of poisons. Who says second-hand smoke doesn't kill?"

He waved the other implements on the tray away and thumbed in the direction of the Mossad agents. "They gave an interesting story. One I have to admit I've never heard before. In fact, it made me curious. They said they weren't sent to kill me. Rather, their assignment is to kill the two of *you,* by any means necessary, but preferably to make it look like an accident."

David blurted, "We told you—"

"Yes, yes." Schroeder stepped over to the Mossad agent who stood against the wall, and stared into his defiant eyes. "But of course, it could just be the most brilliant of covers. Totally fabricated, along with your lady's faked resignation from the Israeli Army, *and* the staged drama in Vienna. Very dramatic. So dramatic, it's probably staged."

"One Mossad agent was captured, the other was crippled," David said. "They're both probably going to spend the rest of their lives in jail. That's not a cover, that's a disaster."

"Yes." Schroeder turned to face David, hands in pockets. "But, you see, I simply can't risk being wrong."

As he spoke, he withdrew his hands from his pant pockets, leveled a tiny fist gun at the Mossad agent's face, and pulled the trigger. A flame leapt between the gun and the man's forehead. His head bounced off the wall behind him and he collapsed to the concrete with a pencil-sized hole between his eyes, his limbs jerking spasmodically. The blast of the twenty-two caliber gun buffeted Sarah's ears and reverberated off the basement walls.

The female agent scrabbled frantically on the floor and kicked herself away from her partner's corpse. Her shoes skidded on the damp concrete and her legs slapped the floor. But then her feet caught, and she scooted on her backside into a corner, where she drew herself into a ball. Her face turned to the wall, she cried out her prayers in gasps, her entire body racked with shudders.

Sarah had flinched from the pistol blast, but something inside her went cold at seeing the woman's agony. These Mossad agents had come to kill her and David, and would have done so without the slightest remorse.

A sparkling glint drew her attention to the woman's earrings. *They've taken everything else*, she thought. *How could they possibly have missed those?* The bejeweled, domino-sized golden tablets that hung from her ears looked like they were plundered from a pharaoh's tomb. *Picked up at a local tourist trap,* she concluded. *Worthless fakes. That's why they didn't take them. But all the same—*

"Stand them up," Schroeder said, and waved his tiny pistol in their direction as he fixed his gaze on the female agent in the corner.

chapter 38

THE NEAREST GOON pulled a knife from his pocket, flicked the blade open with a click, and slashed the duct tape that bound them together. Sarah felt bands of steel surround her arms as strong men lifted David and her to their feet, hands still cuffed behind them. She stood, swaying. Then she leaned backward against the steel beam for support. David pulled the handcuffs on both sides, gathered her hands into his and whispered, "It's going to be all right."

"Double-check their pockets," Schroeder said.

Broad hands fumbled in the pockets of her jeans, front and back, and she turned to see the other goon searching David. The search was quick, thorough, and professional. The man's hands didn't stray, didn't linger any longer than necessary to empty her pockets of everything but lint and loose threads. Now, without identification, and with nothing to link her to family or country, she stood fully clothed but felt like she'd been stripped naked.

Schroeder continued to watch the female agent decompensate in the corner of the room, his face impassive. "As you say in America," he muttered, "she can dish it out, but she can't take it." He motioned one of his henchmen to keep an eye on her, and then strode to Sarah's side. Fighting not to allow him to see her tremble, Sarah stared into his soul-dead eyes. Silently, she wondered how he would deal with his own appointment with death, when the time came.

"You're wondering how I can be so cold," he said to her.

"No, I'm wondering how you can be so stupid."

He cocked his pale, emaciated head at her.

"We're working to expose the truth of the Holocaust. For sixty years, the world has only known the Zionist side of the story. If you've been through our apartment like you've been through theirs," she nodded toward the dead Mossad agent, "then you've seen our research. We're trying to expose what really happened—the history the Zionists don't want told. You're not killing just us, you're killing a story I'd think you'd want to see told."

Schroeder snorted, a smirk on his thin lips. "Beautiful words, for a Mossad agent. You four are working together, and those two are part of your cover. I've seen more elaborate schemes in my time, this is nothing particularly new."

This time it was Sarah who cocked her head. "But Novak told us Mossad's protecting you from being found, denying your whereabouts. Mossad's not even *trying* to catch you."

"Catch me, no. Kill me, yes." He stared at her thoughtfully. "Interesting observation, though. Hmm." But then he blinked, and the coldness returned to his eyes. "I haven't survived this long by going soft for a beautiful face and clever words. I'm sorry, but ... " As he raised his pistol, David yanked on the chains that linked him to Sarah and shouted, "Schroeder!"

Sarah planted her feet and tugged back, resisting David's effort to swing her around the beam and take the shot meant for her. The aged Nazi held his gun level between her eyes, but flicked his gaze between them as they wrestled for position. David grabbed her wrist and pulled, but she wrapped her other hand around a steel edge and anchored herself in place. "Hold me and let her go," David blurted out. "She'll never talk. She'll know that you'll kill me if she does."

The Nazi's pale lips twitched. "You sound like a bad movie. Why should I hold either of you, when I can just kill you both?"

"Then kill me first."

Sarah snapped her head to the side and shouted, "No!"

"Your mind is poisoned, Schroeder," David yelled. "You've been hiding for so long, you don't know who's a threat and who isn't."

The aged Nazi sighed and said to Sarah, "You know, this just isn't one of those 'Ladies first' days." As he stepped around to face David, Sarah reversed her hold on his wrist and pulled with all her might. This time, however, it was he who latched onto the steel beam and held himself in place.

"I admire your chivalry," Schroeder said. Then he snapped his arm up and fired.

Sarah felt David's weight slump onto the handcuffs and screamed. But then his weight lifted again. She swung her head frantically from one side to the other, craning her neck to see, while David pushed himself to his full height, raised his head and said, "What kind of sick game is this, shooting over my head? You demented bastard."

"Maybe," Schroeder said with a rueful laugh. "We'll never know. Where my mother is, I can't ask her about that."

This time he raised his gun slowly, as if to savor the moment. His lips twitched into a sneer, his eyes turned ice-cold. Sarah threw her weight to one side and screamed for Schroeder to stop, but David held himself rigid. As the aged Nazi leveled his gun between David's eyes, one of the goons touched him on his shoulder from behind. "Hey boss," he said. "Read this."

Schroeder narrowed one eye at David, and then pumped his gun at him, as if to throw a bullet into his brain. David didn't even flinch, just growled, "You sick psycho, do what you have to do—"

"Boss," the goon said as he poked Schroeder in the shoulder again, but more insistently this time, "you really better read this."

"Don't go away," Schroeder said with a dry chuckle, and turned to his henchman. A moment later, his back still to David and Sarah, he asked, "Where did you get this?"

The man pointed to Sarah. "Her back pocket."

"You missed it when you first brought them in?"

"Sorry, boss. We patted them down for weapons, not letters."

Schroeder about-faced and stood between them. "Are you perhaps familiar with this?" He cleared his throat and read out loud from halfway down the page:

I remind you of your purpose. Don't waste your time recycling the Nazi atrocities. That is a story well known, and the few Nazi war criminals still at large are no doubt suffering the ravages of old age. It will serve little or no purpose to bring them to justice now, because they will face God's wrath soon enough. More importantly, their evil ended long ago, whereas the evil you wish to expose is very much alive.

It is the Zionist collaboration with the Nazis, both before and during World War II, which exposes Israel for what it is—a threat to the Jewish people, to the Jewish religion, and to world peace. That is a story people need to know. Unfortunately, it is also a story the Zionists will kill to suppress.

From an aged Holocaust survivor to a determined young lady, whom I would grieve to lose, I ask you to do what I did— survive, and return to expose the truth.

Shalom,

Grandpa J

Schroeder folded the letter without looking up, and then tapped it against an open palm. Sarah noticed he no longer held his pistol in his hand. "Young lady, you are either the most absent-minded Mossad agent I've ever seen ... or you really are who you say you are. If this letter is part of your cover, it's the trump card you would've played when all else failed. You never would've forgotten it in your pocket when I started throwing bullets around."

He held up the folded page. "When did your grandfather write this?"

"No," David said, wearily. "It's *my* father, Joel. Joel Cohen. My kids call him Grandpa J. He likes it, so ... "

"*Your* father. Hm." Schroeder handed the letter to his goon. "Make them comfortable upstairs while I look into this further." Then he turned to David. "Do you have a number where I can reach your father for a chat?"

chapter 39

WHEN THE SECOND handcuff clicked open Sarah twisted her wrists to free herself and stepped around to find David. As they joined hands, one handcuff still dangling from his wrist, she looked into his eyes and an unimagined life flashed through her mind: a life with David as her husband, his children playing on the living room floor beside them, his unborn baby wriggling in her womb. It was too much to hope for, especially now. Moments earlier, the dream had almost ended before she even conceived it.

And it would still end. Not only did they know Schroeder wasn't really dead, they knew his exact location. He couldn't allow them to leave with that knowledge, and nothing Grandpa J could tell him would change that. But at least her last thoughts on this earth would be that image: of a happy home, a loving family, and a man so steadfast, only death would take him from her.

Fighting back tears, she felt her knees buckle and fold beneath her. She fell into David's arms and pulled him to the floor. As he regained his feet and helped her up he muttered, "Sorry, you caught me off-balance—"

"Hey." They turned at the goon's call, saw him pointing them to the stairs. Following David, Sarah passed by the monster and took two steps, but then looked back. Schroeder stood gazing at her, his hands once again pushed into his pockets. Behind him, the second henchman hovered over the female agent, who cowered in the corner, her hands cuffed behind her back. Sarah felt a hand gently but firmly grasp her arm above the elbow and pull her up the stairs. When she turned to look up at him, David tugged at her again and said, "There's nothing we can do."

She glanced back as Schroeder turned toward the basement's corner. The henchman behind her pushed and she stumbled, caught herself, and allowed David to pull her up the remaining stairs.

They exited the basement into a palatial kitchen, shining with stainless steel fixtures, hanging pots and cooking implements. She reflexively scanned the countertops for knives, but the only ones she saw clung to magnetic strips on the opposite wall. Their naked blades gleamed tantalizingly, but they were hopelessly out of reach.

Their escort closed the door behind him with a click, and they'd just stepped away from it when a party-favor of a pop went off downstairs. Sarah spun to the goon, who stood between her and the basement door. He shrugged and motioned her toward a hallway on the right, down the long wall of the kitchen. As they walked past a bank of built-in freezers and refrigerators, David said, "Remember, Schroeder thought they came to kill *him*."

There was no point to sharing her certainty that they would soon die. "He knows different now," she said, willing her tone to belie her lingering shock. "*We* barely got out with our lives."

"And it's not over yet."

So he knew, just as she did. What is more, his voice sounded as numb as she felt. She took a deep breath and forced a smile. "What were you saying about it being safer to chase a dead Nazi war criminal than a live one?" She stopped at the hallway entrance and squared her body to his. "By the way, thanks for setting me up in the café. 'My partner.' Sheesh. No wonder he thought we were Mossad."

He didn't smile, but a little lightness appeared on his face. "Somehow, I don't think that made any difference. Dad's letter, now *that* made a difference."

She glanced at their escort, turned her back on him, and lowered her voice to a whisper. "Enough of one?"

"I doubt it," he whispered back. She hung onto his arm as they entered the hallway, an excuse to draw near while keeping their escort behind them. "Dad's letter might have bought us a little time," he whispered, "but Schroeder can't let us leave. Not with us knowing he's alive, and where. Our only hope is escape."

"So play it cool, and ... "

"And look for any opportunity. Any at all."

"Any at all? As in, the two of us against the one of him?" She nudged his arm with her finger to indicate the henchman behind them.

"Hm. Worth considering."

Near the end of the thickly carpeted hall, the man grunted, then nodded toward a door to one side. They entered to find a sitting room decorated with intricately carved furniture. "Okay, *now* I can tell I'm in Egypt,"

Sarah said. "This furniture is all of that famous Egyptian last-a-lifetime craftsmanship—" As she spoke, she ran her hands over the woodwork. She hoped to distract the goon as she edged closer to him, and noticed in her peripheral vision that David was following her lead by slipping to his other side. Another step on both their parts, and they would have him in a crossfire of fists.

Despite his bulk, the hoodlum sidestepped as nimbly as a ballerina. With a loud snap the blade of his flick-knife flashed open in his hand, even as he grabbed and spun David into a neck-clamp in the crook of one arm. He pointed his gleaming knife at Sarah with an outstretched arm and motioned her to a chair.

"Sit," he said.

She primly brushed herself off with her hands, then lowered herself into an ornate upholstered loveseat. "Well, if you insist … "

***

"First," Schroeder said, thumbing his chest as he entered the room, "I now go by the name of Omar Caden. No one has used my real name for decades."

"Omar Caden," Sarah repeated, as she stood from her chair out of reflex politeness. "Good alias."

"I thought so. Omar was the second Caliph of Islam, a name that helps me fit in around here."

"So," David said, "I assume you spoke with my father. After all, we're still above basement level, and minus the lead brain-weights."

"It wasn't so much your father, but your daughter who convinced me." He sat across from them and nodded to the maid who appeared in the doorway. "Coffee," he said, and circled a finger in the air to include them. Then he turned to David. "When I asked to speak with Mr. Joel Cohen, I heard her say ... " Schroeder screwed up his face and spoke in a girly voice, "Grandpa J, phone for you ... " He smiled. "That was all I needed to hear."

Sarah was stunned by the realization that he now conversed as though they were neighbors who had dropped by for a social visit. Then she recalled reading that many Nazi war criminals were loving fathers and doting husbands, and some were devoutly religious. In fact, psychologists shocked the world with the suggestion that these mass murderers had otherwise normal psychological profiles. This implied that perfectly normal people could be coerced to commit atrocities under the wrong influence—precisely what Stanley Milgram and Jerry Burger's famous experiments showed. She had studied the subject while trying to understand her American comrades' atrocities in Iraq, and later, the crimes of the Israeli army in Gaza. Watching Schroeder now confirmed the conclusions of these studies. No one would ever guess that a monster lurked within him.

"Did you talk with my father?" David said.

"He told me what I needed to know."

"What did you ... ?"

Schroeder turned his mouth into a frown, screwed a make-believe monocle into one eye and said, "*Ve haf vays* of making people *tawk*." Then he reverted to his normal tone. "What do you think? That I told him I'm holding a gun to your head, and he needed to give me a good reason not to pull the trigger?"

"No, I just—"

"So we can go now?" Sarah blurted.

Schroeder glanced up at the ceiling, then back at her. "Go? Of course not! Now you're my guests! If you go, you'll miss the finest stuffed pigeon and Egyptian duck this side of the Nile, an evening of poetry and scintillating conversation, and the best sleep of your life in rooms fit for a king and a queen. And that leaves plenty of time to … " he held up his hands and stroked air quotes with two fingers, " … 'kill you' tomorrow."

When they stared at him, speechless, he winked and said, "Mossad won't stop hunting you, unless they think you're dead. So if you're going to complete your mission, we'll just have to fake your execution. Exposing the Zionist deception … " He held up his hands, as if in prayer. "That is something I would very much like to see happen."

chapter 40

UPSTAIRS, IN THE vast guestroom into which the maid had ushered her, Sarah found her shoulder bag and suitcase at the foot of the king-sized bed. She showered in water so hot the temperature setting bordered on autoclave, then explored the clothing racks that lined a walk-in closet the size of her studio apartment in New York City. She exchanged her ruined jeans and duct-taped blouse for pink-hued tweed trousers and a mauve, Egyptian-style tunic with a floral burnout pattern. Then she knocked on the adjoining door. After a moment, David pulled the door open from the other side. His pleated wool slacks suited the chill of early spring; the blue oxford shirt and buttercup-yellow tie with turquoise accents added a heavy hand of class.

She followed him into his room, where he donned a charcoal-gray dinner jacket. "One thing you've got to admit," he said while adjusting his tie in front of the floor-to-ceiling mirror, "he's got a solid sense of style."

"I hate to think of how he made the money to support his tastes."

"You're right, let's not think about it."

She sat cross-legged on his bed and watched while he moved about the room, checking for hidden microphones. "David, what happened downstairs? I thought he shot you."

He rose from rooting about in a dresser. "Me, too. But he deliberately missed." He stood silent for a moment. "You know, people who deal in death sometimes develop a macabre fascination with it. They do sadistic things, trying to get a last-minute rise out of their victims. Maybe that's what Schroeder was doing with me—playing some kind of sick game."

"The fear alone would kill some people."

"I changed my pants, didn't I?" He flashed her a scoffing grin.

"Is that why you slumped down after the shot? You thought you were dead?"

"Nope. Pure reflex. The bullet struck the steel beam above my head. The shock of it made me duck. That's how I realized I was still alive. Dead men don't duck."

He finished his circuit around the room and stepped to the door. "Come on, this is one host we *reeeally* don't want to keep waiting."

***

They returned to their rooms later that night, fully fed and lightly entertained. And for the moment, still alive. "Well, that was interesting," Sarah said. "An evening with a mass murderer. And yet, it seemed so ... "

"Normal?"

She sat on the wooden chest at the foot of his bed. "Yeah. Who'd've thought?"

"What did you expect? Meatloaf for dinner?"

For a moment, memories of *The Rocky Horror Picture Show* played through her mind. "Don't you take anything seriously?"

"Not often. 'Nose itches' should've taught you that. What's this?" He picked up a note from atop the mahogany dresser and Sarah saw his expression darken as he read it. Then he pinched the corners of his eyes with one hand.

"What is it?" she asked, standing and sliding to his side.

"The Mossad agents. Their confessions," he said, still squeezing his eyes, as if in pain. He held up a manila envelope that accompanied the note he just read. "This contains their signed confessions and a DVD that contains a video of their ... interview."

"Holy cow!"

"Don't say that: It's disbelief. Think about what it means." He sighed, and pushed the envelope into her hands. "Keep these in your shoulder bag. They might prove useful someday." After a moment he said, "Okay, off to your room with you. We'd better get some sleep. We've got a full day ahead of us tomorrow, according to Schroeder."

"You mean Caden now," she said in a half-mocking tone. Shaking her head, she turned to the door that connected their rooms.

"No, I mean Schroeder. I never want to forget who that monster really is."

She stopped at the doorway, her hand on the knob. "I'm going to leave this open, if you don't mind. Sleeping here ... it gives me the creeps."

He leaned against a carved mahogany bedpost. "Goodnight, Sarah."

"G'night." She eased open the door and started to step through.

"Love you."

His words rushed from behind and tackled her. When she got her breath back she turned to face him, a mixture of pain and joy squeezing her heart. "I love you, too. I ... I—"

"Look, it doesn't mean we have to ... to do anything, okay? I just wanted you to know. In case something ... goes wrong tomorrow."

"Do you think something will?"

He shook his head. "If he wanted to kill us, he would've done it by now. Plus, I think he truly wants us to succeed—to expose the Zionists. He even called it 'the Zionist deception.' But I couldn't think of a better time and place to tell you, so ... I love you, and there it is."

All she could do was repeat what she'd already said. "I love you too."

He nodded. "Tomorrow, then." Shifting his eyes away, he shrugged himself off from the bedpost and turned to his walk-in closet while he loosened his tie.

In her own room, Sarah searched the closet and found a jersey track suit that seemed strangely appropriate. Deep down, she knew that if Schroeder's intentions changed, and she had to make a run for it, she wouldn't stand a chance. But she donned the track suit anyway and slipped between her bed sheets, luxuriating in the soft cotton for which Egypt is famous.

The moonlight's glow through the net curtains on the balcony French doors reminded her of a romance scene in a movie, but then she remembered it could just as well be the clichéd prelude to a vampire seduction. Dismissing that depressing thought, she rested her head on one pillow and hugged another. After a while she gazed at the open door to David's room and then, for no good reason she could think of, she kissed the pillow in her arms and closed her eyes.

chapter 41

EARLY THE NEXT morning, just before sunrise, a ragged procession filed out from the villa into the fields of what Schroeder, a.k.a. Caden, had bragged was one of the largest working farms in Beni Suef. The field hands had been confined to their quarters, as he said they would be. He couldn't resist adding, "And on this farm, everyone understands what that means."

Two henchmen flanked each of the dead Mossad agents. They carried them by their shoulders and under their handcuffed arms, propped up as if still alive but beaten senseless. They'd done something overnight to make the corpses hold their heads semi-erect, but whatever it was, Sarah didn't want to know; her own anxiety had her too much on edge to think of anything else. She and David followed, their hands cuffed behind their backs. Henchmen on both sides carried them by their arms and shoulders, just as they did with the dead Mossad agents. They flopped her heads about and dragged their feet to look semi-conscious, as Schroeder had told to do. "I need all four of you looking like you've been beaten nearly unconscious," Schroeder had told them. "It won't look believable otherwise."

When they reached a deep trench at the edge of a privacy row of closely packed poplars, the henchmen forced the four "condemned" to their knees, facing the trench side-by-side in a line. Then they removed the handcuffs. Schroeder, the last man in the macabre procession, stepped forward in his faded khaki killing-suit and worn canvas boots. He leveled his little gun at the first dead Mossad agent with the smooth movement of a man who is practiced in his craft. Fire spat from the gun with a clap, the man's head jerked, and he fell from the henchmen's hands into the trench and rolled to the bottom.

Sarah nearly retched at Schroeder's inhumanity, but swallowed her revulsion. The woman followed, and then Schroeder sidestepped to stand behind Sarah. She felt time slow to a crawl, and each of her senses quicken. The chill spring air on her exposed skin, the fertile smell of freshly turned soil and sprouting grasses, each chirp and warble of every songbird within earshot played like a symphony on her senses. Her eyes settled on the dead Mossad woman in the trench, and she realized her last living thought might be that, finally, they had removed her earrings.

She knew that at any moment she would feel either the cardboard wadding and hot blast of a blank cartridge on the back of her head, or her brain explode from a live bullet. Either way, she had to jerk her head.

Schroeder said, "Wait for it" through clenched teeth, and then counted, "Three, two, one ... " As they had rehearsed, David shouted and tried to stand. Schroeder's men wrestled him back to the ground as fire spat from the gun and Sarah's head jerked. Then she pitched forward and rolled into the trench.

From where she lay, she couldn't see Schroeder step behind David, couldn't hear what he said that made David try to jump to his feet again. All she knew for certain was that this was something they had not rehearsed, and that chilled her to the bone. The men on either side pulled him back down to his knees. Schroeder said something else to him, laughed, muttered words she couldn't hear, and then fired a jet of flame at his head.

chapter 42

SARAH LAY ON her side in the moist black earth, her limbs thrown haphazardly in front of her. "Are you okay?" she mumbled, struggling to not move. With one ear pressed against the earth, she strained with the other ear to hear his answer over the chugging of the tractor. Parked at the far end of the trench, it started up as soon as they'd fallen, and now revved its piston-pinging diesel engine. Instead of answering, David's body shuddered, one limb twitching. The only thing that restrained Sarah from jumping to his aid was the knowledge that a single movement on her part would ruin everything. "Oh my God," she said, her own body twitching from fear. "Oh, David. No—say something, *please.*"

"Nothing by halves," he muttered. "Just playing it for all it's worth."

Sarah sighed and choked back a sob of relief. After a couple of shallow breaths, she asked, "What did Schroeder say to you?"

"He asked me if I trusted him to have loaded blanks."

"And then?"

"He told me to say hello to his mother, and laughed. Then he did his countdown."

"You're right, he's a psycho."

"Told ya."

"Something else. Did'ya have to land with your knee in my ribs?" She squirmed millimeters, but quickly realized his knee was there to stay.

"I just landed where I fell. Schroeder told us not to move a muscle until he gives the signal. Sorry."

"Uh-huh. Now tell me how your hand ended up where it is right now."

"That might be harder to explain."

"Well, tough guy, I've got just one thing to say to you."

"What's that?"

"Your nose itches."

***

Schroeder watched David tumble and fall before pocketing his pistol. He motioned one of his men to the tractor. The engine turned over on the second try and belched puffs of sooty exhaust as the man at the controls revved it. Then he sat with the engine on idle, waiting.

"Well?" Schroeder said into his ear-clip communicator.

"Thirty seconds," came the reply.

Half-a-minute later the disembodied voice spoke urgently: "Sky's clear. No Israeli satellites. You have twenty seconds."

"Go!" Schroeder yelled.

As if Schroeder had fired a starter's pistol, David flipped himself onto his hands and knees and scrambled along the trench to the metal culvert at the near end. The second he lifted his weight off her, Sarah followed. They entered the culvert on all fours and crawled ten feet before they stopped, their knees banging against the rough corrugated iron. Then they sat and watched as the tractor skimmed the ridge of earth from the far side into the trench, filling it, and forcing a tumble of earth into the mouth of the culvert.

"That could be us, buried back there," Sarah said.

"As far as Mossad knows, it is." David nudged her and added, "Don't forget them in your prayers. They might have come to kill us, but their deaths could save our lives."

She raised sad eyes to meet his. "I have a hard time getting past the 'came to kill us' part."

He turned to the culvert's open end and started crawling in the direction of the early morning light. With a shrug, she followed.

chapter 43

SHOWERED AND CHANGED, they waited for Schroeder at one end of the banquet-length rosewood dining table. Chafing dishes simmered over burners on the serving counter to one side, venting puffs of steam and delicate odors from beneath their spotless stainless steel covers. A uniformed servant poured coffee from a blue spruce-pattern porcelain pot, then withdrew to his station by the service entrance, at the far end of the room. A second servant nestled a porcelain sugar and cream service between them before noiselessly slipping away to a station opposite that of his companion.

David lifted the porcelain cup to his lips, took a sip, set it back down with a clink. Sarah touched a sugar cube to her coffee and watched the dark liquid invade the crystal matrix. When it was saturated, she leaned over her cup and popped it into her mouth.

"Wow, that redefines the concept of taking coffee sweet."

"Nothing by ha ... ," she shook her head with a shiver and smiled bitter-sweetly in his direction. "Um, you know what I mean." She dunked another cube and crunched it. "I thought I lost you."

"Don't worry. I'm becoming a professional at surviving head shots."

A few minutes later, Schroeder entered the room in a flood of servants and henchmen but, one by one, each drifted away with minimal instructions, leaving only Schroeder.

Showoff, Sarah thought, watching.

"First," he said to David as he took his seat at the head of the table, "good acting! I especially liked the 'trying to stand to defend your woman' part. Now," he reached over his shoulder with an open hand, and a waiting servant slipped a file folder into his palm. "It's time I gave you what you're looking for. Or perhaps I should say, my part of it."

Another servant laid a matching folder on the table between David and Sarah. Sarah flipped it open, and together they read while Schroeder gave an impromptu introduction.

"Prior to World War Two, Jewish leaders declared economic war on Germany. They then used the predictable anti-Semitic backlash to convince able-bodied Jews to emigrate to Palestine. You see, sixty percent of European Jews were businessmen and professionals. Many more were artisans, clerks, and students. These were not the kind of people who would abandon civilization for a kibbutz in the Judean desert without strong motivation. So the Zionists terrorized Jews into leaving. Prior to the war, they fanned the flames of anti-Semitism, publicly denouncing it but secretly exploiting it. That game has continued to this day."

He laid his folder on the table and turned a page, and they followed his lead. Then he continued: "During the war, Zionist leaders recognized the Holocaust as their bargaining chip, one they could redeem for a Jewish homeland after the war. Assuming the Allies were victorious, of course. Western Zionist leaders held no affection for their anti-Zionist European Jewish brethren, and abandoned them to their fate. They knew the Jewish death toll would generate the world sympathy they needed to obtain their objective."

"But," David said, his finger sweeping lines in the middle of the page, "toward the end of the war, Germany knew it was losing."

"Exactly." Schroeder snapped his fingers and then twirled one finger in the air. Sarah tensed, until she saw uniformed servants lift the covers from the chaffing dishes, pick up plates and start to fill them. Ignoring her reaction, Schroeder turned a page and locked eyes with David.

"I was one of Eichmann's deputies. This ... " he tapped the page with a pale claw of a finger, "this is documentation of the blood-for-goods deal. Also known as 'blood for trucks.'"

He paused to allow them to skim the page, then said, "Heinrich Himmler, head of the SS, ordered Eichmann to sell a million Jewish lives for ten thousand trucks, to be used on the Eastern Front. He also demanded tea, coffee, soap and other goods. The deal was offered to Joel Brand and brokered through Rudolf Kastner: two prominent Hungarian Zionists. When the British detained Brand in

Aleppo, Kastner became the chief negotiator with Eich-mann."

"Aleppo?" Sarah said. "Where's that?"

"Syria. On the border with Turkey." Schroeder leaned back as a servant set a full plate in front of him, then said, "Brand was betrayed by a Zionist organization known as the Jewish Agency for Israel, which he had approached to help save the Hungarian Jews."

"I know something about that case," David said. "We can't say for sure that it was the Agency that betrayed him. The British—"

Schroeder launched himself to standing and slammed an alabaster fist to the table, accidentally catch-ing the edge of his plate. Scrambled eggs, fried potatoes and fruit salad catapulted to one side in a confetti of food. "We offered you American Jews a chance to save them! We offered you their *lives!* And you turned your backs on them. You just kept your cherished money in your miserly Jewish pockets and let them *die!*"

Sarah flinched and felt David stiffen by her side. She'd seen the rage and insanity in Schroeder's eyes, and instantly realized that beneath his charade of civilized hospitality, a seething hatred burned in his heart. She pat-ted the air in his direction with both hands. "Not us," she said, gently. "Not us. We're against the Zionists too, re-member? We weren't even born back then."

For a moment she thought she'd lost him, but then the wrathful contortion of his wretched features eased, and the wildfire in his eyes subsided. He lowered himself into his seat while servants scrambled to clean up the mess and provide him with a fresh plate.

"My apologies." He waved a tremulous hand at their place settings. "Please, have something to eat."

Sarah looked down and found a vegetarian breakfast in front of her. David's plate was the same. In the same moment, she realized there wasn't even the smell of meat in the room. *His best effort at kosher,* she reflected. *How thoughtful.* But then she remembered that just seconds ago, he could have killed them in rage. She pondered that her emotions toward him, like his toward them, oscillated between reflexive courtesy and deeply rooted prejudices. She tolerated him out of necessity, but knowing him for what he was, would consider it an honor to put a bullet into his brain.

"I think we've gotten off track," she said quietly.

Schroeder rubbed a smear of egg from his hand into a napkin, and twitched a smile at her. "Yes. We have. Please excuse me." He accepted a fresh plate from a solicitous servant, picked at the potatoes with his fork. "What I wanted to tell you is not about the deal, but about Rudolf Kastner—"

"What's this?" David asked, and held up an envelope. "It's between two pages of the folder."

Schroeder stared at him thoughtfully, as if considering whether to spit in his face for interrupting. Sarah tensed for another explosion, but Schroeder glanced down at his plate and said, "That is your next stop. Leon Bauer. I've told him to expect you."

"The other name Novak listed as living here in Egypt?" David said.

This brought a terse smile. "Not all of us hid in South America. I would also send you to Dr. Aribert Ferdinand Heim, but he died a few years ago."

Sarah found herself questioning Schroeder's reliability, because she'd come across reference to Heim, a.k.a. Dr. Death, in her research. A number of reputable sources reported that Heim died sixteen years ago in Cairo. But she decided this might not be the best time to question his mental faculties.

"Leon Bauer will educate you regarding the most critical details to your research," Schroeder said. Then both his voice and expression tightened. "You think you're on the right track, but you're only on *one* track. What you don't realize is that you've completely missed the biggest train."

Sarah stood and strolled to his end of the table. "You were going to tell us about Kastner," she said, and patted the aged Nazi's shoulder as she passed behind him. He craned his neck and swung his head, eyes on guard, to follow her as she stepped to the service counter and filled a plate with fruit salad.

When she returned, she sat to one side of him and lightly touched the sleeve of his dining jacket. She reflected that somebody still had the panache to dress like a squire for breakfast. "We appreciate all you're doing for us," she said. Then she plucked a spoon from his place setting and filled it with fruit.

"My dear *Fraulein,*" Schroeder said, his eyes smiling now, "a man doesn't reach my age without understanding something of the machinations of women. Nonetheless," he gave a courteous nod in her direction, "I surrender to your calming influence."

After a moment, Schroeder explained that Kastner accepted a human bribe from Eichmann. In return for his cooperation, Kastner was granted safe passage for 1,685 Jews of his choice from German-occupied Hungary to neutral Switzerland. Many of the saved Jews on what came to be known as the "Kastner train" were his friends, relatives, Zionist leaders and wealthy sponsors.

Partway through his explanation, Schroeder directed them to a quote from an interview with Eichmann, published in *Life* magazine. "See there?" he said. "Eichmann stated that Kastner 'agreed to help keep the Jews from resisting deportation—and even keep order in the collection camps—if I would close my eyes and let a few hundred or a few thousand young Jews emigrate illegally to Palestine. It was a good bargain for us.' Those are Eichmann's own words."

But then he snorted. "Of course, *he* thought it was a good bargain, too. What we feared most was a Warsaw Ghetto-like battle in Hungary. Kastner kept that from happening."

"He saved nearly two thousand Jews," David said as he picked up his plate and strode the length of the table. He sat on Schroeder's other side, opposite Sarah.

"*Tens* of thousands could have escaped, if he had warned them," Schroeder said. "They could have hidden or run away, forged documents, bribed their way to freedom, or formed a resistance movement. But they didn't, because Kastner deceived them into believing that the death ride to Auschwitz was simply a resettlement program."

He pointed to David's folder. When David slid it toward him, Schroeder flipped a page, then another, and then spun it back to face his guest. He pointed to a passage, and David read, "The judge in a libel suit stated that Kastner, quote, 'sold his soul to the devil,' and that his acceptance of the human bribe was, quote, 'collaboration in the fullest sense of the word.'"

Leaning back in his chair and ticking off on his fingers, Schroeder said, "He collaborated with the Nazis, negotiated for the lives of a privileged few at the expense of the masses, facilitated our extermination machine at Auschwitz, and intervened on behalf of Nazis at their Nuremberg war crimes trials. Kastner negotiated with Himmler's envoy, SS officer Kurt Becher. After the war, he intervened on Becher's behalf, even though Becher was Commissar of the German concentration camps. In addition, Becher was in charge of converting Hungarian Jews' body parts and belongings into cash. As a result of Kastner's support, Becher avoided trial *and* became one of the wealthiest businessmen in postwar West Germany."

David chewed slowly. Then he swallowed and cocked his head at Schroeder. "You know, the way you're talking right now, I can't tell whose side you're on."

Schroeder placed his fork on his plate and then raised one finger, whereupon a waiting servant removed his plate. "Coffee," Schroeder murmured. Then he turned back to David with a smile. "This generation is taught to believe we Nazis were the problem. I'm just saying the Zionists had a heavy hand in the horrors as well. Do you want to see how similar we were, in some ways?"

"I fought in Gaza," Sarah said. "I've seen it with my own eyes."

"Ah. Well, all the same, this is what Eichmann had to say."

David read aloud from the passage Schroeder identified in the folder: "In the years that followed I often said to Jews with whom I had dealings that, had I been a Jew, I would have been a fanatical Zionist. I could not imagine being anything else. In fact, I would have been the most ardent Zionist imaginable."

Sarah jumped in her seat. "Where did you get that?"

Schroeder smiled. "Well, of course, I knew it first-hand. But you can find it in a *Life* magazine interview with Eichmann. Written by a Dutch journalist in 1955 ... ." His finger drifted down the page until he found the dates. "In two parts, November 28 and December 5, 1960. Now, read what Eichmann had to say about Kastner."

David flicked his gaze to Sarah, his eyes wary, and then dutifully read, " ... an ice-cold lawyer and a fanatical Zionist ... . With his great polish and reserve he would have made an ideal Gestapo officer himself."

"So there you have it," Schroeder said, "Eichmann could have been a fanatical Zionist and Kastner, a fanatical Zionist, could have been a Gestapo officer. And these two negotiated with one another. A match made in Hell, no doubt."

David stood, the folder in one hand, and paced the room while still reading: "Eichmann said, 'As a matter of fact, there was a very strong similarity between our attitudes in the SS and the viewpoint of these immensely idealistic Zionist leaders who were fighting what might

be their last battle. As I told Kastner, "We, too, are ide-
alists and we, too, had to sacrifice our own blood before
we came to power." I believe that Kastner would have
sacrificed a thousand or a hundred thousand of his blood
to achieve his political goal. He was not interested in old
Jews or those who had become assimilated into Hungarian society. But he was incredibly persistent in trying to
save biologically valuable Jewish blood, that is, human
material that was capable of reproduction and hard work.
"You can have the others," he would say, "but let me have
this group here." And because Kastner rendered us a great
service by helping keep the deportation camps peaceful, I
would let his groups escape."'

Sarah's mouth worked, but she could only come up
with, "My God."

David shrugged his eyebrows. "I'm thinking these
two didn't have our Creator on their agenda."

"Don't *think*," Schroeder said, saluting him with a
raised cup of coffee. "Be sure. Be one hundred percent
positive they didn't have God on their agenda. This, then,
is what you need to tell the world."

chapter 44

"YEESH." DAVID SAID as Sarah followed him into his room upstairs, "You're good. Slick, even."

"Somebody had to calm the storm down there."

"Sorry about that. I didn't know I'd set off a bomb."

"You nearly set off two."

David scrunched up an eye as he scratched behind one ear. "Yeah, well, it's a good thing we serve his purpose."

"I'd hate to think what might've happened if we didn't. You know, if I have a woof-look, that's your meow-look."

He stilled his fingers behind his ear and raised an eyebrow at her questioningly.

"That eye-scrunch while scratching your ear? It reminds me of a cat. In any case ... " She waved the thought away and said, "an apology from you would've gone a long way toward keeping the peace back there."

"*Your* apology might have saved our lives. I just ... couldn't. Not to that creep. I'd rather he'd have shot me."

"You might not feel that way if he decided to oblige you."

"Hey, he's pulled a trigger on me twice now."

She stepped back and appraised him coolly. "You're a rock, you know that?"

"Rocks turn to sand over time."

"Yeah, well ... don't. Sand can be irritating."

She left through the connecting door, and returned wearing Ponté knit trousers and a shirred blouson top, her black cavalry coat draped over one arm. "Ready to go?

He threw a final pair of socks into his bag. "I see you've made good use of his warehouse hospitality."

"He offered, I accepted, learn the lesson."

He picked up his carryall bag and followed her into her room, where she grabbed her shoulder bag and new valise. She cast a glance at her old suitcase in the corner. "Who'd've thought?"

"Well, me for one," he said. "That metal detector I bought just wasn't sensitive enough." He pinched something from her bedside table and held it at eye level. Peering at it with one eye closed, he said, "The size of a grain of rice and paper-thin. Mossad could've hidden this anywhere. It's a good thing Schroeder had a *real* bug detector. If not, the moment we started moving again, they'd have known that stunt in the field was a ruse."

He placed the tracking device back on the table and gave her a tight smile. "Come on, let's get out of here. We've got a date in Cairo."

"It's hard to believe he's letting us go."

"He might not've, if he wasn't foaming at the mouth to see us bring the truth to light. All the same, let's not push our luck. Let's get out of here before he changes his mind."

chapter 45

"MIXED NEWS," LANDAU said into the red telephone's receiver. The chief was at his desk in Tel Aviv thinking that finally, today, he would be able to relax and enjoy his lunch. The news wasn't perfect, but in his opinion, the end justified the means. Surely the prime minister would feel the same way.

"What's the good news?" PM Rosenfeld asked.

"Operation Bud Nipper has been concluded. Both flowers have been plucked."

"What's the bad?"

"Our two gardeners quit."

There was a long silence on the other end of the line. Landau thought, *Okay, so maybe I won't relax over lunch after all.*

The silence ended when Rosenfeld said, "Hold for my secretary."

The line clicked and went mute. A few seconds later, a woman's voice picked up and said, "The prime minister would like to see you in his office today at four. He says you're to bring an electronic compilation of the Operation Bud Nipper files. Can I confirm?"

Landau glanced at his calendar, saw he was already double-booked for that time slot. "That'll be fine. My day's wide open."

***

The prime minister was pacing the vast, patterned-marble floor of his oak-paneled office when Landau entered at precisely four p.m. He kept his eyes drilled on Rosenfeld, wondering what had him so disturbed, even as the PM pointed to a chair across from his desk. Landau sat opposite the third man in the room, alarm bells going off in his mind as he recognized Elan Glick. Tall, muscular and in his mid-fifties, Glick had served as the Director of Mossad for the past seven years.

"First of all, Vienna," Rosenfeld said. "Everything just got worse. Ari Pinsk turned state's evidence."

"What?" Landau prided himself on keeping cool and circumspect, even in the most distressful circumstances. But today he jumped from his chair. "How? What made him ... *Why?*"

Rosenfeld scratched his head and pointed to Director Glick, who turned in his seat and said, "Some nut sent an SMS message from one of *our* ports to the senior toothpick's cell phone. The message read, 'After inviting David and Sarah to the party, be sure to invite Pinsk. Please confirm.'"

Landau threw himself back down in his chair and sputtered, "Nobody here's stupid enough to send that!"

"We know," Director Glick said.

"We're tracing it?"

"As we speak." Rosenfeld halted his pacing at one wall, and stared at a flawless reproduction of one of Monet's water-lily scenes. He spoke to the painting, sweeping his eyes over it like an appraiser searching for defects. "Whatever we find, the damage is done. The police showed the message to Pinsk, he panicked and made a statement. He's now in protective custody. Even if we find an explanation for that message, we can't communicate with him to turn him back to our side."

Landau rubbed his forehead. "And if he's already made a statement, he won't be able to retract it anyway, without perjuring himself. Great. So now Austria has both assassins and not just one, but *two* direct links between them and us."

Rosenfeld turned from the painting, a sour expression muddying his face. "The assassins were employed at our embassy, and now our turncoat informant, Ari Pinsk, has testified to their criminal activities. Chancellor Zuckerkandl knows he has the upper hand, so he called this morning." He turned up a fist, his little finger pointed toward the ceiling. "He's switched from squeezing my pinkie with pliers to crushing my head in a vice."

"Just your head?" Glick said through a thin smile.

"Hm." The prime minister eased himself into the chair behind his desk and sat gingerly, as if in pain. As he hitched forward in his seat, the door opened with a knock. An advisor crossed the floor quickly, handed a folder to Director Glick, and retreated back out the door.

Glick read the paragraph of text inside the folder, then passed it to Rosenfeld. While the PM scanned it, Glick turned to Landau and said, "This guy is amazing.

Phone records show that moments after David Cohen took our man down in Vienna, he used the agent's cell phone to place a missed call to his own cell. That gave him our man's phone number. Later, he hacked into one of our portals and sent the fake SMS, making it look like a message from Mossad."

Landau's face went blank with disbelief. Then he said, "This David Cohen thinks fast on his feet. Too bad he's dead. We could've used him."

"We did," Glick said. "He worked in our tech section for three years, before he returned to the states. Let me tell you, he steers a laptop the way a fighter pilot flies an F-16. His practical skills were pretty good, but not good enough to qualify for field work. Where he really stood out was in computers."

For a moment, Landau's lips moved, but nothing came out. Then he managed, "Why isn't that information in his dossier? If I'd known this, perhaps—"

Rosenfeld spun the file in his hands onto his desk like a flying disk. "Some things are still above your clearance level, Simon. Let's see your closure on Operation Bud Nipper."

Landau sat frozen for a moment, unblinking. Then he stood mechanically and stretched an arm to Rosenfeld over the massive wooden desk. Rosenfeld opened a desk drawer and fed Landau's DVD into the electronic slit within. He spun a dial and the room lights dimmed as the wall-screen lit up with an aerial image of a farm.

"Toss me the remote," Glick said.

Giving the Mossad director a curious glance, Rosenfeld slid the remote over the smooth desktop. It skidded off the edge and fell into Glick's hands.

The satellite was one of Israel's newer models, so the resolution was good enough to make out facial detail. Rosenfeld bent his head toward his desk during the agents' executions. After David tumbled into the trench, he stood and walked over to stare at his Monet. Landau and Glick continued to watch in stony silence. After a thirty-four-second loss of satellite coverage, the recording cut in to show the tractor smoothing earth over the trench and the execution team walking back to Schroeder's palatial villa.

Landau stood from his seat. "Well, that's about all there is to—"

"Hold on," Glick said.

Rosenfeld turned from his water lilies and Landau glanced at him questioningly, but then lowered himself back into his seat.

On the replay, Glick stepped from his chair to the wall screen and peered at it, as if searching for detail. On the third play, he stopped the recording at the moment of David's execution.

"What are you looking for?" Rosenfeld said while he stepped to the tall man's side.

Glick shook his head as he toggled the rewind and play. "The head snap seems wrong."

"Wrong?" Rosenfeld raised an eyebrow and propped both fists on his hips.

"Maybe. I can't be sure."

A few more minutes of rewind and frame-by-frame inspection, and Landau said, "Shall we send it to Annie?"

Glick nodded slowly, still staring at the screen. "Annie" was Mossad's euphemism for their analysis department. It was perpetually swamped with work, but Glick said, "Make it top priority. I want an answer before I blink."

chapter 46

LEON BAUER RECEIVED David and Sarah in his two-bed-room rooftop apartment in the Shobra district of Cairo. Bald, bespectacled and pleasantly rotund, he lacked the posh circumstances Felix Schroeder wallowed in. Also unlike Schroeder, he was unabashedly jovial and seemed to thoroughly enjoy life. "Heil Hitler, Heil Hitler," he said, snapping a heel click and flashing the Nazi salute when he met them at the door. A broad smile widening his chubby chipmunk cheeks, he ushered them into his apartment. "Please, make yourselves comfortable."

"Is he messing with us?" Sarah whispered once he stepped out of the room to fetch refreshments.

"He's either a complete social retard," David said as he glanced about the room from his seat on the thread-bare sofa, "or he's a total loon. Unless, that is, Schroeder didn't tell him who we are. Come to think of it, how many Jews do you think Schroeder ever sent to this guy's door? Living ones, I mean."

"Maybe we should tell him we're Jewish."

"Maybe we *shouldn't*."

"Two psychos before lunch." Sarah sighed. "Throw in a homicidal, necrophiliac cannibal, and the day will be complete."

***

Over soft drinks and tinned butter cookies, Bauer explained that many Nazis saw Hitler's extermination program as a unique opportunity for human experimentation. "Everybody knows about Josef Mengele, the 'Angel of Death' at Auschwitz," he said. "What most don't know, however, is that Mengele was just one of many doctors who capitalized on the traffic of human guinea pigs. Some, like Mengele, committed atrocities. Others, like myself, pursued more humane studies."

Bauer stood from his rickety folding chair and pulled a photo album from a nearby wall shelf. As he laid the album on the folding coffee table between them, Sarah braced herself for what he might show her. Yet the first few pages contained only faces. Each was photographed from different angles, with calipers clearly showing the span of certain facial features.

"What I studied," Bauer said as he bent over the album from his standing position, "was external racial similarity. I wanted to define the facial and body traits that would allow us Nazis to identify Jews." He paused for a moment to let this sink in, then turned the page. The next group of faded black-and-white photographs showed miserable crowds of the condemned being herded into cattle cars. "It was a difficult task, but we needed to identify those who polluted the innate superiority of the Aryan race."

Sarah stiffened and glanced at David, who listened calmly, head bowed, as if absorbing a scientific lecture.

"Many Jews lived undetected in our midst," Bauer said. "They were shielded by forged documents or concealed genealogies. So I wanted to define the features by which we could distinguish Jews, just by looking at them."

"Or measuring them," David said without raising his head.

"Why, yes, *exactly!*" Bauer's broad face glowed, as if a respected colleague had suddenly recognized the brilliance of his work, and he slapped his baggy pants with a pudgy hand.

"What did you find?" David reached out and turned to the next page. Sarah gasped at a collage of severed limbs, and he hurriedly flipped the page again and left the album open to sheets of mathematical calculations and statistical analysis.

"What I found," Bauer said, puffing out his chest as if to receive a medal, "has now been verified with modern scientific methods. And that is that the majority of Jews are not of Hebrew origin. In fact, they descended from the Khazars!"

"Khazars?" Sarah said, befuddled. "Who are the Khazars?"

David coughed into his fist and cleared his throat, then said, "Um, well, in its day, Khazaria was one of the largest countries in the world. It spanned more than a million square miles, from the Hungarian-Austrian border at its Western aspect, all the way east to the Aral Sea. From the Caucasus Mountains in the south, it extended north to the upper Volga. We're talking *huge*. In addition, its fighters were some of the most feared of their time."

"Did you two go to the same school?" She waved a finger between the two men. "Or what?"

"I minored in European History," David said. "I was going through a discover-your-roots phase."

"But did you know," Bauer said, "that the whole of Khazaria converted to Judaism between the seventh and eighth centuries?"

"Hw-*What?*" David said, his jaw visibly slacking.

Bauer slapped his swollen thigh and let out a huge guffaw. "Ha! This is history the Zionists don't want the world to know. Faithful Jews don't care, or at least, they *shouldn't*, because it doesn't affect their Jewishness. They put their religion before the Holy Land ... "

" ... believing one will follow the other," David said. "Our Creator will miraculously award the Holy Land to the righteous, regardless of their ancestry, in a future messianic era."

Sarah coughed against the back of her hand and shot David a warning look. He rolled his eyes in apology for his lack of caution, but Bauer failed to see that both David's gesture and his words pointed toward his religion. Blinded by his exuberance, the fat Nazi turned to his new star pupil with glowing appreciation and said, "Precisely!" He tried to snap his fingers, but the pudgy digits bounced off his palm noiselessly. "The Zionists are the exact opposite," he said, unfazed. "Their priority is on the Holy Land, based not on their religion, but on their race. So for Zionist Jews, this information is poison!"

He jumped to his wall shelves and grabbed an armful of books. He handed two to David and one to Sarah, and set a small stack on the table in front of them. "It's all in there," he said, stabbing his finger excitedly at the books in their hands. "Published knowledge, forced out of print as soon as it hit the stores. Some say Khazaria's king preferred Judaism to the other monotheistic faiths, others say he chose it to maintain his autonomy: He didn't want to subjugate himself to the Pope as a Christian or to the Caliph as a Muslim, so he made Judaism the religion of his realm."

Then, in the strangest act of spontaneity Sarah had ever seen, Bauer spun in a circle like a dancing bear, sang an incomprehensible German anthem, and strutted around the small room like a puffed-up pigeon, beating his chest with his hands. She shot David a wary glance; he cocked an eyebrow and shrugged in return.

"After all of Khazaria became Jewish," Bauer said, halting at the far end of the room, "their empire disintegrated following the Mongol invasion in the thirteenth century." He walked over to a wall map and splayed out his fingers in the middle of Eastern Europe. "The Khazars spread out in every direction. Unlike their Hebrew cousins, they freely intermarried, vastly expanding the numbers and diversity of their descendants."

David sat back in his seat and strummed one knee with his fingers. "I think I see where you're going with this."

Bauer spun around from the map. "Can you?" He grabbed a notebook from his shelves and laid it on top of the pile of books in front of them. "What I found," he said, "is that Khazar's descendants make up roughly ninety-five percent of all Jews."

Fists on hips and leaning forward at the waist, as if to lecture a rebellious child, he said, "Don't you get it? Ninety-five percent of all Jews are not descended from Noah's son, Shem. They aren't Hebrews *or* Semites. They have no historic, racial or religious connection with the Holy Land. Neither they nor their ancestors ever set foot there. The Jews claim God made His covenant with the Hebrews, in the bloodline of Abraham. They say God's covenant was made *not* with Jews, as a religious body, but with a specific blood lineage, namely the Hebrews." Bending backwards, he balled up his fists and shook them at the heavens, his face enflamed. "They have nullified their own claim! Ninety-five percent ... *NINETY-FIVE PERCENT* of Jews aren't Hebrews!" Folding himself forward at the waist, hands braced on bent knees, he brought his face level with David's face and locked eyes with him. Dropping his voice to a whisper that belied the intensity of his emotions, he said, "They descended from non-Hebrew converts, not from Abraham's bloodline. To say that modern-day Jews have a claim to the Holy Land is like saying that Russian Muslims have claim to the oil in Saudi Arabia! Russian Muslims are not Arabs, and modern-day Jews, for the most part, are not Hebrews. By their own scripture, they have invalidated their claim to the Holy Land."

"Wait a minute." Sarah swung the book in her hands to the top of the pile in front of her, then stood. "For sixty years, the Israelis have accused their detractors of being anti-Semitic. Now you're saying—"

Bauer clapped his hands, spun another dancing-bear circle. "That it's the biggest farce of the century. Excepting the *very* few Israelis who are Hebrews—true Semites—ninety-five percent of Jews are not even Semites to begin with! In fact, it's the *Israelis* who are anti-Semitic. They attack the Arabs who, along with the Akkadians, Canaanites, Phoenicians and Ethiopians—the true descendants of Shem—are *legitimate* Semites. It's the biggest farce—"

"Of the century," David said. He stood and strode over to Bauer's wall map, to where Bauer had blackened Israel from the Middle East with a marking pen. He said, "So this is why Israel protects you and the other Nazis on Novak's list?"

"Of course." Bauer lowered his ballooning body into a metal folding chair. "If they put us on trial for our crimes, we'd expose their lies to the world, and reveal that ninety-five percent of Jews have no legitimate claim to the Holy Land. *We* might lose our lives ... but *they* might lose their country."

chapter 47

"I COULD'VE DONE without that 'Heil Hitler' hello and goodbye of his," Sarah said as they stepped onto the sidewalk. "One thing's for sure. For all his research in recognizing Jewish features, he still doesn't know a Jew when he sees one." She squinted into the unfiltered sunshine.

"That's the point." David slipped on a pair of Blast Chiller sunglasses and scanned the street in both directions. "If all Jews were Semitic, we'd look the same. But we don't, because most of us descended from the Khazars, who mixed their blood all over Europe."

"He certainly convinced you pretty quickly," Sarah said.

"Not just him, but also his books. We looked those over together. Tell me you're not convinced as well."

She nodded her head thoughtfully. "Nope. I'm on board too."

"Okay then. Anyway, it certainly explains our genetic diversity. It also explains how you found your near-twin in Slovakia—you and Hava Östberg must come from the same genetic stock."

Not to mention the facial similarity between you and Sergeant Kyle, Sarah thought with a painful pang. She gazed at his sober profile as he scanned the street and realized that, except for that initial instinctive reaction, her mental association with Kyle had finally died. When she looked at David now, she saw nothing but a man who had gently, with her barely noticing, eased the embittered warrior out of her. A man who had caused her, for the first time in her life, to dream of children, a settled home, and peace.

But this wasn't the time to share her vision. She said, "I guess it also explains where ruddy-complexioned, red-headed Jews like Hymie come from."

"That would be the Caucasus region of Khazaria," David said. "It's where the word *Caucasian* comes from." He swung open the rear door to Schroeder's black Mercedes sedan and held it while she slipped in, then followed while she scooted to the far side. The Egyptian driver eased into traffic, and Sarah leaned her head back into the contoured headrest.

"I could get used to this," she said with a sigh, once again slipping into the daydream of a happy home.

"Me too. If I could just stop thinking there's Jewish blood all over this car."

Even those words failed to rub the daydream from her heart. Gazing at his dark, masculine features as he stared straight ahead, she felt a softness rise within her. Suddenly she wanted nothing more than to be pampered, cherished and protected by the man she loved. *Dang. Does this mean I have to let him do all the fighting from now on?*

***

Director Glick charged into Prime Minister Rosenfeld's office, pushing past a secretary, and said, "We've got a problem." He waved an aide out of the room, slapped a report on the desk, then stood back as the PM began wading through it. After a moment, Glick threw his hands into the air and said, "Annie took twenty-four hours, but there it is. There wasn't any blood in the blowback from our agents' heads. When they fell and rolled into the trench, their bodies were stiff from rigor mortis. They hadn't been beaten unconscious—they were already dead."

Rosenfeld rested his finger midway down the first page. "The head snaps for David Cohen and Sarah Weizmann's *were* off, just like you said they were."

Glick nodded. "Delayed. There wasn't any blowback from our agents' heads, because they were already dead. No blowback from Cohen and Weizmann, either, but for a very different reason—Schroeder didn't shoot them, and their reflexes were slower than a speeding bullet. Something else ... " He leaned forward and flipped a page, tapped the paragraph at the end of it. "The tractor sat there, engine idling, spewing smoke from its exhaust. Why didn't it fill in the trench immediately? What was it waiting for, if not for a blackout window in our satellite coverage?"

"GPS?"

"I'm guessing from the house. Our tech department is analyzing the pings on our satellites. We should have an answer within the hour. It figures that Schroeder's been monitoring our satellites since we sent in our first team to eliminate him, nine years ago."

Rosenfeld slapped his desk and pushed himself from his seat. He stood, bent over the desktop with his hands straddling the report, arms braced on the polished wood. "So he shot our agents with real bullets, but faked Cohen and Weizmann's executions. So where did they escape to?"

"That," Glick said, "is what we've got to find out."

***

Ten minutes later, Meyer watched while the chief took a memo from one of the prime minister's aides, read it, and then rose from the meeting he chaired and followed the aide from the room. He wondered why Chief Landau left so suddenly and, more importantly, why he'd glanced at Meyer, anonymously tucked away at the far end of the table. That was something he almost never did. *Since the day he asked me about Sarah Weizmann, he acts like I don't even exist.* Then he shrugged, raised his fourth cup of morning coffee to his lips and washed the thought away with a serious swig.

chapter 48

"WE FOUND THEM," Director Glick said, grabbing a handful of salted cashews from a decorative bowl on a sideboard as he entered Rosenfeld's office. "They boarded a flight to America sixteen hours ago."

It was mid-afternoon, and Landau was in the office too, having been summoned by Rosenfeld for an update. Neither man expected this news, however. Hearing Glick's announcement, Landau blurted, "Why weren't we notified when they went through passport control in Cairo?"

Glick and Rosenfeld exchanged glances. Glick said, "I'm betting Cohen bought a new laptop and did some of his Internet kung-fu. No doubt, he altered the records."

"When do they land?" Landau asked.

"Twenty minutes."

"Enough time to arrange an intercept at the airport?"

Glick tossed back a couple of cashews, crunched. "Don't know. We made the order. Now we wait."

Landau slipped a pipe from his inside jacket pocket and tucked it into the corner of his mouth. "Perhaps it's time you told me *exactly* what's so special about this David Cohen we're chasing."

Glick glanced at Rosenfeld, who leaned forward, arms crossed on the desk in front of him. The PM met Glick's eyes and nodded, but Glick shook his head. Rosenfeld shrugged and turned back to Landau, "I'm sorry. It's strictly need-to-know."

Landau raised his Dupont lighter, but Rosenfeld waggled a finger at him. He dropped his lighter back into his pocket and puffed his pipe cold. "Don't you think I need to—?"

"No," Glick said from where he'd sat opposite him. "The only thing you *need to know* is to go to your office and stay there until I call."

After the door closed behind him, Rosenfeld said, "That was a little harsh. Remember, he's a good friend of mine."

Glick rose from his seat and walked to the sideboard by the door, refilled his fist with nuts and turned. "We'll have to hold somebody accountable for this. Friend or no friend, we're in this up to our necks, and in the end somebody's going to go under. Better that it be the chief of a department than the Director of Mossad." He flashed a thin smile, sat, tossed nuts into his mouth and crunched.

Rosenfeld leaned back, a steeple of fingers resting on his lips. "We'll have to think about that."

"What do you think about our David Cohen now?" Glick asked.

Rosenfeld jerked his chin at him in response. "You first."

Glick resettled himself in his chair. "Cohen left his tech job with Mossad years ago, after a big blow-up with his boss. There were a lot of hard words and hurt feelings. Cohen's parting shot was that he claimed to have inserted a mutating access port, a MAP, into our security system. Everybody thought he was just spouting off, but his boss said he really did it. On the other hand, we couldn't trust his boss completely, because he hated Cohen. So we didn't act on his accusation."

"Remind me," the PM said. "Why couldn't we just scan our system and delete the ... whatever a MAP is?"

Glick jumped from his chair with the balance and poise of a gymnast, grabbed a letter opener from Rosenfeld's desk and walked over to the service bar to one side. "You have to remember, David Cohen is the Jason Bourne of computer-hackers. He does stuff nobody else can do, and by nobody else, I mean in the world. So when he said he wrote a mutating access port, we got scared."

"Because it's a ... ?" Rosenfeld's brows furrowed, one hand waving through the air, sifting it for an answer.

"Basically, it's what we tasked Cohen to develop: a software backdoor that can't be detected. A theoretical entity, until he said he'd done it. The idea is that it infiltrates the infected software like a worm, but it mutates as it bounces around the database. It's like a shape-shifting ghost. Only the operator can find it, and the only way to get rid of it is to delete the entire database and any existing backups."

He turned to the service bar, grabbed a soda from the concealed mini-fridge and stabbed two holes in the top with the letter opener. "We hired Cohen to build a program that would allow us to infect and infiltrate other countries' databases. When he had that falling-out with his boss, he claimed to have sabotaged ours instead." He tilted his head back and poured a long stream of soda down his throat, raising the can from lip level to arm's length in a show of bravado more befitting a teenager than a grown man. Then he leaned back against the bar. "We didn't know whether to believe him. If what he said was true, he could sell our secrets to the highest bidder. It would have been so detrimental to our national interests that he'd have to have a death-wish to actually do it. At any rate, we couldn't detect the MAP, and we certainly couldn't delete Mossad's entire database. The only thing that kept us from killing him was that your predecessor didn't believe his claim, thought he was just spouting off."

"I remember that part," Rosenfeld said, and swiveled in his seat to follow Glick's movements. "We had a team of programmers study Cohen's notes, and they not only said it wasn't possible, but that he wasn't even close."

Glick nodded as he flipped the letter opener in the air and then caught it by the handle. "And now we know he didn't do it. If he had, he would've accessed our system to know how we're hunting him. But he hasn't."

"Would we detect it if he did? It sounds like he would know how to cover his tracks—"

"I trust my tech guys on this one." Glick tilted his head back for another arm's-length stream of soda. "But just in case … "

Rosenfeld rose from his seat and strode to face Glick beside the service bar. "But just in case," he said as he stared into Glick's winter-gray eyes, "let's not tell Landau."

"Exactly." Glick flicked the letter opener into the air. As it came down, spinning, Rosenfeld reached out and caught it by its tip.

chapter 49

"ARE WE BEING followed?"

"By about a t'ousand cars," the taxi driver said, his Russian nationality obvious by his thick, guttural accent. Seeing David glaring at him in the rearview mirror, he said quickly, "In morning rush-hour traffic? At JFK International? How can I tell?"

"Take every exit and re-entrance," David said. "When we get to the city, drive circles around the blocks for thirty minutes. I'll give you fifty—no, an extra hundred if you spot somebody tailing us." He turned to Sarah and lowered his voice. "It won't be safe to go home until we have this sorted out, so we might spend a couple nights dropping in on friends and crashing with them. Never two nights in the same place, though."

"That'll put them in danger too," she whispered back. One look at his stern face and she added, "No choice, though. Right. We'll explain and give them the option to refuse." After a moment she said, "I'm glad we left our bags behind. We need to travel light. Did you talk with your kids?"

"It's not safe yet."

She felt her eyes well up and turned to the side window so he wouldn't see. "They must be going crazy."

"I get the impression you miss them as much as they miss you." When she nodded without turning he said, "Let'em go crazy. Katie and Dad can handle it. A few days of crazy might make the difference between live parents and dead ones."

Startled, she lowered the tissue from her eyes and turned to stare at him, wondering if he meant what he'd said. But this time *his* face was turned to the window. She said, "Live *parents*? Is that your way of ... I mean, are you ..."

He nodded slowly, but kept his face toward the window. "If we survive this, and if you'll have me."

She sniffled, and said what Katie would have told her to say: "Well. It's not the most romantic proposal a girl ever got, but considering the circumstances, it'll do."

He combed his fingers through his hair and turned to face her. "If we die, I want it to be together. If we live, I never want to let you go."

After arriving in midtown Manhattan, and after interminable random circling until David deemed it safe, the taxi driver watched David hold the smoked-glass door for Sarah at an Internet café frequented as much for its Internet as for its café. After she entered, the driver pulled away from the curb, dialed a number on his cell phone, spoke the address and hung up. "If you die, you want it to be together?" he muttered with a glance in the rearview mirror at the receding café. "So be it."

***

"Explain this to me again," Sarah said, then sipped her coffee and wedged her back more firmly into the corner booth's cushions.

"You're watching my back, right?"

She nodded. "And the street."

"Okay, like I said, a completely undetectable MAP proved impossible." He loaded a DVD into his new laptop, checked his watch, and then talked as fast as he typed. "The only way I could design it to avoid detection was to put a time-lock on it, like they do with bank vaults. When the time-lock is shut, I can't access their database, but they can't detect the MAP. When it's *open,* I can access the database and, during the same period, Mossad can detect the MAP and shut it down. The reason they never detected it before is that I always kept the unlock periods so short and far-between, they never had a chance. Reason being?" He raised his eyes to meet hers and shrugged. "I dropped programs into their system that did my work for me. The next time I logged on, I only needed seconds to download the program results."

"And you missed your last chance in Vienna, because we were in police custody when the time-lock opened."

"Right. It only stays open three seconds, unless accessed." He inserted a flash drive into the laptop and typed a command, then sat back. "Now we wait. When the port opens, this program will drive a wedge into it and keep it open until the download's complete. Then it will upload my message to Glick and Rosenfeld, and exit automatically. If we're lucky, we'll be gone before they even know we've been there."

He glanced at his watch again. "Four-thirty in the afternoon, Israel-time. But as for me, I need a croissant."

She gazed past him as a thick-built, average-height man in tracksuit and sneakers strolled past the café windows, straining to peer through the darkened glass. Just then, the computer blinked and displayed a window that read: "Connection established," followed by "Requested information located" and then, "Downloading ... "

The progress bar inched painstakingly slowly to completion, neared the end ... and stalled.

In her periphery, she saw Mr. Track Suit cruise past the café window again, this time from the opposite direction. She glanced at the laptop, saw the meter surge to the end and the window flash "Uploading files ... " A split-second later it flashed, "Upload complete: disconnected."

"Got a visitor," she said. "Somebody's casing the joint."

David carefully glanced out the sidewalk window. "The guy in the red-and-yellow tracksuit?"

"Uh-huh."

"Red and yellow. Subtle, real subtle. Keep an eye out for his partner." He scanned the downloaded file and scrolled through the information to the bottom. "Okay. They haven't rescinded the assassination order against us. That means we have to evade until they come to their senses. Have you identified his partner?"

"It's just a wild guess, but it might be the guy standing beside him, leaning against the mailbox. Blue tracksuit, broken nose."

He glanced again. "Yeesh. They stand out like pork chops at a bar mitzvah, dontcha think?"

"Well, the slick approach didn't work. Maybe they've decided to hit us head on, make it look like a mugging."

He nodded three beats, but then shook his head. "Something's wrong. How'd they know where to find us? We took forever getting here, to make sure we weren't followed."

"We'll have to figure that out later. Let's get out of here before they come inside."

"Breakfast time," he said. They got up from the table together and walked quickly to the line at the service counter.

"You won't miss your laptop?" she asked.

"I don't like the color. I've got my flash drive and DVD right here." He patted his jacket pocket, his eyes combing her black cavalry coat. "*Matrix* fashion has nothing on you, that's for sure."

"Speaking of *Matrix,* how'd you turbo charge that laptop, Neo? It booted in less than a second, and uploaded in a bunny-breath."

He stepped forward as the line advanced and patted the DVD in his pocket. "Your idea. Casting out nines. It accelerates start-up and upload times by a factor of ten thousand. It's unidirectional, though—it does nothing for downloads, only working on information the computer processes and sends. That'll change if communicating computers have the same software."

She stared at him as he advanced another step toward the counter, then slid up beside him, her neck craned forward. "By a factor of ten *thousand?* That must be worth a fortune."

"Ten fortunes, actually. Maybe a hundred. But only if I live to negotiate a deal." He ordered stuffed croissants, and pointed the server to the table in the corner with the open laptop on it. Sarah slipped off in the direction of the bathrooms. After he paid, he followed.

chapter 50

THEY KEPT THEIR pace casual while they bypassed the bathrooms. As soon as they slipped out the back door and into the shopping mall on the other side, she felt David's nudge, and they sprinted toward the mall exit.

Sarah heard shouts from behind, and turned her head to see the two tracksuits burst from the café. She pushed through the mall doors and bolted out onto the street, David at her heels.

"Break right!" he shouted. She pumped her arms and flew to the corner, then across the street to the other side, dodging traffic. Honking horns and a squeal of tires told her David was doing the same on the opposite end of the block, as they'd planned. She stopped at the corner and saw him leap to the pavement, then wave her on as he disappeared around the block of buildings, running east on West 33rd. She looked back and saw the two tracksuits explode from the mall and skid to stops, bouncing on their feet, furiously scanning the street. The thinner man in the blue tracksuit stabbed his finger at her and shook it, then sprinted down the pavement. The heavier man stood, chest heaving. On the last backward glance she dared, she saw him take a few tentative steps, but then stop and pull something the size of a large cell phone from his jacket.

She turned and ran east on West 32nd. More honking horns told her Broken Nose had crossed the street behind her.

Three-quarters of the way down the agonizingly long block, she risked another glance and saw him gaining on her at an alarming rate. Pulling for air, she reached the corner and swung herself around onto Fifth Avenue. Then she forced wind into her feet.

Head down, she raced forward, aware of a parting in the crowd down the block. *David. But will he reach me in time?*

Next glance backward, she saw Broken Nose whip around the corner. Pumping her feet to break the pavement, she heard shouts behind her and glanced back in time to see the thug narrow the gap to three strides. She flicked her head forward to the parting crowd of startled faces, and David exploded from its midst. As she flew by him, she glanced back to see Broken Nose reach for her flapping coat. In that instant, David took advantage of the man's focus on her and straight-armed him across the throat.

The thug reverse-cartwheeled in a swirl of sneakers and blue tracksuit, landed on his shoulders and neck with a bone-crushing thump and skidded, rolling, to a stop in a crumpled bundle. Then David was upon him, bent over at the waist and running his hands over his body. He pulled something from the man's clothes and stuffed it into his own waistband, under his jacket.

A pimply faced teenager stepped forward from the gathering crowd and eagerly said, "I know CPR." David glanced up. Taking advantage of the distraction, Broken Nose rolled over and grabbed David's wrist, his eyes narrowed. He reached with his other hand and mouthed something, but Sarah stepped forward and kicked him in the face before the words could come out. David twisted from his hold and jumped out of reach, and the two of them bolted from the crowd and into the street.

***

"See anyone else?" David panted while he checked over his shoulder for the tenth time.

"His partner hung back at the mall," she said, also glancing backward.

"Shame. I was hoping to see you tackle the guy on *my* tail."

"Me, too." For a moment she mused over the fact that since they'd been together, David had dominated events, with her tagging along like a soldier in his army. A vision of Katie filled her mind, and she knew instantly what her friend's advice would be: *Let him be the man. If he thinks you're stronger than he is, your relationship's doomed.* She hadn't had much opportunity to flex her own muscle. *But maybe that's a good thing.*

They speed-walked down the street and jumped into the first taxi that stopped. "Central Park," David told the driver.

"He saw us leave," she said, staring through the rear window.

He hitched himself sideways in the seat and looked back as well. The thug was shaking off the well-meaning strangers who'd helped him to his feet. Once free, he stumbled into the street, one hand bracing his neck from behind, and glared at the retreating car. Then he spun a circle and waved for another taxi, but none were stopping.

Then traffic filled in the spaces behind them, and they were in the clear.

***

Inside a taxi two cars back and one lane over, the passenger in the front seat said, "Don't lose them, Ivan."

The blond, bullet-headed passenger in the backseat said, "Who were those other guys?"

His partner in the front seat was his complete opposite: deeply tanned, with straight black hair and dark eyes, a deep scar along the length of his jaw filled out his swarthy appearance. "Amateurs, whoever they were. Any pro knows in New York, you secure a ride before you do a job. The only thing dumber than not having a ride," he said, twisting in his seat to glare at his partner, "is for a freckle-faced blond to wear a blazing yellow hoodie while working a tail."

"They called us in on short notice," he said, and stuffed his hands into the hoodie pockets. "I didn't have time to go home and change. Just be glad I wasn't wearing my light-up sneakers."

"Headed uptown," Ivan said, his heavy Russian accent nearly obscuring his words.

"Just keep them in your sights." Scar-Jaw slipped a Glock automatic from his inner waistband and checked the chamber. Then he re-holstered it and pulled his jacket closed to cover.

chapter 51

"CHANGE OF PLANS," David said to the taxi driver. "Swing back to Pier 86."

"The *Intrepid?*" the driver asked.

"Yeah."

Sarah looked at David, befuddled. "What's going on?"

He watched through the rear window as the taxi turned. "There's too much traffic to tell if anyone's still following us. We can't afford not to know."

"And?"

"And the emptiest streets I've ever seen in New York City during the day are in the red-light district, near the wharf."

Soon after, they exited the taxi at the Intrepid Sea, Air and Space Museum, beneath the hulk of the retired USS *Intrepid* aircraft carrier.

"Come on," he said, "We need a cup of coffee. We also need to stand around and see who else is standing around." He led Sarah over to a street vendor, and they took their coffees to stand in the admission line for the museum. Halfway through their cups and three-quarters of their way through the line, he said, "We'll walk away now, and watch to see if anyone leaves the line behind us."

***

"More amateurs," Scar-Jaw said to his yellow-blond partner. From inside their waiting taxi, they watched David and Sarah leave the admission line. Scar-Jaw snorted derisively. "What'd they think? We'd follow them inside? There's only one entrance and one exit. Even if they went inside, all we'd have to do is wait until they come out again. Then they're ours."

He watched the targets head east on West 46th Street, away from the wharf.

"That's our cue," Scar-Jaw said. He instructed his Russian colleague to circle around and wait four blocks away, then jumped from the taxi. "Let's go," he called to his partner, who already stood on the pavement beside him.

chapter 52

SARAH FOLLOWED DAVID north, and they wove through the streets and avenues. She noticed that as he had described, this part of the city was more deserted during the day than midtown Manhattan was at night. After two blocks, she saw nothing but darkened buildings and the refuse of night-trade on the streets. The neighborhood that hustled at night slept during the day.

"Did you see those two behind us?" David asked.

"They split up. One block back, they were together. I think Banana-Man peeled off to go around the block."

"Banana-Man? *Peeled* off? Cute. Which direction?"

"The yellow-hoodie'd cone-head?" She pointed north.

"In that case," he said, "let's turn south at the corner."

"You grabbed that guy's gun, didn't you? After you decked him?"

He unzipped his jacket and held it open for her to see the Ruger automatic wedged into his waistband.

"Check the chamber."

He held her gaze for a moment. Then he drew the weapon and jacked the slide halfway. "Empty chamber. A *cautious* hit man. I'm telling you, something's not right." He jacked the slide all the way to the rear and slid it forward, chambering a round and replacing the empty blackness with the golden glow of brass casing. "What would I do without you?"

She smiled. "Die?"

***

Seven time zones away, Elan Glick strode past his secretary and advisor and asked, "Any bulletins?"

He threw his eyes to the wall clock that told him he should think about going home. Behind him, his advisor said, "No."

"Right." Glick pushed through the solid Oak door, pillowed with studded oxblood leather, and strode into his office. He grabbed a can of cola and ice from the sideboard, then lowered his muscular frame into his desk chair, taking pride in the silence of his movements.

He leaned forward and tapped his computer's touch screen, to bring it to life so he could check his end-of-day messages. He sat back, his left hand wrapped around his drink, and flexed the fingers of his right hand as though he were playing a musical instrument.

The monitor flashed bright white, and then filled with a photograph. Glick shot upright and dropped his drink. It landed with a shatter and a splosh as broken glass and ice cubes skittered across the smooth marble floor.

The photograph on the screen blinked off, replaced by a text message. As he read it, a knock reverberated off the office door. When he didn't answer, the door opened and his assistant peered inside. "Sir," he said, "is everything all ri—?"

"Fine, fine, go away." Glick flapped a hand at him, eyes glued to the monitor. The door closed with a click while he read: *I knew Mossad had a lot of dirty laundry, but I didn't know it was* this *filthy.*

Another photograph flashed onto the screen, and he gasped. The screen then flicker-framed through a series of shocking pictures Mossad never intended for the eyes of the public. The message then appeared: *Let's not hurt one another.*

Another photo followed, showing Glick seated at this very desk, holding pen to paper, his laughing face turned up to Rosenfeld's. The prime minister stood behind Glick, also laughing, one hand resting collegially on Glick's shoulder.

Glick's eyes went to the webcam at the top of his computer monitor, and he swore. As if to confirm his suspicions, the picture on the screen zoomed in on the paper beneath his pen, flipped it, and filled the screen with one of the most damning memos he could remember having signed. The computer stunt then repeated the act, each time showing Glick or Rosenfeld signing a similarly damaging memo or order.

Another text message appeared: *If I do not live, a program will automatically dump these photos onto thousands of viral websites, reaching every corner of the world. Call your dogs off, and I'll stop it.*

A new photograph appeared, of such sensitivity and shamefulness Glick clenched his lids shut with a groan. In his mind's eye, he saw his career and reputation not just destroyed, but vaporized. Rosenfeld's as well. He eased one eye open as a bright yellow smiley-face blinked on beneath the picture, along with the caption, "Have a Nice Day."

Glick sat stunned for a moment, then snatched the redline phone from his desk. He fumbled it with both hands and caught it on the first bounce off his desk. Then he stabbed the connect button.

Rosenfeld answered on the first ring. "No," he said to Glick's question, "I haven't checked my computer. I was just getting ready to leave ... ." A moment later, the PM blurted, "What? He hacked our ... *WHAT?*"

Rosenfeld leaned forward in his desk chair and jiggled the mouse to boot his computer out of its sleep. The screen flashed white, then went dark with a sickening photograph. He yelped as if physically struck. The image changed to a well-focused video, complete with sound, and the prime minister dropped the phone in his hand, jumped to his feet and grabbed the monitor with both hands, as if to steady it against his disbelieving eyes.

chapter 53

SARAH CALCULATED TEN paces from the street corner before she risked a glance over her shoulder at the swarthy man behind them, literally the only other soul on the otherwise deserted streets. Her idea that the Al Pacino-Scarface lookalike was just trolling for a quickie or a fix ended when he lowered his cell phone from his ear and into his pants pocket, then reached across his body and inside his jacket.

"Run!" she shouted, and pushed David forward. When they reached the end of the block, she yanked him by the shoulder of his coat and whipped him to the left. David ducked as he turned the corner behind her, just as the explosion of a shot rang out. Across the street, a car's windshield shattered in a spider web of broken glass. The eerie warble of a passing bullet cut the air, followed by another blast. Then they were around the corner ... and they both skidded to a stop in front of the two thugs in tracksuits. Sarah threw a punch that Blue Suit swept aside, throwing her off-balance. Out of the corner of her eye she saw David whip his hand into his jacket, but Red Suit leveled his gun before he could draw. In the same motion, Red Suit fired and thrust himself forward.

The burning gun blast blew through the space between Sarah and David, followed by Red Suit, who drove himself like a wedge between them.

Not comprehending, Sarah felt the big man's shoulder toss her aside as David spun off Red Suit's other shoulder, his gun-arm swinging in an arc. With dismay, she watched the pistol fly from David's fingers as the same eerie warbling skimmed past from behind, blowing a puff of material from the shoulder of his jacket.

Never let go of your gun—never! the soldier inside her screamed. The moment she'd seen the gun in his waistband, she had wanted to take it for herself. Only fear of insulting his manhood and damaging his love for her had restrained her. Now, as she watched the gun fly through the air away from her, she realized her misjudgment could cost them their lives.

She stumbled to the curb, barely catching herself from falling. In her peripheral vision, she saw David land in a crouch with one hand against the brick wall. Red Suit stepped past the corner of the building in a shooter's stance, his back to them, his pistol cradled in both hands and bucking with recoil. Across the street and down the block, Banana-Man spun as a puff rose from his shoulder, and spun again from another puff at his hip. Flame leapt from his gun as he turned, throwing his return shot wild. A third puff rose from his yellow hoodie as Red Suit's bullet punched him in the back and pitched him forward onto the pavement.

Too late, Sarah realized that when the two assassins had split up, Banana-Man had run around the block. Then, when she and David turned the corner, they had run from Scar-Jaw's line of fire right into his partner's killing zone. For some reason she couldn't fathom, Red Suit had saved their lives by killing Banana-Man, but now he had exposed himself to Scar-Jaw by stepping past the edge of the building. Of one mind, she and David yelled, "Watch out!" As the words left their mouths, a pink plume blew out of the left side of Red Suit's neck.

In a flash of blue tracksuit, Broken Nose snatched David's gun from the pavement and circled around the car parked at the curb. Incredibly, Red Suit remained frozen in a shooter's stance. Two more shots double-tapped him in the head, blowing gore out of his left temple, but leaving his body upright.

Sarah motioned David to her as she stepped toward the rear of the parked car. She watched him push himself off the wall, and then grabbed him by his coat when he ran to her side. Together, they slid between the parked cars and into the street, behind Broken Nose.

Down the street to their left, a taxi turned the corner, and David pulled her toward it, running. With the squeal and smoke of burning rubber, the car fishtailed toward them but flew past. Sarah spun to see Scar-Jaw flash a peek around the corner of the building. Broken Nose crouched on the street side of the parked car, his arms leveled on its hood, and his gun spat two jets of flame in Scar-Jaw's direction. The first shot disappeared, but the second gouged a chunk of cement from the building as Scar-Jaw ducked back out of sight. The taxi plowed into Broken

Nose, crushing him against the parked car's front fender and spinning it, wrenching its rear end into the street.

The taxi driver jumped from the cab, leveled his hands over the roof of the car in a double-fisted grip at where David and Sarah stood in the street and yelled, "Freeze!"

They froze.

Scar-Jaw flashed another peek around the building, saw it was clear, and slipped around the corner. He bumped Red Suit as he passed and toppled the dead man to the ground. His gun remained trained on David and Sarah. He cupped his right cheek with his left hand; a rivulet of blood snaked down his arm and dripped from his elbow. As he cleared the rear end of the parked car, gun steadily trained on them, the driver lifted his black leather-gloved hands from the roof of the taxi and blew imaginary smoke from an index finger. Not until then did Sarah realize he didn't even have a gun.

"Our airport driver," she side-whispered to David. "The Russian one. That's how they knew where we were. They didn't need to tail us from the airport, because the tail was *driving* us."

Her eyes on the Glock in Scar-Jaw's hand, she cursed her second fatal error. She had noticed the Russian's black gloves on their ride from the airport, and had thought it an odd affectation for a taxi driver. But she now realized he wore them not out of vanity, but to avoid leaving fingerprints on a stolen taxi. When he'd double-gripped his hands together on the car's roof, she'd been so distracted by the battle she hadn't realized his two black fists were wrapped around nothing but one another. Unbidden, her mind conjured up memories of legendary battles that were won on bluff. "Some soldier," she muttered. "I've killed us twice today."

"Huh? What's that?" David said without turning.

Too numb to explain, she shook her head.

The driver slipped back into the taxi and reversed the car away from Broken Nose's fallen body and shattered legs. Keeping his eyes upon them, Scar-Jaw swung his gun to the right, flicked his eyes to Broken Nose and pumped two shots into his blue tracksuit. While the taxi driver slipped from the cab and strode over to check the body, Scar-Jaw turned the gun back to them and mumbled, "I hate amateurs."

Sarah watched the assassin raise the black tunnel of his automatic pistol to the level of David's eyes.

And the air screamed with a shrill squeal.

The assassin hesitated.

A mechanical voice shouted, *"Abort. Abort. Abort. At all cost, abort. At. All. Cost. No exceptions. Abort, and confirm."*

Scar-Jaw dropped his left hand from his face, where Broken Nose's bullet had carved a deep furrow in his cheek. He dug into his jacket pocket and extracted a device the size of a deck of cards, checked the display, and shook his head as he stuffed it back into his pocket. "Sorry," he said as he returned his eyes to theirs, "but you've seen my face."

He raised his gun again, and Sarah felt David's hand stiffen within her own as the barrel leveled. She closed her eyes and felt him flinch from the gun blast, and then the street fell silent.

chapter 54

SARAH REFUSED TO open her eyes, fearing what she would see. David's hand remained within hers, but she'd seen a dead man standing only moments before.

The dream of a happy marriage and a peaceful home drifted through her mind like a cloud that could be seen, but never captured. With tears in her heart but dry eyes, she clenched her teeth and waited either for her bullet, or for David's body to fall away from her. His previous testimony of love and commitment floated through her memory, and she spoke to the darkness of her shuttered eyes: "If we're going to die, we'll die together."

"And if we survive, I'm never going to let you go," David muttered, and squeezed her hand.

Her lids sprung open to see Scar-Jaw sprawled flat in front of them, a bloody crater in the back of his skull. The Russian taxi driver stood up from where he had crouched beside Broken Nose's body. He dropped the spent Ruger to the ground and shrugged. "Order said at all cost. No exceptions." He waved at Scar-Jaw's prone corpse. "He no professional." Then he hurried around to his open door, slipped inside the mangled taxi, and pulled away with a lurching of gears.

A long moment passed before she felt David release her hand. She watched him step around Scar-Jaw's body to stand over the man in the blue tracksuit. He crouched and rested his hand on Broken Nose's chest. Sarah went over, crouched beside him and watched as David's hand rose and fell. The idea that the man still breathed made her flinch.

David reached out and rolled his head to face them. With a flutter of eyelids, Broken Nose opened his eyes.

"Who are you?" David said.

The man licked dry lips with a pasty tongue and whispered, "Schroeder ... sent us. Watch ... over you."

He closed his eyes and rolled his head away. Sarah reached out and rolled his head back, and the man opened his lids again, but only halfway.

"How did you find us?" she said.

"Tracking ... device." He coughed foamy blood to his lips, gagged on it, and swallowed weakly. "He ... tagged you."

He closed his eyes again, exhaled a raspy breath and lay still.

Sarah stood and laid her hand on David's shoulder. He covered her hand with his own and rose to stand beside her. She then tugged him to the sidewalk, where they both slipped to sitting positions against the building, their backs to the cool brick wall. A shrill squeal cut through the wail of approaching police sirens, followed by the mechanical voice, *"Abort. Abort. Abort ... "*

chapter 55

TWO WEEKS LATER, Sarah sat with Katie and David in Chez What?, across the street from Benyamin's Brooklyn apartment building.

"So," Katie said, "Schroeder removed one tracking device but planted another."

"Uh-huh." Sarah thumbed in David's direction. "In his wallet. Good thing we didn't get mugged."

Katie turned her eyes to David. "And that MAP-thingie?"

"I couldn't give that to Mossad," he said. "They'd misuse it. But yesterday, when the time-lock deactivated, I left it open so they could delete it from their system. Call it a peacemaking gift. Otherwise, I'd spend the rest of my life looking over my shoulder. Mossad's enemies would kill for it, to have access to Israel's deepest secrets. And Israel's next prime minister might murder me to cover up its existence."

"Tell you what, though," Katie said, "from what you guys just told me, if I ever need a hit man, I'm hiring a Russian. Shall we order?"

"After," Sarah said, and checked her watch. Then she glanced out the window. "Here they come."

She thought she would need twenty minutes to present her findings to Hymie and Benyamin. She told them of Zionism's role in instigating the Holocaust, of the Zionists' refusal to rescue fellow Jews when the Nazis offered them the opportunity to purchase their lives, because it didn't serve the Zionist purpose. She followed with the post-war Zionist demand for a Jewish state based on the Holocaust they themselves contributed to.

Next, she explained the illegitimacy of the Zionists' claim to the Holy Land, that less than five percent of all Jews are the Hebrews to whom they claim God promised the Holy Land in the first place. She explained the farce of anti-Semitism for the same reason—that ninety-five percent of all Jews aren't Semites. She spoke of Zionism's rebellion against God's commandment not to return to the Holy Land as a body before the Messianic redemption.

Twenty minutes, she figured. Thirty tops.

It only took ten. The two JSA leaders started spouting brainwashed slogans and parroting the same tired fallacies she'd risked her life and David's to expose as untrue. In the end, Benyamin said they were going to take the Holy Land, will of God or not.

"This isn't about religion," Hymie said as he stood from the table, "it's about land." And with that, they stormed out.

"Whew. Well ... I'm glad we got *that* straightened out," David said. He stood and pulled out his wallet. "Now, what can I order for you two?"

At the counter, he gave Tony his order for Kat's tea and two biscotti, and for Sarah's house blend with a shot of espresso and a raspberry scone. Tony shouted the order letter-perfect down the counter. His counter-mate sidled over and said, "What're you yammering this time, Loco?" Then he peered over Tony's shoulder at his order pad. "Oh. A sock in the wash, two fence posts, boot polish with a spit and a speckled doorstop. Why didn'tcha say so?"

***

"When we finish writing this up," Sarah said while they waited for a taxi, "do you think anybody will believe it?"

David shrugged. "Let's see ... . We've got the video of that guy searching your room in the hostel, the police record of the failed hit in Vienna, the DVD and confessions of the Mossad agents in Egypt, and the monster mess-up here in New York." He smiled at her. "Even with all that, we're up against the Zionist-controlled media, most of which think a lot like Hymie and Benny. So will anybody believe our side of the story? It depends on what they want: truth, or politically correct lies."

A taxi cruised to the curb and Sarah pulled the rear door open. "When you tell this story to your grandkids, will you mention how you flinched when the gun fired?"

He strode around to the other side. "You know, I don't think anybody ever gets used to *not* being shot in the head." Then he jacked the door open and slipped inside.

chapter 56

"HE'S A GOOD friend," Rosenfeld said as he stood to stare out his office window. The overcast sky was further blurred with dust dug up by storm winds off of the Judean desert. Glick sat in front of the PM's desk, ankle propped on his knee, fiddling with a broadsword of a letter opener.

"Somebody has to take the fall for what happened," Glick said. "It's not going to be you, and it sure better not be me."

"Landau and I go back a long way. Okay, maybe we should have elevated this to your level sooner, but what's done is done ... " Rosenfeld turned from the window, snatched one volume of the file labeled "Bud Nipper" from his desk and paced the room while leafing through the pages.

"There's no other choice. We'll have to sacrifice someone to the media." Glick rose from his chair, flipped the letter opener in the air and caught it on the spin by the handle. "In the meantime, the MAP is history, and we've informed our media contacts to minimize dissemination of the story. In three months, the world will have forgotten all about it. Sooner if we can dominate the headlines with suicide bombings and Jewish casualties."

The PM nodded thoughtfully, and shut the file in his hands with a slap. "If we push the Palestinians hard enough, one or two are bound to snap and do a suicide bombing." He thought a moment. "We only give them two hours of running water a week in the occupied territories. Cut that in half?"

"Among other things," Glick said. He strolled to the service bar and pulled a strawberry soda from the mini-fridge.

Rosenfeld tossed the file onto his desk with a thump and picked up a book from beside his blotter—Ron David's exposé of the history of Zionism and Israel: *Arabs and Israel for Beginners*. He nodded to the book in his hand. "Loved by seekers of truth for its honesty, hated by Zionists for its accuracy. Remember, terrorists aren't born, they're made."

"And right now, we need to manufacture a few to take the heat off of us." Glick stabbed the letter opener into the soda can, bringing a tortured hiss and a splutter of pink foam.

***

"Is this really what you want?" Landau asked. He sat across from PM Rosenfeld's desk, toying with the pipe in his hands. "My resignation?"

The PM shook his head, genuine sadness washing over his features. "It's the *last* thing I want. But I don't have an alternative. I have to hold someone accountable in the eyes of the public."

"Well," Landau said, standing, "if *you* don't have an alternative, *I* certainly do." He slipped his pipe into one corner of his mouth and clamped down on it with a clack of teeth.

***

Meyer smoothed the few greasy-gray strands across his balding pate with one hand, and checked his appearance in the elevator mirror. He'd never been called to his department chief's office, much less to the prime minister's. A flood of insecurities swamped his mind, and he stumbled when he stepped from the elevator, two paces behind one of the prime minister's trusted male secretaries. Dressed in an immaculate suit and striped tie, the secretary could have passed as a CEO. Meyer glanced down at his own rumpled brown blazer, brushed some stray cracker crumbs off with his hands. He pulled it closed to button it, but let it fall open again when his belly kept the two sides from meeting.

"Follow me," the secretary said. He led him from the elevator, through the secretarial buffer zone and into the PM's office.

Rosenfeld stood at his office window with his back to the room, once again staring out at the gloomy day. Chief Landau sat in front of the desk, puffing on a cold pipe and reading that morning's *Ha'aretz* newspaper. As Meyer entered, Landau lowered the paper into his lap with a rustle of crumpling pages.

Rosenfeld turned, a sheaf of papers in his hand, and motioned Meyer to the chair opposite Landau's.

"As you know," he said as Meyer took the chair, "we've had trouble over this Sarah Weizmann affair."

"It's no fault of mine," Meyer blurted, and stood. "I said we should kill her."

Rosenfeld waved him back down to sitting, and lowered himself into his own chair behind the desk. "We know that—as per standard operating procedure, you and all present signed the minutes of the meeting where you recommended her elimination." He tossed the papers onto the desk in front of him and leaned back in his chair. "No, the problem is that your kill order caused this mess."

Meyer felt his insides turn to a gurgling stew. His voice squeaking in a whine, he said, "My order ... ? I don't have the authority ... . It was just a recommendation."

"A recommendation that we unfortunately ratified, albeit considerably later." Rosenfeld brushed lint from his jacket lapel. "In a strange way, however, this might work in your favor."

Meyer felt a stirring of hope, and tried to mold his face into a mask of confidence. He glanced at his chief, who smiled at him benevolently, then folded the newspaper in his lap and plucked the pipe from his mouth. Landau pointed its stem at Meyer and said, "We appreciate the commitment you show to the Zionist cause. Because of that, we're giving you a choice."

Landau turned to Rosenfeld, and the PM gave his nod. Landau lowered his gaze into his lap. "Your choice. You can accept the blame for this mess, in which case the world's media will crucify you. In addition we will apply disciplinary action with suspension of salary and lowering of your pay grade."

Then he raised his eyes to meet Meyer's, still with a curiously benevolent gaze, and said, "Or we will fire you and lay the blame on you anyway."

Meyer's fingers twisted knots between his knees. "Wh ... what kind of a choice is *that?*"

"A simple one, really." Landau lifted the newspaper from his lap and started to unfold it again. "You've been with us fifteen years, and have no hope for advancement. If you cooperate, in three months, when the world has forgotten you, we'll reinstate your position with advancement of two grades. You'll coast the final years to retirement at the level of G6. If you *don't* cooperate, you'll be on the street from the moment you walk out of this room."

Landau shook the paper open with a snap, clamped his pipe into the corner of his mouth and peered at Meyer over the edge of the newspaper. "So. What do you say?"

A few minutes later, Meyer shuffled toward the prime minister's office door. For the first time in his dim life, he truly recognized Chief Landau's wisdom. He'd always wondered why Mossad retained his employment when a computer could do his job faster and better. Now he understood. Computers can't take the fall for somebody.

As he reached the door, PM Rosenfeld called out, "This woman, Sarah?"

Meyer turned, his head bowed, and stared back across the room with mournful eyes. Rosenfeld nodded at him over the expanse of his desk. "She's intelligent, tenacious, and a force to reckon with. I assume she acquired those qualities from her mother's side of the family. Shalom, Mr. Weizmann."

Meyer Weizmann stared a few seconds longer, reflecting on the ruin the Zionist ideal had brought upon him. He was such a loser, his ex-wife in America had told his own children he was dead. Then she changed her address, so he'd never been able to find them. Not that he'd tried, he admitted. *Even in that respect, I'm a loser,* he considered. *I didn't even search for my own daughters.*

And when Sarah miraculously reentered his life, he sacrificed her for his career, all in the name of Israel. Shaking his head, he turned to the door, his back bowed and shoulders slumped lower than ever before.

Epilogue

"GOSH, I'M JUST so happy for you," Katie said as she reached up to pin the intricate diamond, ruby and sapphire brooch to Sarah's wedding gown. "So happy. Just so, *sooo* happy ... " She poked the pin straight through the ivory fabric.

"Hey!" Sarah flinched and recoiled as she felt the pinprick, pulled the dress's high collar open and snuck a peek. No blood. She glared at Katie. "That's not funny!"

"Just so, so, *verrry* happy for you," Katie said between giggles, and play-stabbed the broach's pin at her. Then her giggles turned to guffaws. She clutched her abdomen with her free hand and bent at the waist in gales of laughter.

Sarah turned and winked at Hava, who sat on one of the hotel room's twin beds, her face glowing from the light of her smile. "You're my best friend, Katie," Sarah said, unable to suppress a chuckle. "You're supposed to want what's best for me."

Katie straightened and faked a serious face. "And you're simply too good for him. Tell you what. Just leave David for me, and I'll see if your Prince of Brunei has any unexpected openings for a new wife. How's that?" As she spoke she pinned the broach on for real, then patted it flat against Sarah's lace collar.

Sarah fingered the exquisite broach in the mirror. "I told you, this is from his mother, not from the prince. It was her way of thanking me for tricking him into buying her the best fur in the store."

Katie answered the knock on the door, and a younger and chubbier hippie version of Sarah sauntered into the room. "Here's the package the front desk called about," Carla said. Then she threw herself onto the unoccupied twin bed and stretched out on her back, one knee bent, her black sneaker on the bedcover. "They said a courier dropped it off. Now is that, like, totally cool, or what?"

Sarah stared at her sister's multicolored, beaded hair and spiderweb neck tattoo and silently thanked her for excusing herself from bridesmaid duty. "Who's it from?"

Carla stared at the ceiling and shrugged. Sarah flicked open the message card taped to the package.

From Grandpa C

Then she read the signature below it. She thought of the kind, gentle man she'd come to know as Grandpa J, who despite his age, had jumped from his chair and kissed David on both cheeks when he asked his father's permission to marry her. She muttered at the card, "Omar Caden, you're no 'Grandpa' to me."

"May I?" Katie reached over from where she stood beside her and flicked the message card open. "C for Caden? That's not, I mean, it couldn't be ... "

Sarah sighed. "The guy I told you about. Schroeder. Omar Caden's his alias."

"Unbelievable. A Jewish wedding gift from a Nazi war criminal." Katie clapped her hands together and rubbed them against one another. "This has *got* to be a first. You going to open that?" She nudged Sarah with an elbow, then scrunched down and turned big, baby-Thumper eyes up at her. "Huh, huh, you gonna?"

"Kat, you're, you're ... nuts. You're just nuts." She tore off the wrapping and lifted the lid on the wooden jewelry box inside it, to find a heavy gold necklace of a design that could only be Egyptian.

"Jackpot!" Katie murmured. "That's got to be worth a fortune. And look, there's a second level."

Sarah lifted out the top tray, and her guts writhed a snake's dance at what she saw.

"Wow," Katie breathed. "The necklace is great, but those earrings could be museum pieces. Except for the splash of brown on that one," she said, pointing. "But even so ... "

Sarah replaced the top tray and shut the box on the domino-sized golden earrings. "Cheap imitations," she said, teeth clenched. "Dime a dozen in Egypt." Willing the snakes in her gut to still, she plunked the box onto Carla's exposed midriff, where it landed with a click against her bellybutton stud. "Here, Sis. For you. Just clean off the ... brown stuff. Wear gloves. Those ancient Egyptian pigments can be dangerous. Dig?"

While Carla sat up and balanced the box in her lap, Katie shot Sarah a questioning look. "Don't think too deeply about this," Sarah said, out of the corner of her mouth.

Katie scratched over one blonde eyebrow, her lids scrunched closed. Then both eyes widened. "Ah. The brown stuff—it isn't paint, I'm guessing. Are you going to tell me what this is all about?"

"I'd sooner talk about Iraq."

"Wow," Carla said, and held one of the earrings up to the light, "*Cool!* Are you *sure* you don't want these?"

I never want to see them again in my life. "Nope, I'm sure. They're all yours, little sis."

***

The happy couple twisted tradition by stomping on the glass together. This kicked off their "Snapple" celebration, complete with *hora,* the chair dance. After the traditional blessing over the ... well, in this case, over Snapple Iced Red Tea, conducted by pouring two glasses of the tea into a single glass to symbolize the union of marriage, a few guests called for a toast from the happy couple.

Sarah trailed her eyes around the suddenly still and silent hotel ballroom, filled with the expectant faces of friends, neighbors, relatives and coworkers from a variety of sects of a number of religions. Her gaze embraced the Jews, Christians and Muslims of Grandpa J's interfaith group; the Orthodox Jews of their neighborhood and of David and Leah's True Torah circle; and the moderate Christians and Muslims with whom all of them had forged friendships.

Nearest her stood Katie and Hava in their designer dresses. Little Yosef wore his black morning suit. Miriam, who since Sarah's return had never strayed far from her, jostled with young friends to one side in her charming satin miniature wedding dress. Nearest of the adults were

Grandpa J and Mr. Klein, the teddy bear of a greengrocer who'd been so keen on their union.

For a moment, Sarah's heart shrivelled. So many familiar faces, and still she pined for the one face she didn't see, longed with the heartache that accompanied her mother's illness. Yet she knew if her mother could have, she would be here today. Still, she felt her mother's spirit, and found some solace in that.

As she scanned the crowd, she was struck that these were her people: men and women of diverse origins and beliefs, all devoted to the principles of peace, love, charity and goodwill. These were friends who neighbored together in mutual respect for freedom of religious choice, who struggled daily to make the world a better place for all, regardless of race or religion: Golden Rule non-Zionist Jews, moderate Muslims, and middle-of-the-road Christians who welcomed David and her into their marital union with best wishes of health, love, happiness and prosperity. These were people not of persecution, suffering and death, but of *life*.

Of life. Eyes melting with joyous tears, Sarah turned to her new husband and raised her glass. "And if we survive ... " she whispered.

"And if we survive," David said, "I'm never going to let you go ... . unless, that is, you don't know how to cook. Then we'll have to talk."

She cocked her jaw and shot him a sideways glance through narrowed lids.

"Oh, ouch—I mean, *woof.*" He leaned forward and sneaked a wink at Katie. "Major woof."

"So we're agreed?" Sarah said, and lifted her glass again.

Smiling back, he raised his glass beside hers. "Deal. Granola bars and MRE's will do."

Gazes fixed on one another, together they pronounced the traditional Jewish toast, "*LeChaim!*—To life!"

And the hall exploded with hundreds of resonant voices, raised in hope and cheer, all shouting back, *Le-Chaim!*

Which Parts of *The Zion Deception* Are True, And Which Are Fiction?

SOME READERS MIGHT question whether American forces ever committed My Lai-like massacres, such as the one described in this book, in Iraq. Time and history will tell. Reports have surfaced regarding atrocities inflicted upon innocent civilians, but the veracity and scope of such claims remain largely unproven.

Lest I be accused of overdramatizing events, the Israeli slaughter of the mother and daughters described in this book is based on an actual news report. This was just one of many war crimes reported to have been committed by the Israeli military during their December 2008 through January 2009 incursion into Gaza. In the February 2, 2009 issue of *Arab News,* Uri Avnery, a brave and forthright Jewish journalist, reported on an Israeli soldier gunning down a mother and her four children from the security of his tank turret. The soldier had little need of protection from the armor that surrounded him; Avnery noted that the mother and children exited their home waving white handkerchiefs. Furthermore, he stated that testimonies reported similar war crimes on more than one occasion.

The year 2009 was peppered with accusations of Israeli war crimes, culminating in Justice Richard Goldstone's damning report to the United Nations. Among other crimes, Palestinians and peace activists claimed Israel deployed white phosphorus in violation of international law. After a year of denial, Israel responded to the pressure of Goldstone's report by formally reprimanding two senior Israeli commanders for firing white phosphorus "in a populated area." The populated area in question just happened to be the UN's agency for Palestinian refugees (UNRWA), in which forty refugees, mostly women and children, were killed. Those who believe there was ever even the slightest doubt about the matter can search the internet for "white phosphorus in Gaza," and examine the photographic evidence with their own eyes. At the same time they should note the evidence of Israel having used white phosphorus not just once, but on multiple occasions, in multiple locales.

Can we expect future confirmation of other Israeli war crimes? How many "scandalous" accusations of today will prove to be horrid realities tomorrow? How many "Goldstone reports" will it take before Israel turns a critical eye upon itself and accepts objective, outside investigation into the accusations against it? When will Israel abandon the smokescreen of self-righteous denial, self-serving media blackouts and sympathy press? When will they open their borders to outside journalists and grant them free movement and reporting? When, in short, will Israel hold themselves accountable for their actions?

If the history of Israel has taught us anything, it has taught us not to hold our breath for answers to questions such as these.

Moving along, some believe all Nazi war criminals from World War Two have either died or been brought to justice, but they are sadly deceived. Of those who remain alive, most have evaded their pursuers and will undoubtedly die free men and women. Even at this late date, however, Nazi hunters pursue open cases. The example of Ivan John Demjanjuk bears witness to this fact. In May of 2009, shortly after I completed the second draft of this book, Demjanjuk, aged 88, was arrested in Ohio and deported to Germany. He is alleged to have been a notorious prison guard, nicknamed Ivan the Terrible, at Sobibor death camp. He is scheduled to stand trial for having participated in the mass murder of 29,000 Jews.

Three months later I was polishing what I hoped would be the final draft of this work when I learned a Munich court sentenced Josef Scheungraber, a 90-year-old ex-Nazi officer, to life imprisonment for his World War Two crimes.

Other suspects remain at large, and up to the writing of this book, the struggle to bring them to justice continues.

Regarding the issues relating to Zionism, I do not consider myself qualified to either validate or refute the references, opinions, and view of history expressed herein. I am not an accredited historian. Rather, I am an author who finds the anti-Zionist evidence compelling, and who feels the anti-Zionists and revisionist historians deserve to have their collective voices heard. Only by challenging history can we hope to clarify it. Hence, this book profiles characters who express views encountered among anti-Zionists and revisionist historians but leaves you, the reader, to examine their evidence and draw your own conclusions. Let us not forget, however, that the fictional adventure in this novel is my own creation, and should not in any way be misconstrued as fact. In particular, the inner workings of Mossad, the length to which it goes to accomplish its objectives (i.e., does Mossad assassinate Israel's non-combatant ideological opponents?), and the makeup of its members are entirely my creation for the purpose of the fictional story.

Those who wish to research the history, references and opinions expressed herein can do so through my sources, which follow. I invite you to investigate these sources and decide for yourself whether the "Zionist deception" is truth or fiction.

Websites:

- **www.truetorahjews.org** ****A MUST-VIEW****
- www.israelversusjudaism.org
- www.jewsnotzionists.org
- www.nkusa.org
- www.jewishvoiceforpeace.org
- www.ijsn.net
- www.NormanFinkelstein.com

Videos:
- *Peace, Propaganda and the Promised Land*: available on YouTube and Google videos.
- *Occupation 101*

Books (Arranged first by subject, then in order of personal preference):
The Palestinian/Israeli conflict:
- *Arabs and Israel for Beginners, by Ron David.* ****A MUST-READ****
- *Zionism, The Real Enemy of the Jews, Volumes 1, 2 and 3,* by Alan Hart

- *The Ethnic Cleansing of Palestine*, by Ilan Pappé
- *Israeli Apartheid,* by Ben White
- *What Price Israel? 50th Anniversary Edition 1953–2003*, by Alfred M. Lilienthal
- *Taking Sides: America's Secret Relations With a Militant Israel*, by Stephen Green

Jewish opposition to Zionism
- **A Threat from Within: A Century of Jewish Opposition to Zionism, by Yakov M. Rabkin ***A MUST READ*****
- *Ben-Gurion's Scandals: How the Haganah and the Mossad Eliminated Jews*, by Naeim Giladi
- *A History of Zionism*, by Walter Laqueur
- *The Zionist Connection: What Price Peace?*, by Alfred M. Lilienthal
- *The Zionist Connection II*, by Alfred M. Lilienthal
- *Genocide in the Holy Land*, by Rabbi Moshe Schonfeld

Zionist collaboration with Nazi Germany:
- *Zionism in the Age of the Dictators*, by Lenni Brenner
- *51 Documents: Zionist Collaboration with the Nazis,* by Lenni Brenner
- *The Unheeded Cry*, by Abraham Fuchs
- *Perfidy*, by Ben Hecht
- *The Transfer Agreement: The Untold Story of the Secret Agreement Between the Third Reich and Jewish Palestine*, by Edwin Black

- *The Holocaust Victims Accuse: Documents and Testimony on Jewish War Criminals*, by Reb Moshe Shonfeld
- *The Yishuv In The Shadow Of The Holocaust: Zionist Politics And Rescue Aliya, 1933–1939*, by Abraham J. Edelheit
- *The Holocaust Industry: Reflections on the Exploitation of Jewish Suffering*, 2nd Edition, by Norman G. Finkelstein
- *Perpetrators, Victims, Bystanders: The Jewish Catastrophe 1933–1945*, by Raul Hilberg
- *While Six Million Died: A Chronicle of American Apathy*, by Arthur D. Morse
- *The Abandonment of the Jews: America and the Holocaust, 1941–1945*, by David S. Wyman
- *The Seventh Million: The Israelis and the Holocaust*, by Tom Segev
- *American Jewry and the Holocaust: The American Jewish Joint Distribution Committee, 1939–1945*, by Yehuda Bauer
- *The Politics of Rescue: The Roosevelt Administration & the Holocaust, 1938–1945*, by Henry L. Feingold
- *America and the Survivors of the Holocaust*, by Leonard Dinnerstein
- *Heroes, Antiheroes and the Holocaust: American Jewry and Historical Choice*, by David Morrison

The non-Semitic heritage of most Jews:
- *The Jews of Khazaria*, by Kevin Alan Brook

- *The Invention of the Jewish People,* by Shlomo Sand
- *The Thirteenth Tribe*, by Arthur Koestler
- *The History of the Jewish Khazars,* by D.M. Dunlop
- *The Myth Of The Jewish Race: A Biologist's Point Of View,* by Alain F. Corcos

Made in the USA
Middletown, DE
06 July 2019